MIT OUT SOUND

A NOVEL

By

Rick Lenz

Mit Out Sound

Chromodroid Press
ISBN: 978-0-9996953-7-1 (Trade Paperback)
ISBN: 978-0-9996953-8-8 (eBook)

Book Interior and E-book Design by Amit Dey (amitdey2528@gmail.com)
Cover Design by Grace Trees

Mit Out Sound was previously published as *Impersonators Anonymous.*
The manuscript has been substantially updated.

Publisher's Cataloging-In-Publication Data

Names: Lenz, Rick, author.
Title: Mit out sound : a novel / by Rick Lenz.
Description: [Los Angeles, California] : Chromodroid Press, [2025]
Identifiers: ISBN: 978-0-9996953-7-1 (trade paperback) | 978-0-9996953-8-8 (ebook)
Subjects: LCSH: Women motion picture producers and directors--Fiction. | Triangles (Interpersonal relations)--Fiction. | Siblings--Fiction. | Celebrity impersonators--Fiction. | Ambition--Fiction. | Betrayal--Fiction. | Family secrets--Fiction. | BISAC: FICTION / Media Tie-In. | FICTION / Literary.
Classification: LCC: PS3612.E557 M56 2025 | DDC: 813/.6--dc23

For Frances, Riley, and Aaron

Also by Rick Lenz

North of Hollywood

The Alexandrite

Hello, Rest of My Life

A Town Called WHY

“Imagination is everything, it is the preview of life's coming attractions.”

— Albert Einstein

AUTHOR'S NOTE

Along with the principal characters, movie stars James Dean and John Wayne are also players in this story. The more deeply I researched their histories, the less I understood who they were. I am reasonably sure that anyone who hoped to gain real insight into the psyches and souls of those two icons would need to dig through every little thing that touched on their complex, sometimes tortured histories, and even that might not be enough to make comprehensive portraits of those two men possible.

For that reason, when those "characters" appear in *Mit Out Sound*, it is always as my version of their mythological movie star selves.

I

THE PRODUCER

1961-1973

"What is it?" Faye Bennett, wearing a plaid shirt and gabardine slacks, ran from her bedroom to the top of the stairs. *"It sounds like someone shot you out of a cannon."* She stared down at the foyer below.

"Mama!" Emily shouted for the seventh time, each time louder than the one before. "You'll never, *never* guess!" She went back and slammed the front door shut. "Never in a trillion years!" She swooped up her Pekinese, Suki, from the border of the tidy little rock garden that occupied a corner of the foyer.

From amidst a meadow of bone-white stones, Saint Francis, surrounded by plaster sparrows gathered at his feet, kept his focus on his birds and ignored Emily, who was furiously petting Suki. "You know that show we saw last night about the new vice president's wife?"

"Yes?"

Emily squeezed her eyes shut, sucking in a fierce breath. "She's my new teacher!"

"...*Who* is?"

"That *woman*. The one from last night. The lady who's married to the vice president." She glanced down at Saint Francis's flock. "That Lady Bird."

Her mother came down the stairs. "I don't understand, darling. Your new teacher is named Mrs. Johnson?"

"No! She's *named* something else. Mrs. Nichols, I think. But she *is* that vice president's wife from last night." She set Suki back down next to St. Francis and the sparrows. "*You* know, Mrs. Lady Bird."

"You're teacher is Lady Bird Johnson … then who is Mrs. Nichols?"

"They're the *same*," said Emily, running to her mother. "*They're exactly the same.*"

Faye Bennett sat on the third from bottom step and put her arms out to her daughter. "No, darling, they're not." She stroked her cheek and took hold of her shoulders, looking her in the eye. "Your new teacher is Mrs. *Nichols*. You learned her name today. Right? … I'm right, yes?"

Emily looked down and in a small voice said, "Yeah."

"Then she *can't* be the vice president's wife, can she?"

Emily collapsed into her mother, burying her head in her stomach. "Why doesn't anybody ever believe me?"

Faye stroked her hair, petting her. "Your father and I believe you, honey. We just don't know what to make of all these … *people* you keep seeing." She felt dampness through her blouse from Emily's tears. "It'll be okay, love. You'll see. We'll get everything straightened out."

Emily had *no* idea what she meant.

• • •

It wasn't until high school that she was given a brain scan. MRI technology was still in its infancy, its earliest use was primarily as a diagnostic technique. Earlier neuropsychological assessments had labeled her a victim of a form of prosopagnosia, a term derived from Classical Greek, literally meaning "face" and "non-knowledge." In the late nineties it would come to be commonly known as "face blindness," after sufferers' inability to recognize the faces of familiar people.

The disorder is still little understood. No one knew the cause of Emily's occurrence of it. There was no evidence it was genetic or that it had been trauma induced. A brain scan demonstrated there was no sign of a lesion. It was something she would have to learn to live with. Many others had. Famous people who did or would later suffer from the syndrome included actor Brad Pitt, neuroscientist/author Oliver Sacks, zoologist Jane Goodall, playwright Tom Stoppard, Apple co-founder Steve Wozniak, and many more. The argument could be made that if the affliction didn't halt the careers of these and other highly successful people, why should it hold Emily back?

Also, according to all of the diagnosticians she had been sent to, Emily's case was "not seriously debilitating."

Emily disagreed.

She had one atypical symptom: an inability to distinguish ordinary people from those in the public eye, primarily celebrities. The effect of this syndrome was to bring two images of a person together into one, as with the focusing mechanism of a camera. The new, combined picture was of someone she recognized from film or television or wherever, and could often think of by name.

Dr. Aaron Withers, a pricey psychoanalyst to whom she was sent by her father, decreed that Emily's presentation of face blindness was likely aggravated by the fact that she lived in Beverly Hills, California, where the girl was raised and had spent most of her childhood.

If you spend any time in Beverly Hills, in the post office or the local markets, drug stores, parks, movie theatres, and so on, celebrity sightings are an almost daily occurrence. Emily had seen Jack Nicholson, Natalie Wood, Rock Hudson, Lucille Ball, and hundreds more, oftener than she could count, although in the end she wasn't absolutely sure if she was seeing those celebrities, or if it was someone who looked—to her—like whichever celebrity it either was or was not. She saw roughly 2 percent of the people she took the time to focus on, wherever she went, as this or that well-known personality. Some of them, because of where she lived, actually were the celebrities she thought they were.

Most were not.

• • •

Because her case seemed mild and not always an issue, Dr. Withers showed her his most *benevolent* smile one day and called her *celebrity-challenged*. “Look at the happy side,” he said. “Most people with your ‘little problem’ feel constantly threatened. At least, you’re able to recognize some of the strangers you run into.”

In the back of her mind, she heard the words “little problem” almost every school day; her classmates could be unkind about it. The good news was that Dr. Withers turned out to be useful. She learned, when goaded, not to take the bait. With Dr. Withers’ support, she devised an “off switch” for those confrontations with other kids and teachers that could easily turn into clashes. The danger usually passed.

Meantime, Dr. Withers helped Emily trace the beginnings of her condition back to childhood days when she was home from school, sick, looking at movies with her mother, her beloved Suki wedged between. They would get lost, watching Fred Astaire, Ginger Rogers, Katharine Hepburn, Bob Hope, and the rest. Emily found herself—in a game-playing way at first, she thought—imposing the people from her movie world onto the people in the real one. Mr. Lassiter, her history teacher, became Jimmy Stewart; Ms. Pesetsky, her home economics teacher, was magically transfigured into feisty character actress Thelma Ritter; the mailman was James Cagney, and so on. From the beginning, her ailment had seemed to be incurable. It wasn’t with her all the time, but it was like a cunning leprechaun, often escaping from the nighttime of her unconscious into the glaring sunshine of her wakeful mind, gleefully wreaking its mischief.

It was not enough that the logical part of her knew that Lew Ayres, star of the original (1930) *All Quiet on the Western Front*, was too old to be her brother, that her mother had not really been Myrna Loy, matriarch of the family in the Academy Award classic, *The Best Years of Our* Lives, and that she had to have been hallucinating that first day she'd stared at her own father's profile and realized with dismay that she was seeing the usually benevolent, older, Academy Award-winning (*Hud*) actor Melvyn Douglas.

Her father was far too mean to be Melvyn Douglas.

• • •

An additional wrinkle to Emily's problem was that, having lived in the world's major geographical concentration of actual celebrities for most of her life, she developed an all-consuming desire to *make it* in film.

Despite the supporting roles of the music and television businesses in Tinseltown, the movie industry was still the reason Hollywood was Hollywood. If you wanted to truly *be somebody* amongst that gathering of pixies, you did it via the movie industry.

From the beginning, she knew that was not as easy as a lot of old films make it out to be. She couldn't compose music scores, sing, dance, choreograph, write, or design scenery. She had little knowledge of cinematography or film editing. She'd had some success, acting in school and community theatre plays—one local reviewer even called her "radiant"—but she never forgot her high school drama teacher calling her "perky." It was a strong enough message to start her thinking about more commonsense roles in the movie business.

But nothing small. She didn't mind not being in the spotlight—as long as she was able to believe that someday, the world would recognize that she was special and, by the final reel, understand that in fact it loved and cherished her. She realized that along the way some people might misinterpret her ambitions as delusions of grandeur, and that anyone aware of her "little problem" might look at those ambitions as a desperate attempt to escape it, but she wouldn't let herself worry about what those people thought.

• • •

For a short time, she worked in a studio mailroom, then, for an even briefer period, in the menial, thankless job of on-set Directors Guild of America trainee. She soon dismissed any directorial ambitions, deciding that profession was unsuited to her periodically timid nature, not to mention her face blindness—although, by the time she reached young womanhood, she had begun to develop some limited skill at disguising her condition.

She decided to be a producer.

That wasn't so easy either. She didn't know anybody in *the business* to teach her the ropes or open important doors.

In the beginning, in 1971, after she'd graduated from UCLA (the College of Fine Arts), she found herself a job as a personal assistant to a TV series star of the time, a gorgeous young man who had been an overnight sensation and whose name, by the following season, nobody knew. Emily's star was cancelled along with the beauty's series.

She tried nonunion extra work, bit parts, and even a stint as an assistant casting director. She wanted to become familiar with the film business from as many points of view as possible and, at the same time, demonstrate that she *was* sure of herself—sure enough, at least, to be a movie producer.

As is often the case with people who go into show business, she longed for certainty.

II

THE LOST FILM

1

1973

Emily Bennett stumbled onto the legend of *Showdown* while doing a tiny part on an episode of a long-forgotten television series being shot at Fox Ranch in the West San Fernando Valley. She found herself talking to an extra who claimed to have worked in one scene of a fourth major James Dean film, a film that had never been released.

She was more than startled, since to common knowledge there is no such film.

The man, a rosy-faced talker named Miles, said it had been filmed toward the beginning of the last year of Dean's life, 1955—before *Rebel Without a Cause* began production. "It was shot in Arizona. That's where I was living at the time," he said, unsmiling. He never smiled.

Miles morphed into prodigious-nosed character actor Karl Malden in Emily's mind. It occurred to her that no matter how nutty what he had just said was, if she were to tell him who she was seeing him as, he would get that fey look people do when the guy in the next seat on the bus or subway leans in to you, looks you straight in the eye, and tells you he's not wearing underpants.

"Why wasn't this … um … *lost* film ever released?" she asked Miles. She knew she was being put on.

"Because it was never completed. His costar quit."

"Who was his costar?"

He regarded her belligerently. "Consider yourself special," he said. "I've never told this to anyone. It was John Wayne."

"NO! *Noooo.*" She giggled. "Come on."

"God's truth."

Emily shook her head reflexively, flicking her long, chestnut brown hair across her face. She scooped it back and tried to repress a grin. "Why don't I know about it? Why doesn't *everybody* know about it? Why isn't it common gossip?" She was ready to leave this extravagant old liar and go watch the shooting just over the hill.

"Because," he said, "some tough-looking guys told us to keep our mouths shut, and it was easy to see they weren't kidding. One of the extras had some Hollywood experience—he was older than I am now. He told me people had gotten in deep doo-doo for opening their mouths in this kind of deal." He pushed his nose to one side, an expression, she assumed, of gangland intimidation.

"So why are you telling me now?"

When he told her he'd been diagnosed with a brain tumor and felt he *had* to tell the story to *somebody*, Emily restrained herself from rolling her eyes and saying, "Sure... *riiight*."

Two months later, another extra told her Miles had died.

• • •

Several months after that, she was working for Richard Boone, the craggy Western star, as a personal assistant. Boone was a devilishly charming man, as well as a masterful actor, who liked whiskey. He and Emily became close friends, a fact that quietly thrilled her. Although he was a roughhewn bear of a man whose tippling, like so many Hollywood "men's men" of that time and earlier, occasionally approached "problem" level, Emily found him only kind, generous, and with her anyway, always a gentleman.

One night, as they were doing some drinking together, Emily asked him if he'd ever heard of a movie called *Showdown*.

Boone blinked and squinted at her with his patented, dangerous *Have Gun—Will Travel* smile. "Where did you hear about that?"

"Never mind. Did you?"

"I saw it," said Boone. "Well, maybe two minutes of it." He took a draw on his Pall Mall, and then, at the bottom of his warm, raspy register, intoned: "What the hell."

This is the story he told her:

• • •

"One morning I got up and found a brand-new Cadillac in my driveway. Duke had bought me a car, to thank me for doing Sam Houston in *The Alamo*—I'd worked for pocket change since he was producing it and footing the bill. Well, hell, I didn't know what to say. I figured I ought to say thanks for a thing like that, so I jumped into that beautiful black Caddy and drove over to the office he kept in Culver City.

"He was kind of embarrassed and so was I, so to help kill that he got out a bottle of sippin' whiskey, which we went through in short order. When we were near the end of it, he said to me, 'I want to show you something I never showed anybody.'

"He took me into a little screening room, set up and started a reel of film, then returned to the front, sat down a seat away from me, and glanced back and forth between me and the screen as I watched.

"A cowboy rode up over the crest of a hill off in the distance, moving toward the camera. Then the angle shifted to include the profile of a boy—a young man—in the foreground, watching the cowboy. The boy reached into his jacket pocket, drew out a bag of chewing tobacco, opened it, tore off a chaw, and put it into his mouth. I started to say something, but Duke said, 'Watch.'

"The cowboy dug a spur into his mount, a big old bay, and galloped toward the camera and the boy, whom I could now make out clearly. I said, '*What is this*?'

"Duke growled. 'A reminder of all my sins.'

"I said, 'When did you do this? And what in great fucking hell were you doing with James Dean?'

" 'It was a long time ago,' he said. 'I did half a damn film with the little prick. It ought to be worth a fortune, but it's not. We had to shut down.' "

• • •

"*Why? Why* did they shut down?"

"Duke wouldn't say. He turned it off. Said he couldn't look at it anymore."

"Did he have more footage?"

"Evidently."

"Where did it come from? How did it get made? Why hasn't anything ever been written about it?"

"There are good reasons. And I'd advise you not to go passing this story around. I shouldn't have told it to you."

Emily frowned at him, her intelligent eyes narrowing. "Why did you?" She reddened. "Did you just make this all up?"

Boone looked at her somberly. "You know me better than that. And I told you about it because you're trustworthy."

This was the moment, she would realize years later, that marked the point from which there was no turning back. The *Showdown* legend had hooked her.

For now, she knew she couldn't make anything of what Boone had told her; after all, she was "trustworthy," which, looked at from the point of view of a "Hollywood girl" with ambitions, can be an awful burden. But it *had* reminded her of her personal plans. Even though it was more than typically manic of her, she had begun to feel—*some of the time*—like Don Quixote in search of *honor*. She'd be a "trustworthy" Hollywood producer.

About as likely as a kindly hit man.

Also, in the case of her movie industry ambitions, Emily was not at all certain she had the necessary linear relentlessness of character to be one of the Hollywood killers.

"You're too soft for the job."

To further complicate things, her developing self-image was plagued with dualistic messages. Her other voice seemed to enjoy quibbling with her, goading her, repeatedly asking questions she didn't want to think about, let alone answer.

"A film producer has no time to feed and water prisoners."

"I can be tough."

"So can a sponge—until it's soaked up all the tears of the world the way you do. If there were such a thing as a producer's aptitude test, the only question about something like, say, "compassion" would be: are you able to ignore yours?"

"Leave me alone."

Because of her doubts and all the insecurities that accompany most dysfunctional upbringings, and partly because she could see a growing currency in doing things unconventionally, she decided to make what she thought of as a bold move. She determined to approach her career from outside Hollywood, which mainly in those days left New York City.

• • •

1974

The first thing Emily discovered while living and working in Manhattan was that her lifelong "little problem" did not go away. For years, she'd been sure her celebrity face blindness had been mostly a result of being raised in Los Angeles, where it was not at all odd to run into, for example, Martin Sheen at Sears, looking for a sheet of HardiBacker ceramic tile underlay. Celebrities had been unavoidable in her experience. It was, she understood, at least *part* of the reason she'd moved to New York.

She found plenty of them there too. Unsurprisingly, a good deal of the time she didn't know the difference. Her roommate's father had once come to town, and he hadn't been a plain-faced Iowan as he should have been, but a middle-aged version of Laurence Olivier.

She worked at a series of jobs in Manhattan: secretary at an advertising agency, assistant to a talent agent, reader for a movie production company, assistant editor for a publishing firm, and finally, assistant vice president in charge of acquisitions at Sterling Films, a respected independent production company. She became the youngest executive they'd ever had.

She told herself: "Finally, I'm knocking at the door." She knew she was now on standby for success, and she hoped—although she hadn't quite worked this part out—honor.

During her final six months with them, Sterling released three pictures, all bombs. Her boss (Emily saw him as Walter Brooke, the actor who said, "Just one word … plastics," in *The Graduate*), with whom she'd had a brief, tempestuous fling, and who had been respectful of all of her suggestions until then, suddenly became unresponsive to everything she had to say, even though she'd had nothing to do with choosing the properties that failed. She'd been instrumental in the optioning of two novels during her fourteen months at Sterling, but neither of them had been scheduled for production and Emily was "dropped."

Crushed, she left New York's endless buffet of stimulations, frustrations, triumphs, and disasters, went back to Los Angeles, and moved in with—*please God, temporarily*—her father, Dr. Benjamin Bennett, a Los Angeles internist, and her brother, Ben Jr., "currently unemployed."

It would have to be temporary. Her father had recently been diagnosed with lymphatic cancer. Only the prospect of being able to spend time with her brother made the notion of playing nurse even imaginable.

Ben Jr., six years older than Emily, was an actor who'd recently undergone his second plastic surgery and was reminding her more and more of Lew Ayres in the role of the young, regretful, and alcoholic brother in the 1938 romantic comedy *Holiday*, at whom Katharine Hepburn looks sadly one evening he's gotten blind drunk and says, "Oh, Neddy, you're dying." Emily hoped a little of her outlook—she told herself it was still essentially optimistic—would rub off on Ben. She wanted to do everything possible to save him.

• • •

January 1976

A week after she'd moved back home, convinced all over again there was a short in her brain's electrical wiring, she got a telephone call from Richard Boone, asking her if she'd be available to help him out while he was in Hollywood and Nevada working on what would turn out to be John Wayne's last film, *The Shootist*.

"Yes!" she cried, recoiling from a shotgun blast of adrenalin. She remembered the tiny bungalow she'd rented when she'd first moved out of her father's house. The rental agent had told her the place had "some history," that Lon McCallister (a blandish juvenile leading man who played mostly callow roles in the late 1930s and early '40s) had lived there when he was breaking into the business.

What if she had once rented a house that James Dean had *briefly* lived in, approximately twenty-two years earlier? It was perfect. It would give her an opening gambit to question Wayne about *Showdown*—if she could just find the guts and a moment alone with him. Certainly it wouldn't be dishonorable to talk to Wayne about it—if he was willing.

"Yes," she said to Boone. "I'll do it!"

It should be inserted here that Emily didn't think she had a problem with celebrities themselves. She felt comfortable with Boone. At first, she thought it was because of his rough, homely face, but realizing that it was also in its way a beautiful face, she decided it had to be something else. Maybe, she thought, it was because with actual celebrities, she knew where she stood. Richard Boone was Richard Boone. John Wayne was John Wayne. She had convinced herself that she was not awestruck by celebrities, just baffled by a world where she didn't know who was one, and who wasn't.

In Richard Boone's case, she felt more at ease with him, celebrity or not, than she had with anyone since her mother. Maybe it was because their affection for her was so consistent and easy.

• • •

Boone had not talked to her about *Showdown* since that first time, three years earlier. She assumed he forgot he'd mentioned it—they had been drinking that night. She knew he wouldn't want her saying anything about it to John Wayne, but this job, working for Boone on *The Shootist,* hooked into the *determined* corner of Emily's psyche, a hidden alcove she was again beginning to explore simultaneous to her unexpected, rekindled belief in the authenticity of the *Showdown* legend. Just talking about it wouldn't be a comment on her trustworthiness.

"*That's how it begins,* said her other self. "*Boone called you trustworthy.*"

"*That's how what begins?*"

"*Skewed definitions of truth.*"

"*A certain amount of pragmatism is necessary if you want to survive.*"

"Got it. Survival on one side, and on the opposite shore—"

"I'm simply thinking of TALKING *about it to somebody who already* KNOWS *about it. What honor does that violate? I'm not going to wait for the prince to show up with the right sized slipper. I'm going to let myself dance free for a change.*

The truth was, she did have her own kind of relentlessness. She was sure of it. She'd learned it in New York. A young woman doesn't go to Manhattan and survive for two years without a stockpile of desperation, first cousin to relentlessness. She'd been wrong in her earlier judgment of herself. The fact was, that when she was at her strongest, when she really grabbed on to something, she had the dogged persistence of a trial lawyer. At this moment, her pendulum had swung all the way in that direction. She intended to find out what John Wayne would have to say about *Showdown*.

"I can do it. I can do it."

"From your lips to God's ear, honey."

• • •

She hadn't counted on how sick the old man was.

"Duke" had almost no time for off-camera conversation. He would show up just before the director, Don Siegel, said, "Action," and leave as soon as the shot was over. In his trailer, he was unapproachable to her. Emily could never find an appropriate moment to get away from her obligations to Boone and talk to Wayne alone. She was introduced to him briefly, but that was it.

Boone's role in *The Shootist* wrapped, and Wayne disappeared as usual into a limo that waited for him at the edge of the set.

It was late winter. Boone would soon be on his way to his home in Florida and have no more employment for her for the time being. She put out half-hearted feelers for other personal assistant work, but no one responded.

Her self-confidence pendulum swung all the way back to her un-dogged, timid side.

• • •

Benjamin Bennett Sr. couldn't have helped seeing his daughter come into the room, but he didn't look away from Dian Parkinson, the gorgeous young blonde model on *The Price Is Right*. She wore an eye-popping bikini in the Showcase Showdown, fondling a Lucky Jet Ski. A dead man couldn't have looked away.

"Dad?"

Emily picked up the remote lying next to him on the bed and turned the sound off. "Please talk to me. I want to know something. This is going to seem very strange—an odd thing to ask your own father at my age, but this is something I really need to figure out. If I don't ask you now, I'll never be able to.

"I came across something. I know it's silly … I found Ben's old baby book. Here's the … *curious* part: you have an entry under the section about potty training. It's in your handwriting. It says Ben was potty-trained at three months, and that you started the process at five weeks. Do you remember that?"

Her father's eyes flicked toward her, then back to some point in the space between Emily and the television.

"At *five weeks*? she said, "You *know* that's insane. You're a doctor. The thing I need to find out is, did I get the same treatment? Ben won't remember, he's barely conscious." She waited. "Can you answer me, Daddy?"

Her father's mouth tightened. It hit her like knuckles in the ribs.

"Did you make Mama hold him over the potty too? I picture you gripping him under his arms when he was two or three months old, too roughly; his head is lolling off to the side. Little Ben gazes around, tries to make sense out of any of it, then, one day, he's accidentally successful while you're holding him there—or maybe you just *scared* him shitless."

She gazed out the window at the manicured yard. When she looked back, he was watching her.

He turned away, casually, and closed his eyes.

Dian Parkinson had vanished from the TV screen, replaced by a close-up of a pristine bathroom sink, thanks to Bon Ami cleanser.

Emily sat on the edge of the bed. "The thing is, I know you did the same thing to me when I came along, whenever you got your hands on me." She giggled. "I told you this was strange. But I've *got* to talk to somebody about it. Ben won't listen. It probably wouldn't bother him any more than it does you. I've talked to a couple of 'professionals,' but they just look knowing and nod and utter platitudes."

She got up and moved to the window, glancing down at the Crayola-green lawn. "See, Daddy, I think this might be worth giving some thought to. It's not going to change you, I understand that. And maybe this is mean of me, you being sick and all, but I'd like you to know, just to say it one time, that the spic-and-span way you look at the world isn't—"she giggled again"—well, it isn't the world, is it? It's something else … not sure what. Anyway, my brain's threat detection system, thanks to your sanitized view of life, is incessantly on standby …" She glanced at the heavy wooden beam in the ceiling, directly over his head, reminded that they lived in earthquake country. "I guess what I'm saying is that sometimes I'll look at you or Ben and see something that's in all three of us. I don't know what to call it—sort of an essence of despair. Other times, I'll glance at either one of you and feel a … it's more than just melancholy, more than just a sad aimlessness, because underneath it, there's a sharp flavor of … There's only one right word for it: rage."

Benjamin Bennett Sr. turned his head slightly and looked her directly in the eye. "Is this why you came up to see your father? To vomit this sort of trash on me?"

Emily recalled coming home from school once. Her father told her that her mom was sick. "I've taken her to the best people at UCLA," he'd said. "She has leukemia."

Emily had asked him if there was a cure. When he told her there wasn't, she said, "Could all the pills you give her have anything to do with it?"

"What kind of question is that? Not, what can we do for her? How can we make her feel better? How long does she have? But, is Dad responsible?"

"How long does she have?"

He'd stared at her as if willing her into the cornfield. "A year, maybe two. It's hard to predict with this kind of leukemia."

"Could it be longer?"

He could have been addressing a medical conference: "The prevailing professional wisdom is that it's possible."

"Then why don't you try to get her off of the drugs? She doesn't need them."

"I'll be the judge of that. She needs them more than ever."

Now, today, Emily watched him turn away from her. She studied his profile.

It was unmistakably the profile of Melvyn Douglas.

"You think it's all about you, Daddy, but it's not. You think you're the only crazy one in this family, but you're not."

2

When she finally did get a telephone call, it was from an aunt who lived in Missouri. The gist of it was that Emily had a young cousin, on vacation in Southern California, who wanted to go to Disneyland. Since the cousin was in town and his father would be driving up from a business meeting in San Diego, could Emily take him to Disneyland to meet the father?

On her way back to LA, having delivered the sweet but shy little eight-year-old to his dad, she stopped to get gasoline in northern Orange County. Seeing a Stater Bros. Market near the gas station, she decided to pick up a few things.

As she went into the store, she was aware of a commotion off to one side of the parking lot. She didn't pay much attention, but as she was checking out she noticed that people were gathered around a makeshift stage, looking up at a tall, broad-shouldered man who was talking into a microphone.

"What's going on?" Emily asked the young checkout guy, who looked like a convict lost in daydreams of escape.

"We've got John Wayne here today."

"What?"

"*You* know..."

Emily shook her head.

He snapped out of his reverie. "He's an impersonator."

"I beg your pardon?"

"He *plays* John Wayne."

"Really?"

"It's a regular thing here. He's an impressionist, but, like, more so. He gives a talk, and a bunch of doofuses hang on his every word like he was the real guy. It's a one-man John Wayne show, and jeez, what a crock of ..." He remembered he was talking to a customer. "... garbage."

Emily had heard about the '70s phenomenon of the "supermarket show," but she'd never seen one.

"They bring in lots of impersonators—everybody from Mark Twain to Humphrey Bogart. Been doing it all this month, to celebrate the opening of the market." He clicked his tongue and looked at his watch.

She went outside and found herself heading toward the show, edging into a place close to the stage.

• • •

She watched him in amazement, at times feeling almost faint. It was not just some Elvis impersonation, some tacky homage, the kind of thing she might have thought it would be, given the smell of hotdogs and popcorn that permeated the air. She'd never seen anything like it. If he hadn't been decades younger than the original, he could have *been* John Wayne.

Impersonators are almost always disappointing. After a closer look, they're obviously not the stars they superficially resemble. This performer didn't have to think about that. With only the slightest tickle of Emily's imagination, even up close, he was wholly convincing. She was spellbound.

He wore a red placket-front shirt, jeans rolled up at the bottom, boots, and a cowboy hat. His performance consisted of friendly, surprisingly un-corny banter with the audience and several anecdotes, told in first person, about John Wayne's life and career. Then, he moved on to talk more generally about America and Hollywood, mixing it up with bits of folksy sagacity, borrowed more from Will Rogers than John Wayne. He managed to heighten his John Wayne in such a way that, while it was a good facsimile, it was also a concentrated rendering of that part of Wayne's essence that for whatever reason has always appealed at a gut level to most people.

She wondered how much her reaction might have to do with her "little problem," but this was not like those other experiences. She knew from all her previous years of grappling with face blindness that this was an entirely different thing.

As he was winding up his performance, the impersonator quoted John Wayne: "Talk low, talk slow, and don't say too much." He smiled, nodded, and left the stage.

Off to the side, he spoke with several members of the audience, signed autographs, and did some business with a man in a shiny tan suit. He was walking toward his car when Emily approached him.

"You're a wonderful actor," she said, feeling wobbly.

"Thanks."

Amazingly, he looked even more like Wayne up close, although Emily would have admitted hers was a suspect opinion. He looked to be in his late twenties and was handsome in an outdoorsy way.

"Do you enjoy it? The work?" She felt like some super-goofy fan. "I'm a ... an actor, too ... sometimes."

"Really?" The man seemed sincerely interested, not the usual reaction around LA.

He told her his name was Tom Manfredo.

"But you can call me Duke if you like." Reading her embarrassed smile, he shrugged as if to say, *What can I do? It's what most people who come to this kind of thing seem to want.* He gave her a card that identified him as an "Actor and John Wayne Impersonator."

She told him she'd recently been working on a film with John Wayne.

When she asked if he'd ever met him, he flushed and said, "No … no, not really."

"I'd love to introduce you, but I'm, uh ... wrapped on the picture."

Tom smiled forlornly. "I wouldn't know what to say to him anyway."

Emily liked him on the spot. He seemed easy and sort of innocent. When she asked him where he was from, and he said he'd been raised in Forest Hills, Queens, she raised her eyebrows involuntarily, surprised. There was a lost quality in his eyes and a kind of rural directness about him she wouldn't have expected from a New York-bred entertainer.

Another thing: she felt as if she knew him from film or TV, but not as John Wayne exactly. She struggled to figure out from where, feeling even more disoriented, but too shy to question him about it.

When they'd gone through as many pleasantries as the encounter would bear, Emily smiled, told him she'd enjoyed meeting him, and repeated what a wonderful job he'd done.

He grinned like a huge, pleased puppy.

When she got home, her answering service had a message for her.

Richard Boone was to have two more days work on *The Shootist*. They were adding him to a sequence of pick-up shots, mostly with Wayne.

• • •

Even though *The Shootist* was a Paramount movie, the backlot filming was done at Warner Bros. because they had better Western sets—left over from the spate of Warner television "oaters" of the fifties.

On the first morning, as they were setting lights for a scene in front of the sheriff's office, Emily saw Boone and Wayne standing alone together, talking.

She'd been given her moment.

She gritted her teeth, marched up to them, forcing a smile, and said, "You'll never guess who used to live in the little house I'm renting."

Boone had a hangover, and Wayne looked worse than he had earlier in the shooting. He'd been in the hospital with flu and bronchitis since her first time on the film. Don Siegel had been forced to shoot around him for two weeks and Wayne was reportedly not in a good mood.

Boone and Wayne gave Emily looks that told her there was no punch line she could come up with that would atone for her interruption.

But she had momentum. "James Dean."

They both did long takes on her, then as if choreographed, they looked at each other.

She wasn't afraid of being found out—there are lots of places in Hollywood that people claim were formerly occupied by such and such a star.

Boone cocked his head and scratched his chin. Wayne, who despite his illness, dominated the set of *The Shootist* like a redwood in a cabbage patch, whispered, "How the hell did you …?" He scowled, murmured something else low and deep in his throat, then turned and walked away.

"Sorry," whispered Emily.

Boone iced her, then sighed. "Ah, never mind. Don't worry about it, Em. It's not what you think." He looked after Wayne, moving slowly toward his trailer. "It isn't you. He's dying. It's not easy."

• • •

Later, Emily was doing some mimeographing for Boone and noticed a picture of James Dean mounted on the office wall. He was smirking at her. It gave her chills. The picture was out of place on the wall of the production office for a John Wayne film. She guessed a diehard James Dean fan on the staff had put it up. The week before, she'd been browsing in a Hollywood memorabilia store and had seen separate pictures of Wayne and Dean next to each other at the center of a display of legendary stars. Other actors' pictures were positioned around them, but Wayne and Dean were featured in the very center, together.

Then, still early in the morning, having nothing to do for Boone at the moment, she was alone on an idle backlot street, sitting in a canvas chair with the name "Harry Morgan" stenciled on it. She was feeling blue. She wouldn't get another chance to approach Wayne. She'd be afraid to do it anyway.

She heard a familiar voice, behind her.

"Did you know Siegel used a double for me while I was in the … while I had that touch of bronchitis?"

She turned around, looking up dumbly at John Wayne. She couldn't make herself say a word. John Wayne was *not just* John Wayne. She shook her head, unable to make sense of the moment.

"A couple of shots in this thing are going to show some other guy being J. B. Books," he said, staring down at her like one of the monolithic *moai* statues on Easter Island. Wayne's axe-gash mouth appeared to break into that famous crooked grin, but

Emily realized it was a wince of pain. "Say, how'd you know about *Showdown*?" She felt another jolt of adrenaline when he added, "Boone told you about it, didn't he?"

She stammered out her story about Miles. When she was done, Wayne said, "I don't ever talk about that." He continued to gaze down at her, but as Emily looked back, still frozen, she saw a change come over him. His displeasure seemed to modulate into something deeply considered—something close to the dignity of John Bernard Books in the film they were shooting, a man who knew he was dying and was trying to do it with elegance.

"The kid cost me a fortune," he said finally. "He worked real slow, real Actors Studio. We got behind and he had to go on to other obligations. It was supposed to be a quickie we were going to fit in." He looked off toward the buzz of activity on the set of his last picture. "But it was a good script. We determined to finish it up later."

"What happened?" asked Emily.

He blinked. "Son of a bitch went off and killed himself. For a while, people talked about using a double for him, to finish up. I didn't give it serious thought. I never liked the idea of doing that kind of thing." He shrugged. "Then, years went by and I got too old to play myself." He smiled sadly, baring a heart line not commonly associated with him.

"Why didn't you recast it and start again?"

"I couldn't do that. It was more than half shot. Life's too short."

A cloud on Wayne's brow advised Emily that she had maybe one question left. "Who directed it?" she said.

He raised a hand, as if shielding his eyes from the sun, and looked at her sideways, squinting.

Then he shook his head very slightly, turned and walked away.

• • •

After that final day's work was done, Emily sat with Boone on his trailer steps. Boone poured her a generous glass of bourbon and watched her with a bird of prey look she knew well.

"I thought you weren't going to talk about that," he said. "And then you go and bring it up to him."

She blanched. "Sorry."

He made a hissing noise and looked away, shaking his head. "Forget about it. I should have known you couldn't contain yourself."

She told him about her conversation with Wayne and the framed picture of James Dean in the production office. "I keep being struck by images of John Wayne and James Dean," she said. "And those images are always coming together—like a boxed set. Doesn't that feel weird to you?"

"Chalk it up to topology." She frowned, as Boone took a meditative drag on his Pall Mall. "In a world of infinite connectivity," he said, "you've got to expect infinite singularities."

"What's *that* mean?"

"It means infinite combinations are possible ... infinite clusters of combinations. Why *shouldn't* those two pop up together to somebody? They've left tracks all over the planet. It's kind of poetic. These are archetypal guys—order and chaos, possession and loss, strength and weakness, masculine, feminine, maybe even love and hate."

"That's all very interesting, but why should they be popping up to me?"

"Why *not* you?" He leaned over and gave her a fatherly pat on the top of the head. Although they would have a few telephone conversations in the next few years and his serene and all forgiving nature (with Emily) would remain his gift to her, it was the last time she would ever see him. "Especially why not you?" he said. "You're an inward-turned girl, but you're also an open wound of a romantic. You create what you need same as we all do. In a manner of looking at it, you've conjured your John Wayne, James Dean complaint in order to survive."

"But I don't invent outside occurrences."

"Who says?"

• • •

He was sitting on the steps of his trailer, looking over Emily's shoulder. "Speaking of infinite singularities." He raised his voice: "Hey, Jack! Come here and meet a friend of mine."

A little man, about sixty years old, shuffled over to where they sat. He was wearing wrinkled chinos and a shiny paisley shirt. He had a bug-like face with features drawn together toward the middle and skin covered with large, pale freckles. His thin strawberry blond hair was cut short in military fashion.

Boone shook hands with him and put his other hand on Emily's shoulder. "This is Emily Bennett. She's my girl Friday. Emily, meet Jack Butterworth."

Butterworth studied her and said, "It's a pleasure to make your acquaintance."

"Jack's one of the best editors in this town."

Butterworth raised one shoulder slightly, took a well-sat on card out of his wallet and handed it to her. It read: "Jack Butterworth, A.C.E."—American Cinema Editors, an honorary society of film editors.

"What are you working on?" Boone asked him.

Butterworth shrugged and said, with a sidelong glance at *The Shootist* set: "Not this."

"It's their loss. You're keeping busy though, right?"

"A little of this, a little of that." Butterworth lifted one shoulder again, then raised his eyebrows in expression of something he couldn't say in words, or wouldn't with Emily there. "Good ta meetcha," he said to her, then looked at Boone again, tugging at a forelock he didn't have. "Dick." He turned and scuffed off to wherever he'd been going.

When he was out of earshot, Boone said, "He edited *Showdown*." Before Emily could speak, he added, "Don't think what you're thinking. Nobody asks Jack about that."

"How come?"

"Because Duke would hunt him down and shoot him like a dog if he said a word about it." Boone slow-grinned. "This has really grabbed you, hasn't it? I'll tell you something else: he once hinted to me, in strictest confidence—Jack is not exactly gossipy—that *maybe* he'd made off with the 'A' negative of that film. That's the part I thought you'd find especially interesting."

Emily's jaw dropped. "How could he have done that?"

"It's happened before."

"Are you saying you think he's still got it?"

He shrugged.

"Even so, it would probably be falling to pieces by now, wouldn't it?"

"Maybe."

"Whatever happened to Wayne's copy, the one you saw?"

"I'm not sure," said Boone. "There was a rumor he lost a lot of his personal film to vinegar syndrome."

"What's that?"

"If it was an acetate copy, which it had to be at that time ..." He frowned. "A lot of good stuff gets lost to the breakdown of molecular bonds; it smells kind of like vinegar. That happened with some of the best film handlers. Acetate didn't burn up like nitrate film, but it still fell apart pretty fast if it wasn't constantly watched over. I'm not sure, of course, but I imagine that's what happened to Duke's copy of *Showdown*." He gazed off toward the set of *The Shootist*. "It never would have been an issue if they'd gone ahead and shot the rest of it right after Dean got killed. They already had most of it in the can."

"How could they have done that?"

Boone flashed his trademark devilish smile. "Doubles."

3

Emily got up in the middle of the night, unable to sleep, and took Jack Butterworth's and Tom "Duke" Manfredo's cards out of her wallet. She looked at them side by side. She'd taken a pill to sleep, then another one, but her mind was still racing.

She studied herself in the mirror of her vanity table, scooping a lock of silky hair from in front of one un-drowsy, delft blue eye. She tried to straighten her tangle of thoughts. Unless *Showdown was* a Hollywood legend, an elaborate practical joke, repackaged by a growing number of sadists to drive her even crazier than she already was, it had to exist. It was only twenty-one years later. It made no sense that whoever had the only surviving copy would let it fall prey to vinegar syndrome.

The film hadn't been made by one of the major studios. It would have to have been independently shot in great secrecy, as she'd been told. In that case Wayne had almost certainly owned it—or a piece of it—especially if it had been shot as a quickie. Nothing else made any sense. Wayne had had more movie star clout than almost anybody in 1955. If he'd had control of it, he either hadn't wanted it to see the light of day for some personal reason, or he'd somehow *lost* control. That seemed possible, even likely. Why else would he not have pursued it to its logical conclusion? She was positive he wasn't faking his regret over its incompletion.

Movies had gotten lost or stolen before. By a freaky coincidence, one of the most famous was a John Wayne Western, *The Oregon Trail*, from 1936. Emily had read about it in a battered edition of Leslie Halliwell's *Filmgoer's Companion*. No prints or still photos were known to exist. So it seemed credible that Jack Butterworth or *someone* had made off with the negative. But if so, Emily couldn't understand why the old editor hadn't confessed it to Wayne years earlier, faced up to his responsibility, and maybe suggested that some attempt be made to complete *Showdown*.

On the other hand, perhaps it was naïve to expect anyone, especially a man who made his living in Hollywood, to admit to John Wayne that he'd stolen from him. Maybe Wayne, like most of the straightforward characters he played, was a man who couldn't easily forgive something like that. Or, maybe Butterworth was just a weird, withdrawn, fringy guy, or simply crazy.

Emily was certain Wayne was a practical man, who could probably be approached now. The idea of doubles, even if he didn't like the notion, had been on his mind. They must have gotten close to completion during the original shooting in 1955, no matter how slowly Dean had worked, or they would never have started. Wayne would without a doubt be open to the idea of seeing the promise of *Showdown* fulfilled.

Emily didn't know anything about the movie itself, not even who had written or directed it, but she felt sure it was out there somewhere and that her idea was not madness. If Tom Manfredo, John Wayne's youthful doppelgänger, was asleep somewhere in Los Angeles, then there had to be someone who could do a convincing James Dean, someone who could be filmed in such a way as to persuade an audience that he was the same actor as the James Dean they were seeing in the close-ups.

She looked up and saw alien, strobing images of her flushed face in the mirror, then moved to her bedroom window and looked out into the night, at the looming silhouettes of the Santa Monica Mountains. She had almost no technical knowledge of filmmaking, despite her time with Sterling, but she was sure it was worth a try. The commercial potential was enormous. Dean was a legend by that time—Lord, he was a legend the day he died. His nearly pathological vulnerability to hurt and rejection had, in only three movies and a few odd television appearances, left an indelible mark on two generations of teenagers and an ever-widening demographic of people who were finally beginning to understand his cultural significance.

John Wayne had reached mythological proportions, and he was still alive—a *living* legend—arguably the most popular male movie star of all time, a larger than life character who pursued impossible tasks with iron determination.

Dean and especially Wayne were more familiar entities to a lot of people than most of their relatives.

An absolutely unique endeavor had been laid neatly in her lap. It was luck and, for all she knew, destiny; not to mention there was a fortune to be made. Any savvy movie investor would jump at the chance. Wouldn't they?

"Or are you simply mad?"

"I'm not. I'm finally doing something. It's happening. I am about to be a film producer."

Her other side felt like a skeptical Nina Simone: "*Uhhh-huh.*"

• • •

She spent two days at the Los Angeles Public Library, but had her major success in the Academy of Motion Picture Arts and Sciences Margaret Herrick Library in Beverly Hills. She pored through production records of earlier examples of films that had not been completed for a variety of reasons. She wanted to be as familiar as she could with precedents, with the history of projects that bore any resemblance to what she had in mind.

Other films had been interrupted for various reasons and never completed: Errol Flynn's *The Story of William Tell*, Orson Welles's *Don Quixote*, *Something's Got to Give* with Marilyn Monroe (Billy Wilder later completed it—with Kim Novak in Marilyn's role—as *Kiss Me, Stupid*). Sergei Eisenstein's ¡Que viva México! wasn't finished for financial reasons, and Fred Zinnemann's *Man's Fate* turned out to have a thwarted one. When a film shuts down or one of the leads dies or gets too old to play his role, the option—if there's enough money—of finishing with doubles is rarely chosen. It's happened a few times, Emily learned. The producers finished *The Night They Raided Minsky's* after Bert Lahr (most famous as the Lion in *The Wizard of* Oz) died, but his major scenes had already been shot and they were able to film his double, from behind only, for the rest of the picture and get away with it. Robert Walker died during the filming of his last movie, *My Son John*. The producers borrowed unused footage from his next to last film, Hitchcock's *Strangers on a Train*, to fill in missing moments.

That's interesting.

Emily had trouble pulling herself away from the Margaret Herrick Library at the end of her two days there. If you want to know the history of film in Hollywood or of movie-making, period, it's practically all there, under one roof. One of the things Emily learned was that the vogue of "the Western" had started on stage in the year 1900 at the Herald Square Theatre in New York City, of all places, with the production of *Arizona* by Augustus Thomas. It was a smash hit and spawned endless imitations, including: *New Mexico*, *California*, *Wyoming*, and, notably, Owen Wister's *The Virginian*, which featured dialogue like: "When you say that, pardner, smile." It didn't take long for movie "Westerns" to become a craze that has never entirely ended, at times being by far the most popular single film genre. Emily still had pangs of anxiety, but she was also beginning to feel a mushrooming sense of promise about "her project," a growing faith that had her imagining a new resurgence of Western mania—all because of *Showdown.*

• • •

She understood the research had to be done, but it felt a little like sharpening pencils before the writing begins. Now it was time to get to the tasks that would not be so easy. She knew what her next step had to be.

She called Tom Manfredo, reminded him who she was, and told him she was putting together a movie pitch. She said that if it worked out, she would need a John Wayne and wondered if he would be interested in talking about it, adding that she couldn't imagine anybody better. She told him there was no money yet, but that she wanted to be prepared when it was time to raise it. She hated to use him on the come that way, but she knew she had to act with every bit of resolve she could summon if she was to have a prayer of succeeding. Tom seemed open to talking about it.

"Could we meet this evening?" she said. "Anywhere you say."

"I've got an I.A. meeting."

"I.A.?"

"Impersonators Anonymous."

"You're *kidding.*"

"No," said Tom. "It's like A.A., only for celebrity impersonators. We meet the second Tuesday night every month. … Umm, it's not really anonymous, but you understand."

"Would it be okay if I sat in?"

"Yeah, I guess. If you'd like."

When the phone call was over, Emily whispered, "Only in Hollywood."

• • •

She met him at a scrubbed, age-worn church annex, built in the 1920s, on Seward Street in Hollywood. It was the size of a small school gymnasium and had a 14' x 20' stage at one end for church theatricals and so forth, with an oak podium, downstage center.

When they met, she again felt like Alice, disappearing down the rabbit hole.

"Nice to see you," said Tom.

She smiled back at him, blushing.

After some awkward chitchat, he began to tell her about being a celebrity impersonator and the influence of the star on the impersonator's life.

"After the first shock of it," he said, "when you're startled as hell to realize what you're doing, you don't necessarily lose any sleep over it—"

The impersonators talked among themselves as they came in. Staring at them, Emily felt breakers of vertigo.

"—then it settles into something else and you're hooked, and it can get kind of … troubling. We don't have great self-images, most of us." Tom's frown turned into an appealing smile. "But our stars do. Our stars have everything—love, attention, money. And we get to feel the way those things make them feel, or the way we hope it makes them feel." He warmed to his subject, and clearly to her. "And it's great. They give us a feeling of safety—a little like having your own bodyguard. But there's something else. Maybe the biggest gift they give us is just letting us *be* them. Just the feeling of something like …" He shook his head. "It's stupid, I know, but it's almost their *approval* we want. It's kind of a reward for most of us. Impersonators get to cross a line most people never can. You'd think it might make you feel like a split personality or just silly, but it's the opposite. Once you've committed to it, it makes you feel … whole and focused. Some of them say, when it's really working, it's like being a tribal medicine man."

"And when it's not working?"

"Hard to say. It's a little different for me." He frowned, as if reluctantly remembering an ongoing dilemma never far from the surface. "How do real actors deal with stage fright?"

She blinked. "I don't know. Wait for it to go away, I guess."

"That's no help." He seemed to turn something over in his mind. "The thing John Wayne does for me is to bail me out of my stage fright—sometimes. That's the best thing he does." He gazed at a woman two chairs away, who it turned out was a Gracie Allen—George Burns's fabulously talented comedienne/actress wife—specialist. "The funny thing is ..." He looked back at Emily. "He's also the one who causes it." He scraped at his chin with the back of his hand.

• • •

Emily was disappointed to realize there wasn't a James Dean in the room.

Most of the thirty-five or forty people who had drifted in didn't look as much like their celebrities as Emily had hoped. Clark Gable looked more like John Hodiak, an underappreciated leading man of the '40s and '50s. Lou Costello was Eugene Pallette, the '30s character actor, and the Bud Abbott of Abbott and Costello next to him was unquestionably the 1950s B-picture leading man, Marshall Thompson (*Fiend Without A Face*). The Sally Field, on the other hand, was alarmingly close to looking like ... Sally Field.

The meeting began. Men and women got up from wooden folding chairs, walked up to the podium, and talked about their day-to-day troubles living in and out of other people's skins. Emily had a feeling they were silently, between the lines, betraying deeper narratives than would ever be spoken aloud.

The stories were as many-colored as the testimonies at an A.A. meeting. They were very different, and at the same time, alike.

Some of the performers aroused sympathy in Emily. Others made her want to tell them to stop whining. A man who had done Ed Sullivan for many years broke down and cried because Sullivan had died recently and his livelihood was drying up. Emily was, in a way she couldn't understand, annoyed with herself that she felt so little sympathy for him.

She realized this whole experience was in a way … plain creepy. It was fascinating, just the idea of watching people pretend to be "famous" people, but it also gave her chills. It defied belief that human beings around the country and the world, she assumed, would pay to enter into a kind of whiplash of common sense—stammering in the presence of some poor soul who pretends to be someone who, if truth be told, is "worshipped" for no sensible reason in the first place.

And yet, some of these people, aside from being sad, were fascinating.

A woman who did Marilyn Monroe touched her. She didn't look much like her star except for the platinum blonde hair and a nice figure, but as she spoke, she began to lose her professional detachment, impersonator and celebrity merging in a way that hinted at mental illness. Using Marilyn's breathy voice, she said she didn't know why she'd even come to the meeting—that touring the country as Marilyn was the most satisfying thing she'd ever done and that she didn't need the support of a support group. Then, giving no impression she knew she was doing it, she *became* Marilyn.

"I started off wanting the world to know me," she said quietly, looking puzzled. She isolated her attention on the Tony Perkins and the Tab Hunter in the front row. "I have this child in me, and I know that's a good thing for an actress, in a way. … Sometimes my directors just keep the camera rolling after the take is over. They want to film me being myself, but then I never know when I'm performing and when it's … you know, *real*." She shivered. "I never know when I'm 'on' and when I'm supposed to be … 'living.' It's like I'm in a cavern, way underground, and I can't find my way out. And there's not enough light to even see who I am."

"She's marooned," said Tom, and despite the insanity of this whole experience, Emily knew what he meant. This Marilyn was only now coming to understand that "support" was impossible for her, harnessed as she had come to be, like the original, to somebody's made-up idea of somebody.

The Marilyn forced a wan smile. "Oh well, if you can't lick 'em, join 'em, huh?" She looked at the people closest to her, watching her, and considered that idea. "But that doesn't seem like much fun either." She shrugged, again smiled her sad half-smile, and left the podium.

"You people drive me crazy," said the Bette Davis with her signature clipped diction. "I thought you were going to teach me how to pick my way up that difficult path to fame and fortune. And what do I get? Pathos. I hate pathos. Makes me want to slap someone."

"She's okay," said Tom as Emily watched Marilyn make her way back to her seat. "Don't feel bad. Everybody in this room is a little bit nuts. That's why we're here."

"You think so?"

"Yeah," said Tom. "Of course we make excuses for … you know … what we do—like everybody I guess. They tell me performers have been using alter egos forever. Their 'other self' can—at least for a while—take the pressure off their real one. I've heard it's kinda like a placebo effect, and that it can be … freeing. These people can express themselves in a way they never could before. And the lure of that keeps them coming back." He hesitated, looking inward. "The only problem is, like with drugs, it … *can* turn out to be a kind of deal with the devil."

• • •

Afterwards, the two of them went to The Regent Bar & Grill, a few hundred feet west of Vine Street, on Hollywood Boulevard. The mahogany-paneled walls were covered with large glamour photographs of Hollywood stars from "The Golden Age"—Cagney, Garbo, Rita Hayworth, Henry Fonda, Spencer Tracy, and about thirty others. At the far end of the room was a huge fireplace with a gas log fire flickering in it. There were quite a few other customers, but Emily and Tom had privacy in a booth near the bar.

She told Tom she knew people might call her crazy for pursuing *Showdown*, and for going on a talent search before she'd found out for sure if the thing even existed, but she had no choice. With Tom's mind-bending likeness to John Wayne and his uncanny ability to impersonate him, she had to stick with it until she found the James Dean she needed. She was determined to have the complete set before she approached Jack Butterworth. If it all turned out to be untrue ... well, she'd apologize and find a way to pay them for their time.

She told him everything she knew—except her sources—about *Showdown*. When she'd finished, he said, "It sounds like it could be a heck of an opportunity. But I'm afraid I'm not your guy."

"Are you *kidding*?"

"You know the stage fright I was talking about? It's for real."

She remembered what she'd seen him in. Tom had played a John Wayne archetype, a classic American hero in a modern Western that had never gotten a commercial release and had gone directly to cable (it was among the first to do so). Burt Reynolds was the lead, a character physically and spiritually lost, who keeps seeing a heroic type off in the distance, played by Tom Manfredo.

"But I saw you work," she said. "And I saw you in the Burt Reynolds film. You were great."

Tom blushed. “It was the best job I ever had. Just a lucky thing.” He chuckled, which made her giggle. “I made a lot of money too,” he said. “They hired me for two days the first week and tied me in photographically with Burt Reynolds’s character. Then they did some rewriting that called for me again. But by that time, they’d gone over schedule and Reynolds had to go off to do something else—a previous commitment. Well, they had me on a daily rate, the most money I’ve ever made. By the time Reynolds got back to finish his stuff, I’d earned enough to make a sizeable down payment on a house.”

“Too bad it wasn’t a hit. It might have made you a star.”

“But that’s what I’m saying. I don’t really see myself that way. Sometimes I try to picture myself playing leads, in movies or on television. I’ll be coming out of a dressing room at Universal and walking toward a limo waiting to take me to the set.” He shrugged his massive shoulders. “But every time, the image falls apart and it’s me driving the limo.”

“But you’re in the business. You get successful acting gigs. My project might turn out to be no more than fantasy, but if it exists and my instincts are right, you’re the only one on earth who can play it.”

He gulped. She knew she had him. “My chief obstacle now,” she said, “before I can approach the guy I think has the negative, is to find somebody who can do James Dean even close to as well as you do Wayne.”

“Don’t you think you ought to make sure it really exists first?”

It was the kind of question that always made her angry. It reminded her of people who were constantly trying to put a damper on her creativity, snipping off her ideas before she’d had a chance to figure out for herself if there was any life in them, treating her like *old Hollywood* so often treated “the girl” in the story.

"I *know* it exists," she said.

He smiled. "If you say so." Then, almost as an afterthought: "I know a great James Dean."

"*Really?*"

• • •

Early the next evening, Emily went to Tom's house to see a videocassette recording of a sketch "Duke" had done with an actor named Jimmy Riley. It had been taped several months earlier at the dedication ceremony for the Hollywood Western Television and Film Museum on South La Brea.

According to Tom, there had been six "celebrities" in the show: Gary Cooper, Barbara Stanwyck, Randolph Scott, and Joel McCrea—along with John Wayne and (which one doesn't fit?) James Dean.

"Why would they have James Dean in a show about Westerns?" Emily said.

"They were counting *Giant,* although you're right, it's not really a Western—more like a contemporary Western, soap opera. They were trying to sell tickets and Dean's legend is bigger than ever lately. He's a hell of a lot better draw than, say, Hopalong Cassidy."

Emily found the playlet Tom did with Jimmy Riley, as John Wayne and James Dean, embarrassing. It was a clammy little piece about patriotism and "Western values"—whatever that meant—played in front of an American flag, in a wash of red, white, and blue light, accompanied by a sepulchral choral recording of "The Battle Hymn of the Republic" lifting to periodic orgasms of sentimentality.

Jimmy Riley was good. Without seeming effort and despite the nauseating material, he had the head tilts, the pained angularity, and the smoky demeanor of James Dean without being an impressionist's cliché of memorable poses from Dean's three movies or the exhaustively circulated still photos.

The problem was his look. It was close, but didn't quite make it. Emily knew it was implausible that the James Dean character could be shot from behind only, as they had Bert Lahr's double. She realized that Tom had set an unmatchable standard for her. Jimmy Riley was not in the same league.

"He's really good," said Tom after it was over. "They didn't have us lit very well." He cleared his throat. "I could get a hold of him. You could meet him."

"No thanks." She felt her resolution dissolve. She spread her hands, palms up. "I guess there's a reason nobody does this kind of thing."

She'd learned the reason while she was doing her research. Aside from the complex technical demands, the look of the players has to be dead-on or an audience won't buy it. She knew it would shatter the suspension of disbelief if the James Dean character, even with the most skillful lighting and camera work, suddenly looked like somebody else. She'd pored over every available source on doubles and celebrity impersonators and had come up blank on James Deans.

"I'm afraid he's not what I'm looking for. I'm sorry." She lifted her shoulders in resignation.

"I'm sorry for you," said Tom.

"You're sweet, but you're the one who's been put out. I should have known a long time ago this wasn't going to work." She told him about the research she'd done and apologized again, her spirits now in a sharp nosedive.

She glanced around the large, elegant living room. "I like your house."

"I put every penny from the Reynolds movie into it," he said, good-natured about whatever disappointment he felt—or probably, Emily imagined, relieved. "I think, when it was all over, I'd made nearly as much as Reynolds had. I knew it would never happen again, so I bought this place. The payments keep me hustling, but it's worth it to have my own little retreat in the middle of the city. I've done most of the remodeling myself."

It was a white California-Spanish hacienda in the hills, with polished oak floors and a view of the San Fernando Valley. She gazed at the trappings of this man's slant on the world. The living room was furnished with an eclectic variety of interesting pieces. The comfortable overstuffed sofa she sat on was covered with a buckskin-colored fabric. The nearly foot-thick walls had been recently repainted; they were pure white and there was an interesting assortment of pictures and woodcuts on them. At one end of the space, French doors opened onto an inviting courtyard with a recycling water fountain set into an adobe wall, and a walkway of Mexican paver tiles wending through a well-tended garden. At the far end of that was a fifteen-foot explosion of bougainvillea, completely overwhelming the trellis it had been trained on.

"This is just beautiful," she said.

He looked around, grinning, as if seeing it for the first time. "Thanks. Sometimes, I imagine I'm a big old movie star. Or that I had rich parents. That would have been nice, I suppose."

"My parents were pretty well-off," said Emily. "It's not the most important thing." She frowned. "I mean, I know coming from money can be a blessing … if you've got a healthy family life to go along with it." She saw that he was gazing in the direction of what could have been a Picasso print on his wall: a young nude woman, seated, her back to the viewer.

"I never knew my folks," said Tom. "They died in a traffic accident." Glancing back and catching the look on her face, he added, "This was when I was a baby, so it's no big … I mean I don't even remember them."

If a look on a face can express open arms, Emily's look did that. "I'm so sorry," she said. After a beat, gazing around: "You got all this from one movie?"

"Most of it." He smiled, got up with athletic grace for a big man, but felt awkward in the moment anyway, went off to fix her another gin and tonic and brought it back, along with a Pepsi for himself.

• • •

Emily sat on a canvas lawn chair in the backyard. Tom had one foot propped up on a fallen silver maple tree and was smoking a cigarette. The sun, an orange and crimson ball, was beginning to disappear beneath the horizon. The smell of lemon blossoms floated on the breeze as the evening darkened and they watched the first few thousand lights begin to speckle the San Fernando Valley.

They'd been talking about show business—how tough it was to figure out, then to decide on a path and follow it. If you guessed wrong, you could end up butting your head against an invisible wall your whole life. Emily told Tom about her brother Ben's short career. Tom remembered him, not in much detail but with a good opinion of his work.

Watching the lights of a commercial jet rise toward the west out of Burbank Airport, Emily said, "So you think I'm crazy?"

"I'm sorry?"

"You said everybody in that room was a 'little bit nuts.' *I* was there."

"I don't know you well enough to say that. I know I am—crazy. And we seem to get along. Do you think likes attract likes?" He smiled, blushing.

She thought about it. It was true that at the moment she didn't feel a bit nervous with him. That was unusual. Were they likes? She didn't know. *She* was certifiable. She knew that.

She wondered if he could tell.

He flicked his cigarette to the ground, crushed it out with the heel of his boot, sat on the silver maple; then, sounding exactly like John Wayne, he said with good-natured self-mockery: "I was just talking, little lady, about the ones of us who swallow all this Tinseltown hogwash like it means something."

Emily smiled. "What happened to your tree?"

He looked down. "Oh, wood bees got to it.

"What are wood bees?"

Tom gazed at the point in the trunk where it had given way and fallen. "They're also called carpenter bees. If you don't pay attention around here and you've got softwood trees like this poor old guy"—he patted the tree trunk he was sitting on—"big ol' wood bees will make their homes in it, and they don't seem to care whether it's standing or fallen like this old guy.

Emily shook her head minutely. "Poor old guy."

Tom reddened in the twilight. "Yup, poor old guy."

• • •

He had been thinking of the kind way Emily had about her. In the fading light, he had studied her full lips and elegant brow, and even though the sun had now disappeared, it felt to him as if, at five feet away from her, he could *feel* the warmth of her radiant, satiny skin.

4

MARCH 1979

In the almost three intervening years, Emily hadn't done a thing about *Showdown*, primarily, she told herself, because of her family responsibilities. Her father hadn't died. His cancer had gone into remission. But by that time, he'd developed congestive heart failure and his personal physician recommended that he not resume his practice. The medical wisdom of the time recommended as much bed rest as possible with only short morning walks to keep up his strength. Emily and Ben (when he was sober—rarely) ran the house, a large Tudor-style dwelling that fit appropriately into its neighborhood and the Beverly Hills tradition of cramming as many architectural styles as possible into a Christmas card town that looked more like a movie backlot than a community where people actually lived.

Emily was far too busy, she'd convinced herself, to do any work toward resurrecting the forbidden *Showdown*. She'd had half a dozen jobs; all but one of those she'd hated. That one had been watching old movies and writing three-sentence reviews for a publication that had been offending some of its younger readers by continuing to rate current movies by the standards of 1930s, '40s, and '50s Hollywood.

At least part of the reason she was sorry to see that job end was that it had been a neat rationalization for her latest and longest-lasting attack of *indecisiveness*. She was afraid the right word was *laziness*. She had not fully confronted herself with the fact that her precarious film project, *Showdown*, had become overwhelming to her—and, ironically, as she unconsciously on purpose continued pushing it down into her bin of unawareness, too real.

Despite the fact that it had been her only professional goal, she continued not to think about it.

• • •

She was staring at the muted television one evening, doing her best to ignore her father's new companion, a Chihuahua her brother had bought for him and dubbed El Poochino, whose only virtue was that his bark seemed muffled, as if he were wearing a collar that was too tight and it pained him to produce even those sounds. His bark came out sounding quietly angry, like a pillow being shaken into its case: *Wheeff wheeff wheeff.*

Ben got up from his favorite easy chair and concentrated like a tightrope artist on making it to the bar.

"Like something?" he said with a stiff, haunted look.

El Poochino watched Emily suspiciously.

She stared at Ben, shocked again by his face. He'd recently had his third plastic surgery and looked too tightly stretched to be real.

"Have a spot. Do you the world." He spoke, as always, with a smorgasbord of British idioms.

"White wine," sighed Emily. "Heard anything from your agent? You never talk about your career anymore."

He poured her a glass of Chardonnay. "Fuck 'em and the 'orses they rode in on. You never talk about yours either."

She ignored that. "Then why do you do that to yourself—have yourself chopped up and put back together on a regular basis?"

Ben ignored that. They could have been in a Harold Pinter play. "I'm going to call my drowsy sodding agent as soon as the swelling is down. I want to play some comedy for a change." He crossed his eyes at her, added some Scotch to his Scotch and soda, handed her the glass of wine and sat back down, idly pointing at the ceiling. "How's the oracle?"

"Asleep."

They watched as El Poochino made a sudden decision to set off for the foot of the stairs; then, pumping and clutching with his tiny legs and claws, he worked his way one cliff-like obstruction at a time, up toward the second floor.

"Where's he going?" said Emily.

"I don't think Al likes us."

"Al?"

"Poochino."

"Ah, of course. Well, the feeling is mutual."

Ben managed a wicked, mouth-only smile, not disturbing the rest of his face. "Oh sister woman, you are a chilly wanker," he stage-whispered with a perfect cockney accent, sounding eerily like Michael Caine in *Alfie*. "This 'owl Daddy thing is turning you right glacial."

Ben had trained at the Royal Academy of Dramatic Arts for four weeks. Then he'd gotten "homesick," moved back to Los Angeles, and finished his education at UCLA. The main thing he'd brought away from his nineteen days at RADA was a belief in the theory that the only way to speak properly on stage and in front of the camera is to speak properly all the time—which apparently to Ben meant any British dialect.

His career had been brief, although most of the few people who remembered him thought of him as a decent enough actor. He was handsome in a not very distinct way, with blond hair, even features (evener now) and a presence that somehow made you watch him. At the same time, after he'd made his exit, you had trouble remembering him. He was in a couple of B pictures, "costarred" in fifteen or twenty episodic television shows, and was scarcely ever seen again. "Doesn't look that bad, does it?" he asked, returning to his favorite subject, his face.

"It's hard to tell *yet*." She forced a smile. "It looks more or less like a face."

"Thanks a bunch." He turned toward a mirror and ran the fingers of one hand along the line of his chin.

Emily looked at his profile and wondered what had gone wrong. The features were perfect but not quite right. The clay had been reworked too often, or maybe the sculptors had tried a little too hard. She had a brand-new brother, but she wasn't sure she liked this one. For a fleeting moment she saw him one late summer when he'd come home from being a camp counselor, healthy, tan, full of life.

"It's a little puffy, and I know the scars are still red, but they fade in a fortnight or two."

Emily nodded, looking deadpan. "Yeah, the eyes look fabulous."

Ben flashed a scowl. Then, recovering from whatever resentful shot had ricocheted off his dimmed perception, he blinked his shiny, still-swollen eyelids. "Right. Eyes are the main thing in film acting, isn't that so?"

"For sure. Absolutely."

"Bugger me, what we do for love, eh?"

"Not much lately."

He carefully formed a new smile. "I know the casting director on a new film at Universal: *Coal Miner's Daughter*, starring Sissy Spacek. There are several good male parts, according to the breakdown. It takes place in the South, and English actors do the best Southern accents."

She stopped herself from saying, "But Ben, you're not English." Nobody says "fortnight" or "bugger me," or, for Christ's sake, "chilly wanker" in this country.

"I was up for the Chris Walken role in *Deer Hunter* a year or two ago. Remember I told you?"

"Uh-huh."

"If I'd gotten that, I'd have an Oscar today." He shrugged and stared down at his drink. "I wish I'd been attracted to the intoxicants business."

"Why didn't you become a doctor like Daddy wanted you to?"

"Because Daddy wanted me to."

She remembered him having a confident sense of himself. Now there was something … *sticky* about him mixed with the remains of his old charm. What she found most troubling was that in recent years his aura of being someone a little jinxed had turned, unobserved behind his series of masks, into a mantle of doom.

"There was a call today from Phil," he said faux-casually between sips of Scotch.

"What'd he say?"

He looked up with something close to confusion or dread in his eyes. "It's back."

"What? *What's* back?"

"The cancer. Daddy's cancer. I wonder how long—"

Emily felt a burst of relief and rage. "Why did you wait until now to tell me?"

"I'm a little arse over tit today. What are we going to do?"

She glared hard at his new face. "Pray he dies this time."

Ben sucked in a sibilant breath. "Crikey. You've turned into a right twat."

• • •

Two weeks later, they were watching television and drinking. It was the first day on the job for the hospice nurse, Ms. Morovec, who was upstairs with her charge.

The local station Emily and Ben were watching cut to commercial just as a gang of stuntmen and character actors were about to be driven into a ravine on the old Republic backlot. The commercials stacked up on top of each other. The seventh was for Walker Chevrolet, a local new and used car agency. A young man, seen only from the rear, was looking for a car of a certain vintage. And whaddayaknow, the Walker people had a classy little convertible that was the answer to his prayers.

Then, for the first time, they showed the young man from the front. He walked toward the car salesman (and camera), accepted the keys with a shrug, and after drawling a low but charged "Hey, thanks," stepped into his new purchase, and zoomed off.

The young man was James Dean.

Of course he wasn't, but he was a living image of him.

Emily sat up and shouted at the television, "*He's the one!*"

Afraid Ben, alarmed, might spit up his pills on their father's favorite chair, she lay back down on the sofa and began to formulate a plan.

She felt as if a decision had been made for her.

• • •

The following day, after several calls, she reached a prickly young male voice at Steiner and Belding Advertising in New York and told him what she was looking for.

The man rustled through some files, then said, "There was just one on-camera talent on that commercial. It's a 'wild spot.' They're only using it in the Western states." (The name of the specific automobile agency—Walker—was superimposed over the basic commercial.)

"Can you tell me the performer's name?" asked Emily.

"That's an unusual request."

"I know that. I'm trying to find him for another job."

"We're not a talent agency, ma'am."

"I realize." Emily smiled ingratiatingly through twenty-five hundred miles of AT&T connections. "But if you could just help me out, you'd save me an awful lot of trouble."

"All right, miss. All right." Her amiable tone had briefly appeased some long-standing wrong. "The actor in that spot was hired out of Los Angeles. His name is Jimmy Riley."

She was poleaxed. It simply could not have been the same actor she'd seen in the sappy, taped pastiche Tom Manfredo had shown her.

She watched for the commercial and saw it several more times. Each time, Jimmy Riley evoked James Dean to an eerie near perfection. He didn't look exactly like him, but he captured him completely. The people from Steiner and Belding had used a first-rate director and an excellent cinematographer who'd understood exactly what they were going for.

The next evening, she was watching television with Ben when the commercial aired. "Why would a car dealership hire a James Dean look-alike to sell a sportscar convertible?"

"Haven't you noticed?" said Ben. "Everybody's a little in love with death these days."

• • •

Even though it was certain her father was really dying this time, Emily found herself again, after her three-year power failure, thinking of nothing but *Showdown*. She started to let herself remember how sure she'd been that Wayne and Boone had *not* been putting her on.

Once more, she took tentative steps toward actually doing something. She stared at the copy she'd had printed, after more research, of production companies that had paid licensing fees in 1955.

She looked at it again. In black and white, between *Seven Brides for Seven Brothers* and "Sol C. Siegel Entertainment": "Showdown Productions."

"That doesn't necessarily mean anything."

"That CANNOT be coincidence."

• • •

She called Tom Manfredo and brought him up to date on her thinking about *Showdown*. She told him she wanted to get together with him and Jimmy Riley. If Jimmy was right for the job after all, she would need them both. She felt guilty, bringing the whole thing up to Tom again. She was afraid she'd acted the big Hollywood mogul before, throwing him a bone, then snatching it away.

He hadn't held it against her. Emily had fallen out of touch with him for almost three years. He'd left her two or three messages, but she hadn't had the heart—or, she later admitted to herself, the courage—to return them.

But things seemed to pick up exactly where they'd left off. "We can get together here," said Tom. "I'll call Jimmy, and cook us dinner on the night."

There was a silence. "You *know* him? I thought you'd just worked together once."

"No no no. We're friends. We met at I.A."

A chill ran through her. "Talk about infinite singularities."

"What?"

"Nothing. It's … it's nothing. Sorry."

"Pardon?"

She made a nervous popping sound with her lips. "It's nothing. … Or rather, it's something I can't explain because I don't understand it myself."

Her impersonators—if it worked out—*knew* each other. She understood she shouldn't be surprised by that, not in a community of entertainers like Hollywood, but she was dazed anyway. It was a new instance in her adventure of ... *she didn't know what to call it*—not simply one more coincidence, but an out of the blue disclosure that she sensed might fall neatly under the heading of Richard Boone's topology: a convergence of singularities.

"It's nothing," she said again, clearing her throat, wondering if maybe he'd been right three years earlier when he suggested she might be crazy. "You cook?" she asked him.

"I follow directions," said Tom. "What if this movie doesn't exist? Your licensing printout doesn't prove anything."

She stifled an impulse to lash out. "I understand that, but I believe it *does* exist, and if it *does*, and Butterworth has the only copy of it—and that's as plausible as his having taken it in the first place—then I've got to know as much as I possibly can when I pitch him the idea and tell him I have the perfect performers." She imagined the puzzled look on Tom's face. "What night do you want to do this?"

"I'll call Jimmy," he said. "When's good for you?"

She hit the stop button on the voice that told her to hang up on him and go sit in front of the television with Ben and watch Gene Autry in *Tumbling Tumbleweeds*.

"Time to hit the off switch, my lovely—the one that when you wanted to run home and hide, at least kept the kids out of your face."

"I can't ever use that switch again."

"God, you're stubborn. Of course you can. Jimmy Riley? Are you kidding me? Do you really feel up to working with a kid who makes his living pretending to be the most difficult actor in the history of difficult actors?"

"If I don't face up to this now, it's like giving up for good and I won't do that anymore."

"Okay, girl. You win. You're talking about an impossible task, but there's not enough time or crayons for me to explain to you why."

5

1962

Jimmy Riley's association with James Dean began one evening during the summer he was ten. His mother and father had driven him and his four-year-old sister Marie Grace (Gracie) to a tiny town in central Arizona. They were on their way to dropping Jimmy off the next day at Camp Cottonwood—"Building Boys with Character." That evening, they went to see a movie.

There was only one movie house. It was almost directly across the highway from the motel where they were staying. They were playing *Rebel Without a Cause*. Even though it had premiered seven-and-a-half years earlier, a month after Dean's death, the attention paid to the movie, and Dean, was still periodically snowballing.

After the show was over, Jimmy asked repeatedly if he could stay for the second screening.

"Why shouldn't he?" said Gerald. "If he really wants to see it again that much?"

Vivian said no.

• • •

Even though his father had told him, "These are the good times, Jim," the next day, Jimmy's stomach was a knot of apprehension as they got closer to the camp. It didn't go away until the counselor of the cabin he'd been assigned to took him aside for a one-on-one talk and a walk around the extensive campgrounds.

Skip Bennett was a friendly nineteen-year-old with broad shoulders, a blond flattop haircut, and an aura of self-confidence. When they met, he grinned, shook hands firmly with Jimmy and said, "What do you say, mate?"

After they'd toured the well-equipped facilities, they climbed up a low, rocky escarpment and passed through an outdoor chapel that had a dozen split log benches and a crude altar. They stopped on the other side of it in a gathering of late afternoon shadows cast by a nearby stand of pine trees.

"It ain't LA, is it?" said Skip.

Jimmy looked at the vista below them. The camp was separated from the desert by a poorly graded service road that extended to the top of a small hill and back down the other side to the main road. Two miles in the distance, a purple block mesa glowed with a phosphorescence that, in contrast to the muted gray-greens of the desert lichen-covered rocks around it, gave it the impression of being lit from within.

"How come it's so green here?"

Skip picked up a stone from a patch of gravel. "This bit is fed by an underground river."

Jimmy pointed at an A-frame cabin farther from the camp, along the way they had been walking, half-hidden among more pine trees. "What's that?"

"Storage," said Skip. "Old gymnastics equipment mainly." He threw the stone at the chapel, striking one of the benches, and tousled Jimmy's hair. "We'd better get back."

• • •

Not long after he'd gone to bed on the second night, Jimmy slipped down from his upper bunk, got a dry pair of pajama bottoms out of his trunk, and moved quietly out of the cabin. He didn't have much trouble seeing—the moon was nearly full, the cloudless sky laden with stars.

He didn't look up. All he saw was the path to the latrine.

About halfway there he passed a pile of cinder blocks at the side of the path.

As he came even with it he was grabbed around the waist, lifted into the air, and plunked onto someone's lap.

A lantern snapped on, the beam aimed at his face.

He felt as if his heart had stopped. He heard Skip's voice: "What are you up to, mate?"

Jimmy couldn't make any words come out.

"I just came out to have a ciggie," said Skip, his hands resting on Jimmy's shoulders. "Do you know Wally?"

The owner of the hand that held the lantern aimed the beam at himself.

It was a distinctly unpleasant face, almost square like an old-fashioned robot with loveless eyes and a large, thin-lipped mouth that was curled into a hard parody of a smile. Its owner had blond hair cut in a flattop like Skip's. He took a drag on a cigarette. Jimmy could see that he had another cigarette in the hand that also held the lantern. It gave off an odor he didn't recognize.

Wally said, "Booga-booga, kid."

Jimmy looked up at Skip. "I was just gonna go up ..." He pointed toward the latrine.

Skip smiled at him. "Feeling a little homesick?"

"No," said Jimmy in a small voice.

Skip nodded. "This is a good kid, Wally." He looked at the pajama bottoms in Jimmy's hand. "What have you got there?"

"Nothin'."

"Okay." He lifted Jimmy off his lap and set him on the ground. "You go where you're going, and get back to bed, hear?"

"Okay."

As Jimmy headed off toward the latrine, he heard Skip ask Wally if he had a handkerchief.

The only other words he was able to understand came out in a snarl from Wally: "Jesus H. Christ."

• • •

Jimmy played baseball, tennis, and swam, and was pretty good at all the games and activities. The one he liked best was Theater Games, led by a stumpy, unaffectedly charming man with a lively enthusiasm for his work. Three counselors, including Skip, and a dozen of the campers took part. The games were improvisational, set up so that no one felt he was being judged. It was exhilarating, like breathing pure oxygen with a dash of laughing gas. It was spontaneous and more wide awake and alive than he thought he'd ever felt in his life. When a session was over, he counted the hours until the next one. After he'd come home from camp though, and he tried to describe it to his mother, she didn't seem to get it. Even his father, meaning to be kind, could only respond, "I guess that kind of thing appeals to your great imagination." Reflecting on it long afterward, Jimmy said it felt like trying to explain "happy" to people who weren't.

Toward the end of summer, some of the campers and counselors, including Jimmy and Skip, were discussing the possibility, albeit long-shot, of becoming actors someday. For Jimmy the best part of the experience may have been having Skip Bennett in the group, learning with him, enjoying the camaraderie with him. Skip didn't hold himself above anyone, including the kids, and Jimmy respected him, almost idolized him, for it.

• • •

One evening after dinner, Jimmy was playing Capture the Flag in a dark, wooded field. The only light was a pale half-moon sliding in and out of a gathering thunderhead. He had come into a clearing, deep inside the other team's territory, and was approaching their flag, pinned to a large mesquite tree. No one was guarding it.

He crept through the high grass on his hands and knees. Looking to both sides, he stayed low so that anyone glancing in his direction from a distance wouldn't be able to see him in the moonlight that sifted through the scattershot clouds.

When he was about a yard from the tree, he realized he'd have to get to his feet to reach the flag.

He smelled a familiar odor and felt a deadening sense of shame. He dropped back down.

Too late.

He felt himself dragged by an ankle around to the other side of the tree.

He recognized the teeth before he could take in the lumpish face of their owner.

"You're mine, asshole."

Two other kids and another counselor bounded into the clearing.

As he was being escorted away as a "prisoner," he looked back and for a motionless instant, everything was lit up. The source of it was off beyond the horizon, but it set the sky aglow. One of the boys who'd captured him, pleased by his own worldly wisdom, said, "Sheet lightning."

It flashed again, turning night into eerie daylight.

Wally was still standing there. Jimmy got a clear look at his face.

The robot eyes were watching him.

• • •

He remembered getting back to cabin 12 that night, but nothing else until he woke up the next morning in the camp infirmary.

A nurse was standing next to his bed. She said, "He's a little groggy. He's still got a fever."

Jimmy could hear Skip Bennett's voice: "I won't stay long." He sat on the edge of Jimmy's bed as the nurse walked away. "How are you doin', mate?"

Jimmy opened his eyes and looked at him. "I'm okay."

"Glad to hear it."

"Just a little sick, I guess."

"Of course." He put a cool hand on Jimmy's forehead. "You take it easy now and get better. And remember what I told you."

Jimmy nodded, embarrassed that he had no idea what Skip was talking about.

• • •

He was sent home from Camp Cottonwood with a "low-grade flu," some bruises, and a recurring nightmare.

In it, he was walking along a wide, hard-packed dirt path, illuminated only by the moon and stars. He could see a pile of cinder blocks ahead of him; beyond that, a wooden cross and past that, a large cabin—away from the others—surrounded by pine trees, at the top of a small hill. He approached the pile of cinder blocks, feeling shame because his pajamas were wet.

Then, he realized he wasn't alone. In front of him, walking along the path in the same direction, in a flickering of rhythmically oscillating yellow light, was a young blond-haired, square-jawed man, illuminated by the eerie glow of the lantern he carried.

Jimmy couldn't tell his family what had happened to him the last night at camp because he didn't remember; this enraged his mother and she accused him of lying.

"I'm not a liar!" he told her.

He didn't think it was hatred exactly—that wouldn't make sense—but his mother looked at him with such joylessness, he understood that whatever was going on in her mind about him was heartfelt.

Later, Gerald told him what had happened to Vivian when she was seventeen.

"Her father smoked heavily ever since he was a boy," said Gerald, "even though he had a circulatory ailment. You see, Jim, he had to have one of his legs amputated."

Jimmy stared at him.

"Her aunt and uncle, from San Bernardino, decided Vivian was the one to look after him during his recuperation. They always had money worries and didn't have enough to pay someone. Vivian was the oldest and a good student, and they decided she could afford to miss a few days of school.

"Late in the morning on the first day of nursing him, your mother was reading a newspaper when her father rolled over toward the wall and went to sleep.

"When she tried to wake him to give him his lunch, he was gone."

"Gone?"

"He'd died, Jim. Well, some of the family, the aunts and uncles, blamed your mom. But you see, it wasn't her fault."

"Of course it wasn't!"

"Life isn't always fair."

The lesson this story reinforced for Jimmy was that he must always be on guard. His mother had good reason to be angry.

• • •

He had a talent for mimicry, and in his early teenage years began to do impressions of a few movie stars, mainly James Dean. For a while, he immersed himself in James Dean lore, reading everything about him he could find. He got so good at the impersonation he sometimes wondered if his "gift" was a blessing or a curse, although his friends were impressed and told him he should go into the movies, which didn't seem like an entirely bad idea. At best, the sensation of channeling James Dean made him feel he was finally unveiling himself, in an energized, spontaneous way, and he was able to close his mind to the dread that went along with the irresistible pull of it.

When he was fifteen, several months after his father's death, his mother finally agreed to let him take acting lessons. "I don't see how I'm going to stop you." She knew she would have been angry at him, if he wasn't her own son, for giving her no choice in something that was not meant to be anyone's call but hers.

Feeling an awakening sense of power, Jimmy turned away from her, combed his oiled hair back with a black pocket comb, and wiped his hands off on his jeans.

Vivian stared at him in the mirror.

"You know what it means, don't you?" he said in a monotone. "I'm going to learn to do exactly what I want to do." She looked at him balefully.

He sensed the fear beneath the look.

• • •

Nobody "discovered" Jimmy Riley. He did not become a teenage acting sensation. Most of the girls in the class (and a couple of the boys) were hypnotized by his sensual magnetism, his myopic intensity. His teacher believed he had talent, but it didn't lead anywhere.

He auditioned for a couple of agents. They were reminded of James Dean, but in the business, James Dean was old, dead news.

6

Tom took Emily out to the courtyard. He was dressed in John Wayne's characteristic Western outfit: a dark, semi-military placket-front shirt, faded denim jeans folded up at the cuff, and worn elk skin cowboy boots.

Jimmy hadn't arrived yet, which heightened the jitters Emily already had from trying to stay in the same film as her host. He served her a gin and tonic (he had a Pepsi) and she tried to give in to the moment and the gin without leaving the impression she required liquor to be sociable.

The setting sun, slanting in on the wall, drenched the bank of bougainvillea, igniting it into a blaze of translucent magenta. The smell of pink jasmine hung in the air and gradually, vaguely aware of the wall fountain's quiet trickle, she began to relax. Drinking her second gin and tonic and having a reasonably comfortable conversation with Tom about superficial things—springtime in LA, the Santa Ana winds, living in the San Fernando Valley as opposed to the more fashionable side of the Santa Monica Mountains; nothing, really—she started to feel quite serene.

Then Jimmy arrived.

• • •

He was about five feet nine with short to medium-length light brown hair, allowed to lie this way and that in the style of James Dean.

Emily and Jimmy drank gin and tonics and Tom had Pepsi as they talked mostly about show business. Jimmy had idealistic notions about the entertainment industry. He moved his arms expansively as he spoke, underscoring his points, although Emily had the sense that his words and his body language were not quite in sync and that the source of his emotions was disconnected from the unfolding conversation. She felt as if she was being maneuvered quickly backward, having to make instantaneous adjustments to an erratic dance partner.

His look was arresting. He had a noble brow like Dean's and cerulean blue eyes that either bored through Emily or didn't look at her at all. One time, he'd stare at her intensely, a second too long—as if trying to make out the composition of her soul; the next, he'd look away quickly, embarrassed it seemed by his own being. The following moment, he'd erupt in a torrent of enthusiasm, the tumble of things on his mind spinning out one on top of the other.

"You can't *not* do what you've got to do," Jimmy was saying, not quite appropriate to what had gone before, "just because you don't know how it's going to turn out. I mean, look around you. You see people all over the place leading dwarfed, frustrated lives because they didn't do what they needed to do. And I'm not just talking about show business."

Emily frowned. "You should see what show business has done to my brother."

"Is he an actor?"

"A good one," said Tom, scraping a knuckle across his chin. "But he's had some tough times lately. I mean, it's not easy. Well, shit, you know that." He flinched. "Sorry."

"What for?" said Emily.

"Well … I just usually try to watch my language around ladies." He was blushing. "I guess I don't need to worry about the occasional—"

"Poop?" said Jimmy. "Emily doesn't seem like someone who'd mind if you're a little cussy once in a while." He looked at Emily. "Right?"

"Right."

"How about you?" Jimmy asked. "How serious are you about acting? Duke told me people thought you were pretty good."

"I don't know about that," she said. "And I'm not serious about it." She glanced at Tom, who looked as uncomfortable as she felt. "I was always afraid I'd get lost in my role." She laughed lightly. "And never find my way out."

She sketched her limited history as a performer, realizing as she talked that she'd better suppress her impulse for a third gin and tonic and try to regain focus on what she'd come there to do. She wondered if Tom had said anything to him about *Showdown*.

"Duke told me your father is sick," said Jimmy. "I'm sorry. I know how that can be." There was an awkward silence. "I mean I hope the doctors are wrong."

"Thanks. I suppose I should tell you why I wanted to get together with the two of you." She stared at Jimmy and for a split second, having no idea where the image came from, pictured him as a child, sitting on a broken curb amidst a concrete field of industrial trash, scrap iron, and razor-sharp metallic junk.

"I have strong reason to believe that a film was begun in 1955 that starred John Wayne and James Dean, but it was never completed." She left a silence but neither of them filled it. "Okay, so maybe you can guess why … I mean *what* I have in mind … here … to talk about … today." She drew in a low hissing breath between her tongue and teeth.

"Is this about *Showdown*?" said Jimmy.

• • •

She felt like she'd told a shaggy dog story and just before she'd gotten to the punch line, somebody had blurted it out, and she felt stupid and embarrassed and that she'd made a terrible mistake to bring it up. One moment Jimmy had seemed exactly right to play James Dean—the next, not at all. Now she was certain of it. He was dead wrong. She felt Tom watching her.

"I didn't tell him a thing," he said, with the same self-consciousness he'd had when he'd been "cussy."

She stared at Jimmy. "Where did you hear about it?"

"It was years ago. A friend of mine—his father was in the business—told me. I figured it was just like 'one of those stories.' *You* know. So did my friend."

"Well, it's *not* one of those stories. It's *true*. And I think I know where the negative is. I think the film is half or more completed. And I believe it's possible to shoot the rest of it with doubles."

Looking like he'd been injected with caffeine, Jimmy turned to Tom. "You knew about this? Is this why you invited me here?"

Tom nodded without looking at him.

Jimmy looked at Emily. "You actually think it *exists*?"

She felt a sharp pain behind her eyes. "Yes, I'm pretty sure."

"And you're both sitting here judging whether I can do James Dean or not, without telling me that's what's going on?"

"It's my fault," said Tom. "Don't blame Emily. She didn't want to dangle a biscuit in front of you, then snatch it away if she decided you were wrong. Her motives were … kind, and that's not the point anyway. I know how smart you are. I should have known. We should've been up front."

Emily forced a smile. "The whole thing may turn out to be undoable anyway."

"What have you decided about me?" said Jimmy in a near monotone.

"I'm not really sure. I'm not sure the kind of thing we're talking about can be acted anyway. At least not on film." She wished she'd shut up.

"I think you're wrong," said Tom. "His look may not be quite right without good lighting and makeup, but he's the most gifted impersonator I've ever known."

Aware of the buzz of a lawnmower a few houses away and the intermittent calls of mockingbirds, Emily looked at Jimmy, then back at Tom, and saw them as she knew she would if she were standing next to them in a bank line. At this moment, they were not just look-alikes—they *were* the originals.

Christ, I'm the most unqualified human in the world to be doing this. Tom is probably not even right for it. What possible excuse do I have to be making a decision like this?

"I'm not sure I'd want to do it anyway," said Jimmy.

She stared at him. *It's HIM. HE'S the problem. It's not me. It's this boy. It's this fucking ... James Dean boy.*

"What are you talking about?" Tom was staring at Jimmy. "You love what you do."

Watching Emily, Jimmy shook his head slowly. "I like performing. I just don't like doing *him*. Not anymore."

Why not, you prick?

But what she said out loud was, "Why not?" It didn't come out as sweet-natured as she'd hoped.

Jimmy hunched up his shoulders like James Dean and did a long, intense take on her, stroking his lower lip with a forefinger. He spoke with the same conviction James Dean might have had playing the scene: "Because I hate the bastard."

Then why the fuck do you do him?

"Then why do you do him, for God's sake?"

He studied her. "You're asking the question like you think I'm just being an asshole, but I'll give you a serious answer. I started because ... I *could*. I thought the passion—even what I now think of as the childish part—was cool. He made the raw nerves and sort of gloom I felt when I was a kid seem okay." He gave a sidelong look at Tom. "Now I do him because"—he barked it like a bank robber telling the customers to hit the floor—"I have NO FUCKING CHOICE!"

Emily leaped up. "WELL WHY THE FUCK DIDN'T YOU SAY SO?"

Tom looked at them like an oversized bear cub discovering his parents fooling around. "I guess I won't have to worry about an occasional … off-color remark, huh?"

Jimmy and Emily suddenly laughed, two locomotives back from their journeys, their boilers chuffing off steam.

• • •

They sat at a high, white-tiled breakfast counter in the kitchen, watching Tom prepare a Bolognese sauce.

"Why'd you quit acting?" Jimmy said to Emily.

Conscious that he was rapidly scanning her face as if reading movie subtitles, afraid of falling behind, she tried to be casual. "I guess I didn't have the crucial manic obsession. No offense." She unfastened her gaze from Jimmy's and looked at Tom. "Do you work through an agent?"

"A manager," he said, "kind of a booking agent. I mostly do John Wayne gigs." He stirred the sauce. "I'm not really an actor anyway."

"Yes, you are," said Jimmy. "You just need confidence. You aren't limited to John Wayne. You can do anything you want. You should be stretching your muscles, trying other things."

Tom stuck out one helpless palm, then finished cutting Swiss cheese and porcini mushrooms into strips for a salad.

Emily lowered her eyes to a pendant he was wearing. "What's that—around your neck?"

Tom looked relieved at the change of subject, but maybe not too thrilled with the new one either. He took the chain and amulet off and handed it to her.

She turned it over in her hand. "It's heavy."

"Yeah, platinum—from Cartier. It was a gift."

Emily stared at it: a horseshoe charm, with eight tiny green stones for nails, and the letters D-U-K-E spanning the open center like a minute bridge. "Who gave it to you?" She thought it might have been a rude question, but couldn't take it back.

"Someone I barely knew—an old friend. It doesn't mean anything." He shook his head. "It's a superstitious sort of ... just a, you know, lucky horseshoe."

"Do you want some help?" Jimmy asked him as Emily gave the pendant and chain back to him.

"I'm fine, thanks." He put the amulet back on, mixed the mushrooms and cheese, and carefully added four tablespoons of olive oil.

Unsettled by the silence, Emily smiled at Jimmy. "Does I.A. really help?"

"Yeah. Most of us have problems with separation and reintegration."

She muffled a giggle.

"Don't laugh. The illusion we create acts like a drug—but it's a useful one. The downside is, if we cross over completely, which we have to do in order to be convincing, and if we stay there too long—and it's hard not to do that sometimes—then we're lunatics, right? Anyway, that's what the world thinks."

"Oh, come on. Who do you offend by having a ... an uncommon profession?"

"In the end," said Jimmy, "a lot of people reject us for pretending to be rich and famous when *they* aren't. They wouldn't hassle us if we were *really* 'somebody,' but something about us being counterfeit celebrities makes it okay for them to give us what they feel they get from '*important people*' in the world: contempt." He slapped his hands together, lost in thought. "I mean, they feel they're *better* than us because when the blush is over, *whatever* they may be, at least they're real. But us? We're phonies." He glanced at Tom. "Right?"

"So, don't hang around people like that," said Emily. She turned her head to watch Tom spoon the salad onto plates.

"Who *should* we hang around with?" said Jimmy.

"I guess that would be up to you."

"Right. That's why Tom and I have our sort of mutual sub-support group. We get together once in a while outside of meetings to reassure each other we're not crazy and that there's nothing phony about us. It helps."

Tom made up-and-down Groucho eyebrows. "Even though we *are* crazy." He looked at Jimmy. "You want to help with dinner, Mr. Authentic, shut the fuck up." He grinned at Emily.

She laughed. "But *you* seem entirely sane to me."

"Do I?" He picked up his Pepsi, put it down without drinking from it, and handed them their salads. "My craziness is almost always hooked up with performing and with … the old man—with Wayne."

"How so?"

He looked at her from an unexpected corner of wariness. "I've told you. It comes out as stage fright."

"Really? What do you do when you're not up to it, but you have to go on anyway?"

"I just … *do* it."

"So where does your will, your resolve, come from if you don't enjoy it?"

"They pay me. If I don't go on, nobody'd ever hire me again."

"But I'm curious. Most performers have that constant show-off thing. You don't seem to. So, what *do* you have? What makes you do what you do?"

He shrugged. Emily couldn't tell whether it was unexplored territory for him or if he was simply unwilling to say any more about it. "I don't know exactly. I guess it's just something I can do."

"He's being modest," said Jimmy. "He just got a great acting job."

"Oh? Doing what?"

"It's not a big deal," said Tom. "Only a commercial."

"Tell her where you're shooting it."

"Italy." He beamed. "It's for an Italian wine. I leave in a week. I'll be gone for ten days."

"And I'm house-sitting," said Jimmy.

• • •

After dinner, as Tom and Jimmy were drinking coffee and talking, Emily was wandering around the living room, looking at the art. She stopped next to the print she remembered from the first time she'd been in this room, the nude with her back to the viewer. As she'd guessed three years ago, it was by Picasso. She even remembered the title now: *Blue Nude.*

"*Oh thank you, College of Fine Arts. Wise investment.*"

She tried to shrug off the wine she'd had with dinner, and looked at the painting next to *Blue Nude.*

Chills surged through her.

It was a 2 x 3-foot oil, a pretty decent Western scene. It hadn't been there three years ago. She would have remembered.

It was a picture of four people and four horses on a stretch of desert, dotted with Joshua trees, yuccas, a few other scrub trees and bushes, several kinds of cacti, and a couple of tumbleweeds in a beautiful beige and coral desert wilderness. The faces of two of the people were unmistakable. One of the men looked very much like Tom Manfredo—or John Wayne. He stood next to a horse, and was looking off toward a light brown-haired woman and a man who was kneeling by the remains of a campfire. The kneeling man looked exactly like James Dean.

The fourth figure, the other man, stood in the background. He had nondescript, even features and was in the act of drawing a pistol from a holster, although you didn't know where he planned to aim it.

"What's this?" Emily demanded, her eyes entirely round.

"Another gift," said Tom. "Actually, it may be the reason Jimmy and I got to be friends. Somebody gave it to me, then later, I told Jimmy about it and invited him over and showed it to him."

"It wasn't here three years ago. I would have remembered."

"It hadn't been given to me yet."

She smiled distractedly and stared at the painting again. "This is one of the spookiest things I've ever seen. What's it supposed to be?"

Tom shrugged. "Just what you see." He got up and came over to look at it with her. "A couple of guys who look a little like Jimmy and me … or … you know who, along with another man and a woman."

"Jesus. It doesn't look a little like you. It *is*—" She stopped mid-sentence, looking back and forth between them. "I'm not a good judge. You didn't model for it?"

Tom shook his head.

She looked back at Jimmy. "Do you know the painter?"

"Neither of us modeled for this," he said. "It's not even a good picture, just a tacky depiction of John Wayne and James Dean. It might as well be on black velvet."

She stared at it again. "It's an infinite singularity."

They stared at her.

• • •

Later, Emily watched Jimmy, who was wrapped up in a point he was making: "...You've got to be able to give yourself to whatever it is, use that ... *thing* that distinguishes you from everybody else. If you don't, it's like having ... I don't know, say, the *gift* to comfort people, but choosing to live like a hermit instead, and suddenly you're old and you can't figure out why you feel so empty."

"Where do you get stuff like that?" said Emily. "You're still a kid. What do you know about emptiness?"

"He knows," said Tom. "In a lot of ways—he hates to admit it—he *is* James Dean. I really don't see why you don't think he'd be right for your movie."

She felt blind anger. *Why is he saying that*? The whole thing had been dispensed with. Now he was bringing it up again. The boy was dead wrong. So was Tom for that matter. Goddammit.

She looked up and saw Jimmy watching her. "What are you staring at?"

Tom said, "You've already delayed acting on your idea for three years. He may not like playing James Dean, but that's what he does. What's wrong with you?" There was no criticism in his eyes, only a curious air of trying to remember something he'd forgotten. "He may not look like Dean—here, in this light—but when he does his thing and it's put on film by pros, he's unreal."

When Emily didn't answer, he looked at Jimmy again. "For pity's sake, show her."

Jimmy sighed and looked off, as if seeking invisible guidance. "What would you expect James Dean to be like?" he said finally. "Here, now, in this room?" He was shaking his head minutely, gazing at Emily from what seemed to be the beginnings of a trance.

"How the hell would I know?"

"Uh-huh."

She felt a sharp chill as Jimmy leaned in toward her.

He spoke quietly: "You'd find somebody who was smart, compassionate, selfish, volatile ..." He grinned as if they'd known each other forever and shared some tantalizing secret. His voice had changed timbre; his words seemed to be coming from a different part of him, tumbling out in an adenoidal mumble. "He got close to you," he said, "whether you were in the front row or the balcony. He was hostile, egotistical, confrontational ..."

She gaped at him. Even though his face didn't match up feature for feature with James Dean's (how would *she* know?), every nuance evoked him.

He inspected her carefully. "There was sexual content in his every motion, every look." He pulled back slightly. "He was exasperating, garrulous, lonesome, clipped, blunt, tedious, just about impossible to carry on a conversation with. But he could be, within the same conversation, diplomatic, sweet, endearing, gifted with language and infectious laughter." He grinned broadly and laughed a sudden staccato sequence of high-pitched guffaws that made Tom burst into laughter. "He was infuriating, sensitive, delicate, breakable, easy to get along with if you agreed with him about the inevitability of his getting his way."

He sprang up, like a cat. "He was an athlete, a fluid, rushing, careening landmine. When he came into a room, he had enough momentum to walk up a wall. He was a show-off"—he turned away—"who was just as much James Dean from the back as he was from the front."

He lifted his shoulders slightly and, without the slightest self-consciousness, cocked his head in a way that recalled from the visuals compartment of Emily's brain most of the publicity photographs of James Dean. "He was outrageous and he made you crazy, like any exhibitionist does, but he was an artist at being James Dean." He turned back to her and sat down again, staring intently into her eyes.

"And so am I. I've got a second to none collection of insecurities, but not a single one about *doing* James Dean." He swatted at the air like he was after a fly. "The prick."

• • •

Without seeming effort he had transformed himself into the essence of James Dean.

Tom grinned. "What do you think? Emily? What do you think?"

"Jesus," she said finally. "Jesus." After another long moment, she said it again: "Jesus … God." She stared at Jimmy as her brain did a speed check of its hundred billion neurons, looking for any reference point at all. "You've got the part."

Her timid side said: "*If that means anything.*"

• • •

Jimmy had kept his guarded eyes on her as she was trying to come up with words to say to him after his performance. She was especially beautiful that evening. She'd had her shiny chestnut brown hair cut to a medium-long length recently and although it couldn't be called stylish, it framed her face nicely and drew attention to her beautiful eyes.

7

Emily knew she had to talk to Jack Butterworth, but she couldn't imagine why some squirrely, reclusive guy who had met her only once should want to discuss sharing his life's treasure with her. She also knew she'd never find out if she didn't ask.

Maybe he'd like to trade his riches for something more rewarding than a few cans of celluloid—if they existed. Her timid side told her these impersonators were probably no more than standard celebrity impressionists, so why bother?

"They're uncanny."

"Shut up."

Jimmy Riley called and asked her if she'd like to go see Tom do a supermarket show on the following Saturday.

After hesitating, surprised he was calling her for any reason, she said, "Sure, I guess. Okay." When they'd hung up, she resisted the impulse to call Tom and see if he knew why Jimmy might be calling her. Instead, she found Butterworth's card and telephoned him. She was relieved when no one answered. She left no message.

"Goddammit. You said you were going to do this. He probably went out to get a loaf of bread or something."

She thought about Miles, the extra who had told her about *Showdown* in the first place. She knew what liars people can be, and that in any case Miles had been someone likely to behave as if he was an insider.

"You're the best. You can rationalize any timid road you want to slink down."

"What if "Showdown Productions" IS nothing more than coincidence? And what if Boone and Wayne WERE just having a laugh at "the girl's" expense?"

"But how do you know it doesn't exist until you know? You're folding up into yourself again."

"All right! I'll call him back, and this time I'll talk to that hideous machine. By the way, which side are you on in this thing?"

"That's a very savvy question, I'm not quite sure lately."

She wondered how many brain cells she'd lost to her family's cozy little alcohol and pill habit.

Fifteen minutes after his first call, Jimmy Riley phoned her again. He surprised her this time by cheerfully asking, "Would you like to have coffee with me tomorrow?"

It caught her off guard again. They had not exactly hit it off their first time together, but he asked her in a tone of voice that was warm and boyish, almost pleading.

• • •

The next day, they met at a coffee shop on Doheny in Beverly Hills. Emily was startled to find herself chatting easily with him this time. He seemed less defensive in the middle of the day—even so, she couldn't entirely rid herself of a feeling of restlessness with this impersonator.

"What a bizarre thing to do for a living. Performers are so strange. Acting, period, is such a weird way to make a living. It's like saying I don't like this world; I think I'll live in this other one where things are more under control."

"Except they're not under control there either."

"I have to apologize for the other night," said Jimmy. "Sometimes I can get a little ..." He frowned, looking for the right word.

"Pretentious?" said Emily, sipping her coffee.

He examined her face the way he had when he was doing James Dean at Tom's house, a smile forming as he half-lifted a shoulder. "Yeah, okay, maybe a little um … a little bit of that sometimes." He shrugged again and grinned.

"No," she said, "quite a sizable bit. For a while there it was like you were explaining the meaning of life to us—the way show business works, the human mind … just about everything else, actually."

Jimmy gave her a mock-hurt look, injured innocence, then chuckled. "Yeah, okay, maybe sometimes I can be a little … know-it-all." He frowned. "But I work on myself. I don't think you get to be who you want to be right away in this life, do you? I can't believe that right this minute you're exactly who you want to end up being."

"Touché, I guess," said Emily, giving him the doubtful look fourth grade girls give little boys who are trying too hard. "But isn't that what living is about? To learn as you go how to figure things out, and try to become a little more 'adult' along the way?"

Jimmy looked puzzled. "Isn't that what I just said?"

It felt to Emily as if he was scanning her—like that device with the other-worldly red light in *2001: A Apace Odyssey.*

"I never met you before the other night," he said. "So why do I have the feeling we know each other? … Or maybe …" He trailed off. "Anyway, I felt like we *kinda* began to connect."

She smiled. *We kinda* yelled at each other."

Jimmy chuckled. "Yeah, we did, didn't we? … But it wasn't like … lethal yelling, was it?"

Emily's eyes reflected the light streaming in through the coffee shop window. "No, I guess it wasn't, but there was something about what you were saying that felt …"

"Arrogant?" His smiled broadened.

It wasn't warmth exactly that washed over her, but whatever it was, it surprised her. Not only did she realize they were a little alike, there was also something raw and lost and—she hadn't expected this—sexy about this James Dean boy. Vulnerable and … sexy.

She'd have to be careful about that.

• • •

Emily had one more out of the blue inducement to proceed with her project, her final call-to-arms to produce *Showdown.* She had earlier phoned a specialty act manager she'd met at a party and left a message for him to please give her a ring. Possibly because he knew Emily was "nobody" in the business, it had taken him a while. He finally rang her back the morning of the day she had lunch with Jimmy Riley.

Knowing you never, never linger over hurt feelings in Hollywood, she asked him if he'd ever heard of Tom Manfredo.

"John Wayne?" said the manager.

"What?"

"John Wayne. Tom Manfredo, the John Wayne impersonator."

"You know him?" she said, surprised. "As a John Wayne—"

"—impersonator, yeah. Why do you ask?"

"Oh, somebody mentioned they … were looking for an actor who fit that general description and I … told them I knew you."

"I see. Well, there's nothing you'd call 'general' about this guy," said the manager. "The only way I ever heard of him is as a John Wayne impersonator. He's … I don't know. … The guy's just … I have no word for what he is. He's beyond amazing. Why are you calling me? I don't represent him. The only thing I know him from, is one time the Morris office was doing a presentation for some sitcom package they were putting together, I forget what, and they hired this guy, Tom Manfredo, to do a John Wayne thing. I was there on some other project and I saw it."

"And?" said Emily.

"And holy shit," said the manager. "I've never seen anything like it in my life. It was full gallop freaky."

"How so?" said Emily.

"If you ever catch his act, you'll know," said the manager. "This guy redefines the word look-alike. If this ... *performer* walked into a bank and said, 'I want to withdraw all my money,' they wouldn't ask questions, they'd just hand John Wayne his money and maybe ask him what kind of vitamins he takes because he looks almost exactly like John Wayne did thirty years ago. Dead ringer."

At this moment, now, having coffee with Jimmy Riley, Emily realized she was doing the first thing a producer must do with a project like hers. She knew enough about movie making by now to understand that no two productions were ever the same, and that whatever her personal feelings about Jimmy and Tom might end up being, her first obligation, her only one for the moment, was to woo these two men. They would be the pivot point of her project.

• • •

Tom's show was at a Pioneer Market in Saugus, east of Magic Mountain amusement park, near the Angeles National Forest.

They didn't talk much on the drive up. Tom was nervous and rehearsed his program to himself most of the way, gazing out at the ragweed-covered hills, noiselessly moving his lips, trying to focus his attention on the stories he was about to tell in front of two hundred people.

Emily and Jimmy watched the show with the look people get when they see a glass blower or a gifted dancer or Yoyo Ma playing the cello.

Afterward, Tom said, "How do you think it went?"

"You were godly," said Jimmy.

"Nah, come on."

"No, I mean it; it was nice work. When you get rolling with it, you weave a spell. You never touch politics. How come?"

"I'd lose the ones who hate Wayne's politics," he said. "And turn it from entertainment into something else for the others."

Emily looked at him like a deer in headlights. "The whole show is just … it's breathtaking. How do you do that?"

Tom shook his head. "No idea how. Or, to be honest, why."

• • •

The next week, the three of them spent hours together. Emily saw herself and the boys as three kids or puppies that had just met in the park—sniffing, running, and jumping together, or as a trio of physically challenged people who feel at ease with each other because they all have similar challenges and are less self-conscious about their own, at least for a short, beguiling while.

Even though it was the furthest thing away from what she'd thought would happen, she recognized that there was a chemistry taking shape between them. Tom was unquestionably attracted to her. Jimmy was smitten in his way, too, although with him, there seemed to be a sense of not wanting to get caught at it. She thought she might be developing a crush on Tom—but *probably* not. The sense she'd had at first of an instant loathing of Jimmy, had changed into something much different: intense curiosity, mixed with … other feelings she did not plan to let herself think about. Whatever the something deep within his eyes that intrigued her was, it was nothing she would ever act on.

"He's just like us, just as high-strung, volatile, and breakable. Not to mention, he's kind of a bum, not the type who typically appeals to us."

As for Tom, he was just plain lovable, but that kind of thing was always a problem for her. She knew that lovable and her were not a natural fit.

There was something else scratching at the back of her mind. When the boys had picked her up a few days earlier, Ben had gotten to the door just before she had, and Jimmy had said hello to him, as if he was surprised at encountering an old acquaintance. She decided he'd probably remembered him from one of Ben's old TV appearances. God knows she could identify with that.

• • •

One day they took the San Diego Freeway over the Santa Monica Mountains, got off on Sunset, and drove the five and a half winding miles west, through opulent Brentwood to Will Rogers State Park. Emily had packed a wicker basket with sandwiches, wine, and sodas for Tom.

They passed Will Rogers's well-kept polo field, his time-warped Western-style house (all the rooms complete with their original furniture), and the still used stables. They hiked up into the hills where they found a picnic spot that overlooked Santa Monica Bay and the Pacific Ocean.

After they'd eaten, Emily said, "What's it like, being John Wayne? What's he like?"

"You mean *my* John Wayne?"

"Yeah, sure, yours."

"He pretends to be open-minded, but he wants you to behave like he wants you to behave, and he's not happy unless he gets his own way."

Emily stared at him. "You take this seriously."

"You have to," said Jimmy. "They won't be ignored. I've tried to kick mine out. It never works."

"Mine just appears," said Tom. "Uninvited. The first time I did my act, he showed up afterwards and said"—he shifted effortlessly into his John Wayne—"That was the sappiest piece of tripe I've ever witnessed. You make me sound like a damned hayseed.' "

Emily stammered, "What did you ... What did you say to him?"

"I told him I was only trying to take advantage of his public image. And he said, 'Well, that's real depressing.' Then he vanished. But he's always nearby, ready to tell me what he thinks I ought to do, what I shouldn't do."

"You mean he shows up to you ... *physically*?"

He stared at the ground. "Not exactly. But he's there. I can see him."

"But nobody else can?"

"Of course not."

"Have either of you considered the possibility that you're just, oh, nuts?"

"Constantly," said Tom, looking at Jimmy, who nodded vaguely. "That's why I don't usually tell this to people."

"Why are you telling me?"

He studied her, puzzled. "I don't know. ... Maybe it's just ... time."

"Where did you get the name Tom Manfredo? You don't look Italian."

"I've told him he ought to call himself Zack Brophy or something more leading man," said Jimmy.

Tom reached into his back pocket, took out his wallet, and carefully produced a laminated picture of a young couple in their early twenties. The man had a thin, ordinary face and dark brown hair like Tom's. The woman was half a head taller, blonde and pretty, with a nice smile. "My mother and father."

"I guess except for your hair, you favored your mother," said Emily, although she didn't think he looked much like her either. "How old were you when they …"

"A few weeks."

"Where'd you get the picture?"

"I'm not sure," said Tom. "I've just always … had it. I'm pretty sure it came from the people, lawyers and such, who processed me into the first place they put me after the accident—kind of an orphanage, really." He glanced at Jimmy and down at the ground. "Then later, I had foster parents and I had their name for a while, but I got it changed back to Manfredo, the name on my birth certificate." He frowned. "Too much information, huh?"

"Didn't your real parents have any relatives?"

"Not that I know of." He indicated the picture of his parents. "This is not the original, of course. I've got copies of it." He put the picture back into his wallet, and looked out at the bay.

Emily touched his hand, then, after a long moment, said, "I think I should tell you ... I see people as celebrities. … Jesus. I cannot believe I said that. I have a problem with allowing people to be who they really are." Her features recomposed themselves into a quirky, resigned smile. "My mother was Myrna Loy. My dad is Melvyn Douglas. My brother is Lew Ayres. And you are ... well, you know who."

There are some secrets she thought were too personal and peculiar to tell anybody. Like this. She had never said that last part, about her family—to anyone, not even Dr. Withers. She had no idea why she'd broken her rule, but she went ahead anyway and outlined the history of her "little problem."

Tom was staring at her. "What happens as you get to know us?"

"I don't know." She spread her hands, palms up. "Maybe it doesn't matter. I know it's stupid, but I don't seem to be able to do anything about it. Maybe there's something too comforting in it to make the effort to let it go, even if I could. … Don't misunderstand. I still like you as *you*—if you know what I mean."

"But John Wayne is alive and living down in Orange County," said Jimmy.

"I know."

"And you know I'm Jimmy Riley. And this is Tom Manfredo."

"Of course. I *know* the difference. I can even *see* it. It's just that the effect of my … condition is so powerful that I don't always *feel* the difference. In the end, what I'm actually seeing doesn't really matter. I know that's confusing. It is to me too, and it is *not* fun. People look away from me sometimes, sensing I'm … kind of strange, almost like they're accidental witnesses to something they weren't meant to see and their animal instinct tells them to look away from 'that girl.' Pretend she isn't there."

Jimmy had been watching her with lamblike eyes. "At my worst, I *am* James Dean." His look turned 'tortured,' like James Dean having to say something he didn't want to say. "I'm twenty-seven. When he was my age, he was … dead. I've lived longer than he did. I have a more solid basis in breathing reality than he did. And at times it feels like he's the knock-off and I'm the original. Or else it's *Invasion of the Body Snatchers*, and I'm the one getting snatched."

Emily slowly formed a smile and, after a moment, they all grinned at each other, acknowledging that three relative strangers had just confessed to each other their deepest, most insane secrets.

• • •

At home that evening, Emily thought about the peculiar kinship among the three of them. It was as if they were all in the same flock flying north to the same destination, even though their histories were entirely separate. They didn't understand those instincts; they just had them.

"Are you dense? All these singularities have to mean something. They are goddam well to be heeded—acted upon."

"Leave me alone. I thought you were on the other side of this thing."

"We're exchanging places. You are going to find and complete this film."

• • •

Jack Butterworth answered the phone at nine fifteen the next morning.

"My name's Emily Bennett. I met you on the set of *The Shootist*. I was with Richard Boone."

"You a friend of Dick's?"

"Yes, I am. I'd like to talk to you if I may."

"What about?"

"I've got a movie idea."

"You lookin' to hire an editor?"

"Yes, but it's more than that." She didn't want to blow the whole thing with a clumsy pitch over the phone. "I'd like to talk to you in person."

There was another silence before Butterworth said, "What's Dick up to?"

"He *was* in New York, teaching," she said. "But he's living in Florida now."

"Let me have your number. I'll think it over and give you a ring back."

"Promise?"

"Yeah sure, promise. I just said so, didn't I?"

8

JUNE 1979

At nine o'clock on a Monday morning, Tom Manfredo got on an Alitalia plane bound for Milan and the best job he'd had since his film with Burt Reynolds.

The American casting director, hired by an Italian advertising agency, had come across Tom's picture in the Academy Players Directory, called him in to tape an audition and, after the agency had made its choice, booked him for a six-day shoot in Corniglia on the Ligurian coast, south of Genoa.

They didn't fly him first class, but he was lucky enough to have a vacant seat between him and a middle-aged man with thick gray hair and bushy black eyebrows who slept from Utah to Ireland.

In the air, drinking a Pepsi, he reflected on his lack of success with women, then lost his train of thought looking at a young pregnant woman across the aisle, leafing anxiously through a copy of Italian *Vogue*.

"You ought to try to learn to hold one thought for ten seconds," said John Wayne.

Tom didn't move his lips or actually speak. "What are you doing here?"

"Reading your mind. How the hell do people stand these middle seats?"

"Would you please whisper? People are not exactly understanding of our ... association."

"Nobody can hear me, but you'd better be real subtle on your end."

"I've met a girl," said Tom. "She's beautiful. She looks at me like I'm something special. And now I'm leaving the country. How's that for timing?"

"You've got to make a living. And if she's anything like most of your women—not that you've spent much time with women of any description ..."

"I've had relationships."

"A ram has relationships. And every once in a while a ram gets banged about as meaningfully as you do."

"This one's different."

"Yeah, they're all different. And crazy."

• • •

From the age of five weeks, when his parents were killed, until he was six years old, Tom lived in an orphanage in Queens, New York. From six to ten and a half, he lived in a foster home.

The father was almost always gone, and Tom didn't like the mother. His main memory of those years was hard work and a frigid home atmosphere. They were a family of seven, Tom the youngest, and when he wasn't in school, he served as a combination maid and janitor to the rest of the family. He thought of himself as a male Cinderella. His foster mother was the evil stepmother.

When he was still ten, his foster father ran off to Atlanta with a woman golf pro, and since Tom was beginning to rebel against the forced labor his life had become, his foster mom gave him up, and he ended up back in the orphanage, also in Queens.

The discipline was undeclared but systematic for the older boys. When they misbehaved, they were strapped. One young male staff member, a self-styled hippie, disliked almost as much by his colleagues as by the kids, liked to talk about peace and the kinship of all life, but found the strap not quite adequate to make his point—especially with the bigger boys like Tom. He used a heavy leather pouch on them (favored by some police departments around the world for inflicting pain without leaving a mark). He found Tom especially resistant, and passed his peace-loving message on to him by using the leather sap on his mid-torso and whispering how blessed they were to be sharing *His* righteousness.

By the time he was thirteen, people were already calling him Duke because the adult he was beginning to take shape as reminded them of John Wayne. As a result, he gave a lot of thought to the other Duke. He had only the mostly chilly, offhand guidance of the people who ran the orphanage to show him the way, so he took some comfort in such thoughts and felt a growing rapport with the old movie star. After a while, he found himself confiding to him almost as if he were there.

Then, one night, as real as the darkness, he was.

He heard the familiar voice say, "I'm going to have to take you in hand. Close your mouth and pay attention. I'm here to help you through some of the difficult times ahead. First of all, you're drinking too much. You're fifteen years old. You shouldn't be drinking at all. Don't do it. You've only got one life."

"It's just a few beers," said Tom.

"It's not just a few beers. I've seen you drink three six-packs in one night. You're already developing a shaky memory. Drinking, the way you do it, is bad for you. It's bad for people's impression of you."

"People can't tell."

"People *know*," said Wayne. "And they dismiss you in their minds. They might not appear to, but they do, even if they're drunks themselves—*especially* if they're drunks. That's just what happens. I've been around a long time. I know about these things."

"But I'm big, like you. I can handle it."

"Can you? Well, consider this: booze and the kind of drinking you and I do, and the life that goes along with it, are killing me, and you have no idea how fast it's happening."

"Please tell me why I'm haunted by a ghost who isn't even dead."

"I'm not a ghost. I'm a presence."

"But why am I actually seeing you?"

The presence shook its head. "How the hell do I know? I guess you sought me out."

Tom frowned. "Are you saying you're a ... *reflection* of me?"

"I am *not* saying that," said Wayne. "I can't stand that kind of crap."

"But it has to mean something like that."

Wayne looked disoriented. "Does it?" He shrugged and vanished.

For the first time in his life, Tom considered the possibility that he had not been given the right pieces to solve the puzzle of his life.

Then, instantly dismissing the notion, he felt, for a few minutes, more peaceful than he could ever remember.

• • •

Tom was only a year out of high school when, one day as he walked from Eighth Avenue toward Broadway on Forty-fifth Street, a slight, suntanned man in his late thirties, wearing an Armani suit and with the easy familiarity of a salesman, stopped him in front of the Golden Theatre and said, "Good God, boy! You're a dead ringer for John Wayne. Are you an actor?"

Tom grinned at him and shook his head no.

The man handed him a card that identified him as a producer of commercials for the Carter/Strong Advertising Agency. "Would you like to *be* John Wayne for two days?"

"What?"

The man blinked and re-focused on him. "Except, holy crap, you already *are* him. … Listen, please come up to my office tomorrow—555 Madison Avenue, ten in the morning. Will you do that?"

"What would I have to do?" said Tom, looking down at the man doubtfully.

The producer looked perplexed. "Basically … nothing."

The next day, after he was cast and the subject of licensed employment came up, Tom told the producer he didn't have a Social Security number, or even a legally valid birth certificate. "All I've got is the one from the hospital I was born in, and that hospital no longer exists."

"Somebody must have that record."

"You'd think so," said Tom. "The New York City Health Department is supposed to, but it turns out they never received it from the hospital."

Tom had already learned that a Social Security number couldn't be issued to him until he could prove he was who he said he was. He had no idea what he would do when the time came for him to get a proper job.

The Carter/Strong producer nodded emphatically and said, "Now that I know you exist, I am not doing this campaign without you."

So it happened that Tom got his first acting job, and along with it, a Social Security number and US passport, which latter document the producer produced in order to make possible the acquisition of the former. Legitimately a US citizen by birth, Tom Manfredo finally had "hard proof" of it.

• • •

He got paid eight hundred dollars for playing a high school football player who reminded some pretty girls of a young John Wayne.

Later, he got six thousand dollars' worth of residual payments for that day's work and accepted an offer from an agent who couldn't wait to represent him. First, he joined the Screen Actors Guild and the American Federation of Television and Radio Artists. Soon afterward, he became a member of the American Guild of Variety Artists when someone asked him to impersonate John Wayne in an industrial show (for the employees and prospective ones of a fertilizer company based in Secaucus, New Jersey).

He had made a career decision. The only problem was that performing terrified him. When he asked Wayne how he dealt with stage fright, the old man said, "I don't have that. What's it like?"

"I don't know what it's like for most people, but every once in a while, I get so nervous I faint."

"You *what*?"

"You heard me. Sometimes I get so scared I black out. Don't you ever get scared?"

"Well, I feel a little … *fretful* sometimes, but I certainly don't faint." He said "faint" as if it had an unpleasant odor. "I'm a professional."

"Don't professionals have stage fright?"

He looked surprised. "I don't know. I never thought about it."

"Listen, no offense, but maybe you're not the mentor I need."

"How about if I need you?"

Tom squinted at him. "What?"

Wayne looked at him intently. "I need you to be awake. You're not really present in your existence, boy. You're headed in a direction that's not going to do either one of us any good." He looked around with distaste at the living room of Tom's cheap Hollywood apartment and vanished.

• • •

Tom gazed at the pregnant woman across the aisle from him, wondering if she was flying toward the baby's father or away from him.

"And what about Paige Leone?" said Wayne.

"Who?"

"The woman who left you the pendant."

"I don't really remember her."

He took a sip of Pepsi as his mind drifted to the Mark Key Detective Agency. He had hired Mark's older brother, unhappily named Donald, to try to track down his birth records. It hadn't worked out. Don had seemed more than eager to help, but his investigation had turned up "nada," he reported, obviously glum at having failed. Mark later told Tom, a little defensively, that his brother was highly thought of in his profession, although he didn't say by whom. "In fact," said Mark, "we'd planned to give Don top billing, and we would have—him being the older brother—if it hadn't been for the awkwardness of having our marquee read: *Don Key Detectives.* 'Donald' would have been almost as dicey. And just billing ourselves 'Key Detectives' makes us seem limited in scope. You understand."

The funny thing was that Tom and Donald Key became friends. Don kept trying to find Tom's legal birth records even after Tom could no longer afford the agency's fees. It seemed to Tom almost as if Donald Key was taking it as a privilege to work for him—the only problem being, Tom concluded, that Don had probably not been the brightest student in his detective school class.

He looked at the pregnant woman again, then out the window, smiling as he mouthed the words "Don Key Detectives."

The plane trembled, flying over the Rocky Mountains.

"*Per favore, attaccate le cinture di sicurezza,*" said the pilot. He spoke a few more sentences in Italian, and then a female voice said, "Please fasten your seat belts. The flight captain says it's going to be a little bumpy for a few minutes. After that, he says it should be pretty smooth flying the rest of the way to Milan. Please keep your belts fastened anyway, just as a precaution. If you look out either side of the airplane, that's the Continental Divide below us."

Tom heard the click of the microphone being turned off as he looked down at the westward gliding Rocky Mountains.

• • •

One day in 1977, he found a message on his machine from a Philip Hopper.

When he returned the call, a man with a thin, metallic voice said, "Oh yes, Tom Manfredo. This is Philip Hopper. I was a friend of Paige Leone's."

"Is that right?"

"You know she died." Tom heard his own audible intake of breath. "She found a lump on her breast and died six months later. That was five weeks ago."

"I'm sorry."

"Are you?" There were seconds of dead air. "I'll tell you why I called you. I have some of her personal belongings. You probably know she had no family. I'm calling you about a painting and a pendant with a chain that she left you."

"What kind of pendant?"

"I don't see any point in describing it to you."

"Why would she leave me anything? I didn't really know her."

"I got the impression it was quite serious."

"It wasn't." He decided against asking this man how he happened to be in charge of distributing the woman's possessions.

• • •

At noon the next day, Tom opened the door and entered the Blue Martini Cocktail Lounge on South Hill Street in Los Angeles.

He walked through the tavern's vestibule. An antique brass coatrack stood in front of a dark blue velvet curtain, behind which were extra tables and chairs.

As his eyes adjusted to the dark, the same unmusical voice he'd heard on the phone, now coming from behind the bar, said, "Welcome to the Blue Martini, Mr. Manfredo. I'm Philip Hopper."

As Tom approached the man, he glanced around him at the elegant interior of the place. There were about a dozen round glossy wooden tables, each with two comfortable looking chairs, set on an expensive looking floor of intricate black and white mosaic tile, designed in geometric art deco fashion. It was hard to make out the source of the room's lighting, but its blue-tinged aura was dramatized by a high, brushed tin ceiling, characteristic of many such urban buildings built between World War I and WW II. The bar was of dark wood with a polished milk-white marble top that reflected and amplified the blue light atmosphere of the room.

"What a beautiful place," said Tom.

"Isn't it?" Hopper pointed to a padded barstool, covered with deep purple leather. "Please have a seat." He was a hard-featured man with gray-brown hair that curled in large ringlets, like a head on a Roman coin.

The geometric mirrors behind the bar reflected Tom as he sat. He noticed they also doubled the sparkling, colorful bottles of liquor, elegantly arranged on thick glass shelves. On the walls between and around the mirrors, were framed black-and-white pictures of LA city landmarks, as well as additional sources of room lighting: shaded lamps and frosted wall sconces. Next to him, at the center of the long bar, a glass front cabinet held boxes of cigars. The Blue Martini saloon reeked of early mid-twentieth century opulence.

"With your permission," said Hopper, "we'll do our business right here. We don't open until two o'clock, and I've seen to it that we'll have privacy." He didn't wait for an answer, or permission. "What can I get you?"

"Anything soft would be good."

"Really? I understood you were a drinker."

"Not anymore."

Hopper moved to one side behind the bar.

The sound system was playing a Lennon-McCartney tune, about a blackbird with broken wings, singing, waiting patiently for the miracle of flight, so it could finally feel what it means to soar.

For no reason he could think of, Tom felt the dull ache of a beating he'd gotten in the orphanage from the pious hippie with the leather sap.

"Paige and I lived together for almost two years," Hopper called out over the music. "We met here, at the Blue Martini. I'm a businessman," he added unnecessarily. "I do rather well, as you can probably imagine. Paige was the most important thing in my life. She didn't need to die." He stood in front of Tom again. "She'd become a Christian Scientist, not a good one, I'm afraid." His voice sounded oddly buoyant. "She was too impetuous for the discipline." He handed Tom a glass of Sprite with ice and poured himself a white wine. "I'm sorry, the kitchen's not open yet."

"I'm not hungry."

Hopper smiled thinly, his gray eyes studying Tom as if he were a curious new museum exhibit. "I've seen your work," he said. "At a supermarket in the Valley and in the film you did with Burt Reynolds. We watched that quite often."

"Why?"

"You should know I feel no personal animosity toward you." It seemed as if he were about to read the will. There was something else, ominous, quivering beneath his civility. "I began in Paige's affections where you left off."

"I don't understand any of this," said Tom. "I only ever spent a few evenings with her and that was two or three years ago."

"That's not what she told me." Hopper reminded Tom of the grotesque illustrations in a children's book at the orphanage titled *"Manners"—Starring Mr. Do & Mr. Don't (Pointers for Little Persons).* Philip Hopper looked like Mr. Don't.

"What did she tell you?"

"I'm afraid that's between her and me," said Hopper.

Tom put his Sprite down on the bar. "May I have the picture and pendant, please?" He stood up.

Oddly cheerful now, Hopper smiled. "Of course."

Taking a key ring out of his pocket, Hopper moved to a cupboard and, out of Tom's line of vision, opened what Tom imagined was a safe. After relocking it, he came back with a brown leather drawstring pouch, which he handed to Tom.

"You might find this a little … unsettling," said Hopper. "You'll want to sit down again."

Tom frowned, but did as he was told, thinking about the abrasiveness in the man's voice. "Except for her … passing on, why should I be unsettled?"

Hopper's smile faded.

Tom opened the pouch, emptied the contents into one hand and studied his bequest.

It was a silver horseshoe, heavy, with eight small green stones for nails. His nickname, "Duke," bridged the center in capital letters. The whole thing was half again the size of a quarter and was on a relatively long, thin chain. He turned it over and found an inscription: "To D from P."

"Obviously," Hopper said with a mirthless smile, "it was something she'd planned to give to you."

As Tom looked up at the man, he felt a shudder rise and settle in his upper spine between his shoulder blades. "Why are you so angry, Mr. Hopper?"

Hopper blinked several times. "I watched her sit through your Burt Reynolds movie endlessly. I would have thought it was impossible for anyone to hate someone like you that much." He moved to the other end of the bar, produced a 3- x 2-foot package that Tom hadn't noticed earlier, and started to untie the string around the plain brown wrapping paper.

"Don't unwrap it, please. I'll do it when I get home."

"I think you should look at it now." He finished taking off the paper and held the picture into the light so Tom could get the full impact.

Tom stared at it. "What's it supposed to be?"

"You don't know?"

He shook his head. "It looks like James Dean and John Wayne."

Hopper nodded. He was smiling broadly, a ham actor, playing to the back row. "She did it for you."

"She painted it? I didn't know she was an artist."

"Oh, she had many talents."

"If she hated me, why would she leave me anything?"

"She liked to imagine the look on your face when you saw these things. Maybe she's satisfied now." He watched his guest as if he were waiting for the drugs he'd slipped him to take effect. "Paige said you might have to study the painting and wear the pendant for a while before you'd know."

• • •

"*Do* you know … *now*?"

Tom looked at Wayne, crammed into the empty seat next to him as they flew eastward. "You know I don't."

"But you're still hoping to. Is that why you wear it?"

Tom smiled mechanically. "I wear it for luck."

Wayne snorted. "You only took this woman out … how many times?"

"I imagine you know the exact number better than me. I was drinking a lot in those days, as you know, and sometimes I have orphan's memory. I only remember two or three nights with her."

"Are you all right, sir?" A slim stewardess, with what Tom thought were judge-like eyes, stood next to his seat. "Can I get you something?"

"Oh, no thanks. I'm trying to figure out some … business things. I guess you caught me thinking out loud. Sorry."

"No need to be, sir. I talk to myself sometimes." Not smiling, she moved on down the aisle.

"He wasn't talking to himself," Wayne called after her. "He was trying to explain himself to an aging movie star."

Tom spoke under his breath. "You stayed here on purpose. You knew she was coming this way. You like to make people think I'm crazy."

"They don't need me."

Tom looked past the sleeping Italian woman and out the window. "How come you talk like John Wayne sometimes and sometimes not?"

"I only use it to get your attention. Otherwise, you boob, there's nothing so tedious as living your life as a damned caricature." He had aped his own slow-going drawl perfectly, enunciating "caricature" with his signature cadenced ease.

Tom grinned. "Now *that* was a great John Wayne."

Wayne stood up, stepped over Tom into the aisle, and stretched. "I think maybe I'll go up front and see if I can give Signore Capitano a hand with this thing."

"Just don't touch the controls."

"You'll hurt my feelings. I'm experienced. Don't you remember *The High and the Mighty*? I brought that one down pretty neatly."

"That was a movie."

"Yeah? … And?"

"It was a movie," said Tom, "Just a story."

Wayne looked puzzled. "What do you think your life is?"

Tom frowned at him. "It's got to be more than just … some *story.*"

"Who says?"

Tom looked lost, hurt. "Well, doesn't it?"

"I'm not sure," said Wayne. "Either way, don't you want to turn yours into a good story, a happy one?"

Tom gazed out the window at the clouds below, cushioning him, he liked to imagine, from anything bad. When he looked back, Wayne was gone, up in the cockpit, he guessed, talking to Signore Capitano.

• • •

The commercial called for him to be on a big palomino in thirty-eight separate cuts in and around the village of Corniglia. He rode across the beach, through the water, down cobblestone streets, past the ruins of an ancient abbey, and over a seaside field of century plants blooming twenty-five feet into the air.

In every shot he carried a bottle of La Spezia wine on a tray. It wasn't easy to keep the product upright. He dropped several bottles—his arms were aching—and twice, nearly fell off his overworked horse.

Between shots, he dismounted, stood next to his palomino, and looked out at the orchards, gardens, and vineyards reaching away from the Mediterranean. He felt this might be a rare opportunity to begin to understand himself.

Then, with no penetrating questions answered, or even formulated, he climbed up into the saddle again.

Sometimes, without having meant to, he imagined he was John Wayne riding his mount with elegant ease, moving with the horse as if he and the animal were one.

He had mixed feelings about that image.

The director and crew gave every sign of liking him, but sometimes he also heard giggles and whispers: "John Wayne. *Il Duco viva. Lui e* John Wayne." He could see that it didn't matter that his name was Manfredo. A couple of people asked politely where his family was from. But even if he'd known, he didn't think it would have mattered. He was still a foreigner. He felt about as Italian as a Dodger Dog.

Or John Wayne.

On his fourth night in Corniglia, he drank four bottles of La Spezia.

• • •

Standing next to a newsstand near the Duomo di Milano, a weary-looking woman stood over Tom Manfredo, who lay on his back on the sidewalk, unconscious.

A man approached and said, "*Che pasa? Chi e?*"

Looking down at Tom, the woman said, "*Guarda, caro. Vedi? E John Wayne.*"

"*Non e possible,*" said another woman, pointing to a display copy of an Italian tabloid.

The others looked at it and saw the headline:

JOHN WAYNE E MORTO.

9

Emily and Jimmy traveled north on Highway 101 to 170, then on the Golden State Freeway to San Fernando Road, which they remained on when it became Bouquet Canyon Road. It was late morning on a weekday. Jack Butterworth had called Emily back and agreed to meet with her at his house. She'd brought Jimmy with her because, she admitted to herself, she was scared to go alone.

There wasn't much traffic. Jimmy, who was also nervous about this meeting, drove slowly.

A few miles north of Santa Clarita, Emily rolled the window of Jimmy's VW Rabbit all the way down and held her right hand out in the dry dusty air. "When I was in college," she said, "and later in New York, my friends thought I was … moderately wise."

Jimmy glanced over at her. She was letting her flattened hand surf the backdrafting currents of air.

"You know what I mean?"

"No."

"I was usually moderately stoned. Moderation was the key. I was always above the fray. Not too far, just enough so that nothing was risked—in any direction. My moderation was moderate." She pulled her hand in, held it to her cheek, and stuck it back out. "I don't want to be moderate anymore. There are no rewards in that." She frowned. "I've always had the people I was with to think about—my parents, my brother. My mother always acted like everything I had to say was a precious gem. But I never believed her. She loved me. She thought I was smart."

She turned down the visor in front of her and looked at herself in the makeup mirror. Sighing, she flipped the visor up again. "What I really was, was baffled. When I first got to New York, I roomed with Mitzi Gaynor and later, Magda Gabor; they don't have to be *stars* necessarily—any half-assed celebrity will do. I mean Magda, not Mitzi."

Jimmy smiled ambiguously at her.

Since the day at Will Rogers Park, and even more since Tom had left for Italy, Emily had found herself talking freely with Jimmy. "I'm only now realizing there's something wrong with me. I'm feeling that if I could mix in a little more and try to take, you know, a real hand in my own fate, that I could reform a lot of these private images I've saddled myself with." She peered sideways at him, trying to imagine what he was thinking.

He glanced back at her. "You have kind of a wild animal look today," he said. "Don't get your hopes up too high."

"I'm not going to let myself think that way. I'm not going to be moderate in my hopes anymore—or schizophrenic."

"Pardon?"

"Never mind." Her fingers fluttered over the passing landscape of featureless, straw-colored hills. "Ms. Morovec isn't there today, and my brother's not exactly sober. I shouldn't be doing this, not today. He told me not to worry—Ben, I mean—that he'd *really* have to drink if Daddy died on his watch. And I have to believe him. I *have* to, don't I?" She didn't look at him or wait for an answer. "Ben scares me lately. Beneath all the booze, he seems very sober sometimes—a little like my father. Too gathered, too … neat. Like he's trying to bury an especially rough siege of collywobbles."

"Collywobbles?"

"That's a Ben word. He says it's a severe case of nerves that grabs you deep in your tummy and doesn't want to let go." She held her hand out the window just long enough for a three second flapping in the wind before she pulled it in and held it to her cheek again. "Daddy once told me about a woman he'd known before he met my mom, a woman he'd planned to marry. One day, this woman was in a minor car accident and was brought into the hospital where Dad was serving an Emergency Medicine internship. He told me that when he examined her, he saw that her feet were dirty. I knew right then, knowing my father, how that story was going to turn out. 'She had filthy feet and I never saw her again,' he said. She shook her head. "I always imagined finishing that conversation with him. 'You rejected a woman you'd planned to marry because on one day she had dirty feet? What if she'd been wearing sandals, working in the garden but had to rush out of the house suddenly? Why didn't you at least try to find out *why* her feet were dirty? Maybe she had a good reason. Maybe she made her own wine and her feet were stained from grapes.' You've got to at least take a glance beneath the surface of things."

She nodded her head decisively. "It's time to make a mess."

• • •

Near the top of a hill, they found a motley jumble of a one-story house that had evidently been constructed room by room over a period of years with a variety of makeshift building materials: stucco and cheap aluminum siding wedged in among clapboard and yellow brick. The parts of the house that called for it had been repainted recently. It was not untended to, just chaotic and confused, as if it had been designed by a mad architect on crumpled drafting paper.

Except for cacti, weeds, a couple of Chinese elms, and an unhealthy mesquite tree, there was nothing growing on the patch of hardened dirt around it. There was no way to tell where the road they came in on ended and where the yard began. Jimmy parked next to a primer-spotted Oldsmobile with a rag stuffed into the gas tank.

Getting out of the Rabbit, he looked up at the roof and wondered if the severely canted chimney would stay where it was during the next earthquake.

Emily knelt down to pet a rheumy-eyed, black and gray foxhound/pointer mix, grateful for the attention.

A crackly voice spoke with raspy urgency. "Yes? What do you want?"

They looked toward one of the elm trees and saw an old megaphone-style speaker attached with wire to the lowest limb. The still-live speaker creaked and yawped, demanding a response.

As soon as Emily had identified herself, the voice said, "Who's that with you?"

"My associate and friend," said Emily.

"You didn't say you were going to bring anybody."

"He's my … partner." Static. "He's a stand-up guy. I vouch for him."

The speaker continued to quack and crackle for several more seconds, then the voice said, "I guess you'd better come in." The speaker went dead.

They walked up to the house and onto a narrow cement slab that served as a front step.

Butterworth stood behind a screen door. He hadn't aged much. The features of his face were still gathered toward the center, like the three "eyes" on a coconut. His hands were half-clenched with arthritis, he had what looked like a recently self-administered haircut, and his face was red and puffy. It looked like he'd been crying.

"Hi, Mr. Butterworth," she said, sensing that it was a bad idea to call attention to his emotional condition. "I won't ask if you remember me."

"I'm not an old man. I remember." His voice was thin and shaky. "I wouldn't be likely to forget somebody that looked like you."

She blushed. "This is Jimmy Riley."

Butterworth peered at him closely, frowning.

"I'm happy to meet you," said Jimmy, flatly, almost in a monotone. Emily recognized by now the speech pattern he took on when he was nervous, or feeling defensive.

Butterworth took a handkerchief out of his pocket and dabbed at his eyes as he scrutinized Emily.

"Thanks for seeing us," she said.

"I was curious. I don't put myself out into the world much, but that doesn't mean I'm not interested in people." He hiccupped, opened the screen door, and they followed him into his front room.

It was a tumble of discount store cupboards and shelves, piled high against all the walls and jutting out at one point into a peninsula of stacked storage boxes. Butterworth threw some papers and magazines off an old, dark, overstuffed chair covered with an unidentifiable fabric. He gestured for Emily to sit in it, then pulled a folding chair out from underneath a card table, stacked high with papers and videocassettes, and placed it in front of Jimmy, staring at him. He dabbed again at his puffy eyes and sat down opposite them on an old swivel desk chair on casters.

"Did you hear about Duke?" he said. Emily looked puzzled. "John Wayne. It just came over the radio. I can't take it in. He died." He swiveled away, wiped his face with the handkerchief, and turned back to them. "I'm sorry. It's hit me hard."

It hit Emily hard, too. It was the first they had heard of it. She later told Jimmy she'd felt at that moment like leaving and going out to find the nearest liquor store.

Butterworth pressed his lips together, which seemed to lead to a clenching of all his facial muscles. Looking like a grieving weasel, he exhaled a long, slow breath, opened his eyes, and dabbed at them once more with his handkerchief. "What's this all about?"

Jimmy looked at Emily, who blinked and took a deep breath. "We understand you have several reels of *Showdown*."

Butterworth didn't move. His gaze swung slowly to Jimmy, then back. "Did Dick tell you this?"

"Yes, but I'd heard a rumor of it before."

"You're here because Wayne died and you want to exploit it. That's it, isn't it?"

"We didn't know he'd died until you told us, but yes, we would like to … do some capitalizing."

The old film editor stared at her. "Suppose you tell me what you have in mind."

Jimmy found just enough nerve to speak. "Emily used to work in … well, *for* … Sterling Films in New York. In acquisitions …" He trailed off again, leaving only a feeble smile.

"Mr. Butterworth," said Emily, "if you have an uncompleted movie with John Wayne and James Dean working together, we think people should know about it."

"Izzat right? And why do you think that?"

"Because anything else would be a sin. Keeping it to yourself is a sin—if you have it."

"Don't be tossing words like 'sin' at me, missy." He glowered at both of them. "Maybe the two of you ought to turn around and go right back to Hollywood." He said "Hollywood" with undisguised distaste.

"We aren't trying to take advantage of you, sir," said Emily. "I figure after twenty-four years, you aren't that easy to take advantage of."

"Damned straight. I've also got a nice gun collection—just so you know."

"We're not that way," said Emily, not knowing what she meant by that, or for that matter, what *he'd* meant. Was he threatening to shoot them? She didn't *think* so."

"You're a friend of Boone's. He told me so." He narrowed his eyes like Robert Redford's Sundance Kid, just before he admits he can't swim and he and Butch jump off the cliff.

Butterworth looked over his shoulder, scanning the shelves, cupboards, books, boxes, and papers around them; glanced at Emily again, got up, and shuffled to the nearest window. He lifted up the closed venetian blinds, just enough to peer out, looking in all directions.

He looked back at Jimmy, then settled his gaze on Emily. "How long you known Boone? When'd you first meet him?"

"Winter of '73-'74."

"And when did he first bring up the subject of *Showdown*?"

"He didn't," said Emily. "*I* brought it up. I'd heard the rumor of it and asked him if by any chance he had. That wasn't long after I'd gone to work for him."

Butterworth frowned. "And when I met you on the set of *The Shootist*, that was … what? Early 1976?"

"Right."

Butterworth sat back down in the caster chair, looked at Emily again, and after another long pause, said, "I've got the negative." A prideful smile broadened his compressed features. "I've got about seventy minutes—edited sequences of footage you wouldn't believe." A look of astonishment crossed Jimmy's face. Emily, wondering if her new friend was about to come apart, redoubled her concentration. "Do you have the only copy, sir?"

Butterworth breathed in deeply. "I'm not sure. I think at this point, probably." He frowned at the backs of his hands. "I used to be a hard drinker, for too many years. Then one night about six months ago I had a lot of drinks, went to bed and woke up an hour later with a pulse rate over two hundred. I drove to the hospital. They gave me a lot of drugs and got it back to normal." He made his sour face again. "And how that changed me is that I don't know what to do with myself anymore. I can have one drink if I want it, but that's not the kind of drinking I enjoy. I can't afford to go anywhere. And now, for the first time in longer than I can remember, it pesters me that I can't get hired in my profession. Except for crap work around the fringes. Industrial films—stuff any schoolboy could do."

"Why can't you get hired to do what you want to do?" said Jimmy, his voice skipping momentarily into an adolescent squeak.

Butterworth stared at him. "I think it goes back to *Showdown*."

Emily left no dead air. "Why hasn't anybody ever heard of it?"

"Who said they haven't? More people than you think know about it."

"Then why isn't it common knowledge?"

"It's common rumor." He glanced uneasily at Jimmy. "And the thing about common rumor is that after a while, it gets to be so common, nobody pays attention—like one of those yarns that goes around. You know. In people's minds, they say, 'Yeah yeah, sure,' and dismiss it out of hand."

"What about the crew?" said Emily. "Why didn't word get out from the crew?"

"It was a skeleton crew—eighteen, all men but the script supervisor and the makeup girl. It can be done—if it's the right people.

We were all given a substantial bonus to ... *persuade* us not to talk about it."

"But *why? Why* did production shut down?" said Jimmy.

Very slowly, he said, "I don't know."

"Mr. Wayne told me the reason was that they fell behind because of the way Dean worked," said Emily.

Butterworth squinted at her. "You talked to *Duke* about *Showdown?*"

"Yes, sir. For about five minutes on the set of *The Shootist.*"

"Well, pardon me, but why was Duke talking about this to *you*—a young woman I'm guessing he didn't really know."

Emily squinted back at him in the puzzled manner of someone who's been asked a question she's been meaning to ask herself. "I don't know," she said. "I think because Richard Boone seemed ... comfortable with me, and that was enough for Mr. Wayne."

Butterworth nodded. "Yeah, all right. I guess that's why *I'm* talking to you." He glanced at Jimmy, then fixed his gaze on Emily again. "I don't think they fell behind because of the way Dean worked. Duke might not have wanted to tell you the real reason. They were pretty close to their timetable. Dean managed to convince Duke it could be done on a short shooting schedule. They hired the best crew." He pursed his lips, thinking. "It mighta had to do with Duke's people."

"What people?"

He sucked through his teeth impatiently. "His *people.* All those dipshits and their hangers-on whose bread and butter depend on a movie star, like a medieval fiefdom. You know as well as me who they are."

Jimmy said, "But why wouldn't they want him to do it?"

Butterworth frowned at him, then took in a deep breath and leaned back. "I think it goes back to John Ford. Duke practically worshipped the handkerchief Ford chewed on. Despite Ford's self-image of being a man's man, he also thought of himself as an artist, although he'd never have said such. And he did artistic films, when the studios would let him get away with it—*My Darling Clementine, The Man Who Shot Liberty Valance, The Long Voyage Home*, and especially *The Fugitive*—not the Richard Kimble one, but the one that came from a book by Graham Greene about a whiskey priest—Henry Fonda as a priest with a moral failing. It was probably Ford's artiest film, and it didn't make ten cents.

"Well, Duke not only adored 'Pappy' Ford, he also had a father-son thing with him, and since Ford was a man who liked to beat on people, in a manner of speaking, it wasn't exactly what they call a 'healthy relationship.' Duke wanted like a son of a bitch—pardon me, young lady—to outdo him, give Pappy a good thumping.

"That's where Dean came in. He got to Duke with the king of all Western art projects—*Showdown*. And the 'people' can always smell it when their meal ticket is going all artsy on 'em and it makes 'em jumpy, and they start applying that kind of shifty pressure they're so adroit at."

"*How'd* Dean get to him?" said Emily.

Butterworth laughed. "Ah, well, Jimmy never lacked *cojones*. He just walked onto the set of the picture Duke was working on at the time—*Blood Alley*, terrible piece of … Anyway, he said, 'I want to speak to Duke.' Well, the whole town was talking about Dean in those days, so Wayne let him into his dressing room and they had a conversation. The story is that Dean said, 'I'm going to direct a film. I want you in it.' Dean later told a friend that after Wayne had a good laugh at that, Dean swore, 'It's going to be the best, most carefully-crafted Western ever made.' "

"On a fast shooting schedule?" said Emily.

"It was all in the preparation, according to Dean—although what the hell he should have known about something like that, I have *no* idea." He frowned. "But of course Duke obviously thought it could be done too."

Emily regarded him skeptically. "You're saying John Wayne did a little art film because James Dean asked him to?"

He spread his hands. "In a nutshell, yes. Duke believed he was getting involved with something that could be important. And he could see a pot of gold at the end of the rainbow, working with Dean." He lifted his eyebrows and spread his fingers wide in sign of grudging respect. "And Dean did have a way with him—at least during first encounters. If he told you he was going do a thing, it didn't take a lot more words than that to make you believe him." He shrugged. "And Duke was a gambler, especially back then. This was the same guy, recall, who put every penny he had into *The Alamo*—which flopped like a flounder."

Jimmy said what Emily was thinking. "But I thought *Showdown* was Dean's project."

"Well, see, you have to remember Dean didn't know his entire life's output was going to amount to three films. He felt like this was just the beginning of his career. He was establishing himself. His interest was in directing it and acting in it. He didn't care about anything else. Whoever held the purse strings, Dean didn't much give a damn. At least that was the rumor. He'd have done anything to get Duke on board. He was a gambler, too. You don't get where either of those guys got to without a broad streak of the high roller in you—and that is a rule. Then later, on location, when whatever the hitch was that came up ..." He trailed off as he thought back. "I wasn't there, I was home in LA, but I was told Dean was real unhappy they couldn't fix on a time to finish it.

"Then, of course, a few months later, Dean took that little ride in his Porsche." He raised his eyebrows again, this time to indicate: *The moving finger writes; and having writ, moves on.* "So time passed and, as I understand it, nobody talked much about it, and then—"he spread his arms, palms up"—the whole project slipped into the category of myth."

Emily was concentrated on him like a hawk. "But why did Wayne let himself get talked out of it? Is that what happened? That has to be it, right? I mean, if he believed he was doing something important?"

Butterworth stared at her. "I don't know. I just ... don't ... know."

Emily looked around at the disarray, then back at Butterworth, who was, in her view (she later told Jimmy), drifting in and out of being the versatile Mercury Theatre character actor, Everett Sloane (*Citizen Kane*). "And how did you come to be in possession of the footage you have? Do you have the original negative?"

After a perfect dramatic pause, Butterworth nodded, musing. "I suppose it's still possible for somebody to sue me, but offhand I can't imagine who. At least one opinion was that Duke, or whoever owned it at that point, had the whole thing in the hands of surrogates, and that they lost interest completely when Dean got killed because they had the rest of Wayne's empire to worry about."

"What about the writer?"

"James Dean was the credited writer."

"You're kidding," said Emily, sitting up even straighter in her chair. "I had no idea he was a writer."

"He was a brilliant kid," said Jimmy.

Emily put a hand on Jimmy's arm. "Do you think he might have been fronting a blacklisted writer?"

Butterworth shook his head. "Uh-uh. No. Duke would have smelled it and never got involved."

"How do you come to have the negative?" said Emily.

Butterworth's frown contained a hangdog smirk. "I was assistant editor on it. Most of the time, I was in the lab where they were processing the film." He hesitated.

"And?"

"And I got fired. The editor was a son of a bitch. We didn't get along. When I went back to get my stuff, I'd been drinking." He scratched at his chin. "I was—pardon me, young lady—pissed off. The guy who filed the films was having a cigarette. I went in and snatched the negative."

Emily stared at him. "That's *it*? Didn't they come after you? Or call the police?"

"I'm not sure. I was scared they would, so I left town for a while."

"How long?"

He showed them a balmy smile. "Five years. After I took it, I sobered up a little and suddenly realized I could be in deep shit—pardon my French again—for what I did, so I left pissant Tinseltown." He looked into the distance, perhaps remembering his five-year sabbatical from pissant Tinseltown. "But when I came back ..." He squinted his eyes in puzzlement, which caused the mottled skin on his forehead to crinkle like a wet rag. "Nobody said anything about it."

"Ever?" Emily and Jimmy chorused.

He shrugged.

"Is the negative well-preserved?" asked Emily.

"Damned straight. It's the only thing I have of any value. I've got it in hermetically sealed cans. It's my only investment. It's more than that. I look after it like it was my own child." He looked at his hands. "I thought if Duke died before I did . . ." He shook his head. "I thought I could take it to somebody and turn it into a documentary. . . . Although the thought of that gives me the creeps."

Emily stared at him, blinking, took a deep breath and leaned forward. "We would like to complete *Showdown*."

Butterworth lifted his gaze to hers. "How in hell would you propose doing *that*?"

"It's 1979," said Emily, "the dawn of a new age in filmmaking. You know that. With the aid of computers, it's possible to do things that were never dreamed of before. Disney is in pre-production for a movie, called *Tron*, that's going to be all computerized effects." She blinked. "But you already know this, don't you?"

Butterworth didn't say a word.

"Our idea is to find a good director, hire two doubles to fill in for John Wayne and James Dean, and with the aid of computers, voice-overs, creative long shots, and postcard photography of the locales, piece together a complete film." She watched him with laser eyes. "But of course, maybe we're crazy. Maybe the scenes you have won't lend themselves to that."

Butterworth drew in a breath. "I'm not sure. You might be able to do it with the first part of the film. I have most of that; they'd shot all the tavern scenes at one time and, you know, recurring location scenes." His eyes flicked around as he thought about it. "What they didn't get is the beginning—the stuff that takes place back East. And they've only got isolated scenes for the end of it." He made his sucking noise with his mouth. His brow creased. "I don't think it would work. You'd have to linger too long on your doubles. People would know."

"Not necessarily," said Jimmy.

Emily nodded. "Not if you had the *right* doubles."

"But there's no script to cover the ending and the beginning," said Butterworth. "I don't have a copy of it. I'm not sure one exists. They were real tightfisted with them."

"That's the least of our problems," said Jimmy, flushed with the moment and the fever of the pitch, but also wishing he didn't so often think of several things at one time. He wondered what Emily was thinking of him. "She'll get a good screenwriter," he said. "She'll come up with *something*. She'll ... She'll ... If you've got half of a film starring John Wayne and James Dean, I know it's … it's possible. … It could be … I mean it *WOULD* be …"

Jimmy continued trying to get the words to come out right.

Emily wondered if he was doing a James Dean moment. Maybe—she had no way of knowing—he'd been doing him since they'd gotten there.

Her moment had arrived. She was terrified of what might come out of her, knowing she wouldn't get it right. Jimmy was a huge disappointment, useless as a pitchman. It hit her again that she didn't really know why she'd brought him. Maybe she'd thought he would be worth something as a visual aid. But Jesus, it wasn't that. She'd brought him because she had hoped he would somehow magically jump in and save her. She felt a mist of perspiration on her forehead and wished her brother were there. Ben was a solid performer when he was sober. He could think on his feet, under pressure.

Jimmy was still stammering. "It can be done if you ... you know, just go about it, like … like really, *really* carefully …"

Butterworth was looking intently at him. "Let me guess. You're the James Dean double?"

Emily drew in a thin, hissing breath. "That's true, Mr. Butterworth. I know he doesn't look exactly like him, but in his makeup, he has an astonishing power to *become* James Dean."

Tasting flop sweats, Jimmy looked as if he were about to cry.

"Yeah, well, I can see the Dean ... thing." Butterworth looked uncomfortably back at Jimmy even as he made a sort of shrug of acknowledgement. "But I don't think it would work." He stood up, shaking his head. "No, I don't think so. You put doubles into this, computers or not, long shots or not, people are going to know. You'll have to get close enough for the audience to be able to stay with the characters. And when you do, they'll see that the performers are doubles. And that'll piss them off and they're going to want their money back." He contemplated Emily. "What exactly is your stake in this?"

She glanced at Jimmy who, now aware he'd failed in his mission today, felt rejected, humiliated—like jackals had caught his scent and the only way not to die was to remain still as a corpse. He knew it wouldn't last long. It never did. He simply had to wait it out and everything would be ... bearable.

Emily went pale. "I'm sorry, Mr. Butterworth." She shook her head; her brow creased as she stood up to face him. "We've wasted your time."

Jimmy pivoted in his chair and gawked up at her.

Looking at him, Emily saw the most unstable part of herself.

"Christ, look at this poor baby, this poor little child."

"*What* are you DOING? What is the MATTER with you? You want to live, or would you prefer to lie down and die—right now, next to this 'poor little child'?"

"Don't much like that idea—'my lovely'. *Sometimes, you are about to observe, you underestimate us. Check this out:"*

She glanced back at Butterworth, then slowly sank back into her chair.

Not lifting her eyes to the old editor's, she spoke evenly. "Okay, my *stake* in this ..." She worked her jaw involuntarily. "I'll *tell* you: I sought you out because I found two actors. And I was struck with a feeling in my ... in my *bones* that maybe there was some reason for my professional background coming together with meeting Jimmy and a brilliant, on-the-nose John Wayne impersonator."

She looked up at Butterworth. "If there *was* a reason, it had to be *Showdown*. I don't usually believe in things I can't see or touch or explain. But I can't see or touch or explain away meeting the possessor of a lost John Wayne, James Dean film on the day John Wayne died, only a few weeks after being introduced to two actors who were born to portray those two men. I know this sounds crazy, but whatever the demands of your film are, I'm betting this is possible. If you've got seventy edited minutes, that's ... what, almost two-thirds of a movie? I'm guessing with that much film in the can, that if the rest of it were smartly directed and edited in, using all the technology that's been developed since 1955 and doubles so skilled at doing the originals it's surreal, that we would have something astonishing."

Butterworth sat back down, not taking his eyes off her. "What about the rights to it?"

"It's chancy, obviously. Twenty-four years have gone by. It's unclaimed property. But if the film is completed, I don't think any court in the country would prevent us from distributing it." She spread her arms. "And even if we were sued, at that point, whoever it was would probably want the thing released in order for the suit to be *about* something. I think it's worth the gamble. Don't get me wrong. I have a misgiving or two—if we were able to come after you, so could somebody else. On the other hand, there it is—in your possession. For the moment at least, it's still yours to do whatever you want with."

"But you haven't even seen the footage," said Butterworth. The crooked smile crept across his face again.

Emily beamed back at him. "Then show it to us, Mr. Butterworth. Show us your work."

"I didn't know you had it in you. Very nice!"

Jimmy looked at Emily with something like the adoration a toddler has for his mama.

10

John Wayne swung easily out of the saddle, gave a tug on the reins, and walked toward the distant foothills.

James Dean pulled at his appaloosa and followed him. "Where are you headed?"

"Nowhere. I'm gonna go find a place to sleep," said Wayne.

"I meant tomorrow."

"Up to high country."

"What are you going to do there?"

"You're awful damned curious."

"I figure since it looks like I'm going with you, I got a right to know."

"Right?" Wayne unloosed a burst of cynical laughter as he moved toward a patch of late afternoon shadow cast by a stand of junipers. "You don't have any rights at all."

"I go by what I see," said Dean, grinning at him insolently.

"Then you see precious little, youngster." He let go of the reins of his large bay and the horse began to feed on desert grass.

In a separate shot, Dean dropped his reins and leaned awkwardly against a natural bench of pink sandstone. He stared off toward the setting sun and the dimming forms of cactus that seemed to stretch all the way to it. "I never seen the sun go down that way before, all red like that."

Dean's concentration seemed to switch gears, then he said, "Cut. End slate."

The screen went to black. Butterworth said, "That's the last of the unincorporated scenes. You can probably guess I've remixed the whole thing recently."

From beginning to end of what they'd seen, Emily and Jimmy had been spellbound. It was a simple story with unembellished elegance, the hallmark of a great movie Western. Emily felt sure that if it had been completed, it would have been a good film, maybe a great one.

There wasn't much plot. Years ago, a man named John Barnes fell in love with a woman called Sarah and was set to marry her. She was the widow of an unpleasant character named Edgar Scanlan who died in the Civil War.

On the day of the wedding, Scanlan, with whom Barnes had long shared a mutual dislike, comes home. Obviously he didn't die; he was one of the few survivors of Andersonville Prison. There were no scenes from the beginning of the film. Butterworth said they were to have been shot last, and they didn't get to see Scanlan or Sarah, who had not been in the part of the film that was shot in 1955.

Barnes, played by John Wayne, has said goodbye to Sarah and headed west. Nineteen years later, he's on the run. He's been an outlaw (it's never made clear *what* law he's broken) ever since he left home.

One day, Barnes goes into a bar and gets drunk. After a fight, he's kicked out onto the street by a couple of burly thugs. With the camera close on him, he makes a decision not to get up and allows himself to pass out in the mud.

He's alone, and realizes he's going to become an old man without ever having done anything with his life.

He hears a voice and looks up to find a young man standing over him. His name is Gabriel. He's hostile, defensive, and sad. He's Sarah's son by Scanlan. Gabriel tells Barnes his daddy left them and his mama died soon afterward, which depresses Barnes even more, and he tells Gabriel to go away.

Gabriel says, “Mama told me to find you. She said you were a good man, that you’d help me. I’m glad she can’t see what you turned out to be.”

Barnes says, “How old are you?”

“Eighteen.”

“You’re a grown man. Go away. Leave me alone and help your own self.” Barnes gets up and goes off to find a bottle.

In the next section, Miles, the extra who’d first told Emily about *Showdown,* shows up briefly—he had grown much older by the time Emily had met him, but she recognized him—as a customer in the background, in a short scene in a country store.

Months later, Barnes is worse off than ever. He comes upon a group of men about to hang an outlaw. He doesn’t try to stop them—he doesn’t want to get involved, but he’s gotten curious despite himself and rides closer to take a look.

The man they’re hanging is Gabriel.

Barnes starts to ride away. *Something* stops him. Slowly, he turns his mount around and, gaining momentum and purpose, rides down on the men.

Except for three other short, disconnected scenes that told little about the plot, it ended.

Gabriel was literally left hanging.

• • •

“Emily?” said Jimmy. “Are you all right?”

Emily stared back and forth between him and Butterworth, eyes dancing. “Maybe I’m not the best judge right this second,” she said, “but I think the artistic sensibility is beyond …” She shook her head. “… Not to mention it’s vibrant, color-rich … You’d think it was shot last week.”

"No difference," said the film editor.

Emily looked at him with something like lust. "Mr. Butterworth, in my time with Sterling, I never saw anything with this kind of promise, artistically or commercially. Is there anything I can say that will persuade you to let us do this thing?"

Butterworth studied the light in her eyes. It took him a moment to find his voice. Finally, he said, "I don't know. Maybe I should." He opened and closed his hands several times as he looked around at his piled-up possessions. "Would you deal straight with me? If you can convince me you'd deal straight with me, I might. I think women are a better bet in business than men." He stared at Jimmy, lit by a single beam of daylight slicing down from a dormer window above a sleeping or storage loft.

Jimmy's face was glowing as if it were encased in polished glass. Emily looked at him, too, and saw grief in his eyes. She had the impression that the mask he wore was one-way; that inside his skin-tight mirrored cell he was powerless to see any intelligible reflection of himself. And again, she didn't know if he was acting James Dean or if this was just who he was.

Butterworth looked back at Emily. "I've got to take a chance sometime."

He got up more abruptly than Emily would have guessed he could. "Here. Look at this." He put another cassette in his VCR player and turned it on.

The screen displayed a series of shots of John Wayne and James Dean, all well lit, filmed in front of neutral matte backgrounds. There were shots of the two actors looking up, looking down, to the sides, staring toward both sides of the camera; appearing pensive, suspicious, angry, amused—the gamut. James Dean as director, likely with Wayne's approval, had used John Ford's occasional custom of getting a series of medium portraits and close-ups of his actors that were simply a palette of reaction shots on the "off chance"—Butterworth told them—that they might later be useful in the editing room. It wasn't "artistic" on the surface of it, but Emily understood how valuable it could be, especially in a complex drama where it's vital to have something to cut to.

In the case of *Emily's* project, words couldn't express what a piece of good fortune these shots might be, especially when complemented by the other resources they had. She thought of *My Son John*, Robert Walker's last film. The self-destructive actor had died during production; Emily recalled that they used footage of Walker from *Strangers on a Train* to complete *My Son John*.

As Butterworth turned the VCR off again, she offered a silent prayer of thanks. To the two men she was with, she said: "I could just hug you both to death."

Jimmy smothered a smile. Butterworth sucked in a mouthful of air through clenched teeth and exhaled heavily. "What kind of arrangement did you have in mind?" he said.

"I have a friend who's a producer," said Emily. "I can't make any guarantees, but I know her and she's going to want to work with us on this. She's honest and discreet."

"Is she with an independent company?"

"No, but she's experienced, knowledgeable and understands independent production as well as anyone I know. We'll be forming our own company anyway."

Butterworth scratched at his cheek with a knobby hand. "A small company is good. The smaller we keep it, the better the chances. What about the money?"

"We'll come up with it."

"You gotta do it without giving away what we're sittin' on."

"I know," said Emily weakly.

Butterworth leaned in toward her. "And we got to come to a personal arrangement."

"Fine." She steepled her hands to her lips. "Mr. Butterworth, were there any outtakes?"

"Not a one. I mean, of course there were other takes and other angles on scenes, but if you're asking is there any footage covering Duke and Dean out of their roles as Barnes and Gabriel, the answer is no." He frowned. "I've got no idea why. You normally expect a little out of character stuff to show up in the printed footage … but somebody didn't want that to happen." He shook his head. "So … zilch." He stared at Emily. "One more thing."

"What's that?"

"No major decision is made unless I agree."

"All right."

He narrowed his eyes, again like Redford as Sundance. "Okay." His voice had become husky. "I love this project. It's the only noble thing I ever had in my life—despite how I got it—and it scares the shit out of me to let it out in the air. I'll make you a cassette." He looked down at his gnarled hands. "I've got to do this. This is a story of salvation. If I'm going to learn anything from it"—he looked around at the tangle of his sanctuary—"I've got to face the fact that nobody gets saved, livin' in the dark."

Emily smiled at him. "Why didn't you ever go to Wayne about this?"

Butterworth looked at his hands again and shook his head. "I don't know. I suppose I was afraid to." He blinked. "One more thing. If the cassette gets out, I'll kill you."

11

On the drive home, they talked about what would have to be done to put *Showdown* together. Emily said they'd need to form a production company, hire a director, and, most importantly at the moment, find someone to write a beginning and an ending for the movie.

"But do we want to leave that in somebody else's hands?" she said.

"Of course," said Jimmy. "You're not a writer. I think you should run it a few times for yourself, so you have a practical understanding of the whole story. Then, you can hire the writer and sketch it out with him … or her."

Emily was quivering with excitement. "I was only trying to psyche myself up before. Now I really believe we can make this work. I feel like Judy Garland and Mickey Rooney—gonna put on a show!"

Jimmy looked queasy.

"The first thing I have to do is form a limited liability company. Go step by step." She chewed her bottom lip, thoughts racing. "Hey, don't you think it's odd that Wayne would have wanted to play such an unsympathetic role?"

"No, I don't think so. He was already in preparation to play Ethan Edwards in *The Searchers*, one of the meanest protagonists in the history of Westerns. He was probably thinking he could make *anybody* sympathetic by the end of the story."

"You are a film buff," said Emily, impressed.

"More like an escape artist."

She gazed at him, then drew in a deep breath. "I'm getting over-stimulated." She felt a craving for a family-size bottle of Chardonnay—or almost any fast-acting sedative would do. "My daddy would have a stroke if he knew what we're up to."

"Why?"

She laughed sharply and crinkled her eyes repeatedly, like a hyper six-year-old. She watched the flickering silent movie effect it had on the scattered hills and rock formations.

Glancing at her, Jimmy said, "I'm afraid you're going to vibrate through the upholstery. Tell me about your father."

"Ahhh. Daddy. My shitty-ass excuse for a fucking father." She blinked. "Jesus, I'm that *Exorcist* girl." She shook her arms and hands, making a conscious effort to relieve the tension in her body. "Well, I have perpetually clean feet because of him." She giggled. "What's to tell about Daddy? He never did anything I could point to. He never beat me. If you told him about physical abuse of a child, he'd be outraged. But occasionally he'd get a … dead look, staring at me. And with no warning, he'd say calmly, even with a … sorta smile, 'It's not an easy thing for a father to have to face the fact that his daughter is an idiot.' In his defense—"

"—His *defense*?"

"Yeah. I think he told himself he was being funny. He'd say things like that to me sometimes in a flat, conversational manner. He might as well have hit me in the face with his fist. And then he'd show me this crooked little smile, as if he'd told me a slyly funny joke." She made an idle mouth-popping noise. "But he never touched me. I wish I had a scar, a trophy, anything that I could say, look at this: this is what the son of a bitch did to me.

He never shed a tear when my mother died. … But he's my father. Doesn't my peace of mind demand that I look for the best in him even if …"

She trailed off, not catching Jimmy's sad smile, and gazed out the window as they came down into the foothills. "Don't you think we should work in a love interest for at least one of them?" She looked back at him. "How would you feel about some little tootsie of a sweetheart for Gabriel?"

He concentrated on his driving.

She studied his profile. "How about you? Ever been in love?"

"Nah. I hate that Hollywood romance crap."

"It's not *all* like that."

"Most of it."

"First you're an anything-in-this-world-is-possible dude, and then you're as cynical as anyone I ever met."

"Yeah, maybe. I don't know."

"Were your mother and father ever in love?"

"No," said Jimmy, "we didn't have that in our family."

• • •

He could feel her watching him and tried to keep his mind on his driving as the outskirts of LA began to materialize around them. It was still desolate enough that it could have been a sci-fi movie setting, dotted with only patchy signs of humanity at first: gas stations, minimarts, a hillock of rocky debris covered with bits of glass and aluminum siding, an uninviting picnic table at a ravaged rest stop, power lines, a truck weigh station—a flat-roofed box of a building made of cement blocks. There was no one working there, judging by the dilapidated sign.

A leaf of melancholy fluttered up inside him. He remembered his father crying after his first heart attack, hugging him and saying, "These are the good times, Jim." He saw him riding his bicycle in Pacific Palisades, where Jimmy was raised, then the card he'd been given at the funeral. A fleshy, wet-eyed man with peroxide streaks in his mouse-brown hair had handed it to him. The card had shown a rendering of several autumn leaves and had displayed the dates his father was born and died and a sentiment from Ecclesiastes: "There is a time …"

After the funeral he saw his mother, one side of her upper lip curled up not quite imperceptibly as she looked away from Jimmy, then, without focus, back in his direction. "I loved him the best I could. But he wasn't the man I'd hoped for."

Still driving Emily home, Jimmy saw, in his mind's eye, a broad side street in the city—East LA or maybe San Bernardino. Heavy clouds gathered. Crows screamed, but looking up, he could barely make them out against the darkened sky. The street was empty, desolate except for a few parked cars, so small in the distance they looked like cardboard cutouts. He was sure he had an appointment, but didn't know with whom or how to get there. He sat down on the curb, rested his chin in his hands, and saw a spreading stream of sooty air coming out of a smokestack on a dirt brown brick building across the street. Inside an apartment on the third floor, he could make out the silhouette of a frail-looking young woman, illuminated only by a single bare light bulb. She was fixing dinner or doing household things. He wanted to go across the street and ring the buzzer, but didn't know which tenant's button he would push for her apartment. He couldn't think what to do, so he huddled himself up tight inside his coat.

Looking now at an approaching apartment building on the outer border of the commuter capital of the West, Jimmy placed on the side of it, in his mind, one of those signs that reads: "If you lived here, you'd be home now."

• • •

At Tom's house, the following night (Tom was not yet back from Italy), Jimmy and Emily watched the cassette of *Showdown* two more times. Outside, an angry storm had blown up. Jimmy told her, "I don't know if I can do this. I mean, I *can*. Nobody could do it better." His voice sounded hollow and small.

"What are you talking about?" said Emily. "You did your best to sell the idea *and* yourself to Butterworth."

"I got into it," said Jimmy in his monotone voice. "I was trying to help you."

"Don't wimp out on me."

Thunder cracked in the distance, then closer. They looked toward the window as it was struck by sand or hail or something spattery hurled from the darkness. Emily felt as if the lightning was arcing into her central nervous system.

"I'm not scared of doing the movie," he said. "I'm scared of *him.*"

"But … he's dead."

"So's Dracula. I know it sounds silly; it does to me, but they come to own you. At first they take you in and feed you, and you're grateful for the shelter, but time goes by and you get lulled into thinking they work for *you*. Then one day, you wake up and"—he shrugged—"it's the other way around. And they have that over you." He shook his head. "Sorry."

"What for?" said Emily. "What are you sorry for? … I still don't understand why you're scared today when you weren't yesterday."

"Because yesterday was about making this thing work for you. … But then I left you and went home to my garret—" He stopped himself, looked into her eyes, palms sweating, trying to ignore a distracted, snippet of dialogue from *Rebel Without a Cause*: Natalie Wood whispering, "I love you, Jim. I really love you." They were lyrics he wanted to rip out of his repertoire, except that they were also said to James Dean's (and Jimmy's) favorite character, *The Little Prince*, the lost urchin, wandering through space, wanting nothing more than to get back to his planet and the rose he loves with all his heart, and unable in Jimmy's version to imagine any nicer words than, "I love you, Jim."

He gazed into her eyes, trying to see deeper than he knew was possible "You look at me as if ..." He shook his head. "You looked at me this same way the evening we met. It's not the... *nice* look you give me most times."

She started to speak, but he held a hand up. "Okay, back to your project and ... me." He tapped rhythmically on his forehead with the middle and ring fingers of his other hand. ... "You don't have to tell me that what I do is crazy. I *know* it is. I live here, but the thing is, in the beginning, James Dean gave me somebody to *be*. When I was growing up, I started to have friends because of him—that's the way it felt. I was almost 'hip'. Without him I was ... nobody."

"But he can't hurt you," she said. "He's your invention, and you'll keep him only as long as you need him."

"No, no!" He shook his head. "You're not hearing me. He's not my invention anymore. I started doing all this a long time ago, and I'm not as good at crawling out from under it as I used to be. 'He's' been in here"—he tapped his chest—"too long now. And you know how you can get locked into certain things you do? Certain ways of looking at the world? Well, that's what's happened to me with this ... *pathetic* thing I do. He is no longer my invention; he's a fact and—"

Emily held out a hand to him.

"—Please let me finish. ... And although I know I'm going to have to outgrow all this—just to live—I'm not there yet. And in a way, you're exactly the wrong one for me to be telling this to, because you don't really *want* me to get well, do you? It's in your interest that I stay as sick as I am."

"Tell me exactly what he has over you," she said. "I mean, what ... control does he have over you *right now*."

He took a deep breath. "He gave me something that in the beginning I couldn't let him take away."

"And later?"

"I dunno. It's just that what I want doesn't seem to matter anymore." He closed and opened his eyes. "Habits are a big deal. It's not only alcohol and drugs. IA is not a joke, by the way. I know it seems like one, but the idea behind it isn't even a little bit funny. It has a lot in common with AA. It's not so much about the 'substance itself as it is about not killing yourself and other people—one way or another. That sounds melodramatic. Take my word, it's not."

Emily stared at him.

"And I don't want to be that way with you. *That's* what he has over me right now. I *love* being with you, but it's also complicated. Because of what your project's about, it all runs right back into you-know-who. And he's a son of a bitch. He's screwed-up, two-faced, stuck on himself. And I don't want to be that way. Especially with you."

The sky outside was a chrome green counterfeit of daylight. Emily felt a pang of claustrophobia. "We're talking about an acting role," she said. "You're an actor. You've got some craft. Use it. You want this part, don't you?"

"Of course. It's what I *do*."

Thunder rattled like kettledrums. She'd been dead wrong. She was nothing like this boy. She'd never been as unsure as he was. She hated the attraction she felt for him—for that soft part of him that she wanted to take care of, to touch ... She didn't even mind that he was a penniless loser—a phrase that came so effortlessly to her, she realized the foundation for it had always been a part of her. Her new problem was that he'd made her see with a clarity she'd never known before that she could feel tenderness and, in the same moment, inflict damage. She knew she could feel for him and soothe his pain even as she caused more.

She felt a flood of cruelty flowing out to the tips of her fingers. She clenched her hands into fists to keep it from escaping. He had made her realize she'd always been walking a tightrope and that now the rope was fraying.

"I almost feel I could talk to you," said Jimmy. "I mean *really* talk."

She swiveled in her chair and looked out at the torrents of rain. "Yes, and maybe we will—someday, later—when there's more time."

He gazed out at the top of the one tree he could see, bending in the spiraling winds. "More time," he echoed. "Yeah." He looked away. "I knew your brother. He was my camp counselor when I was ten."

"What do you mean?" A shadow danced across her face.

"He was my counselor one summer in camp. Not for the whole time. I went home early."

She remembered a photograph—a picture of Ben after he'd come back from his summer as a camp counselor and the T-shirt he was wearing.

It read: CAMP COTTONWOOD—"Building Boys with Character."

Watching Jimmy, she could see him now as a little boy—about the same age she would have been at the time.

She could see Ben, too, suntanned, happy, confident, her hero.

• • •

Jimmy's mind moved seamlessly to an image of a log cabin in the woods, off in the distance, but getting closer as he approached it. He was following a man half-lit in the darkness by the glow of his own lantern.

For a long time now, it had been his dominant nightmare, and it refused to restrict itself to his sleeping hours.

III

PRE-PRODUCTION

1

The taxi ride from JFK into Manhattan was especially reckless, but Emily didn't say anything to the driver. She knew if she did, she'd lose concentration on the meeting she was about to have with Joanna Morgan. She felt like she'd won the lottery, or was some Oz-like character, but with real power.

She arrived first at the basement French café on East 53rd Street, famous, among people who care about such things, for its crème brulée. She sipped a glass of red Dubonnet with a lemon twist as she waited.

Joanna had been the only one to make an effort to be nice to her when she'd begun to work for Sterling Films, although others had been courtly. Emily had later dated one of the firm's several vice presidents, who looked to her like Conrad Veidt, the Nazi major in *Casablanca*. He'd had a trim beard and had spoken with an appealing Austrian accent.

But it didn't work out. On their third date, he gave her an ultimatum: "Sleep vis me tonight or it's time ve call it kvitz."

She chose kvitz. His approach had bullied all the air out of her moderate enthusiasm.

• • •

Rehearsing her pitch to herself again, she lost concentration and thought about Jimmy.

After he'd finished telling her about his time at camp and his nightmare and how it was with Vivian, she reached out, drew him toward her, caressed his face, gave him what she worried wasn't a maternal kiss, and rocked him in her arms.

As he'd fallen asleep, he'd said, "I've got another secret I want to tell you. Another time."

She didn't want to know his secret—then or ever. She'd seen him after that time only once and had made sure the conversation was about *Showdown.*

As she was about to leave, he caught her hand, drew her to him and kissed her.

She kissed him back with an intensity that terrified her—not from the animal force of it, but from a reminder of something else, an unidentified hunger. She lowered herself on him, straddling him, and kissed his face and neck as if she wanted to siphon the life out of him.

She stopped, sat straight up and looked down at him with what could have passed for malice.

She'd known she had a weakness for this boy. But this was not only bewildering, it was wrong. For a thousand reasons.

She swung her leg over him, stood up and backed away, staring at him.

"I don't understand," said Jimmy.

"We can't," she said. "That's all. We just can't. Don't you *see* that?" Her look softened, then became uncertain.

Neither of them could think of a word to say.

• • •

Joanna hadn't arrived yet. Listening to her own best guidance, Emily didn't order another Dubonnet. She realized something else was troubling her. She'd called home to check on her father. When Ben told her "the oracle" was fine, but that he (Ben) was "a smidge legless at the moment," she'd said, "Darling, you really ought to give a little thought to the future, to the next day, and the next."

"Why?" he'd said. "All this bollocks about 'tomorrow? It's a fairytale, unfiltered rubbish. They're taking the piss, princess. No one cares what comes next, because tomorrow is just … *there.* We have nothing to say about it. It's a great merciless void we have no control over. We *think* we worry about it, but we don't. All we *really* worry about, when you reduce it down, is *when* we're going to die, *how* we're going to die, and will it *hurt*? But tomorrow? Nah! No one thinks about that; it can't be done. Tomorrow doesn't exist—it's a massive library of books full of infinite murky pages with nothing written on them, in a language we don't understand anyway." He drew in a breath. "But today … Ah, today, the opportunities are blinding." He chuckled. "Literally, sometimes. … With only the slightest effort, I can make this moment, right now, all by myself, warm and wonderful and fuzzy fucking cozy."

"Oh, Ben." Emily sighed. She sighed again and finally suggested he at least give his liver a rest for the remainder of the day.

"Oh please, princess. Don't pick I up before I fall."

She'd thought of the Brothers Grimm's Rumpelstiltskin, extinguishing himself in his fury when things didn't turn out the way he'd planned.

She'd said, "Bye, Skippy," and hung up. As she did, the nagging unpleasantness she'd felt, hearing what he'd said, had, with only the slightest effort on her part, vanished.

Now, even with her most practiced attempt at avoidance, it had returned.

"*We're no longer safe. Neither of us.*"

• • •

Joanna ordered a glass of Argentinean Chablis. "How's your father?"

"Dying, but better. He's sitting up and taking gin."

Joanna smiled. "I'm sorry."

She was an attractive, gingery woman, in a constant battle with her weight. She had frizzy auburn hair and a vivacious friendliness that was open, charming, and impish. She had a defiant streak, but knew how to make life work for her and, as much as she could, those she cared about. She'd begun at Sterling Films as a script reader, moved up to production assistant, and finally to vice president. When she left the firm, frustrated by her lack of influence, her plan had been to produce small films on her own. It was risky; still a man's world. She didn't care—she was ready for the bastards.

She had no success. She optioned several scripts, but couldn't find financing.

As soon as she'd taken the first sip of her Chablis, she said, "What's the project? Why wouldn't you talk about it on the phone?"

"Are you really hungry?" asked Emily.

"Look at me, sweet pea. Do I look like a girl who's not hungry at dinner time?"

"Because I can't wait to show this to you."

Joanna took in the single-mindedness in Emily's eyes. "Well, I'm not leaving this joint till I've had my crème brulée."

• • •

At Joanna's apartment, Emily stopped the video and started to rewind it.

"Do you have any idea what you've got here?" said Joanna, still flabbergasted. "Once you resolve the legal clearances, you could put this together into a documentary. Any one of the majors would pay millions for it. You might be able to spread it out over two or three nights."

"What would it be about?"

"What do you mean? The story of Wayne and Dean working together."

"Very hard to research. I told you; it was a highly guarded secret."

"All the better. That's part of the documentary."

"But what about *Showdown* itself?"

"Use all of it and fill in the gaps with narration and personal footage of Wayne and Dean." Her brain could barely keep up with her words. "*You* know. Load it up. Make a wonderful mystery out of it. Get Orson Welles or one of those guys to narrate it, so that people will know without doubt that *this* entertainment rises above ... *entertainment*, that *this* one has"—her voice dropped to a Welles-worthy baritone—"*gravitas*!"

Emily leaned in toward her friend. "But what if it were completed?"

"I beg your pardon?"

"More than half the scenes are in the can—beautifully preserved, as you can see. It's been recently remixed, and it was shot with an extraordinary amount of close-up coverage for the time. What if the film was completed with doubles—carefully—in long shots, and finessed with computer wizardry? What do you think the potential would be?"

Joanna squinched up her face and sipped the dregs of her coffee. "Where on earth would you get the doubles?"

"That's not a problem."

"Really?" She put the cup down on the coffee table, leaned back, stretching her back and arms, then looked at Emily.

"The better part of a hundred million dollars, domestic and foreign."

2

Despite Emily's insights about the movie industry from years of watching it, reading about it, and more recently, working in it, she was now faced with the fact that when it really came down to it, she knew, as Ben put it, "bugger all" about being a producer. Had it been several years later, she might have found some small comfort in the words of author/screenwriter William Goldman, who, in summing up Hollywood, said, "Nobody knows anything."

For the moment, Emily believed that among industry professionals—ones with signed papers to produce an independent film—she was the only one who didn't have the foggiest idea what to do next.

"I was beginning to think you might actually know what you're doing."

"Give me a break. I'm going to have to figure it all out as I go. Isn't that how you're supposed *to do it?"*

"You're asking the wrong girl. I'm not yet entirely comfortable going to the potty on my own."

• • •

Joanna Morgan got to the Cock 'n Bull saloon and restaurant on Sunset Boulevard an hour early. She was uneasy about meeting the two men Emily had insisted should play the John Wayne and James Dean roles in *Showdown*.

She sat in the back of the very dark restaurant. It was impossible to tell it was still daylight outside. She watched the front entrance.

She had done the best she could to calm herself—first with a cheeseburger, fries, and a gimlet. She had another gimlet, then decided against a third. This meeting was too important. Emily had guaranteed her that her impersonators were "uncanny, the best." But Joanna knew about Emily's lifelong problem. Since the first blush of seeing the footage of *Showdown,* she'd realized that if her friend's judgment was clouded in casting the two leads, and she refused to budge on those choices, then no matter how promising the project, it was doomed.

• • •

Emily had coached Tom and Jimmy to make their entrances in character; they both felt stupid and had protested strenuously, but Emily was adamant.

Jimmy started toward the back of the Cock 'n Bull with a combination of constraint and agitation, moving with James Dean's restless, quasi-matador grace. Tom strode in easily but as if there were perhaps some little out-of-place widget stuck in the works of his walking mechanism. As they neared the back, a familiar androgynous grin began to light Jimmy's face; he glanced myopically back at Tom, who was moving up behind him—leading, as John Wayne usually did, just slightly with his left side.

They saw a stout, attractive woman get up from a booth and stand statue-still next to her table. As they came closer, the woman remained frozen.

Joanna was in.

This was fortunate because the boys were not about to put themselves through that again. Not for Emily, not for nobody. *Most* actors like performing, as long as it's in a performance arena;

but most would also sooner set themselves on fire than be forced to "act" privately, on demand.

• • •

They drove up to Tom's house and screened *Showdown* for him. He was only four days back from Italy and had yet to see it.

Jack Butterworth was there too, and when he met Tom, the old editor unfurled his loopy grin, shook Tom's hand as forcefully as his arthritis would permit, and looked years younger. He gazed at Tom from time to time for the rest of the evening, smiling and bobbing his head like a dashboard doll.

As the film ran, Jimmy and Emily watched Tom almost as much as they did the television screen.

When it was over, Joanna said, "What do you think?"

Tom jerked out of his trance. "What do I think? Holy crap! It's … amazing!"

"Do you think you can do it?"

"Do I have a choice?"

After Joanna and Butterworth had left, Emily and Jimmy tried to convince Tom he had nothing to worry about. "It's a movie," said Emily. "If you screw up a take, it's okay. You get take two or three or four or however many you need to get it right. The pressure is off with a movie. You won't have a thing to worry about anyway. You own this character."

"It's not that I don't want to." Jimmy started to interrupt him, but Tom waved him off. "I'm not … I'm not sure I can. I do little shows. I'm a day player."

"You're way more than that."

"Jimmy! Shut up. Let me finish. I was always able to make myself believe that what I was doing wasn't very important. And even then, you don't know what happens to me inside. If I'd known at the beginning of my Burt Reynolds movie that they were going to use me again at the end of it, and that I was going to be paid all that money, I'd never have lasted. I'd have fallen apart, or had a heart attack."

"But when they did call you to go back, you did it. You were fine," said Jimmy.

"I *wasn't* fine. I kept blacking out."

"You *what*?" Emily and Jimmy said in unison.

"I've been doing it all my life—ever since I was in the orphanage. It's a nerve thing. I've seen doctors. There's nothing wrong with me." He shrugged. "It's one of the reasons I have so much trouble with women. I'm always afraid I'll pass out on them."

"But you don't, do you?" said Emily.

"No … I guess I don't, but I never know when I might … and I did a bunch of times on the Reynolds movie. The only reason they put up with me was that I was already established on film and they couldn't replace me." He looked vaguely in the direction of the Western painting on his living room wall. "If they could have, they would have."

"Damn it," said Jimmy, "you can't be in the life and not be in it. A trouper's got to troop or they kick you out of the spotlight."

"But I don't know how I got there in the first place. I never really meant to."

"Well, whatever your ghosts happen to be, in my opinion, you can't afford to let this pass you by."

"I'm *here*, aren't I?"

"I mean, holy shit, you've got a terrific advantage. You look enough like your guy, you could be his son."

Tom glanced back and forth between them, lifting his eyebrows in surrender. "I know you're right. Listen, don't worry about me. I'm going to do this. I know a good opportunity when I see it. I'm not going to let you down. I've been doing what I do for a good while now, and I'm not going to mess this one up."

But he made an involuntary face that Emily knew had nothing to do with self-confidence.

• • •

Before Emily left, Tom found a moment alone with her and said, "Did you and Jimmy hang out a lot while I was gone?" He said it good-naturedly, making idle conversation.

She gathered a careful smile. "No, I was pretty busy."

A breeze moved a curtain, and a coyote howled from above them in the hills. Tom looked at her with anxious ox eyes. "What's the matter?"

"Nothing. Why do you say that? I'm just nervous about all this, just like you are." Belligerence flared behind her eyes, a bioluminescent spark. Looking up at him, an old cartoon ran through her brain. It was a rabbit or maybe a chipmunk on a railroad track, looking up and seeing the headlight of a gargantuan train bearing down on it and the little creature says, "Gulp."

"I thought about you a lot while I was away," said Tom.

She smiled again. "Me too." She squeezed his forearm. "Could I trouble you for a glass of water?"

She turned and went back out to the living room where Jimmy was waiting.

3

Under the assumption that Butterworth owned it, based on the old "possession is nine-tenths of the law" adage, Emily and Jack Butterworth signed and had notarized a seven-page contract that gave Emily complete control over the intellectual property rights to the movie *Showdown.* The only proviso was that Butterworth had a veto, should he care to exercise it, in every artistic and business decision. Emily could not override him, but neither could anyone they hired (including the director) override Emily's decisions. She was in an enviable position in the film business, much like that of a playwright's ownership of his or her play under the aegis of The Dramatists Guild. No one (other than Butterworth) could countermand her decisions.

Joanna Morgan had a piece of the action and that was enough for her.

Emily and Butterworth (and now Joanna, whose expertise would, in the beginning, be focused on raising money) set about the practical task of putting together what would amount to a major independent movie production.

If any copies existed of the negative Butterworth had appropriated twenty-four years earlier, their guess was that they were in the neglected vaults of people who didn't know what they had. They had no idea whether or not there was somebody out there with provable rights to *Showdown,* somebody who might seek an injunction against them before they could begin production. They didn't want to stir up the water. They were aware that they wouldn't be in a position of strength if a knowledgeable consortium and its battery of lawyers decided it wanted to take their baby away from them.

In the meantime, they weren't sure what the rules were with a thing like this and didn't really want to know anyway, rationalizing that if they didn't capitalize on it, *Showdown* would either never be heard of, or would end up being used for the profit of someone no more morally entitled to it than they were.

That's what they told themselves.

• • •

"We have a little problem," said Joanna. "And I'm not sure little is the correct adjective."

Emily looked up from the day's *Variety*. "Tell me."

"Did you ever read John Wayne's *Playboy* interview?"

"No."

"Neither have most people—not yet, anyway. But my guess is that at some point, someone will use it against him, and that would be a problem for us. It was the May 1971 issue—a couple of years after Wayne's *Green Berets* debacle, at the height of the Vietnam war. He said some things that came out racist and homophobic."

"John Wayne wasn't a bigot!" said Emily. She felt like she'd just found out she was breathing cyanide. "When did you read this?"

"I just came across some unsavory excerpts in *LA Weekly*. If this interview was trotted out into a broader light, it could do damage. If someone wanted to trash him, this interview would be an easy way to start."

Emily shook her head. "How can you trash John Wayne? It's like trashing the American dream."

"I know. It used to be that if you were liberal and you gave it much thought, you didn't like Wayne's politics, but it was a pretty soft dislike, usually outweighed by the warmth of the image in your mind from the first time you saw him ride in at the front of the cavalry and save the women and children."

Emily took in a deep breath. "So, how does this affect us?"

Joanna looked out toward CBS on Radford Street. "My feeling is …" She paused, frowning. "I don't think there's any doubt that in that *Playboy* interview Wayne said some dark things, things that were really offensive to a lot of people." She looked out the window again. "I don't believe that's who he was, but …"

"I've been reading other pieces about him," said Emily, "almost all of them overflowing with nice things people have said since he died. You could fill a book with affectionate words people who knew him and worked with him have said about him. A lot of people who disliked his politics liked him—thought of him as kind and fair." She pointed to the *Variety* she'd been reading. "Here's one. Roscoe Lee Browne, the Black, Gay actor who appeared with Wayne in *The Cowboys.* He said he 'never worked with anyone who was more generous of spirit.' "

Joanna shook her head. "Yeah, but if we put together a PR statement when it's time to publicize our movie, and we recite a list of the people who *don't* think John Wayne was a shit, no matter how long that list is"—she made a sickly face, waving the thought away—"it would be the definition of lame." She frowned. "Em … if right now you had to issue a statement to someone who had the influence, if they chose to, to pillory Wayne on the basis of who he was other than his movie actor self, what would you say?"

Emily stroked one side of her face with a forefinger. "I think I'd say he was a movie star who aspired to the best in himself and in his work, but who didn't always do so well in his personal life."

"Yes, I think that's the way to begin it." Joanna pressed her lips together in concentration. "Going back to the time of that interview … Wayne was furious about the critical reception *The Green Berets* received—and some of his other films as well. He blamed the liberal press. He told people he didn't read his own reviews—which was *not* true. He read all his major reviews, and *The Green Berets* deservedly got lousy ones. His character in that film said things in the same simple way his cowboy characters always did. In one scene, he said to a journalist, *"Out here, due process is a bullet."* He didn't have his finger on the public's pulse anymore—hadn't for a long time—and doves and hawks alike knew it. I mean, as you and almost everybody else now understands, Vietnam was the furthest thing from simple." She broke off. "I think Wayne finally realized it, and it embarrassed him to death. He was not superhuman; he was a guy who didn't do well with embarrassment, with being pushed into a corner. It sent him into a John Wayne-sized rage, and he said those crummy, hateful things, and they angered and hurt people."

Joanna shook her head, then went on with intonations that acknowledged her frustration in needing to justify the gray area of one person's tangled psyche, she said, "He was a human being and, by a long shot, not always who he'd like to be. But I think by the end, he knew it was very likely that he'd been overzealously patriotic—because of his guilt about not having served during World War II. And he was not the sort of man who knew how to get himself out of that kind of quicksand. Did you know John Ford wouldn't speak to him for almost three years because Wayne didn't serve in World War II except in a movie star capacity? We know that Wayne's avid anti-Communism contributed to hurting people during the Hollywood blacklist. I think he'd like to have undone some of that damage. He saw to it that Marguerite Roberts, the screenwriter of *True Grit*, received due credit for her work. She'd been blacklisted before Wayne interceded on her behalf." She shrugged. "Like most people, Wayne wasn't easy to fit into a cubbyhole."

Emily nodded.

"Everything about him, that the public was aware of, was larger than life. He was John Wayne. The big screen could barely hold him."

Both women looked out the window toward CBS.

Emily said, "Did you know when he was shooting *The Alamo*, he was smoking up to six packs of cigarettes a day? This was an obsessed guy, not so full of healthy habits."

"*Everything* he did was big," said Joanna. "Maybe in another lifetime someone would have suggested he get some psychotherapy. But then of course, he wouldn't have been John Wayne."

"Do you know what he wanted on his tombstone?" said Emily. "He wanted it to say: '*Feo, Fuerte y Formal—Ugly, Strong and Dignified.*'"

Joanna smiled. "Yeah, I read that.... He wasn't ugly—although he might have felt that way a few times. There is no question he was strong—and enjoyed being strong. But I wonder why that last word? Why did he want to be remembered as 'dignified'?"

"Maybe," Emily mused, "because, unlike the star he was in his life, he was just a regular guy who made his share of regular guy mistakes, but preferred to be remembered for the biggest and best things he did—for the majestic moments when he was not just a regular guy born with a girly name, Marion Morrison, but the way bigger than life, charismatic, mythical, *dignified* John Wayne."

• • •

They needed a director and a writer, both in one if possible—fewer cooks to spoil the broth. They decided that they should not look for someone with a high public profile. They didn't want pre-production interest in a famous director's project to compromise the secrecy they had to maintain.

Their director would have to be solid. It was no longer the old days when you put together the story, the stars, the writer, and then you hired somebody's brother-in-law to direct it. They had to have someone highly skilled in every aspect of the work. They all wished it wasn't a fact of movie making, but there was no way around it, they needed a strong director.

They didn't think they were being dewy-eyed about it. They were aware that almost all directors have within their souls ego-driven, Type A characteristics. Despite the exceptions, time after time, "moviemakers" prove the theory that power corrupts. The writer/director for the completion of *Showdown* would have to understand that he or she was expected to do the job, using all the pertinent parts of that personality to run the movie set, but with a thorough understanding of the hierarchy that had been established for this production. The goal must be to serve the spirit of the existing film and to faithfully complete it.

It didn't cross either of the young women's conscious minds, or that of the old film editor, that despite what they told themselves, they might be ignoring a hard fact or two about the power of directors in film.

Still, they would not be hiring one of the "old pros" and felt secure in the pecking order they had all put their signatures to.

They had little reason for worry. They were sure of that.

• • •

After watching hours of footage and interviewing more than a dozen writer/directors, they narrowed it down to three candidates, all youngish artists who were hungry for success, an indispensable personality trait for the work.

After screening and rescreening the three finalists' work, they settled on a thirty-four-year-old Armenian-American woman whose parents had immigrated to Southern California when she was a baby. She confessed to her potential employers that she was driven by two things: her love of movies and her determination to be an American success story.

Butterworth, Joanna, and Emily all thought her demo reel was sensational. Although she had directed mostly commercials, her work displayed a technical versatility they'd seen in none of the other candidates and an obvious ability to draw out the best in what were usually not the best actors. She had also directed one Western for a small production company out of Tucson—a contemporary story in the mold of *Shane*, shot with stylish simplicity in Arizona with the look of a painting by Remington, and without being self-conscious or arty.

She got the job as far as Joanna and Butterworth were concerned, although it was still contingent on the approval of whoever put up the money, as was everything else. Butterworth had already dismissed the first candidate on the awkward grounds that "He's a whiny little pissant and Duke wouldn't have been able to stand him." The other potential director had all the qualities and qualifications, and was technically brilliant, but there was something about him that for Joanna inspired what she characterized as an uncomfortable sense of "the man being not entirely present when you talk to him."

"Why do you say that?" said Butterworth.

"For one thing, he counts his fingers. Twice each time."

"What?" said Emily. "What do you mean twice each time?"

"I mean," said Joanna, "during the two interviews we had with him, I observed that he 'idly' pointed at the fingers and thumb on his left hand with the forefinger of his right hand. It was all quite subtle, almost in his lap. I wasn't behind the desk like you were, and Jack, you were on the other side of him. And I started watching his hands. He did it twice each time, and he did it several times, out of your sight, but not mine. He would do it—count the fingers on the left hand, twice—stop for a while, then a couple minutes later, count them again, two times through. Not once or three times through, but twice. He went through that double set of counting his fingers several times during both interviews."

"So," said Emily, "that would mean, he's … got a problem?"

"Enough so that it's a deal breaker for me," said Joanna. "And I'm sorry if I'm being unfair, but I'm afraid I would end up worrying that he was not as concerned with writing and directing our film as he was about whether his left hand still had the same number of fingers it had earlier in the day."

"What's that say about you?" said Butterworth. "You sat through two interviews with that poor devil and counted the number of times he counted his fingers?"

Joanna nodded. "Point taken, but I'm not applying for a job with the three of us—"she nodded at them both"—doing something we are invested in up to our eyeballs."

Butterworth nodded. "Good enough for me. I liked the guy's film. But I do kinda know what you mean. He made me a touch nervous too. Not sure what it was."

Exit the finger counter.

In spite of Emily's back-of-her-brain edgy feelings about her, all three of the producers voted unanimously for Solange Borugian. She would write the script and direct the film.

Emily knew that her misgivings about their new director connected at least partly to Ms. Borugian's easy authority, her piercing hazel eyes, her apparent comfort in her own skin. She was lithe and athletic, but feminine. Emily recalled watching a league softball game in Central Park in New York. One of the pitchers had popped out of the "girls" softball player mold with the brash confidence of an Olympian. That was how Solange Borugian struck Emily and she found it daunting. She didn't have much experience with strong women—her own mother had not been exactly equal partners with her father in their marriage, but Emily was determined to continue her career as a film producer, and she *knew* it was a positive step to start working with a woman who was at ease with authority.

She swallowed her ... superficial misgivings. They weren't even misgivings, really. They had set out to find a director with strong leadership qualities and that's what they'd done. Solange Borugian's sense of sureness was exactly what you wanted your director to have.

No doubt of it.

• • •

They began the pre-production process. A limited liability company was formed under the title of S. D. Productions. The only money in its bank account was from Emily and Joanna's personal savings. They used half of that to pay first and last months' rent on a small suite of offices in one of a cluster of bungalows on Radford Avenue, across from CBS in Studio City, near Laurel Canyon and Ventura Boulevard. The surrounding tenants were primarily television producers and people developing film projects. Like most Hollywood entrepreneurs, they showed little interest in any enterprise that had nothing to do with their own.

Emily and Joanna had not yet signed papers with Solange. Their writer/director was still in the midst of directing a series of commercials for a women's shampoo company, and because there was still no money raised, she didn't officially have the *Showdown* job anyway.

Even so, Solange was to start working on the script between her other obligations. She and Cindy, the production assistant, had adjacent cubicles at S. D. Productions. She came in, between her other obligations, to talk with Emily and Joanna and to work by herself on the script. Solange was more than hungry.

And yes, Emily confessed she had "somewhat" ambiguous feelings about that.

"We need her to be that way," said Joanna.

"Yeah, yeah, I know, but I don't want this magic carpet pulled out from under me. I'm thrilled to pieces she's ambitious and with every other one of her 'strengths,' but I won't say she doesn't scare the shit out of me. I know we hold the cards but …"

"I know her, not well, but I know her," said Joanna. "I know her family. Not only is she incredibly bright, obsessive, and gifted, she's a straight shooter."

"So why do I feel like I'm nine years old when she's talking?"

Joanna wiggled her eyebrows. "Still waiting for the madness to descend?"

"Re-descend, love."

"I hope you don't mind me saying so," Jimmy had said to Emily when he learned about it, "but aren't you worried it's suicide to hire a woman writer slash director? Whatever men you want to deal with are going to fall down laughing when three women walk into the room."

"My God, what's it all about if I don't follow my instincts?" Emily said. "It's 1979, for Christ's sake. Joanna says Solange is one of the smartest people she's ever known, plus she's got brilliant story sense. That's what I'm interested in right now, her story sense. Who cares what fucking gender she is?"

"Jeez," said Jimmy. "Okay. But how do you know you can trust her?"

"Joanna stakes her reputation on her, and I stake mine on Joanna."

"Gulp."

4

Shortly after Tom got back from Italy, he'd had to go to Seattle for a set of supermarket shows. Emily wanted Solange to meet the boys together, so they weren't able to arrange it until Tom got back.

At eight on a Thursday night, Emily and Joanna Morgan showed up at Tom's house with Solange Borugian. Jimmy and Jack Butterworth were already there.

After Solange was introduced to Tom and Jimmy, Tom said to her, "I'd love to work with you again."

"What did you do together?" said Emily and Jimmy, almost at the same moment.

Solange smiled at Tom. "A commercial. I normally hate to have the actors already cast when I direct. But I've worked with Tom. I think he's perfect." She looked at Jimmy. "And I've only seen this young man do little bits and pieces, but he is without question a brilliant actor."

"Why didn't you say anything?" said Emily with a pleasant smile.

"It was obvious I had no choice," said Solange. "So I kept my mouth shut." She added with matching charm: "It wasn't hard. I think you've made excellent decisions with these two." She smiled benignly at Jimmy and Tom and patted Emily's arm.

• • •

Later, in the living room, Solange peered closely at Tom's painting of the three cowboys and the woman by the campfire. "I've been noticing this painting. This is more than a little interesting. Who did it?"

"A woman I knew," said Tom.

They all looked at it.

"What's the story behind it?"

"I have no idea. She died without telling me."

Solange frowned, looked back at Tom and Jimmy, then at the picture again. "You're kidding. You have *no* explanation for this?"

"No."

"Neither do I," said Jimmy. "But that's not me, it's James Dean."

"How do you know?"

"I don't. It just looks like him to me."

"If you're right, the person who painted this has to have been connected to the original production of *Showdown*, or at the least to have been inspired by the rumor of it."

"But a few people have heard that rumor," said Jimmy. "It's not so surprising, is it, that somebody came up with something like this?"

"Well, it surprises the bejesus out of me," said Solange. "I mean, are you pulling my leg? I feel like I just fell through a crack in the Twilight Zone. I can see Rod Serling leering at me. Is this some joke on the new kid? This picture straight-up *duplicates* two, maybe all four leads in our film." She pointed at the painting. "*Look* at them. Which came first?"

Frowning, she took in everyone in the room as they stared at the picture.

"Never mind. I guess we're just wrapped up in a mystery that's a lot bigger than all of us." She shook her head. "Okay, I suppose there's no point in over-dwelling on the origins of this—at least for now." She looked back at the picture. "Who knows? Sometimes these things are simply in the air. Sometimes, artists see them and are able to show them to us. Maybe it's just a big fat coincidence." She again pondered the woman and three men pictured by the campfire. "Because God knows this could be the climactic scene of *Showdown*. Imagine for a second that all of this *is* in the air. Let's see what happens if we go with that.

"Maybe this picture has something to tell us about the story. What *Showdown* lacks now is conflict in current time. All of the friction between John Barnes and Gabriel is based on personality conflict and issues having to do with events that happened earlier in the story. But there's nothing at stake now, not enough to worry about, to fear, to anticipate, to hope for. After John Barnes rescues Gabriel from being hanged, there's nowhere for the narrative to go, even if they're being hunted by the people who were trying to hang Gabriel. There needs to be *more*. All we have to this point, is people out of time and place, outsiders who long for connections they can't seem to make." She paused. "What if Gabriel's father isn't really dead?"

Emily frowned. "But Gabriel *said* he is. Why would he lie about that?"

"He's a teenager. Teenagers lie. Especially when they want something no one is giving them. Or maybe he just feels like needling John Barnes, punishing him for letting him down—for not being who he thought he was. And he begins that by telling him a whopper of a lie."

• • •

Among them, they came to several conclusions about the story:

Scanlan isn't really the father. John Barnes is. They agreed, Solange steering the line of reasoning, that this was a turn the story may have been about to take. Gabriel's mother, Sarah, told him

Barnes was his real father—but she told him that only after he was grown. During Gabriel's childhood and adolescence, Scanlan had been a monster of a (supposed) father and Sarah never stood up for the boy.

Then later, out West, Gabriel sees that Barnes has become a drunk, wallowing in mud and self-pity; he's disappointed and angry that his dream of a real father, a good father, has been shattered.

When Barnes tells him to go away, Gabriel is hurt and angry, and does. What Wayne and Dean had played to that point was ambiguous enough to allow for that.

Then, Barnes goes wandering off. Meanwhile, Gabriel changes his mind and wants to tell him the truth—that they're father and son. He hunts everywhere he can for him, but it's a big country and he can't find him. Then Gabriel goes bad and wanders off to some "far country" and doesn't see Barnes again until Barnes happens along and rescues him from being hanged.

"So far, so good," said Joanna, "But why wouldn't the woman … I mean, why wouldn't Sarah have told John Barnes she was pregnant before he left home in the first place?"

"She didn't know," said Solange. "Then, when Gabriel was born, she was able to convince Scanlan the baby was *his*—that it was premature. Scanlan didn't find out Barnes was the father until Gabriel was grown and had left home." She pursed her lips. "There might be a pivotal confrontation between Gabriel and Scanlan as Gabriel leaves—you know, long held-in hatreds."

Emily said, "Then, when Sarah does tell Scanlan about the baby, he follows Barnes out West, even though it's been almost two decades."

"That's it," said Solange. "It's stuck in his craw for a long time that Barnes, whom he'd already hated, fathered the child he thought was his. Scanlan feels humiliated, and on *top* of all those years of built-up hatred, with every mile he travels west, he gets more obsessed by his need for revenge. Wow. There's a lot of momentum toward revenge in this story."

She looked at the painting, concentrating on the woman. "Okay. And maybe the mother, Sarah—she's not dead, either. We only have Gabriel's word for that, too. Maybe the reason Gabriel doesn't tell Barnes she's really alive after Barnes has saved his life is that his mother is a sorry shadow of what she used to be, having lived a lie all her life, and now Gabriel doesn't want to hurt his real father—even if he is just a sad case when he finds him." She slaps her hands together. "Okay, and then—somehow, we'll figure it out—Sarah manages to pull herself together and follow them west. There were unending convoys of settlers heading to the Southwest and California in those days. And *here's* something *very* useful: we have no film on Sarah, or Scanlan. From our point of view, that's heaven-sent—"

Emily was finding Solange's easy authority irritating; at the same time, she was sucked in. "—And then," she interrupted, "Sarah gets herself into the picture, along with her husband and son and her son's father, for the showdown."

Solange flashed an uncharacteristically broad smile. "Okay. Yes. Good. I think this is a terrific starting point for developing the rest of my—" She laughed lightly. "Oops, sorry. '*Our* story.' I guess I've spent too much time by myself, figuring these things out."

Her Freudian slip and nimble recovery were far from lost on Emily.

"Now, you need to go ahead and do it," Solange continued, "because there's only half a story here. What's on film is fine as far as it goes, but it's flabby, and you're at the point in the picture where it's time for it to pay off. I know what you're hoping to produce is not some art film that happens to have John Wayne and James Dean in it, but a good old-fashioned popcorn-selling *Showdown*, starring John Wayne and James Dean. I mean, Jesus, talk about a cinematic event."

She looked over their heads, ruminating. "I think the old footage and the new can be brought together in a way that will make it seem like it's part of a master plan. A certain amount of baggage has to be manipulated in art as well as life, elements shuffled around for things to come out right. You could insert enhanced establishing close-ups of Wayne and Dean in some of the new sequences, using bits of those John Ford-like matte shots and a little bit of the outtake footage they didn't use. Then we mix those in with long two-shots and over-the-shoulder angles on Tom and Jimmy whenever you need to."

She looked once more at the painting of the three men and the woman by the campfire. "I'd like to see a love triangle, too. It'd be tricky. Maybe featuring something like the bicycle scene in *Butch Cassidy*. Maybe not. That's already kind of cliché. Anyway, you'll run the danger of breaking the suspension of disbelief if you linger on the boys too long. It's something to chew on. This story needs a woman, and I don't think the scenes with the mother that are implied for the beginning of the film, as it stands now, are enough. I'll have to think about it."

She tapped her forefingers on the corners of her mouth. "I'm not sure the love thing wouldn't feel forced." She frowned.

"There's one question that *really* puzzles me. This all feels … *not* so much like a Western as a whodunit." She stared out over their heads again, concentrating. "And who was it done to?"

"Is that your question?" said Emily.

"Not exactly", said Solange, staring at her. "My question now is, who is the showdown between?"

• • •

The next day at the office, Emily said to Joanna, "We've got to screen-test my brother." Her eyebrows arched in embarrassment. "I wasn't able to find the moment to bring it up to Solange last night. But it's something I have to insist on."

"Sweet pea, you're the boss. If you have to insist on it, so be it. Just for my own curiosity though—sorry to ask—is your brother any good?"

"He's a born actor. Some people thought he was very good. He just never took off."

"I'm fine with testing him. But if Solange directs this, she's not going to be happy if we make the decision for her on one of the three remaining roles."

"I understand," said Emily. "Wait a second. What's the third role?"

"Sorry. Brain overflow. Solange and I had a morning talk. She's been thinking about the love triangle idea—a young woman they meet along the way."

"I thought she said she it would feel forced." Emily drew in a quick breath. "Never mind. That's fine. I thought from the beginning they should have a love interest. … Listen, I have to ask you: You're not worried about the power … thing? If it all works out and she does end up directing this?"

Joanna sighed. "No. I know what you mean, but no, I'm not worried."

"*Do* you … know what I mean? My one strong impression from my time with Sterling was that as the ball gets rolling on a production—no matter who has the alleged 'reins' of the thing—the director *often* gains power … almost exponentially. I mean, you and I will be up to our asses in snapping turtles, dealing with a dozen unions, breaking down the script, hiring a hundred-plus people, working out schedules, scouting locations, et cetera et cetera."

"Darlin,' don't be stirring up the ulcer goblin this early in the day. We're going to hire a production manager. We won't be doing all of it."

"Yes," said Emily, unsmiling, "but we'll be responsible for all of it. Meanwhile, the substance of this slips more and more into the hands of a director who's very … *taken* with her own … *capabilities*. I told you I had a *couple* of tiny misgivings about her." She cut herself off. "Am I being paranoid?"

"Yes, Sweetie, I believe you are."

"So I should probably stop wishing we'd hired the finger counter?"

Joanna nodded. "I think it's best."

Emily felt the size of Tinkerbell, only clumsy and not so cute. "Have you found out anything about the Wayne estate?"

"I had to use some questionable assistance," said Joanna, "and beat my way through file sources that are not exactly public domain, but I got the information and you were right. There is no reference whatsoever to *Showdown* in either the John Wayne or the James Dean estates. Whatever deals were made were not incorporated into those papers."

"Is there anything else it might be covered by?"

"I don't think so. No worries about artist fees, just ownership, and there's no statement stipulating anything about that in either of their estates."

"So who does own it?"

Joanna shrugged. "I don't know. But you're right, we should move ahead as quickly and quietly as possible. I know I can come up with matching funds once the first half is raised, but we still have the ancient problem of who puts up the 'faith' money—complicated by the fact that we don't own the goddam thing. Our next step is to raise four million dollars."

"That's not much by today's standards, is it?" said Emily, trying to will it so. "Never mind. It's enough, I know. It'll be enough to do it really well, right?"

"I think so," Joanna made a comic face that said, "I hope to God so."

"Okay." Emily blinked her eyes. "One o'clock, The Regent Bar & Grill."

"You'll have the boys with you? It's important we're all on time."

"I'm aware of that," said Emily. "I am the world's promptest human. I'll have our stars in tow. I've already told them to set every clock they own and maybe borrow a few. We'll be on the dot. … We'll be ahead of the dot."

5

Emily sat in her father's bedroom watching the old man sleep. His breathing was strong and steady. Beneath the ruins of his body, decimated by chemicals and his struggle with disease, was an apparently robust will to live.

It was a restless day. Santa Ana winds were sucking the heat out of the desert and pushing it out across the LA basin to the Pacific. Emily concentrated on remaining still. She knew if her body reflected her mind, it would be a shark, unable to stop moving.

"That shouldn't bother you honey, now that you're one of the soulless Hollywood shark people."

She shifted her gaze to her brother, asleep in the blue corduroy slipper chair on the other side of the bed. In spite of his creaseless face, he looked less alive than their father.

The old man turned his head and groaned. Ben raised his shoulders and held them that way for several seconds, as if he were expecting a loud noise and was terrified of it.

Emily recalled sitting next to him at the top of the stairs outside the door to their parents' room while their father had told their mother she was "a tedious drudge." Her mother hadn't said a word. Daddy opened the door, looked down on them and roared, "Stop sticking your noses in grown-ups' business."

Emily had spoken in the firmest voice she could manage. "We only want you to be nice to her."

Her father snatched her up and pitched her down the hall, like he was throwing away rubbish.

As she'd gotten up and scampered away, her brother screamed, "You leave her alone, goddammit." Which he paid the price for. Ben had always been her hero.

Today, Ben had told her matter-of-factly: "Things are not going well for me, old thing. Never have, to be honest. I have been pissed upon from a great height." She remembered him in his Camp Cottonwood T-shirt. God, she'd loved him. She wasn't sure when the spirit had gone out of him, but now her recurring image of Skippy was as the wounded, fragile Lew Ayres in *Holiday*, playing two-dollar bets at the blackjack table, never doubling down, not caring if he won or lost—one of the players dealers wish would go home.

She spoke to Ben Sr. in a whisper. "What did you do to him, Daddy? He never used to be like this. He used to have some guts, a little life. But you sucked him dry." The old man blinked and twitched his nose. For an instant she imagined she'd gotten through to him. As her disappointment passed, she continued to watch for any sign that he knew she was there.

She looked back at Ben—disregarded, fallow, forced to live entirely inside himself, and had the illusion of being with him in a hall of funhouse mirrors, watching his perfect but blandly warped face reflected further into the distance than her eyes had power to bring into focus.

She hated to leave the two of them together. She was afraid they'd both die while she was gone that afternoon.

• • •

Keith Oakland, a tall, dark-haired man in his mid-forties, listened as Jack Butterworth spoke distractedly to him and Joanna Morgan. Joanna was politely attentive. Oakland, slender as a whippet, looked as if he was smelling something unpleasant and seemed to be staring at the middle of Butterworth's forehead.

"You want to hear why there's no business like show business?" said Butterworth. "I'll tell you why. Because in no other business do you get a bunch of adolescents together, young ones, old ones, but mostly young ones. And if they're lucky—these Hollywood producer-adolescents—they kinda half-ass know what they're doin' and they hire technicians who usually know pretty well what they're doin' and a bunch of other adolescents to do the performing. And the first adolescents have paid a hefty buck for some story that maybe makes sense, maybe doesn't. It doesn't matter, as long as it's got blood and sex and deadly menace. And the adolescents who pay to see it feel like their own life's at stake while they're watching it. And all the moviemaker adolescents go to their premieres, and talk about how they've conquered the art of the 'cinema.' And all the time they're thinking about the tootsie on their arm with the unnaturally pouty lips and how they're going to hustle her off to their unpaid-for hillside house and snort coke and do unspeakable things to the tootsie—but it turns out they can't because their teeny little dinguses can't stand up straight anymore from all the poisons they've ingested while they should have been concentrating on producing a movie that was anywhere near as accomplished as the average kindergartener's crayon drawing."

He refilled his lungs through clenched teeth and scanned the faces of his two listeners. "Of course, I'm not talking about you independent people. I have the greatest respect for you." He stopped and looked warily around him. "Sorry about that." He showed them a Wile E. Coyote smile. "I get nervous around strangers, especially out in public." He sat up in his chair to try to get Oakland to look him in the eyes.

Oakland, who had pale blue ones and manicured brows that looked like two black Magic Marker checks about to collide at the top of his nose and caused him to appear purposeful at all times, simply lifted his gaze so that whatever his purpose was, it didn't seem to have anything to do with Butterworth, or for that matter, with anyone but himself.

"It's kind of like one of those unfortunate medical syndromes I have—you know, where you say the wrong things under pressure." Again, Butterworth stopped himself, blinking. "I don't get out much."

Neither of them looked him in the eye.

He was nursing a Scotch and water. Joanna sipped a glass of Chablis. Oakland had a cup of coffee in front of him that he hadn't touched. They sat at a large, circular, mahogany table near the bar in The Regent Bar & Grill where Emily had first spoken to Tom about *Showdown*. The gas log fire flickered in the fireplace. A television over the bar was tuned soundlessly to a game show. At three fifteen in the afternoon, there were only a few other customers.

"Would you like another Scotch?" Joanna asked Butterworth, afraid he might accept.

"Damned straight. I'd like a lot of Scotches, but I can't." He clenched his lips together.

"Perhaps we could ask you a few questions about your project," said Oakland, focusing two inches above Butterworth's nose. He glanced over at Joanna, possibly gauging the precise dimensions of her widow's peak.

"No offense," said Butterworth, "but I don't want to do that till Miss Bennett shows."

Oakland smiled icily. "I meant only for purposes of making clear precisely what we're talking about."

Butterworth shook his head and frowned. "Uh-uh. I knew when I came out of hiding on this thing that I'd have to take a chance or two. But I want Miss Bennett right next to me when

I have any discussions with additional parties. Don't take it personally."

"Quite all right."

"I'll be honest. I'm feelin' kinda edgy about this whole thing anyway. Where *is* Miss Bennett?"

"I'm sure she'll be here any minute," said Joanna. "She's a promptness freak. She's obviously … dead."

Butterworth raised his eyebrows and pretended she hadn't said that. "I mean, I don't even know her that well," he said. "I think I trust you, but"—he swung his gaze from Joanna to the front entrance—"but this is making me jumpy."

"The last thing I'd want to do is make you uncomfortable," said Oakland. "I have guaranteed Ms. Morgan that I would keep your project entirely confidential. I know she agrees that would be in our best interests."

"Absolutely," said Joanna.

"I'm what is called a venture capitalist. I raise seed money. I'm also an investor. I invest for other people, and I put my *own* money into any enterprise I settle on. My small specialized clientele takes my word entirely on the projects I choose. I am answerable for the details of my choices to no one. In short, I have no reason whatever to compromise the integrity of your project."

Butterworth nodded, barely moving. "Well, that's good to hear ... I guess."

• • •

"I'm sorry we're late. It was my fault. I'm embarrassed to death. I am never, never late."

Emily stood next to Joanna. She was flushed and out of breath. Tom and Jimmy were behind her.

They exchanged meetings and greetings, Emily apologized again, and Butterworth, as always, gazed wide-eyed at Tom.

After drinks were ordered, the attention settled on Emily. "I'm afraid I've had a ... domestic tragedy," she said.

Joanna gasped. "Oh, sweet pea, your father?"

"Oh, no. We had an accident on the way here. It was my fault. I'd picked up Jimmy and Duke, then I stopped back by my father's house to get some papers—we still had plenty of time." She looked forlorn, remembering. "I got into the car again and backed out of the driveway." She cringed. "There was a ..."

"Just a bump," said Tom.

"That's right." She spoke haltingly. "Just the smallest ... *bump*. But we all got out of the car." She held her hands out, helpless. "And I had"—there was a look of incredulity on her face—"killed my father's dog."

Tom shrugged apologetically as though he had been driving. "Flattened him."

"It was just a little dog," Jimmy explained to Oakland.

"He'd gotten out before," said Emily. "I should have known better."

Joanna uttered a sympathetic moan. "Ooooh, that's awful. I'm *so* sorry."

"Thanks," said Emily. "And maybe we still could have been on time, but we couldn't figure out what to do with him. This meeting was too important to call and cancel, but I couldn't just leave him in our driveway. And I couldn't take him into the house—my brother was ... having a nap, and there wasn't time to wake him and explain."

"What did you do?" said Joanna.

"Jimmy and Duke helped me. We picked him up as gently as we could with a ... shovel and put him in a ..." She couldn't say it.

"A Hefty bag," murmured Tom.

"Then we put him in the garage," said Jimmy.

Butterworth couldn't help himself; he started to giggle, then quickly covered with: "What kind of dog was he?"

"A Chihuahua."

"Ooooh, poor little thing," said Joanna. "What was his name?"

"El Poochino."

• • •

When Butterworth was finished telling the history of *Showdown*, with no side comments about Hollywood, Oakland broke the silence. He looked at the center of Emily's forehead and said, "I only have a couple of questions. Who do you have in mind to direct? I think you could attract almost anyone you want."

"I think we should hold off on choosing a director till we've come to an agreement," said Emily.

Joanna had thought this was the best approach with Oakland, and Emily had reluctantly agreed. "He's a hard-nosed, old-fashioned business man," Joanna had told her. "We need to play him like a giant tuna. Once he's seduced by the project, I'm pretty sure we can sell him on the director we want. Let's not throw Solange at him at the first meeting. I'm afraid his balls might retract into their safe, dark place."

"I'll bet she's got bigger ones," said Emily.

Now, she said to Oakland, "May we discuss directors at a separate time?"

"All right. But I must tell you my other concern." He glanced at Jimmy.

Emily was running a finger back and forth over one of her single pearl earrings. "We'd like to take you to our office and show you some film." She tacked on a charming smile.

Oakland ignored it. "I've noticed that Mr. Manfredo bears a striking resemblance to John Wayne. I'm not an expert, but I observed him coming into the room and sitting down. His body language seems to me to contain the elements of the John Wayne persona. I must tell you in all candor, however, that the choice of Mr. Riley puzzles me. He doesn't immediately recall images of James Dean to my mind."

Jimmy got up. They all turned to him as he transformed himself into Dean. Oakland watched, horrified, then mesmerized.

Jimmy played the pitch directly to him.

Emily appreciated again that it was only as himself that Jimmy was self-conscious. As James Dean, he was poised, fearless. For a moment or two, she was afraid he was doing it too well, that he was getting so close to the man, that Oakland might react to him like Raymond Massey had to Dean during the filming of *East of Eden*. It was perfect for director Elia Kazan's purposes in regard to the dynamics of John Steinbeck's story. Massey came to him and complained about Dean's unprofessionalism and among other things, his painful—to Massey—over-intimacy. Kazan said, "Of course, Ray, Of course," sympathizing with him. Then he went back to Dean and told him to keep doing exactly the same thing—except more so.

But Jimmy Riley sensed exactly when to pull back with Oakland, when to attack, and when again to expose Dean's sweet-natured side.

When he was finished, he faced Oakland for his final moment and said, "But that fanatical kid was flawless at playing James Dean. He was a superb impersonator. What he impersonated was his own invention—a universal rebellious character that would appeal on one level or another to almost every kid in America. He was a genius at doing that."

Then he smiled. "And I'm the second best James Dean impersonator—after James Dean—there ever was. And you can add to that, I'm alive."

Oakland was on board.

6

It was the summer of 1979. Hollywood responded to President Jimmy Carter's assertion that American was suffering from a "crisis of confidence" by making more movies than ever. Pictures in production or pre-production included: *Kramer Vs. Kramer*, *Ordinary People*, *Tess*, *Fame*, *The Empire Strikes Back*, *Private Benjamin*, *9 to 5*, *Coal Miner's Daughter*, *The Blues Brothers*, and Martin Scorsese's spectacular *Raging Bull*. The locals were no longer discussing the metamorphosis of Hollywood the movie factory into Hollywood the state of mind; they were turning out films. Very few of them looked up when Skylab fell to earth on July 11. They didn't pay a lot of attention to the voices of Jerry Falwell's Moral Majority. Although there was plenty of speculation about the future, not many got very excited over the wire service stories about the imminence of personal computers and the recent invention, used at the moment only by the military and scientific communities, of email. When the partial nuclear meltdown of Three Mile Island happened in March, only two weeks after the release of *The China Syndrome*, a film about that very subject, there was a feeling among the extremely right-brained in Hollywood that they were actually creators of history. Others, who knew better, did nothing to try to change those fanciful minds, and as the year wore on, continued to sing along with Gloria Gaynor's "I Will Survive."

• • •

In Oakland's office, three days after The Regent Bar & Grill meeting, he predictably balked on Solange Borugian. "Pardon me for saying it," he said with undisguised antagonism, "but the idea of this phalanx of women is starting to make me uncomfortable."

"Why is that?" said Emily, with a dazzling smile. "Don't you think we're as capable as men?"

"Of course you're capable."

"Then I don't understand."

"And I think you're being purposely obtuse."

"I'm not. It just happens that in this case, three women have come together, not as outsiders or tokens, but as the heart and soul of a film project." She added in diplomatic tones: "I'm sure you're not threatened by that."

"Of course I'm not threatened." He tempered his murderous expression with a crimped smile to demonstrate, Emily guessed, that he had a feminine side himself. "It's just that she's hardly a conventional choice"—his sensitive side evaporated—"to direct a goddam Western."

Emily took a deep breath to keep from responding with her caveman side, and Joanna filled the gap by suggesting that it might be a good time to screen Solange's independent Western.

• • •

Not only was it beautifully photographed, but dialogue that might have seemed routine, in lesser directorial hands, crackled with the appropriate tension, clearly demonstrating that Solange was skilled with actors. It wasn't a great story, but the direction made it feel as if it was a good one.

When it was over Oakland said, "It looks fine, but I still think it's a bad idea."

"What would persuade you?" asked Joanna as Emily leaned toward Jimmy and whispered, "Laurence Harvey. *Manchurian Candidate.*"

"I can't think of anybody who could do a better job," Joanna said to Oakland.

Butterworth almost barked: "You want this done the best way possible, don't you?" Emily shot him a look, but he wasn't going to be stifled. "I'm as tough on a director as anybody could be, and this project is my life. If Solange Borugian can repeat the kind of shots, the sorta pyrotechnics she's built into the picture we just looked at, we've got exactly who we need."

"Let me put it this way," said Oakland. "I'm raising four million dollars for this ... *speculation*—one million of it my own money—and we aren't even getting distribution up front. I'm not going to bet my money on some little cookie named *Solange*, who's directed one obscure B movie." He'd said her name with a flat nasal twang, making her sound like a Dodge City whore.

Emily again produced her most captivating smile. "Would you look at another piece of film?"

Oakland sighed heavily. "I'll look."

She put another cassette into the VCR. "This is a commercial for Buick."

It ran fifty-eight seconds. In the opening shot, an automobile drove along a vast desert tableland, making its way north. The sun rose over snow-capped mountains in the distance. In another angle, a cowboy appeared. In the next long shot, the automobile and the cowboy moved toward each other.

Close on the automobile: a midnight blue luxury car.

Close on the cowboy: a young John Wayne, dressed in a blue placket-front shirt and faded denim pants, riding toward camera, moving like he and the bay he rode were one.

In a series of cuts with composition rivaling Hawks and Ford, the car and John Wayne approached each other.

When they had almost met, the automobile and the cowboy pulled up. A beautiful raven-haired woman stepped out of the car.

John Wayne looked at her in front of the Buick for a long beat and said, "That's a beautiful animal."

Then he turned and rode off.

The commercial ended.

Behind a cupped hand, so that only Emily could see her, Joanna crossed her eyes, and in the same continuing fluid motion, unfolded the hand, palm up, smiling graciously, and said, "That was Solange Borugian directing Tom Manfredo."

Oakland broke out his tight smile. It seemed almost genuine. "*That's* what I wanted to see."

He didn't know much about movies, but he recognized a snazzy-looking commercial when he saw it. He looked Emily, then Joanna—in the eye. Later, they claimed it was the only time he ever did.

"I want you to concentrate on getting this thing made," he said. "If you'll agree to what I have in mind for distribution, I'm good for the entire amount."

• • •

Jimmy had arranged a meeting with Emily.

On his way to the production office, the wheels of his brain spun like bald tires on ice, dislodging a warped memory of Gerald's first heart attack. His father, his champion, wept. "These are the good times, Jim," he said, and then he sobbed. Later, Vivian cried too, but her tears weren't from sympathy; they were bitter tears that fate hadn't delivered her a 'manlier husband.' "The more I told him about fatty foods, or *anything* for that matter, the more he tuned me out. I tried to explain … lots of things, but he would not understand. He never tried. He insisted on making friends with people who simply didn't matter—shopkeepers, workmen … nobodies. All my friends thought he was a clown. And they were right."

Jimmy remembered Gerald taking him and his sister on a Ferris wheel. Now, that memory was muddling itself with another uninvited James Dean moment *(he's no longer my invention, he's a fact).* In this case, it's *East of Eden*, Julie Harris saying to Dean: "Please forget what happened on the Ferris wheel."

On Jimmy's Ferris wheel, Gracie cried. Gerald put an arm around her and told her there was nothing to worry about. The image dissolved to the look in his mother's eyes when she told him his father had not been the man she'd hoped for. Jimmy knew she was right, that his father's "word" had always been a lie. And once again he saw the log cabin in the woods, getting closer as he followed the man half-lit by the glow of his own lantern.

• • •

At his camp, in the outdoor chapel, the wooden cross is lit up in a patch of moonlight. In the distance, he sees the A-frame storage cabin among a cluster of trees. A light glows from inside through the window.

Now, he's just outside the window, standing on tiptoes, looking in at the gymnastics equipment pushed together against one of the walls, next to a sink with a single cold water tap.

Even though he has never been near that storage cabin, he recognizes the inside of it.

• • •

Walking into the office, he couldn't help thinking of James Dean as Jett Rink in *Giant*, petty and small, out of place, neurotic, pestery—an opportunist without grace.

"Is Ben going to play Scanlan?"

Emily stared at him. "Where did you hear that?"

"*Are* you planning to cast him?"

"We're going to test him."

Jimmy groaned.

Emily wished she was home, watching … *anything*. "What's the matter?"

"I saw Ben today." He reddened. "Do you call him Ben or Skip?"

"Ben … both, I guess. I always used to call him Skippy. Now, he doesn't really seem like a … I don't know. You saw him?"

"I was riding my bicycle by your father's house, and he was out at the mailbox." He blushed again. "It was on purpose. I've been ... taking rides by your house ever since I first saw him there. Today I talked to him."

• • •

Ben smiles blearily. "I'm a Billy born drunk. I'm afraid I've lost the plot for most of that summer. But I remember you, mate. You were a sweet little chap."

"Do you remember Wally?"

"Say again?"

"He was a counselor too. He was your friend. I have this dream where I'm following him."

"Afraid the name doesn't ring a bell. Wally, you say?"

"That's right."

"Sorry, I can't put a face to that."

• • •

Jimmy studied Emily's face. "Has Ben talked about me?"

"He told me you took an acting class together." She looked out the window. "He's not much for raking up the past."

"That's *exactly* what he said about *you.*" With the tips of his fingers he felt the dampness at the center of his palms. "Listen, I don't think I can act with him."

"Why not? You don't have that many sequences together. He said you were friends."

"Yeah, well I sort of liked him, in a way—as kind of an adult friend, or almost like a father figure." He looked away. He hadn't meant to reveal anything like that. "But now … now, he makes me feel like …" His brow creased. "Like … you know how it is with somebody you maybe … 'respected' too much, and it turns out they've got … you know … shortcomings like everybody else."

"That doesn't mean you can't work with him, does it?"

"I don't know what it means!"

He didn't tell her any more secrets.

Emily didn't say, *He's my brother. He needs my help.* She knew Jimmy would say that he did, too.

She felt a flood of tenderness for him and took his hand. She wanted to pet him until all his pain was gone. "It's me, isn't it? It's my fault you feel this way."

"Nothing's your fault," he said, tears forming. "It's just that if you're not right for me, I don't think anybody ever will be."

She hugged him stiffly and looked over his shoulder at a poster-sized print of Dennis Stock's famous picture of James Dean—ciggie in mouth, hunched up against the cold, hands tucked inside a dark overcoat—walking through the rain in Times Square. She studied Dean's face, wondering if there was anything generous behind the eyes—anything that wasn't synthetic, a cynical invention, lacking in compassion or even mercy. He was exactly what she didn't need. He made her so angry she could barely speak.

"We're no longer safe."

"Never were, honey."

She let go of his hand. "I wish we could be together," she said. "But, we need a happy ending, both of us, and I don't think the way to get it is to do anything we'd be sorry for. I'm sort of resilient. But you feel breakable to me, and I don't want to take that chance."

She knew the resilient part was a lie.

• • •

On her way home, she thought of the look on Ben's face when he'd told her that he'd known her new friend, Jimmy, back when Emily was still a girl. There had been a light in Ben's eye when he talked about that time that reminded her of the way he used to be.

She thought about how indelibly some things were stamped into her DNA and how others had vanished without a trace.

• • •

Tom was cutting back the Creeping Charlie behind his house, absentmindedly singing John Lennon's "Jealous Guy."

"Wull, who are you jealous *of*?" said Wayne, doing a parody of his movie star persona.

"Leave me alone. I'm ... just singing."

"You know, I used to think all that back-of-your-mind crap was just that. Now I'm not so sure. Ya wanna know why I say that?"

"You're going to tell me whether I do or not."

"Listen, kid. There seems to be a great big wall in your path. If you can leap over it, great; otherwise, I suggest you look for a ladder."

"Now you're a ladder?"

"No, smartass, I'm not volunteering to be climbing equipment—although that is interesting, a ladder, a set of steps." He shrugged. "All I'm telling you is you've gone and got yourself in love for the first time in your life. And what do you do about it?

You go to work on Creepy Charlie here. You know what I'd do if I were you?"

Tom clenched his hand clippers shut, hard. "*What*?"

"I'd try to use some common sense. I might flip to a page in my own book. That's a pun, son. Paige. Get it?"

"I keep telling you, I don't really remember her."

"Not even at the Blue Martini?"

"How's that going to help me? I've been to a thousand bars. I don't remember most of them."

"Me neither, pilgrim. Don't bother to open the gate."

• • •

The elements of the production began to come together.

They hired Rush Mellman, a first-rate director of photography, and he brought Art Gallagher, one of the finest camera operators in Hollywood, with him. The set designer had credits that ran back twenty-five years and read like a list of the best films of that period. The rest of the crew was made up of the highest quality artists and technicians, each at the peak of his form. They contracted to pay all of them more than their going price. They had to, because most of them were not even told what they would be working on. Only Mellman and Gallagher knew, and they were sworn to secrecy.

Casting: Solange had written in the love interest for John Barnes and Gabriel. They would rescue a young woman called Prudence, a mail-order bride, from her abusive husband. Then, in a montage with music, they would each "court" and fall in love with her. Barnes and Gabriel had both lifted themselves out of the grim isolation they'd each inhabited when they'd met and now, for a short while, there was room for something between them that went beyond mutual antagonism.

After two days of casting sessions, without having to screen-test anybody, they found their Sarah and their Prudence.

Emily told Tom that Sarah, Gabriel's mother, would be Rosemary Forsyth (*Shenandoah, Texas Across the River*—not surprisingly, Emily saw her as Rosemary Forsyth). She was too beautiful, Joanna thought, but she did have a sort of pioneer presence and was well cast as a silent long-sufferer. They would not be using her until the end of the shoot.

She insisted that nobody test against Ben for the role of Scanlan. She didn't want the pressure of competition to kill his chances but agreed that if he did poorly, they would see other actors later. They were to test Ben the next week and planned to look at the film and finalize their decision at the following production meeting.

• • •

Something else was playing on Emily's nerves. She wasn't sure, but she had a gnawing feeling that if Ben were going to be in the movie, the infinite singularities Richard Boone had told her had to exist in the universe were adding up to something potent enough to threaten the underpinnings of her already shaky world.

She called Boone at his home in Florida.

After they'd chatted for a while and caught up with each other's recent past, Emily launched into the story of their group's connection with *Showdown,* beginning with the Western painting that hung on Tom's wall.

When she was finished, Boone said, "You and your friends have a lot of nerve."

"What do you mean?" There was silence except for some static Emily imagined coming from a frayed line somewhere over Oklahoma. "What do you mean, Dick?"

"I told you that in confidence." Boone's voice sounded frail.

"Yes, but I thought enough time had passed. And now, since Mr. Wayne has died—"

"Maybe you've finally found your niche in this business."

"I don't know whether to be insulted or not."

"Be insulted." He exhaled sharply and then she heard him breathing. "We have to try to understand who we are. ... On the other hand"—he drew in another shallow, raspy breath—"nothing gets accomplished if you don't jump a fence now and then. It sounds pretty irresistible. If I felt a little better, a little younger, I'd join you."

"Why don't you? We could use you."

"I wish I could, but I've got other things to tend to. I'm finally able to spend a little time with Claire. But it's a fascinating thing you're up to."

"You think so? I've been having doubts lately if it's worth all the trouble."

"Hey, listen, if you're going to do it, it should be fun. You've got the opportunity while you're working on this, you and your other dreamers of dreams, to speculate about Wayne and Dean together—maybe even learn a couple of things." When Emily didn't answer, Boone said, "You did understand that when I was talking about Wayne and Dean as archetypes, I was speaking of the allegorical them, not the real guys. In reality, Wayne and Dean were only who they were. You and I know that." He paused again. "Don't we, Em?"

"Sure. I'm sorry I didn't call you."

"I forgive you, dear, but I also wonder what the hell you may be scratching up here. I had the impression that underneath Duke's bravado he was very edgy about that whole thing." He cleared his throat. "So, what's your question?"

Emily realized that she didn't exactly have one—or more accurately, she had a laundry list of questions but that they all felt messy, ill-thought-out. "How do you account for what's happening with this?"

He laughed. "Would you like me to tell you the meaning of life while I'm at it?"

"Seriously, do you have any idea what I'm dealing with here?"

He was quiet for a moment, then, with a zeal undiminished by the beginnings of his final battle with cancer, he said: "It sounds from the description of your friends like what you have in common is that you're all displaced persons. None of you knows who she or he is, or where you're going." Emily started to object, but Boone kept talking. "Take my word on this. I've got a feel for displacement."

"So what do I do with this information?"

"You understand what it brings to bear on your question. It seems to me that you and your friends are at similar points in your journeys. That's why you came together—it feels good to you to compare notes, and to reckon with the possibility that you're not just dreaming anymore, you're … let's call it 'on assignment.' "

"Okay," said Emily. "I still don't understand how the various parts of this whole thing seem to be assembling themselves around us."

"You're wounded people," said Boone. "Wounded people acting together, renovating yourselves into a brand-new intelligence."

"But I don't think it's happening because of us," said Emily. "My impression is that it's happening *to* us."

"How do you separate it? If the concerted energy of wounded, motivated people gets bound up with any of the billions of forces of God or nature, or whatever you prefer to call it, that man doesn't understand except in language we haven't invented yet, and that unfathomable set of pressures has its own continuing momentum—then those combined energies are going to add up to one … mama bear of a unified force. Who the hell knows what can happen?"

"Well, I certainly don't," Emily said to her father figure of choice. "That's why I called you."

"You called me because for reasons that are entirely baffling to me, you seem to have leaped past the cynicism of your youth and onto a new path of"—he searched for the right word—"openness ... maybe *learning*. I haven't a clue how it happened. I suspect we all have a spiritual butterfly that flutters free one day if we're lucky and we've worked our minds into a ... place of appreciation, or at least receptivity. You seem to have suddenly burst through your chrysalis and now you're trying to get the hang of your new little lepidopteran gyroscope."

She stared at him all the way to Florida. "You're just being purposely spooky."

He allowed himself a brief giggle. "Okay, but it *is* rebirth kinda stuff. Not in the born-again sense, but something inside you is trying to renew itself. Maybe what you ought to do is just relax and let what wants to happen, happen."

"Let go, let God?"

Boone barked his signature, croaky laugh. "Yeah. Sure. I like that. Do that if you dare."

7

Between finishing up her earlier commitment and writing the first scenes and the last act of the script for *Showdown,* Solange Borugian found time for a few hours of rehearsal with Jimmy and Tom. Along with Joanna, Emily was tending to the escalating morass of production details, but she meant to be a hands-on producer, so she was in on these sessions too.

Despite Emily's nagging uneasiness about Solange, she turned out to be even more bright and resourceful than she and Joanna had first thought. Solange was creative, but also listened receptively to other people's ideas when they were offered, incorporating and synthesizing the best of them into her own.

One day in her apartment in the Los Feliz district, Jimmy and Tom were reading a tentative scene when Solange interrupted and said, "You're both giving very controlled performances. I hope you understand that sooner or later—and sooner is better—you're going to have to let it all hang out."

Jimmy smiled uncomfortably. Tom said, "What do you mean?"

"I mean you're all somehow timid. That seems to be the hallmark of your little band." She glanced at Emily. "Timid people, knotted together in a bold venture."

"How the hell are we supposed to be?" said Jimmy, not raising his voice.

"I have no idea. What I do know is that you boys are being neat. You have to be messy and let me clean it up in the cutting room." She looked from one to the other. "If it crosses your minds, by the way, to influence your producers, including Emily here, to fire me, my opinion is that you'll risk losing the jobs yourselves. This is business, and this is Hollywood. There are other celebrity impersonators in town."

"Why are you telling us this?" said Tom, with his chronic look of trying to remember something.

"Just telling you my terms."

Tom looked at Emily's unreadable expression and then, along with Jimmy, glanced at their surroundings—a large, high-ceilinged room, agreeably but sparely furnished. The white walls were pictureless except for an orderly little grouping of family photographs near Solange's desk.

Jimmy studied Solange. She was wearing designer slacks and an expensive white sweatshirt, cut off and hemmed at the elbows. "You don't look to me like someone who lets it all hang out," he said.

Solange scanned her living room. "A mess needs to be presentable if anybody's going to choose to look at it. A book needs a cover, printing, sentences, and paragraphs. A messy movie had better have a lot of structure if it's going to be a good messy movie."

Tom looked like a faithful family pet, unaccountably mistreated by his master.

Emily shifted in her chair.

"If you're trying to unsettle us by drawing us into your mess," said Jimmy evenly, "it's working just fine on me." He took a cigarette out of a pack, held the pack out as an invitation to Solange and Emily, and as part of a separately considered afterthought, to Tom.

They all declined.

Solange stared at him. "Are you nervous?"

Jimmy lit a cigarette and put the pack back in his shirt pocket. "Yeah, a little bit. Why?"

"What about?"

"This."

"Nerves are good. Stage fright is good—to a point. After that it's destructive. It takes away from the guts of what's going on. It's crippling."

" 'Let's not throw around words like 'crippled,' " said Jimmy in a measured monotone. His voice got even flatter. "And I've got to tell you this conversation is beginning to piss me off." He took a deep drag on his cigarette.

"I'm not sure I'd know you were pissed off without you telling me so. You're good at doing the volatile side of James Dean when it's not about anything. How about when it is? Put the cigarette out, please."

"I'm sorry?"

"Put the cigarette out. I don't allow smoking in my apartment." Solange got up, opened a drawer in an étagère, took out an ashtray and handed it to him.

Jimmy crushed out his cigarette without looking at her.

"At our starting point, you still hate this man." She nodded at Tom without looking away from Jimmy. "You know he's your father, but you haven't been willing to forgive him for running away and turning into a drunk, even though he didn't know he was your father. It's irrational on your part, but there it is." She turned squarely to him. "How do you feel when it turns out your first impressions of him were wrong?"

Jimmy swung his gaze toward Tom. "I form a new impression."

"Well, sure, but it's got to be *about* something. You're not suddenly a blank page. Your beliefs about what you thought John Barnes was have become a part of you, part of what makes you carry on. When he turns out to be more complicated than that, more than an idealized father, more than a simple drunk, it's got to threaten your picture of yourself, doesn't it? How's it going to make you feel?"

"Not good," said Jimmy. "Angry, I guess. It might make me angry."

"Unless you're a machine or an impersonator, living a secondhand existence, it goddam well would."

"Not everyone needs to be an original," said Jimmy. Although his voice remained even, one side of his upper lip rose slightly, turning his expression into something like a controlled snarl.

Solange's eyes sparkled as she looked over at Tom. "What's the matter?"

"I don't know," he said. "I expected … Well anyway, I didn't expect *this*. Why don't you give us a script so we can …? I'm not an Actors Studio performer. I'm not *Second City or Saturday Night Live*. I need a script and plenty of time."

"You'll get a script. But first, we have to work a few things out—like how you're going to feel if Gabriel doesn't respond to you like you're the complex personality you are. How would you feel?"

"I don't know."

"Yes, you do."

"Okay, I'd be a little pissed off."

"Jesus. You two really *are* related. As an actor, given *these* circumstances, how do you play 'a little' pissed off?"

Tom's brow furrowed.

"Because even if that's something you can do, it's going to be deadly dull for the audience, not to mention disappointing." She softened her tone to what she meant as sweet reason. "Look, everybody wants understanding. When a person goes out of his way to be understood and he's distinctly not understood, he's going to be upset about it. And since the audience is going to be upset on your behalf, they'll be further upset and disappointed with you for not seizing the opportunity to vent the outrage they feel. One of the main reasons we go to the movies is so we can have the chance to 'say things' in a satisfying way that we can't say in life. If you rob the audience of that, it'll make them mad, and they're not going to like anything about you or your movie."

"So what does John Barnes do?" asked Tom.

"For Christ's sake. He's lost everything. He's developed a way of coping that's not working anymore. There's only one thing he *can* do. He becomes fucking enraged. He needs change, and rage is an unrivaled catalyst of that."

"Well, I'll tell you the truth, I *am* angry."

"At whom?"

Tom stared at her hard.

"At whom, please?"

He turned slowly to Jimmy and locked eyes with him. For an instant, he looked to Tom like cornered prey.

Then, as if they'd agreed on the exact moment, they both broke off the staring contest. Tom said, "I don't know who I'm angry at," and looked back at Solange. "At myself, I guess."

Jimmy said, "She wants us back on our heels, Duke. She wants us raw."

"Amen," said Solange.

Tom regarded them both grimly; then, looking at Emily: "I'll show her raw. I'll show her a nervous freaking breakdown."

• • •

In the production meeting that night, Solange did not report that she was unsatisfied with rehearsals, as Emily thought she might. When Joanna asked how it was coming along, Solange mentioned the boys'—especially Tom's—unwillingness to fill emotional moments as fully as she wanted them to, but when Joanna expressed alarm and reminded them that they were going to begin shooting soon, their director responded with categorical optimism:

"I'm not disappointed. I never thought either of them was uninhibited. Neither were the originals. John Wayne was not exactly free as a bird, and James Dean, even though on the surface he was willing to risk anything—chewing the scenery to pieces—he was still at his core extremely guarded." She bit her lip, as if holding back unsuitable glee. "But this is a Victorian era story—the definitive example of times when people wouldn't say shit if they had a mouthful. We have the right actors."

"This is not Henry James," said Joanna. "This is the American West."

"I know, but the American West was part of the Western English-speaking world, and a Victorian, Calvinist air was circulating through all of it. What I'm saying is that the heart of what the boys bring with them is on the money."

"But?" said Emily.

"But within the range of who they are, I still have to get them to open up."

Emily's eyes were blinking rapidly. "It's all hip and off the cuff and everything for you to get them nice and messy, but will they be ready when we shoot?"

Solange regarded her, half smiling. "I see signs of real conflict between them and that's going to help us make some fireworks."

"But aren't the fireworks supposed to be between Scanlan and Barnes?"

"It's *all* supposed to be fireworks. That's what makes drama live. '*Gyanke bare' grage' lezeou ee vra.*' It's an old Armenian expression: 'Life is a dance on a tongue of fire.' "

• • •

The following evening, Solange said, "I've been working on something. I might as well just tell you: I think we have to make some changes in the material."

Joanna and Emily gave her their full attention.

"I'm not knocking … *most* of what we already have. And I don't want to disturb the tone of the piece. But I think there are things we can do that will expand and heighten it." She paused, tapping two fingertips on her lips. "I think Prudence has to go."

"Ouch," said Emily, thinking of the actress.

"I understand. But I'm convinced I know where the writer was going with this. He must have planned a love triangle. The story cries out for it."

"But we've got Prudence," said Joanna.

"We're imposing Prudence on the story. I think the triangle he intended was Barnes, Gabriel, and Sarah."

Joanna and Emily stared at her. Finally, Joanna said, "Are you suggesting that James Dean, or whoever wrote this, wanted a triangle between the father, the mother, and … the *son*? That would mean the son wants to … to … go to bed with his mother…?"

"Yes, but that's not where I'm going."

"Where are you going?" said Emily.

"He wants to possess her."

"Not make love to her?"

Solange shrugged. "Well, yes of course, but that's secondary."

"*Wanting to fuck his mother is secondary*?"

"I'm saying he wants to, but only as a human function that goes along with any love relationship a healthy young man would have."

"*Healthy*? said Emily. "Did you say *healthy*?"

"My point," said Solange, staying calm, "is that Prudence will disappoint the expectations of today's moviegoer."

"Jesus, Solange," said Joanna. "Today's moviegoer will be unhappy without *incest*?"

"In this story, I think so. I think this particular screenplay cries out for it." She looked at both of their faces; then, in frustration: "You ladies have no idea the moviegoer this culture is creating."

"That can't be true," said Emily. "Everybody likes a traditional love story."

"But everybody—and I mean *everybody*," said Solange, "will go to see a movie about James Dean wanting to fuck his mother."

Joanna blinked hard. "Are you *crazy*? People would be *repelled*. They'd stone us."

"No they won't. They'll rent it and watch it in their bedrooms, so as not to embarrass themselves in front of all their friends—who will also be watching it in *their* bedrooms. Then years from now, they'll invite the gang over to see it because that kind of thing will be commonplace. Look, I understand your skepticism."

"*Skepticism*?" Emily shouted. "Try revulsion."

"Think what we have here," said Solange. "This is a good story, but it can be memorable if we take on something truly important. I'm not talking about actual m-effing. But I am talking about the *feel* of it, you know? I'm talking about essential human emotional needs. These men both have a gut need for this woman. They might make an effort to really get to know each other under other circumstances, but at the core, they have something else on their minds. Each of them has a separate history with Sarah, a separate claim on her. She is the lasting pivot point in their lives. In a real sense, it's the old and the young bull locked in combat over the female object of their affections, and it's no little thing. In this story, in this moment, it is blood, bone, and sinew what their lives are about. And anything less from them—any tacked-on romance—will feel like a monumental letdown."

Emily clenched her hands. "And how does that square with your 'good old-fashioned showdown'?"

"It's a vital element of it. When Scanlan sees it and recognizes it, it'll drive him crazier than Anita Bryant at a gay convention."

"And I'm telling you," said Joanna—piercingly for her, "anything approaching blatant incest will not play in Peoria."

Solange looked around, musing. "I'll work on that."

• • •

For his test, Solange had Ben move slowly in a circle, stop, show his profiles, and speak one line several different ways: "I've traveled more than two thousand miles to kill you." There was no trace of the British stage training in his dialect.

He managed to show them a character who had found an object on which to unleash a lifetime of hatred. His even-featured look, along with a vaguely dissolute demeanor, overlay his loathing of whomever he'd conjured in his mind to talk to, creating for the viewer what could be a burnt-out, resentful playboy, or in the appropriate costume and makeup, the perfect Scanlan.

Emily turned her head and looked at the screen only out of the corners of her eyes, like a child at the movies watching the scary part.

Ben was cast. Solange was not unreservedly positive about him but she agreed he had "a rather alarming presence."

Their overall growing confidence was reinforced when Joanna said she'd hired someone who was close to locating Ruth Maggeson, the makeup artist from the original filming, and they were only slightly troubled when she told them that an unknown somebody was making inquiries about their production.

• • •

Time had passed quickly—as pre-production time always does. In three days they would be leaving for Arizona.

In the living room of Tom's house, at the beginning of their last rehearsal before they left for location, Solange pointed to Tom's Western painting and said, "Look: James Dean, Gabriel, and Jimmy Riley are kneeling next to what's left of this campfire. John Wayne, John Barnes, and Tom Manfredo are standing by that bay horse, looking off at Scanlan and Ben Bennett, coming into the scene with Gabriel's mother, Sarah, John Barnes's one-time lover as well as Scanlan's wife, and Rosemary Forsyth—all in one woman. I see"—she looked at Emily, Tom, and Jimmy—"I also see other mothers and fathers."

"Do we really need the Freudian psycho-speak BS?" said Emily.

Solange aimed an innocent smile at her. "All right, let's call it 'family BS' if you prefer. We are made from the same clay as our parents, aren't we?"

Jimmy shrugged. "I'm connected to everybody in the picture."

Solange gazed at him. "So I'm told." She glanced back at the painting. "So, each of you has a preexisting connection to all of this. What do we make of that?"

"Coincidence?" said Tom, forced by her stare to say *something*.

"I don't think so. We don't create our lives out of whole cloth. It's more of a patchwork quilt; a scrap here, a remnant there. Then, with a lot of pricked fingers and swearing and trial and error, it all miraculously comes together—sometimes into something beautiful you want to hang on the wall, sometimes something hideous you want to hide in grandma's cedar chest."

"Are you saying you think there's a pattern to all this?" said Emily, tight-lipped.

"Not a pattern. An interlacing. A filigree. Tom and Jimmy already knowing each other." She gazed at Emily, then the others. "You happening on somebody who had a lost film, half-finished, that starred John Wayne and James Dean. Tom having been given a picture that 'coincidentally' conjures up a scene we've all agreed has to be in this movie. Then, Jimmy tags along with Emily to her house and *happens* to run into his old camp counselor, who just *happens* to be Emily's brother. Jesus."

"So what's it mean?" said Tom.

"I have no idea. But it seems to me we should proceed with a healthy respect for it, whatever it is."

• • •

The day they decided Ben would play Scanlan, Emily came directly home from the office, eager to tell him he's been cast. Ms. Morovec met her at the door. The lines of worry on the hospice nurse's face made her seem much older than her forty-eight years.

"He wants to see the dog," she said.

"Oh, God. What did you say to him?"

"I didn't know what to say. It happened just now. You were driving in. I said I'd come ask you. He's being very insistent."

"Where's Ben?"

"Taking a nap."

Ben had already expressed himself on the subject: "You killed him. You get to tell him."

Upstairs in her father's room, she briefly considered saying El Poochino was at the vet's office but decided against it. "He's gone, Daddy."

"Gone?"

"I'm sorry." She tried to think of a gentle way to phrase it. "He got run over. I'm sorry. He's ... dead."

"Oh my God. I was afraid of that." His voice choked. "He used to sleep next to my bed. Then suddenly, he didn't show up anymore." He looked away from her. "What happened to him?"

"Are you *crying*?"

He gulped a breath of air, then brought one hand up slowly to wipe the tears away, groaning as he did. He was covered with bruises from the blood thinners he was taking. "What happened?"

"He got out of the house and ... a car hit him. ... I hit him. I was backing out of the driveway and I ran over him. I'm sorry, Dad."

After a moment, the old man nodded. "That's what happens. When we aren't aware of consequences."

• • •

Emily had a headache and couldn't get to sleep. She didn't have any choice about her father. She would have to leave him with Ms. Moravec and other hospice nurses in a few days. She knew that. The movie had to shoot now. There was no going back. Ben had become a man possessed when she'd told him he'd gotten his first acting job in four years. The old man might die while she and her brother were in Arizona. But she couldn't blame herself for that.

She gave fleeting consideration to delaying the filming but recognized that would be insanity. Past a certain point, making a movie—according to Hollywood lore—is not unlike a pregnancy; you can't not have the baby. Bonds had been posted, deals set with the crew. At great and meticulous pains, schedules had been coordinated and fixed. Rental deposits had been paid on four million dollars' worth of equipment. Joanna, Solange, and the production manager had taken three trips to Arizona to choose and firm up the locations. (Jack Butterworth had gone on the first two of them in place of Emily; he understood what was needed, knowing the existing film better than anyone.) Lodgings had been booked. Craft services and catering had been hired. An on-the-quiet deal had been negotiated with the Teamsters. Emily was thinking once again that Dr. Bennett's "idiot" of a daughter did have producer skills, the relentlessness of character—or lack of character. She had wheedled, made herself clever, chummy, charming, and devious.

She had done whatever it had taken, along with Joanna and their production manager, to set up their monster enterprise. She'd handled a million details and there were more ahead of her, to try to put this mess into some kind of—please, God—working order.

The pressures were overwhelming and were taking their toll. Emily had created this production, but it had grown and was now carrying her along like a rowboat at flood tide.

And the final fucking shooting script hasn't been finished. Thanks a lot, Mizzzzzzzz Borugian.

"Be nice. She knows what she's doing."

"She'd fucking well better."

"You didn't used to talk this way."

"I didn't used to be a member of this questionable club."

"A little lipstick on the pig and waddaya got? Instant producer."

"But I've still got collywobbles? What do I do about that?"

"Sorry, sweetness. Above my pay grade."

Against her better judgment, she had let herself be talked into making Gabriel's mother, Sarah, "the woman" in the love triangle. Joanna had disappointed her by coming around to Solange's point of view about getting rid of the Prudence character and replacing her with a three-way relationship with distinct Oedipal overtones.

When Emily wouldn't bend, Solange had an adjustment to offer her. She'd said, "Not only is Scanlan not Gabriel's father, but Sarah is not his mother. Before Gabriel left home, Scanlan told him that Sarah took him from a friend who'd died in childbirth. That kind of thing happened in those days."

Emily scoffed, "Are you serious?"

"That way it'll play in Peoria."

"And why would Scanlan tell Gabriel that?"

"Maybe he was trying to make sure Gabriel left. Maybe Scanlan came to believe that Sarah had an unnatural fixation on her own son—and convinced himself the boy was not really hers. We may be able to leave it ambiguous."

"Well, is it true or not, as you see it?" Emily demanded. "Is Sarah Gabriel's mother, or isn't she?"

"If we know at all, it won't be until the end," Solange said with her vaporous magician's smile.

"No no no, This production is my baby," said Emily. "I'll goddam well know if she's his mother or not—right now!"

So, Solange told her and Joanna.

Today, on a dead still, late August day in 1979, Emily was again having serious misgivings about her choice of careers, despite her budding flair for it.

She heard Ben crying.

• • •

Early the next morning, she answered the door and found Tom standing on the front step. He was wearing jeans, boots, and his green placket-front shirt with the sleeves rolled up. His hair was wetted down and combed back flat on his head.

"Are you all right?" he said.

"I'm fine."

"I rang up, but there was no answer so I came over. I saw an ambulance pulling out of your driveway."

"It was for my father. Come on in."

"Is he all right?"

She frowned, and he went inside and stood mutely in the front hall, waiting.

Emily closed the door and headed toward the back of the house. "Would you like some coffee?"

In the kitchen, as she put on the pot, she hummed a strain of the bridge from "(Somewhere) Over the Rainbow."

As she was getting cups out, Tom said again, "Is he all right?"

She shook her head. "No, he's not. I called Ms. Moravec to tell her not to come today, but I missed her." Seeing the confusion on his face, she said, "He passed away. ... It's okay." She opened her arms to him, and he hugged her and patted her back and shoulders. She patted him too, like a caring maiden aunt.

"I'm sorry," he said.

She held still for several seconds, then looked up at him. "I still needed to say things to him. Now, they'll never get said. I was finally ready to do it, to say the important things out loud, not just to myself."

"What happened?"

She slumped back against the counter. "The doctor said it was a stroke. He said it's not uncommon in the state Daddy was in, that it was amazing he hung on as long as he did."

"Are you all right?"

"Yes." She touched his forearm, moved mechanically to the refrigerator, got out a container of half-and-half, and set it down on the counter next to a red ceramic sugar bowl. Even though she wasn't crying, she gulped spasmodically once, then once more for air. "Have you seen Jimmy this morning?" she said.

Something else completely, not compassion, creased Tom's features. "No. No, I haven't." As Emily nodded, he said, "Where's your brother?"

"He's gone to the funeral home."

"You're sure you're all right?"

"I think so. We knew he didn't have much longer."

"Was anybody with him?"

"Ben was. I was in my room. He said he was in the chair by Daddy's bed and had nodded off. When he woke up, he knew something was wrong. He felt Daddy's pulse, but he knew he'd already passed on by the look of him."

"What are you going to do?"

She laughed sharply, then shrugged. "Go on with the show. It's convenient in a way. Now, I won't have to come back from location." She stroked her lips with her fingertips. "I don't have any lipstick on. Daddy liked women to wear lipstick. I've been thinking about *Hud* this morning. I've always loved that movie, even though Hud is a horrible man. I've been thinking about the scene where Melvyn Douglas is lying by the side of the road, dying, and he says to Brandon DeWilde, about Paul Newman's character: 'Hud there's waiting on me, and he ain't a patient man.' Well, now Daddy's dead, and I'm the one who killed him."

"What are you talking about?"

"I told him about El Poochino last night."

"He didn't die because of that."

"I'm not so sure. That might have been the final straw. It turned out he loved that dog, and I never knew it."

"Yes, exactly! You didn't know it! You can't blame yourself for that."

"Why not? I *should* have known. I've been living in this house again—for a long time now. I ran over the dog and killed him. I told my father about it. I said it too bluntly. And then he died. It didn't do him any good."

"You're still not responsible."

She studied his face. "The thing that really bothers me is that all I can think of is my guilt—not my father. I didn't like him, but he was my father. Shouldn't you feel a little something over the death of your own father?"

"I'm the last person to know the answer to that."

She smiled at him, reached out and touched one of his hands, then held it tightly as tears began to stream down her cheeks.

He drew her to him, pressing his cheek against the top of her head.

She breathed in the clean, soap and shaving lotion smell of him.

She felt her arms rise up.

She touched her own tears, then reached further with one hand until it rested on the back of his neck.

He stroked her hair and said, "I don't want you to be unhappy." He squeezed her gently. "Please don't be unhappy. I love you."

She lifted her other hand to his neck and kissed him—softly at first. Then, she began to kiss him harder and to cover his face with kisses.

8

Four days before they were to go to Arizona, Emily and Jack Butterworth took a short road trip to interview Ruth Maggeson, the makeup artist from the original production. Emily drove and put up with Butterworth's male chauvinistic backseat driving.

On their way, they glanced again at the wallet-sized photograph they'd been given of a prickly looking woman in her late forties or early fifties. "I would have thought she'd be older," said Emily.

"She was still a kid, a lot younger than all of the men on the crew. Younger than everyone except the script supervisor."

Joanna Morgan had hired a detective to find Ruth Maggeson. He'd located her in Fullerton, in Orange County, but when he told her he wanted to talk to her about *Showdown,* Maggeson had hung up on him. The detective tracked down her place of employment and the hours they could expect to find her there.

Instead of taking the chance of not getting buzzed into her apartment building, Emily and Butterworth were going to try to catch her as she was getting off her shift at the Los Angeles Convention Center, where she worked as a security guard.

"Funny career change for a makeup artist," said Emily.

"Not so funny," said Butterworth. "Actors aren't the only ones who get phased out of show business. The movers and shakers love to have kids around—the greener and wetter behind the ears the better—who'll believe them when they tell them what great, stiff dicks they've got. Pardon my French."

"Don't worry about it. I was raised by men."

Butterworth looked at her out of the corner of his eye. "You *sure* you don't mind doing this?"

"I'm okay. Really."

"It's a terrible thing—to lose your father. You shoulda let Joanna make this trip. I wouldn't have minded. I swear."

"It's all right. I want to hear what this woman has to say." She glanced from the road to Butterworth. "It's *okay*. We weren't that close."

"Well, too bad for him." He looked at the picture of Ruth Maggeson again. "This doesn't look much like her, but I guess it is. The shape of the face is the same if you take away the jowls."

• • •

The Convention Center was hosting the annual Whole Life Expo. A list of the lectures and workshops was posted on a huge bulletin board in the cavernous lobby: UFOS AND EARTH AS WE NEAR THE GALACTIC MILLENNIUM; CREATING WITH THE ANGELS; GHOSTS—THE ROLE THEY PLAY IN YOUR LIFE; ARCHETYPAL SYMBOLISM: HOW TO EXPLORE YOUR INNER ARCHETYPES; EARTHQUAKES, SHAKING UP YOUR LIFE FOR POSITIVE CHANGE. Emily wondered if maybe what she needed was a good eight-pointer on the Richter scale.

They knocked at the door marked Personnel and were told they'd just missed Ruth Maggeson.

Butterworth looked so pitiful in his disappointment that the woman told him, "She usually stops off at McGreene's. It's a little bar between Olympic and Ninth on Figueroa."

• • •

It was only four fifteen when they sat down at a table with their drinks. Butterworth was having his one for the day, but Emily was feeling too wired from natural causes to risk it and settled for a tomato juice, which made her stomach hurt anyway.

Ruth Maggeson, who had grown stouter since the picture they'd been looking at was taken, was sitting by herself at the end of the bar, her concentration on her drinking interrupted only by an occasional word with the bartender.

After gulping half his Scotch and soda, Butterworth said, "Here goes." When Emily started to get up to accompany him, he said, "Lemme start this alone."

Emily sat back and watched the scene from across the room. At first, Maggeson didn't look at Butterworth when he sat next to her and began talking.

Then, she turned to him in slow motion. From Emily's vantage point, it looked exactly like what it was—somebody presented with a relic of her distant past. She stared at the old film editor, at first with what looked like the pleasure of recognition, then with uncertainty as he continued speaking. She looked vaguely in Emily's direction, swiveled away, and started to get up from her barstool.

Butterworth touched her shoulder with a tentative hand and said something else to her.

She looked at Emily again, but this time, after a few more words, and with Butterworth taking her arm, Ruth Maggeson got up hesitantly, holding her drink, and walked with him to the table.

After Butterworth introduced her, she didn't look Emily in the eye for a while, only at her hands, chest, and arms, as she evaded their questions.

Up close, she was leonine, her salt-and-pepper hair brushed up and out and sprayed to stay that way. She had wide-set eyes and a thin-lipped mouth that seemed too narrow for her strong chin.

As Emily gazed at her, she saw Anne Bancroft as Mrs. Robinson in *The Graduate.*

"We'd just like to know what you can remember about it, Ruthie," said Butterworth.

"Why?"

"I can't tell you."

"Then why should I?"

"It's important." He nodded at Emily. "It's really important to us to work out what went on."

"I've kept quiet all this time," she said. "Why should I start talking now? Not for old time's sake with you, Jack. I barely knew you. I only met you once or twice, and I guess a bunch of us had supper one night. Right?"

"Right." He looked at Emily helplessly.

"Have you really never told anybody about it?" asked Emily.

Ruth shook her head.

"Why? Weren't you dying to?"

After a long moment, almost as if to herself, Ruth Maggeson said, "At first I was, but I was afraid. Later, I got used to not talking about it."

"Why were you afraid?"

"I gave my word. We all did." She frowned at Butterworth. "Didn't you?"

He nodded, and Emily said, "Were you threatened?"

"No, nothing like that," said Butterworth.

Emily decided that Miles, the man who had started the whole thing for her, had probably picked up his notion of a dire warning out of his own imaginings. Or else, with a handful of extras working for only one day, someone had decided to try to scare them into silence with an ominous threat that would instantly get the point across.

"We kept our mouths shut because we were loyal," said Ruth.

"To whom?" asked Emily.

"To Duke, of course." Now, she looked Emily in the eye. "And we were given a bonus and paid top dollar. The day we began, Dean asked us not to tell anybody—even our families—about it, and we didn't."

"Amazing."

"Not so amazing. The first silence had to do with Dean's paranoia about anything getting out about *his* project." There was more than a trace of condescension in her manner when she said his name. "The second silence—the one that's gone on till now—had to do with Duke. I think it'd be fair to say it was Duke that kept us quiet in the long run." She sighed deeply and took a sip from her drink. "Him bein' gone now is the only reason on earth I'm talking to you."

Butterworth smiled at her.

"First of all, you had a pro in John Wayne and a loose cannon in Jimmy Dean. Most of the crew didn't like Dean to begin with. It didn't matter that he was directing—there was something pissy and childish about him. I know he *was* a kid, but still ... The only reason the crew guys behaved so well was because of Duke. They'd have done anything for him. They looked on him as a man's man. He didn't hold himself above them. He treated each of them like a fellow professional, doing his job. And he treated everybody equal by the way; he didn't play favorites. I guess I can't say anything better about him than that he was a gentleman and the men respected him for that." She concentrated on Butterworth. "One day, early on, he assembled all of us and asked us to be fanatical—that's the word he used—in the total silence we'd been keeping."

"But how about before that?" asked Emily. "Before you got there? Why didn't word get out from the crew guys *before* the shoot began?"

"Because nobody was told until the shoot began—nobody, as far as I know. It happens sometimes."

"Go back to Duke," said Butterworth. "Why did he quit? *Did* he quit?"

She closed her eyes tight, as if trying to squeeze the memories back. "I'm not sure. My impression was that there was something about the whole thing that had turned sour for him."

"Do you have any idea what that was?" asked Emily.

Ruth stared through her. "Makeup's an enlightening place to work if you keep your eyes and ears open. You get them in there on a daily basis and their guards drop, lying back, having their faces sort of massaged every morning. They get comfortable. Neither of those two was likely to share their innermost thoughts with me, but I got a strong intuition about both of them. My feeling was that after they'd been shooting for a while, Duke got cold feet." She pressed her lips together and looked in the direction of the bar.

"Would you care for another drink?" said Butterworth.

She eyed the one she was still working on. "No, thanks. I'm going to have to drive home. I don't want to do it cockeyed."

"Why did he get cold feet?" said Emily. "Were there script problems?"

"Damn, you're persistent. Who knew about script problems? Nobody ever saw anything but the scenes we were shooting on the day we were shooting them. Anyway, makeup doesn't much need to see the script, not usually."

"Was it politics?"

She snorted. "Nah. Duke worked with liberals all the time—Henry Fonda, Montgomery Clift; later, Richard Widmark, Kirk Douglas. He liked having them around. Gave him something to shoot at. Besides, he thought of himself as an American first, not a conservative. Some of his best friends were rabid liberals: Paul Newman. Haskell Wexler, the cinematographer. Gregory Peck. Duke and Katherine Hepburn were crazy about each other—well, *most* of the time with Hepburn—I understood she could be pretty starchy.

… Nah, he just got cold feet, for no other reason, I think, than the way Jimmy Dean was. Dean had a way of getting too close to you sometimes, his face too close to your face. And with Duke being the other star, Dean—'cause he was director *and* actor—got real close to him real often, and to be honest, I think he gave Duke the creeps."

"That's it?"

She stared at Emily defiantly. "Maybe."

Uneasy, Butterworth looked at Emily and then back at Ruth. "You've told us how the men felt about Duke. How about the women?"

"Pardon?"

"How did you feel about him?"

She showed them a girlish smile they hadn't seen before. "There were only two women. I guess you can tell how I felt about him. I've never seen much written about his appeal to women. Let me tell you, I was there, and if you were a woman who was interested in men …" Her smile widened. "It was hard not to stop every once in a while and gape at him—not just because he was big and good lookin' and, you know … dignified, but because something in him cried out for comforting. There was a sweet and helpless thing in the midst of all that machismo that set up a … you know, that *feeling* in a woman." She looked at Emily. "You know what I mean?"

"Yes, I do."

She nodded, looked into middle distance and touched her glass to her lips. "Now don't be getting the idea I was in love with him." She swung her gaze back to Butterworth. "I wasn't. He was a married man, and I was no homewrecker—even though he glanced my direction a time or two in a way that was more than just sociable. I had things in perspective. I had a husband at home, and I knew Duke's faults. He drank too much. He had this attitude he wore about 'a woman's place' and all that." She looked away again, remembering. "Still, I'll tell you, I could have been tempted."

Emily interrupted her reverie. "You said two women. Who was the other one?"

Ruth frowned. "Ah. *She* was the trouble. Betty Merrow, the script supervisor. If you ask me, everything else would have worked out, despite the way Duke felt about Dean. She's the reason we folded up our tent."

Emily and Butterworth exchanged glances.

"She was crazy." Ruth's thin lips curled in a flicker of derision. "She was always toying with people, or off dreaming and conniving. You know the type. She *wanted* things."

"What sort of things?"

"Whatever there was to want. She was one of those people who couldn't be satisfied."

Emily disguised an impatience she couldn't have explained. "How would that have had anything to do with shutting down the film?"

"She was one of those women who have influence over men."

She lifted her chin slightly, reminding Emily of a documentary she'd once seen on Benito Mussolini, and she wondered for a second if they'd run into a wall with Ruth Maggeson. "Did you ever see her again?"

"No, but I wouldn't have been likely to. We weren't exactly fast friends, even if we were the only women. We were by far the youngest in the crew, too—but that didn't make us pals. I didn't think much of her professionally. She hadn't done any continuity work at all before. I mean *never*. I didn't understand how the little"—she paused, started to lift her glass and again didn't drink—"how she got the job. She wanted to be an actress; she told me. She could have been one, it seemed to me. But at the same time, she thought of herself as … not good enough or something. It's hard to explain." She flashed a sardonic smile that quickly gave way to what Emily imagined as a jumble of recollections. "She was just

… nuts, that's all. She lived in that twilight world of freaks and the down-and-out. … I don't think she liked herself much."

"What was her appeal?" asked Emily. "Why didn't they fire her? Why did they hire her in the first place?"

"She was drop-dead gorgeous—even though she was still really just a kid." She shook her head as she remembered. "And she *knew* she was gorgeous. She knew it, and yet she didn't like herself." She frowned. "Not only that, I got the notion she only pretended to care about anybody else who might show any signs of liking her. I don't think Betty Merrow could stand James Dean."

"Why do you say that?"

"Because it was obvious to me he was head over heels about her, and she was one of those women who enjoyed hurting men like that."

"But he was the director, and he *was* James Dean."

"Wouldn't matter. I never ran into anyone more completely unimpressed with celebrity than Betty."

"How about John Wayne?" said Emily. "What was her attitude toward John Wayne?"

"I don't exactly know. Nobody really knew her. When she wasn't teasing men, she kept to herself, dreaming, drawing sketches … this or that."

"You think she might still be alive?" asked Emily. "I mean, if she was young, she probably would be, wouldn't she?"

"God knows," said Ruth. "I never heard of her again. I don't know anybody else who did. I'd tell you I think she quit the business, but she was never really in it in the first place."

Emily frowned at her, saw the lift of Ruth's chin again, and asked her, smiling, what specific memories she had of the shooting. Ruth lowered her chin and shook her head. "Dean didn't let us see much. He barred the crew from watching the scenes, all that he *could* bar—like we weren't good enough to appreciate his 'cinema.'" She exaggerated the word contemptuously, then covered with a mischievous smile. "You can tell he got my goat. He was just going after the brass ring for its own sake. His number one concern was the legend of James Dean—almost like he knew what was in store for him. I'm not kidding. He wanted Stuart Stern, who'd written *Rebel*, to write his biography, and Dean was only twenty-four years old. I mean he was talented, I guess. But he was conceited, and after a while it wears you down." She frowned. "Just why the hell are you asking about all this, anyway?"

"We're just trying to learn the truth, Ruthie," said Butterworth.

"That's pretty mysterious."

"But we don't want to tell anybody about it," Emily added. "And we hope you won't either."

Ruth looked back and forth between them. "Well, I'll tell you … in that case, I wouldn't mind making a little money for my information."

"What did you have in mind?"

She thought about it for a moment, then showed them her undersized demure smile again. "Maybe, for now … I'd leave that up to you."

Butterworth nodded, and Emily said, "We'll be fair. But we'd be grateful to know anything at all you can tell us."

"What are you going to do, write a magazine article? A book? If it's a book, then maybe I should make a nice piece of change."

"It's not going to be a book."

Ruth gazed at Butterworth, who looked at Emily and back at Ruth in concurrence with Emily.

"Yeah, okay," said the security guard. "But you'd better pay me equal to my contribution or I'll make a fuss. People earn a lot of money from magazine articles these days—so I hear." Her eyebrows arched up for an instant, turning "so I hear" into "so I hope."

"We'll be fair," repeated Emily, touched by Ruth Maggeson and promising herself to find fair compensation for her, no matter what her information might add up to.

"You'd better." Maggeson looked at Butterworth, checking to see if Emily was okay, then remembered that, other than their nodding relationship twenty-four years earlier, she didn't know much about him either.

She gazed at a shaft of filtered sunlight slanting in through a grimy window. "Nobody wants to be a security guard the rest of their life." She shrugged. "Well, unfortunately for you, Jimmy didn't like to have me around while he was working. If him or Duke needed a touch-up, they'd walk off the set for me to give it to them. I didn't ever do more than powder them down after I did them in the morning. They'd just come to me before camera was set to roll and I'd give 'em a little dusting.

"But I did see a whole big to-do one day. Normally, I didn't care to watch what was going on, on the set. There's nothing more boring, after you've worked crew for a while, than watching a movie shoot."

"Not even if it's James Dean and John Wayne?" said Emily.

"When you work crew on Hollywood movies, you see Hollywood stars all the time. Anyway, one day there was an unusual ruckus on the set. It was a scene in a cabin. They'd been working on it for a morning and couldn't get it to happen." She made a sort of humming noise as the memory floated back to her. "Then somebody told me Duke and Dean were at it, and I went and got myself into the front half of the cabin, and by hunkering down on the floor in the corner—I was more of a petite size then—I was able to see and hear what was going on.

"The first thing I heard was Jimmy telling Duke that what he was doing was a 'John Wayne cliché.' " She grinned. "Well, you didn't say that kind of thing to Duke if you were anybody but John

Ford—especially a first-time director. So Wayne said real slow, 'Are you telling me how to act?' And Jimmy said, 'No, I just need to see you make it a little fresh. Can't you bring some life to it?'

"Well, Duke turned to Gordon Gray, the first assistant director, and said, 'Give everybody ten, Gordy.' Then he looked at Dean. 'Everybody but this little warthog.' And they all cleared the set.

"All but me." Her grin became a smirk. "I was half hidden under a tarp. Nobody saw me. I didn't move, just stayed there. The key grip poked his head in, but Duke waved him away."

"When Duke and Jimmy were the only ones left, Duke turned to Jimmy and said, 'Now you listen to me, you little chameleon prick.' "

"Jimmy looked like he was about to cry, but instead, he picked up a ceramic pitcher off a table, threw it against a wall and said, 'I'm not afraid of you.'

"Duke looked from the mess on the floor over to Jimmy and finally said, 'Aren't you? Because you're giving a pretty fair impression of a kid about to wet his pants.' "

Ruth shook her head, looking only vaguely at both of them, absorbed in her memory of this. "And Jimmy slammed over to the nearest wall, drew back his fist and smashed it into a pine plank. He groaned in pain and spat out, 'I hate you.' Then he started to cry for real, and I swear he said, 'I loved you. I loved you, Duke.' He looked at his fist, held it out towards Duke and said, 'You were everything to me, and look what you do to me.' "

"What did Wayne do?" said Emily, hypnotized.

Ruth stared at her for a long moment. "Nothing. He looked down at the shattered pitcher and said, 'How do you propose we match this goddam thing?' "

"Was Dean's hand all right?" asked Butterworth finally.

"Well, he favored that hand for a while, but he was okay; it didn't get in the way of shooting. ... But I did get the distinct impression that somewhere inside him, Duke was pretty shaken up from that incident." She shrugged. "Or, maybe it was just a carryover of what his feelings were about Dean anyway."

She talked to them for another hour. She told them all the hearsay and movie set rumors she could remember, even things that didn't bear at all on their interests. She didn't mention Betty Merrow again.

That night they reported what they had learned to the two other women, to Tom, and to an especially fascinated Jimmy Riley.

• • •

There were two remarkable things about the funeral service that was held at Saint Agatha's Unitarian Chapel off San Vicente Boulevard. The first was that the modest-sized house of God was packed, which astonished Emily, and the second was that Ben didn't show up.

Emily had expected no more than a handful of people, but almost three hundred came to honor the life of Dr. Benjamin Bennett. She'd never known much about his practice. He'd rarely talked about his work. She'd always had the feeling it was only what he did to earn a living. He was a *healer*, she thought to herself. *Imagine that.* And it looked to her as if he'd been a popular man, or at least a popular doctor.

As she listened to the minister's shockingly affectionate eulogy, she thought about Ben. He'd stopped drinking. She'd told him he'd have to before he tested for Scanlan. Maybe he'd been overstimulated by finding out he'd gotten the movie role and was unable to face the idea of attending his father's funeral on top of what he was already feeling.

When she got home, she found him in Ben Sr.'s room, staring at the stripped-down bed. He barely spoke to her. She assumed it had simply all been too much for him. But when she asked him why he hadn't shown up for the funeral, he said he didn't want his last act in regard to his father to be a pretense.

She wished she could take back what she'd told him next: "Don't you think it's a little late for that?"

She tried to forgive herself. She'd been upset and confused, too. The positive side of her said, she hadn't done anything wrong, but the other side wasn't buying it. She felt an uneasy mixture of carelessness and nerves.

"It's the goddam men in your life."

She wanted the feelings she was having about Tom to vanish—whatever those feelings were exactly; they were professional folly, inappropriate and ill-timed. There was also her sure knowledge that Jimmy was constantly watching them, like he had ownership papers on her.

"And he's more unbalanced than you. If you can imagine that."

She had been showing Jimmy "motherly" concern, trying to keep him stable. She'd learned the technique dealing with her father. But she knew that somebody as emotionally akin to her as Jimmy could see through that.

It was having an impact on Tom, too. One day, Emily had been present at a costume fitting for both of them. Doing the business of trying to make herself and Jimmy happy with his costume, she was arrested by a look on Tom's face as he stood to the side, watching: amiability, poorly disguising what she knew beyond doubt was jealousy.

"God damn both of them!"

• • •

She tried not to think about her brother, but couldn't stop herself. When they'd set the time for his screen test, she hadn't been able to reach him, so she'd driven downtown to his favorite saloon to tell him in person—tell him that if he'd stop drinking, he might have an actual chance to renew his life.

He'd immediately agreed. She knew he'd been able to tell from the look in her eyes that it was the only way he'd get to screen-test.

But Emily had felt as if she was talking to a stranger, even as he'd listened to the good news. He told her he'd have just one last drink, but she would have to join him. He said, "You're the only real chum I have. You know that, don't you? I adore you, old thing."

But as they'd toasted the movie and their future, he had looked straight through her, and Emily wondered why he would drive all the way to downtown LA just to sit by himself, drinking poison, in the amounts Ben drank it, in the beautiful and swank, lonely and bleak Blue Martini cocktail lounge.

IV
LOCATION

1

Southeast of Phoenix, north-northeast of Tucson and east of the San Pedro River, is a vast expanse of high desert called Potsherd Flats, a name that's a joke among the local Apache because the land is not flat. It's a vast, ridged mosaic of scrub grasses and wasteland vegetation, bordered by piñon and juniper country and traversed by a series of mountains and plateaus.

Emily, Jimmy, Tom, and Jack Butterworth arrived on a clear, chilly Tuesday morning, after a plane flight and a two-and-a-half-hour drive from Phoenix.

As they rode through the mesa, terrace, and hill formations, the intoxicating panorama and the pastel colors of the ever-changing desert floor, shifting from blue and amethyst to yellow and russet, Emily's heart lurched again and again. Aspens, blue spruces, Douglas and white firs sorted themselves into clusters near the highway; then, looking from higher ground, ran off into the distance like archipelagos until they became no more than specks on the horizon. She imagined a postcard photographer, as captivated as she was, staring out at the shadow and sun, night and day, earth and fire; forgetting her profession, even her identity, lost in the humbling beauty of it.

It was just before one in the afternoon when they checked into the Trading Post Motel, a serviceable but uninspired motor inn, sprawling and surprisingly large, just outside the town of Ocotillo

Springs, in the southwest corner of Potsherd Flats. Joanna Morgan had arrived a week ago; Solange Borugian, three days after that.

Twenty-four and a half years after the original filming, they were about to shoot the rest of *Showdown.*

• • •

Standing outside the Trading Post, Joanna and Emily watched as the first crew trucks and vans arrived. They carried cameras, lamps, reflectors, generators, cable, dolly track, arc lights, tripods, light stands, and all the other instruments necessary to the craft of making major motion pictures.

It was three days until the beginning of principal photography. They had hoped to have more time to set up and get used to the locations, but financial constraints had prevented it.

"You really think we can pull this off?" said Emily.

"We've got to." Joanna put a sturdy arm around her friend's shoulder. "We've got everything to gain, but almost as much to lose. If we can't make this work, we'll be known as Hollywood's co-queens of lost opportunity."

Emily frowned. "What exactly is our opportunity?"

"Beg pardon?"

"Does any of this really, I mean *really* … *matter*? Sorry. Never mind." She shrugged it off, but realized the question had begun to loiter in the back of her mind recently. "I guess I'm tired from the travel."

Joanna blinked. "Sure. That car ride is an acid trip. By the way, I looked up someone I'd like to introduce you to. I think we should all be there."

"What's it about?"

"I want to put a blessing on the film."

Emily produced a wan smile, not sure where this might be going.

"I'm not kidding. This is Apache territory. I don't think we should do anything until we get ourselves an Apache blessing."

Emily grinned. "Absolutely. Why not? Good idea."

"And I've found just the man."

• • •

Later in the afternoon, Solange, Jimmy, Tom, and Emily rehearsed. Solange had told them her priority was "working with the actors in the actual locale." She was especially excited about this spot, which was to be the setting for the final sequences of the film. By this time they all had scripts that included most (not all) of the scenes.

The four of them stood under the shade of a large aspen tree at the end of a clearing, out of the early autumn sun, their lungs in a state of shocked withdrawal from the chemical soup of Los Angeles air.

Solange took a few steps back and looked at their surroundings. "Does this remind you of anything?"

They all stared at the east end of the clearing. It had the feel of the Western painting that hung on Tom's living room wall, but without the people in it.

It wasn't exactly the same. The large cottonwood was on the right instead of the left, the flowers in the foreground were yellow, not pink, but otherwise, the colors were the same—and more than that, the flavor of it was identical. It felt like a prismatic mirror image, but no less startling than if it had been a photographic one.

Tom said to Jimmy, "It's not so surprising, is it? This kind of scenery is all over the West."

"But it doesn't look exactly like this."

"Sure it does—same kind of plants and red earth. There are hundreds of thousands of acres like what we're looking at in Arizona alone."

Jimmy scowled at him. "I've been all over this state, for Christ's sake. This is the only place that looks exactly like this."

"Let's do what we came here to do," said Tom. "You're always making more out of a thing than it is."

"You're the one who brought it up."

Emily felt a shudder of panic, seeing her stars locked in a no-win pissing contest. Solange, she noticed, seemed to feed off of it. Taking charge, her languid self-confidence and simmering menace suggested Strother Martin (*What we've got here is a failure to communicate)* emceeing a cockfight.

"Let's work on the revelation scene," said Solange. "Right now."

Tom's eyes filled with panic. "I'm not sure of the lines yet."

"Do it anyway."

Emily hands were fists. *Tom! What the hell's the matter with you? Don't let her talk to you that way.*

"He's a great big coward, girl, just like you. You never even demanded a complete shooting script. That should have been set in stone by now."

Jimmy knelt down near a hillock of rocky debris, turned his attention to the ground, and began to summon up an imaginary campfire. "You want another cup of coffee?" he said finally, focusing on the words he'd memorized for this scene.

Tom looked at Solange, but finding no comfort there, turned back to Jimmy and shook his head.

"There's something I didn't tell you," said Jimmy.

"Yeah? What's that, kid?" The words sounded tinny out of Tom's mouth and he appeared to hear it. He looked off toward an impotent scarf of rain evaporating high above the ground, then, frowning, at the melodramatics of the teeming desert around them.

"You're always so sure you know how things are," said Jimmy. "How everything's going to taste before you even get it to your mouth."

Tom laughed harshly.

Jimmy hesitated, then: "You think you know me from a few days on the trail, but you don't. You don't know anything about me."

Tom turned on him, ferociously. "I don't *think* about you." Jimmy flinched. "I've got enough to think about, just living, tryin' to decide every day if I want to trade my good digestion for another cup of bad coffee."

Jimmy stared at him, then picked up a pebble, looked at it closely and tossed it at a patch of buffalo grass ten feet away. "I've got a … a present for you, but I'm not so sure I want to give it to you now."

"Then don't," said Tom. "I don't need anything from you."

Jimmy shot back, without thinking: "Not happy with what you're given, only with what you take, huh?"

Tom took a deep breath and stared at him. "When I was a kid, all the boys expected me to be the evenhanded, fair one, the one who wouldn't get rattled—"

Emily looked at the script. The words weren't there.

"—and I learned to play that role. But some days, I hated being strong and I wanted to kill those boys. But I couldn't. So I blacked out instead."

"And that's why you hate me?"

None of them knew Tom's voice was so powerful. "I hate you because you're so *helpless*!" He looked dazed as the echo rolled back from the cliffs in the distance.

Jimmy raised his voice. "I'm your son."

Tom stared at him and said the right line: "I'm not surprised."

Solange grinned at Emily.

• • •

Back at the Trading Post production office, there was a crisis. Joanna had gotten a call from the agent of the actress, Rosemary

Forsyth, who was to play Sarah. The character, who first appears at the opening of the story and whose scenes were scheduled for the end of the filming, was now to appear in the story's finale—which would be shot earlier in the schedule. When they'd decided that Prudence's function in the movie would be taken over by the Sarah character, they'd contacted Forsyth's agent and told him they would need her sooner. She was on another picture, according to the agent, but her finish date would get her to Arizona in time for her first day of photography on *Showdown*.

Now, the agent had informed them that Rosemary's previous shoot had gone over schedule and that she was contractually obliged to stay and finish the other picture. The *Showdown* schedule couldn't be shifted around to wait for her.

They were without a Sarah.

"We don't have time to go back to Los Angeles to cast it," said Joanna.

"How about finding a local actor?" suggested Solange. "There's a SAG branch in Phoenix."

"You'd have to set up the casting session, get up there and see them. That's two days, with luck. We cannot run over budget."

"What about Emily?" said Tom.

Emily laughed nervously, and Joanna said, "She's a little young."

"So is Rosemary Forsyth. Anyway, Emily's the right age for Sarah's first sequence, and the audience would accept her aging for the finale. Barnes ages—I'll have to, too, with a lot of help from the makeup department. Why *not* Emily?"

"For one thing," said Solange, "she's not an actress, she's a producer."

"She used to act." He fixed his eyes on Emily. "Some people thought she was very good. That doesn't go away."

Emily said, "No. Thank you, Tom. That's nice of you, but I don't think it's the answer."

"Why not? I can't speak for Jimmy, but I'm first a John Wayne impersonator and only after that, a sorta actor. I can use all the help I can get—to focus John Barnes's feelings on what they should be about Sarah. Sarah's not a big role, but it's a damned important one to me." He repeated: "Why *not* Emily?"

Jack Butterworth surprised everyone but Jimmy. "Yes. Why not? She's perfect."

"Jimmy? How about you?" asked Joanna. Jimmy was staring at the floor. "Can you see yourself working with her?"

In a monotone: "Yes, I can."

Solange said, "Well, I think"—Emily shot her a wary look—"it's a fascinating idea." Her open-mindedness appeared genuine to the others, but Emily didn't believe it.

They all turned to Joanna.

"It would certainly solve a problem for us. Maybe this is some kind of sign." She frowned and nibbled on her lower lip. "But after the first day of shooting, if we decided she wasn't working out, we'd have to find the money, take the time and replace her. Agreed, Emily? … Emily? Do you want to give it a try?"

Emily looked at Tom. She could easily read the thoughts behind his milk chocolate eyes. He was practically begging her to.

"C'mon," he said.

She looked at Solange.

"She thinks you won't do it. She called you timid. Fuck her!"

Jimmy looked up from the industrial carpet on the production office floor and shot an anxious look at her. "Go for it."

"Go for it," echoed Emily hollowly. "All right. Okay. Yeah, okay, I'll go for it." She stared at Solange, adding more emphatically than she meant to: "Just tell me if I start to get perky."

• • •

That evening, they met in one of the conference rooms at the motel. Their guest was prompt. His name was Hugh Palmer. He was about fifty years old, of average height, sinewy and strong. He was dressed in blue jeans, plain deerskin cowboy boots, and a faded orange cotton shirt. His hair was gunmetal gray and he wore it combed straight back like a polished helmet.

Emily found herself looking at the floor when she met him and noticed that Jimmy did the same. The man had the most direct eye contact she'd ever encountered.

"It's a happy task for me to invoke the spirit of these lands," he said. He focused on Joanna. "Tell me what you would like."

Joanna, who was as thrown off balance as the others by his gaze, said, "Well, okay, we'd, um … like to get off on the right foot. We're completing a movie that was begun here twenty-four years ago."

Palmer smiled. "And these two gentlemen will be playing the leading roles?" He nodded at Jimmy and Tom, who were sitting across the table from each other.

"That's right."

"I see." He scanned all of the faces, stopping to look at each of them individually. Finally, he crossed the room to a switch and dimmed the lights. Turning back to them, he stretched his arms toward the ceiling with his hands open and chanted in a low, resonant voice: "Oh, Great Spirit of these holy lands, please look on this crazy quilt of white eyes and their movie fable with compassion and equanimity." He stopped as suddenly as he'd started.

They all looked at each other.

Palmer lowered his arms and smiled at Joanna, who nodded and said, "Thank you."

Palmer chuckled. "You seem like nice people, and I should tell you my magic is not much better than you get from tossing a coin in a fountain." He turned the lights back up, stared at Tom, then

Jimmy. "Okay, here: I know a man. His name is Gil Kahcheenay. I think maybe he's the one you're looking for."

Joanna glanced at Emily, who seemed to be lost in Palmer's stare. "All right," she said. "… Sure. We'd love to have his blessing. … Too. If he's willing."

Palmer smiled. "I'm not sure that's exactly what you'll get from Gil."

"What will we get?" snapped Butterworth.

Palmer examined his face carefully. "Wisdom," he said at last. "If it's a good day, you'll get wisdom. He likes to eat. I can have him here at six thirty tomorrow night. Take us out to dinner and maybe you'll hear a little wisdom."

He turned and walked out of the room.

Joanna smiled at them sheepishly.

• • •

During the second day of the Arizona rehearsals, Solange and Jimmy did most of the talking. Emily spoke up occasionally, but for the first few minutes, Tom scarcely said a word. When Solange asked him if anything was wrong, he shook his head. When pressed, he said, "I have no problems. None."

Finally, after Solange had failed to get any contribution from him about his attitude toward Sarah, Gabriel's mother (the role Emily had tentatively been set to play), she challenged him: "Come on. Let's see *something*. You did it yesterday. Let's improvise. You've just found out you're about to see the love of your life after many years. You know that in the meanwhile, you've been replaced in her heart by this kid you've just been told is your son."

"I can't do this. I don't improvise."

"You do too," said Jimmy. "That's just one of those things you tell yourself."

Tom scowled. "You're always saying things like that, but what do you know? I don't tell myself *anything*. I ask myself why I can't do certain things and the answer I always get back is: that's not what I am. I can't pretend things that are unnatural to me are ... natural."

He looked back at Solange. "Listen, my quarrel isn't with him, it's with Scanlan."

"Your confrontation with Scanlan is meaningless to you," said Solange. "It has to happen, but it's of little consequence. Scanlan has a blood feud with you, but you don't have much feeling about him anymore. It's your confrontation with Gabriel that matters."

"But I haven't known him for most of my life."

"You said yesterday, improvising, that you couldn't stand the boy because he's helpless. Is that because you feel helpless?"

Tom almost moaned. "I don't know." He looked at Jimmy and said, "I don't really have a problem with you."

"I can read him like a book," said Jimmy. "I know what he's thinking, what he's worried about." He glared at Tom. "And what he's been up to."

Tom examined him as if seeing him for the first time. "You don't know anything. You're twice as fucked-up as me. You're always telling me what to do, who I should be, what I should call myself, how I should act. First you told me I shouldn't do John Wayne, then I should—when it fit in with what you wanted. Well, I don't need it. I get plenty of advice without you."

"Come on, you guys, we're here to work," said Emily, glancing back and forth between them.

"Tell her where you get this advice," said Jimmy.

Tom flushed.

Solange was studying him. "It might help."

Tom looked up at the sky. He appeared to be in physical pain. Finally, he said, "John Wayne."

Solange blinked. "Oh, come on, you're kidding." She stopped. "You're *not* kidding. Oh my God." She stared at him. "What does he *say* to you?"

Tom shot a look at Jimmy. "He tells me what to do, how to behave." He shrugged. "Things like that."

"Is it … good advice?"

"You don't need to dig into this," said Emily, her eyes still flitting back and forth between the two men.

"With all due respect to the producer, Emily, let me do my job," Solange looked at Tom again.

"I'm not sure," he said finally. "He means well." He turned red all over again, then looked back at Jimmy. "I never told anybody any of this before you. That'll teach me to pick up hurt puppies and let myself trust them."

Jimmy looked like he'd been punched in the face.

Not even glancing back at Solange, Tom said, "He doesn't actually talk to his guy, but they're pretty tight, too. He's not what he pretends to be."

"And what the hell am I?" said Jimmy.

"A beaten puppy, a whiny little boy and not a man."

"Let's work right now," said Solange. She gave them new pages to work from—around the campfire stuff for the trek to high country.

But they couldn't kindle the embers into anything full-blooded, and, to an indiscriminate observer, it might have appeared to be an unsuccessful rehearsal. Neither of them was able to bend from the obstinate guidelines of the new scripted material and bring it to life.

• • •

On the way back to the motel, they stopped off to see the horses for the film. Brownie, a mare—the second horse Scanlan would be riding—was snorting and stamping, fighting off flies. Sarah's mount was a small black mare named Portia. Cimarron and Raindrop were Tom's and Jimmy's horses, respectively. Cimarron was a huge bay, eighteen hands; Raindrop, a roan appaloosa with black leopard spots in a patch of white on her hindquarters. Neither was a dead ringer for the original, but they were close. When Jimmy and Tom got up into the saddles, riders and mounts looked as near to the originals as Emily could imagine them getting. Luckily, Tom was already a skilled horseman; Jimmy wasn't bad either. One of the first things he'd done toward becoming an actor was to take riding lessons at an LA equestrian center that catered to the movie industry.

Emily thought of Joanna's comment about the opportunity that would be lost if they couldn't make their project work. What opportunity? What did it matter? She remembered standing next to Richard Boone, expressing youthful indignation about a report she'd heard that another actor had been cast in a role she thought Boone should play. Boone had pointed at a television monitor on the sound stage they were working on and said, "Look up there. A little story, acted out in a box. I suppose it *is* a … fleeting *sorta* art form. It goes in the side door of our brain and maybe once in a while our *sorta art form* ends up being … constructive. But, I suspect, most of the time, not so much. I mean, our unconscious is increasingly full of the crap people like you and me busy our little heads with for most of our lives, and oftener than not, it ends up—especially after all the insurance and pharmaceutical interests get done sticking in their two cents—being no more than simplistic, lesson-less mythology."

She'd said, "Are you *that* cynical?"

"No, sweetie, I'm not cynical at all. I'm just as pissed off as you about that role. They offered it to me. I didn't take it. My friend Harry Morgan told me, 'It's only a movie, Dick.' Dumb."

He took a deep drag on his Pall Mall.

Emily looked off beyond the impersonators on their impersonator horses. In the distance (a hundred yards beyond Tom and Jimmy, astride their horses), she saw Solange with the director of photography and his cameraman, looking out over the wilderness, like lost Bedouins scanning the derelict face of the desert for an oasis. These people were looking for a place to take pictures of a game of Let's Pretend. And one day—if what Boone had said in chagrin after it had become obvious he shouldn't have turned down the plum role of Doyle Lonnegan in *The Sting* was true—those pictures would be tiny flickers, unnoticed in the background on a TV set in some out-of-the-way restaurant or motel, at the shadowy borders of most people's real awareness.

But neither Richard Boone, nor Emily really believed that. Boone knew, and Emily was beginning to understand that human beings can't be fully nourished without storytelling.

During her time with Sterling Films, she attended a class taught by Boone at The Neighborhood Playhouse. Sanford Meisner, Director of The Acting Department was having his own battle with throat cancer and Boone covered for him for several months in 1974 and '75.

Emily brought a cassette recorder with her to that class.

Boone's passions extended to everything he did. He threw himself into his teaching the same as he did his acting. On the day Emily audited his class, he was talking about the importance of the work the actors in the class would be involved in as storytellers.

A year after that, Boone had called on her to be his assistant again, during the filming of *The Shootist*. At one point, Emily played back for him some of what he had said that day, a year earlier at The Neighborhood Playhouse.

When she later asked him if her showing up at that class had been part of the reason he'd thought to hire her the second time, he laughed and said, "We've got to do some work on your self-respect. I would have asked you in any case. We'd already worked together. I knew you were good. After that class at the Neighborhood, I must have hugged all the air out of you I was so happy to see you. So do you even have to ask if this big old ham is pleased to be working again with an attractive young woman who thinks his words are worth recording?"

Part of what Boone said that day at The Neighborhood Playhouse:

"People love stories. They love to hear them told, they love to read them, and a good case can be made that they love even more to see them. It's our nature to care about stories. The more effectively they're communicated to us, the better they do what they're meant to. Stories help us believe our existence matters. They let us know who we are, and what we can be if we aim high enough. They tell us we can be heroic if we want to, that faced with the inevitable we can do the impossible. They give us perspective and hope. And sometimes—when the story has been told artfully and it hits us at exactly the right moment—it can lead us back to a faith that there's an all-embracing wisdom beneath the bubble-thin pageant of our lives."

• • •

Tom crossed through the lobby of the Trading Post Motel. As he approached the corridor to his room, he glanced to his left and saw a man standing at the door of the third room on the right, down another corridor, turning a key in the lock.

Tom stopped, his face gone still and brittle. He took a step back and saw the man disappear into the room.

He hadn't seen him for a total of more than three seconds, at a distance in dim light, but he couldn't help noticing the man's hard features and the gray-brown hair framing his face in ringlets, like an emperor on a Roman coin.

He walked slowly down the corridor until he stood in front of the man's room. He stared at the robin's egg blue door and the brass-plated number: 153.

2

Jimmy lay down for a nap before dinner. As the first coat of sleep spread over him, he dreamed that filming had begun.

It was a simple ride-in.

A voice came over the bullhorn. He wasn't sure if it belonged to Solange or the first assistant director. "Ready for you, Jimmy. We're rolling." A beat, then: "Action."

He nudged his boots against Raindrop's flanks and the horse began to walk, then trot toward camera.

He saw Tom waiting. The shot was over his shoulder. As Jimmy approached, he let go of the saddle horn. He was still about sixty yards away, but he didn't want the camera to catch him hanging on. He felt surprisingly comfortable holding reins only. He had the urge to test the feeling and boot Raindrop into a gallop, but knew it would ruin the shot. He focused his eyes on Tom.

Closer now, he jerked hard on the reins. Raindrop skiddingly stopped, then circled in a tight turn that almost threw Jimmy off and caused him to clutch the saddle horn again.

The voice on the bullhorn sounded immediately: "What's the problem, Jimmy? Are you okay?"

He didn't respond, but stared in the direction of Tom and the camera crew.

"We're still rolling," said the voice. "We'll be cutting away, so just keep coming. Come ahead, Jimmy. We cannot duplicate this light."

He blinked and kicked his heels into Raindrop's flanks, but now it was the horse that wouldn't continue.

"Please, Jimmy. We need to get this now."

He kicked Raindrop again, still with no result. He kicked her as hard as he could and, against her will, the horse began to move as Jimmy continued to punish her with the heels of his boots.

"I'm sorry, girl," he said. "We have to." They moved toward camera, Jimmy's eyes locked on the man who stood next to it.

He knew him, but he didn't.

It was Duke. But it wasn't *his* Duke.

Jimmy swung down from Raindrop and the voice, no longer on the bullhorn, and not Solange's voice, said, "Cut."

"I'll take her," said a wrangler.

Jimmy handed the reins to him as John Wayne moved off, untwining his distinctive hitchy saunter.

"Duke?" called Jimmy.

Wayne stopped and turned back. "What do you want, kid?"

He couldn't think what to say. "I don't know, but I've got to talk to you."

"What about? I've told you I don't much like acting discussions."

Cimarron appeared, and Wayne mounted him in one fluid motion.

Looking down at Jimmy, he said, "I have no choice in the matter. I gotta ride off into the sunset. There is a time to be born and a time to die." He smiled sadly. "These are the good times, Jim."

• • •

Tom lay in one of the double beds in his charmless motel room, gazing at the horseshoe pendant he'd inherited from Paige Leone.

"What's the matter?" said John Wayne.

"I think I saw Philip Hopper. It's crazy."

"Why didn't you knock on his door?"

"I don't know."

"You should know."

"Shut up!" barked Tom, then wondered if he could be heard by the people in the rooms on either side of him—which again made him think of Philip Hopper in room 153. He tried to envision what Hopper might be doing, but couldn't. He didn't know what a man like that would do by himself in a motel room. He always pictured him drinking white wine at the Blue Martini in downtown LA, exchanging sophisticated repartee with connoisseurs of this and that. He couldn't imagine him just reading or watching television. Maybe he'd brought some girlie magazines with him, or something like that, but how much time could that take? Anyway, he remembered that Philip Hopper had been in the back of his thoughts since the day they'd met, the day Hopper had given him the pendant and Paige's painting.

"I've been meaning to tell you," he said to Wayne. "I'm starting to read your mind. I'll plan to ask you a question, and you answer it without even being here."

"Sounds like a watershed in our relationship."

"Why did you walk off the film? I think you suddenly felt naked."

Wayne frowned and puffed himself up uncharacteristically. "Let's not be forgetting who's the original and who's the copy."

• • •

At six thirty that evening, Emily met Joanna and Solange in the production office at the motel.

"I sent a driver to meet Ben," said a livid Joanna as Emily walked into the room. "He wasn't on the plane."

Emily's fingers went cold; her scalp tingled.

"I called your house, but there was no answer. He hasn't telephoned. What the hell is wrong with him?"

"He'll be here," said Emily. "I'll make some calls. Don't worry. This means everything to him. I'm sure we'll hear from him any minute. I'll leave word with the desk to have me paged if he calls while we're at the restaurant." She looked at Solange, who was fuming, and said, "He'll show."

Emily excused herself, went into the next room and called home. No answer.

She came back into the production meeting, but found it impossible to concentrate. She stared without focus at the others, remembering a piece of film she'd once seen of a backyard swimming pool during an earthquake; the water slapping, sloshing.

"Coming soon to your local theater: Part One: 'Emily's Hifalutin' Little Dreams,' and Part Two: 'Sinking Like a Stone'."

After they'd spent an hour going over the production details in preparation for the first official day of filming, scheduled to begin the next morning, Joanna said, "I've got something I have to tell you both." She crossed her arms, not liking what she had to say. "I'm afraid somebody definitely knows what we're up to."

Solange looked up, startled, then shrugged. "There's no way we could ever hide *completely.* All we could ever hope to do was try to keep a low profile."

"Well, apparently we didn't," said Joanna.

"How do you know?"

"Cindy told me somebody broke into the Radford office."

Emily lurched out of her trance. "What'd they take?"

"At first, Cindy thought nothing."

"And later?" Emily hoped she sounded appropriately concerned instead of sick with fear that the bottom was dropping out. "What'd they take?"

"Our location schedule."

"Why—?" Emily stopped herself. It was a dumb question. Somebody wanted to know where they were shooting. "When did it happen?"

Joanna: "Two or three days ago."

Emily: "And she just told you *today*?"

Joanna: "She didn't realize it until today."

Emily: "How'd she figure it out?"

Joanna tugged at a lock of curly auburn hair on the back of her neck. "She was going to make the revisions." She frowned. "The master copy was gone."

"That's it?" said Solange.

"Did she call the police?" said Emily.

"No. All she could tell them was, maybe the lock had been picked—although there was no obvious evidence of that—and that some papers were missing. The cops would have laughed at her."

The three of them were silent for a long time. Finally, Solange turned up a perfunctory palm. "It's just one more of your snapping turtles we're up to our ass in. Fuck 'em."

"That's easy for *you* to say," said Emily. "All *you've* got to do is direct this thing. We have to worry about every damned detail—like, is somebody trying to steal this out from under us?"

"Steal it back, you mean."

"Screw you!"

"Ladies—" said Joanna.

"You've got a nerve with all your life wisdom bullshit, Mizzzzz Borugian. What the hell do you know?"

"Cut it out." Joanna glared at both of them. "We do not have time for this kind of crap. We begin shooting tomorrow. We have enough trouble without you two screaming at each other."

"I didn't scream," said Solange. "She did."

Joanna nibbled at her lower lip. "Just do me a favor. Let's not look for trouble we don't already have. I only told you what I told you to keep you informed. Okay?"

Emily glowered at Solange. "Yeah, okay."

Solange gave only the smallest nod.

• • •

There were nine for dinner at the Paintbrush Café. Gil Kahcheenay was seated at the head of three small tables, placed end to end and covered with red linen tablecloths.

Clad in blue jeans and a J. C. Penney work shirt, he was a skeleton of a man, seventy years old, with claw-like hands and deep-set, dark, penetrating eyes. He wasn't talkative at first, but he was friendly, with a lit from within smile.

On Palmer's recommendation, everybody but Tom and Butterworth drank *chicha*, a traditional Native American beer, brewed by the restaurant owner.

"Don't worry," Palmer said to Solange, as he poured her a second glass. "This is mild. You won't suffer from it."

"I suffer easily."

"This is central to my religion. There are times when herbal remedies are useful to clear the bridge between body and spirit." He took a big draught.

"I never heard anyone call beer an herbal remedy," said Butterworth.

"That and other extracts of plants; treated and untreated. Whatever works."

"Aren't you talking about hallucinatory drugs?" said Joanna.

Palmer smiled. "Exactly. Plants are for us to use—judiciously."

He insisted on ordering their dinner and it was delicious. They ate green corn husk tamales with red chili sauce, cauliflower salad with ham and avocado, *colache* (a vegetable medley), hot Mexican sausage, and sweet turnovers, stuffed with yam and coconut.

"Apache food is marvelous," said Emily to Gil.

Gil chewed the rest of the bite he was working on, swallowed it and said, "It's Mexican. We don't eat our own food so much anymore."

"Why is that?"

He smiled. "Too much trouble. It's easier to eat Mexican. It's good Mexican, and the owner makes the best *chicha* you can get around here." He shrugged. "I like to go to restaurants, and Apache food doesn't lend itself to restaurant cooking." He put a forkful of *colache* into his mouth.

"Gil's been to Hollywood," said Palmer.

Everyone looked at the old shaman.

After he'd finished chewing again, he smiled equably. "That's true."

Palmer looked at him with pride. "He worked in the movies."

Gil returned the piece of sausage he was about to eat to his plate. "I got bit—went to Hollywood and did some Westerns in the late fifties—on back lots. I was atmosphere." He leaned toward Emily, confiding, "An extra. The final years of the Golden Age of television, they say now. Although the shows I was in weren't so golden, I think." He nodded and looked inward, remembering. "It was a different time." He chuckled. "As often as not, I was the only Indian in my 'tribe' who was an Indian."

"What made you give it up?" asked Joanna.

"Oh, I don't know. Show business makes demands. And I missed my family, my people, my goats."

"Goats?"

"That's right. I was a goatherd long before I went to California. I've been one all my life, except for my time in Hollywood."

"Were you happy to get back?" asked Tom.

"Oh, yes. In the end I was. Goats don't hold out false promise, and families usually keep their word."

"What made you go there in the first place?" said Jimmy.

Gil smiled quizzically. "I'd learned a little about it when …" His smile became fixed. "Didn't he tell you?" He glanced at Palmer. "I was in the first filming of the movie you're here to shoot."

"I do, I do, I do believe in infinite singularities."

• • •

Gil looked at Butterworth. "What do you remember about it?"

"Not much," said Butterworth, who along with the rest was staring at the old shaman. "I was in Hollywood, editing."

"But you came to Arizona at least once."

"How did you know?"

"Because I met you," said Gil. "I was in a scene in a store."

Emily now saw him in her mind twenty-four years younger, in brief left profile in the country store. She couldn't contain her excitement. "Do you remember a pink, fleshy man called Miles?"

"Yes, I do," said Gil. "A very sober fellow. Liked to talk. Is he a friend of yours?"

"I knew him a little. He died."

Gil nodded, and Emily held in her multiplying questions and listened as Butterworth said, "Were you here near the end of shooting? Shortly after I got back, I heard that Wayne had walked off the set. It was the last week."

"What happened?" said Gil.

Butterworth shook his head. "I don't know. I was hoping you would. There were all kinds of rumors. Both Wayne and Dean had other commitments. They'd each gone away and come back more than once—fulfilling some minor obligations. But that had been part of the plan. … Someone said Dean was working too slowly, as director and actor. But that didn't make sense—the dailies were coming back to us in LA more or less on time. Anyway, he had to start shooting *Rebel Without a Cause.* And Duke had his commitments. It must have been something else."

"Wayne told me Dean cost him a fortune," said Emily.

Butterworth shook his head. "I still don't think that's true. He was probably just talking about the fact that they weren't able to complete it."

"Maybe it was the girl," said Gil.

"What girl?" Emily looked startled, but not surprised.

"There was a girl." Gil looked at Butterworth. "Do you remember her?"

Butterworth frowned. "I know about her *now.*" He glanced at Emily, who was gazing intently at Gil. "I didn't *then.*"

"She was beautiful," said Gil. "Pale skin, dark hair. She was the script girl." Emily and Butterworth looked at each other. "I saw both of the actors talk to her, separately, at different times." He looked at Tom, then Jimmy. "I couldn't hear what they were saying, but they both spoke to her in the special way of men who are interested in a woman." He drank from his glass of *chicha.*

"Do you remember where the location was?" asked Joanna.

"Yes, I do. It's the same land you're using this time. When your advance people called council headquarters, they were guided back to the same place."

"That's what I guessed," said Joanna, excited. "You're the first one who's been able to confirm it. Solange and Mr. Butterworth recognized it from the film." She nodded to them. "We all did. We were the location scouts."

"Damned straight," said Butterworth.

Gil nodded, amused. "That land is part of our holy grounds. The first time, there was debate among the elders as to whether it should be used for a motion picture. Finally, they decided that it was not an exploitive enterprise and the filming was allowed."

"Did the elders have anything to do with shutting it down?" asked Emily.

"I doubt it. Once they had given permission, they would have been unlikely to withdraw it. You know what that's called." He chuckled. "They would have been doubly reluctant to go back on their word when holy grounds were at stake." He looked around the table. "Would you like to see it by starlight?"

Emily glanced only briefly at the others. "I can't speak for the rest but I'd love to."

"It's out of the question for me," said Solange with an undertone of defiance. "I've got to be up in a few hours."

Joanna nodded. "Me too. I have hours of work before I sleep."

Butterworth, Jimmy, and Duke agreed to go. Solange seemed to have mixed feelings about the idea, but glancing at Emily, she kept quiet about them.

While they were waiting to pay their bill, and also on their way out to the cars, Emily and Joanna interrogated Gil and Butterworth, trying to find out whatever more they might know about the original production. Neither of them seemed to remember much more than they had already revealed.

• • •

Gil Kahcheenay and Jack Butterworth were still chatting and drove with Hugh Palmer out to the location.

Jimmy and Tom were left to ride together with Emily in her rented Dodge Aspen R/T, an uncomfortably small car for Tom and more uncomfortable, it would turn out, for Emily, sitting in the back. Tom drove because he hadn't drunk any *chicha* and was entirely sober.

He followed Palmer's Ford station wagon under a bright full moon and brilliantly starry sky.

Jimmy had been looking to the side, staring at the rocky hills and harsh jagged central Arizona geology gliding by, dreamlike, for several miles, reminding him of the saw-toothed skin of giant reptiles and movie dinosaurs. "I *know* what's going on between the two of you," he said.

"What is the matter with you?" said Emily. "Don't you have any sense of place and time?"

"I recognize that. That's what liars do when they're attacked. That's what you've both been doing, lying—by your silence."

Emily hugged herself and inhaled deeply. "How did you know?"

"Because you might as well be wearing neon signs, both of you."

Tom looked straight ahead at the highway as it vanished beneath them. "Her father had just died. Don't blame Emily."

"Please stop it," she said. "You're embarrassing me. You have no right to say anything to me, Jimmy. My private life is none of your business."

"Better watch her," said Jimmy. "She'll invite you into her inner sanctum and just as you're about to take her up on it, she'll slam the door in your face."

"Enough. Both of you." Tom's eyes were fixed on the station wagon's taillights as it turned off the main road and headed south. "This is not the time to talk about this."

The Dodge lurched as he steered it over an old train siding and continued following the others along a rutted gravel and dirt road.

The penetrating smell of creosote filled the car.

They all fell silent.

A coyote yipped in the distance.

Ahead of them, Palmer made another turn and stopped the station wagon near a small grove of junipers.

Tom pulled the Dodge in next to him and they got out without a word.

• • •

Everyone followed Hugh Palmer up a long slope of hard-packed sand and alluvial silt, covered with crushed tumbleweeds and broken brush. At the top of a bluff that fell back down gradually toward a dry drainage wash, amid a cluster of scrubby desert vegetation, Palmer stopped and began to pick up desert driftwood. Tom and Emily helped him. "You're building a fire?" asked Butterworth, puffing his way up to the top of the rise.

The only answer was a *fwup-fwup-fwup* of bird wings as a snowy egret, startled from its roosting place, flew through moonlight into broken stratocumulus clouds and the astronomical darkness.

Palmer pushed dried grass under a pile of twigs, laid the driftwood carefully on top, and ignited it with the second of two wooden matches he'd pulled from his shirt pocket.

He fanned the fire. When he was sure it had taken, he helped Gil with a hand under an elbow to sit cross-legged near it. Jack Butterworth plunked himself down, a little more suddenly than he'd planned, between Gil and Emily, who was sitting cross-legged next to Jimmy and across the fire from Tom.

When they were all settled, Palmer crouched, checked the fire again, rose easily to his feet, and produced a small vial from his shirt pocket.

Carefully, he took out the stopper and held the open vial in his right hand, close to his chest. He looked out over the valley that spread in front of them in the moonglow, a magic belt, studded with silver and jade. He nodded to Gil.

The old man lifted his chin, closed his eyes, and began to speak. "Many spirits inhabit this land. They are in the air you're breathing, in the trees, and on the ground around you. They sit on your shoulders. Why is it so hard for us young ones"—he showed no hint of a smile—"to understand that the plants, rocks, fire, and water are all alive, as we ourselves are spirit without end?"

He looked at each of them as he spoke. "The final images of the film you wish to complete were shot here. I don't know why they shut it down, but I know the information exists. It has not vanished. It's in the fire."

He glanced at Palmer who, still standing, raised the vial over his head with both hands.

"Spirits of this land," chanted Gil. "Spirits of our mothers and fathers, and theirs, and theirs; help us to see what is already clear."

Emily felt like a lost puppy, still young enough—at least for the moment— not to be worried that she's lost.

Palmer turned to the fire, emptied the contents of the vial into the palm of his left hand, then carefully blew it into the flame, which briefly flashed blue and green sparks.

When he was finished, he looked at Gil, who closed his eyes again.

Palmer sat down and closed his.

After several moments of silence, Butterworth, annoyed, said, "What was that?"

Palmer didn't open his eyes. "An herb that was ground into powder."

"What herb?"

Jimmy started to get to his feet, looking like he wanted to say something, too. But halfway up, he sat back down.

"A rare and sacred Apache herb." Palmer cupped his hands together, pressed them to his nose and inhaled deeply. "It's called *tarapo*."

"I never heard of it," said Butterworth.

Gil spoke without looking at him. "It would be best to be still for a time."

Butterworth frowned but along with the rest, kept quiet for none of them knew how long.

Emily wanted to say something but could barely make her brain turn over. The first coherent thought she could summon was that her mind had been drugged for so long, with and without substances, that it had long ago frozen out all real hope. This notion turned into something more familiar: a yearning. But this time, it was tinged with a new configuration of promise—as if she was looking at a movie screen inside herself, seeing a familiar apparition looking back, but there was no longer any fear in it, no aching urgency to turn the film off.

After a long while, Gil opened his eyes and looked at all of them, smiling.

Butterworth brought a hand to his brow and looked from Gil to Palmer. "What did you do?"

"It will have no harmful effect," said Palmer. "My people have been using *tarapo* for a thousand years."

"What are we meant to feel?" asked Emily.

"What *do* you feel?" said Gil.

"I don't know," she said. "Kinda ... I dunno, wasted … but also … the opposite of that: energized sort of."

"We're not about to expose our *inner selves* like some damn gaggle of hippies, are we?" said Butterworth. He started to get up, but evidently changed his mind. "Jeez Louise, I'm at a damned *be-in*."

"I don't know what's happening," said Tom. "But I *do* feel something. I want to say something. I want to"—he reached into the air with one hand—"to touch something, but … I … I've got no idea what it is."

"Are you saying we've inhaled fumes from what you blew into that fire?" Butterworth said to Palmer.

Palmer nodded and shrugged at the same time.

"Well, I think you've got a hell of a nerve."

"I just realized," said Emily, feeling a sudden swell of sympathy for Jack Butterworth—*for all of these men*—"I know why production shut down the first time."

"Why?" said Jimmy and Tom.

Emily looked intently into the fire. "Because they were both in love with the same girl: Betty Merrow."

"We've already figured that out," said Butterworth.

"But we didn't think that's why it shut down. Now, if we could just sort out the details of it, we might get somewhere."

Tom glanced at her. Seeing that she was looking into the fire again as if hypnotized, he, too, looked back at the flames.

"If we can figure out why they shut down," said Emily, "we'll have a better chance of solving our mystery."

"What's our mystery?" said Tom.

"We have to learn something from the first group." Her voice was sharp, excited. "From Wayne and Dean; from *every one* of them." She gazed into the fire.

• • •

Did they draw us here for their own reasons? Are we, without knowing it, helping the ones who are gone? It's too late for them to heal themselves, but can we? By doing it right this time? This can't be only about a piece of film. Maybe the ones from before are watching us at this moment. Maybe in a way we can't understand because we don't know the language of it, we are them—except as they see it, we are the light that's been missing. And now, all of us can finally cast our whole undertaking into three dimensions. If we work together, them and us, maybe we can finally grasp the whole picture—light and shadow—and not only repair the damage, but make of it the living thing it was always meant to be, our souls washed clean of the everyday debris we have all but hoarded for as long as we have lived.

"I knew, *girl—like I know the sun doesn't rise, it only looks like it does—that it was a dumb idea, getting you into the same orbit with medicine men. You were born to swallow bait like this. You were already suckered in by Boone's bullshit. And why should* he *know anything? He just looks like he might."*

"Lord, how did you ever get inside me? Who invited you? You worry too much. And it's always about the way things look, what appears to be on the surface."

"Maybe there IS no topology, dream girl, no infinite connectivity, no *answers that make any sense, no answers, no questions, only confusion and grief, born of our frigid backstory, and no God to help us understand any of it."*

"I pray *this is the moment that begins the part when I will no longer have to listen to a word you say."*

She felt wisps of wind lifting her as she fluttered up into the moonlight.

• • •

Gil watched her, his eyes bright.

Palmer said, "Mr. Butterworth, do you remember being here—the first time?"

"How would I know? It's dark. I probably wouldn't remember it anyway. It's been twenty-five years. I don't remember last week." He cleared his throat, raging to himself. "I hate this, but"—he looked at Gil and spoke haltingly—"I do … recall a face that looked like yours. And it … seems to me I can see that face now, inside yours." He held his hands in front of his own face, wiggled them back and forth and crossed his eyes. "And look at me now. I've clearly gone fishing."

Gil lifted his gaze from the fire to the eyes of the film editor. "The old face is always the young one," he said. "It doesn't go away. It becomes a mirage like the rest of what we call our past. And mirages are here and gone on the wind." He gazed up at the starry night. "Then, one day the wind spins back and makes our hallucinations real again, as real as the wilderness, as real as the lost faces of our youth." He extended a hand in front of him. "As real as …" He smiled and lowered his hand and head.

Emily was sure she heard him whisper: "My goats."

"When?" Tom's voice sounded like a dissonant chord on an out of tune piano, the sustaining pedal distorting it further. "When?" he said. "When does what we pray for come back?"

"When we're ready," said Gil. "When we've grown up enough to say a friendly hello to it, when something in us tells us we're finally beginning to grasp the truth."

Butterworth was scowling. "What's gone is gone. You've just gotten us high on that … shit—on the *tarapo*." He rubbed at his eyes. "We didn't volunteer for this. The least you can do is tell us how it works."

Gil smiled gently. "*Tarapo* does no more than clear your head so that you can see things—only not in symbols you've ever used before. … How does it work?" He chuckled. "I don't know. God is within us, but if we were able to recite a list of all we know or can imagine of God's miracles, they would no doubt add up to something extraordinary, but they would not add up to God." His eyes twinkled in the firelight's glow. "That's a hard cold fact of God."

Jimmy produced a long, contemptuous groan. "I don't believe *anybody* knows the hard facts of whatever you're telling yourself … Oh, shit." He recoiled into himself, got up, arms and elbows cuffing the air, and stood above the rest, his face set.

Emily extended a hand toward him. "Come on, Jimmy. We start work for real tomorrow. Be one of us."

He turned on her. "But I am *not* one of you." He made a choked whimpering sound. "I thought I'd found something with you. With …" He looked at the faces around the fire. "I'm sorry." He gulped a breath of air and stepped around the campfire to Tom. "Give me the keys."

"You shouldn't drive."

"I'm stone sober. Give them to me. I'm not staying here. There's room for all of you in the station wagon."

Tom got the car keys out of his pocket and Jimmy grabbed them from him.

He wanted to stop the action he'd begun and go back to his place by the fire, but he didn't know how. He would have been too embarrassed.

He turned and strode toward the car.

3

Jimmy drove toward the motel, then screeched to a stop, made a U-turn and headed west, further away from Ocotillo Springs.

As he gained speed, he played a game with himself. It seemed to be a sensible alternative to sticking a car key into his eye. The game was: go faster, never slower. He knew at some point he would have to end it, but in the meantime, he increased his velocity, mile per hour by mile per hour. He was conscious of the muscles in the toes of his right foot exerting more and more pressure on the accelerator. The first guideline of the game was that it should happen slowly enough for him to savor every nuance of the experience.

He watched the digital speedometer: *48, 49, 50.* It seemed to stay at fifty for a long time, even as he increased the force of his toes on the gas pedal. *54, 55.* Fifty-six displayed for only a fraction of a second. *57, 58.* Fifty-nine persisted for several seconds with a mind of its own. *Sixty.*

• • •

He hears his mother's voice and realizes she is with him, not in some long ago memory.

"Somebody's always sorry in our family," she says. "Why is it that someone is always remorseful? How did we disappoint each other so badly?"

"What are you doing, Mother?" He tries not to raise his voice. "Why are you still with me? Did you plan to stay here forever? There's no place for you in me anymore. I never knew the answers to any of your questions to begin with, and all I know now is that I'm not going to be sorry anymore—for *any* of it. The only thing I can remember hearing in my whole childhood that still seems of any value is the line I learned from the Bible, in the Sunday school you made me go to until I thought I'd suffocate—the line that told me to put aside childish things. Having my mother inside of me is a childish thing. I cast you out."

One-sided fights, or what he always told himself were one-sided fights, between his parents explode in his mind. He remembers being left at the houses of aunts and uncles in San Bernardino, before his sister Gracie was born—relatives he didn't know—who showed no interest in him at all, who seemed to hold him responsible for his parents' loveless marriage.

He remembers he'd moved out of his mother's house and had come home one evening. In that dream he is sitting on the edge of the bed in his sister's room.

Gracie is slumped toward him, her arms around his neck, her face wet from crying, and he understands that in his absence, she has become the only object of Vivian's rage. "Not feeling so strong, huh?" He pets her hair over and over again and says, "These are the good times."

"What?" she says.

"Something Dad used to say, usually when things weren't going so well."

"Yeah, well then, these sure are the good times."

He continues to stroke Gracie's hair and finally they both stop crying.

• • •

His mother sits in the living room, in the semidarkness. "It's cruel to say I hate you," she says.

He thinks about going over and sitting down next to her, somehow making things even a tiny bit better, but he has no confidence he could do that. "I know you don't mean us any harm," he says.

"Harm? My children are the only reason I'm living."

"I understand."

"Do you?" They both listen to the house's silence. "Maybe you got a little of your father's kindness."

• • •

Lying in his bed, he concentrates as hard as he can on not thinking about anything. He believes that if he can make his mind a blank, so that it actually becomes the blue-black emptiness he sees behind his closed eyelids, that he can fall asleep. He takes deep breaths and tries to think of nothing but his own heartbeat.

• • •

The digital sixties on the speedometer go faster than he thinks they should, and he curses his clumsiness. *62, 63, 64, 65, 67, 68*. Sixty-nine: the favorite number of teenage boys.

He sees the little child on the curb. He sees the ravaged building across the wide street and, inside an apartment on an upper floor, the woman who is always there, illuminated by a single, bare light bulb.

He can make out who the woman is now.

She is young, seventeen, looking at a not very old man in his single bed, facing the wall.

He isn't breathing, and the girl doesn't know what to do.

He is traveling eighty-five miles per hour. It feels like his toes are cramping, or maybe his whole body. He leans on his left haunch and continues to apply pressure on the accelerator. *89, 90, 91.*

The aunts and uncles show up in the apartment of the isolated building, but they don't speak to the girl. None of them tells her it isn't her fault—that she is not responsible for her father's death.

She knows it doesn't matter what they say anyway. She knows she killed him.

105, 106, 107.

He realizes he can't see.

He hears his own sobs and hits the brake.

The steering wheel is wrenched out of his hands.

The car takes off.

Jimmy doesn't think of dying. He wonders what he can do to improve himself, to find any way at all to make himself easier to love.

Or maybe, if he can just speed up the hands of the clock—only backward—both of them will get a new chance, another try at it, and play their roles differently this time, and maybe finally get it right.

4

The flight to Phoenix was on Ben's mind.

He walked down the hall to his father's room, carrying a piece of paper in a trembling hand.

He sat down in the slipper chair next to the empty bed.

• • •

"I can't sleep, Daddy. What am I going to do?

"There are a couple of things I want to tell you. You won't hear me, but you won't look away either.

"You always thought you didn't understand me because we didn't speak the same language or we had different histories.

"You were wrong.

"The reason you didn't understand me is that you didn't want to. And the reason you didn't want to is because you thought you'd somehow get caught with your pants down, and nothing could be worse for you.

"I've always wondered what you thought of me, but if I'd been able to see you, I would have known it was the other way around—that you wanted to know what I thought of you. And since I was always afraid to answer that, you and I were stuck, slogging around in the mud together, before we even started.

"But now, I'm taking stock of myself. I haven't had a drink since you passed away. I want to make you proud of me, Papa.

"I wish I'd had the nerve to tell you this sooner, but I always had the feeling you'd hit me if I did—even though you hardly ever did that. How is it you had the power to make me feel the axe was always about to fall? I'm expecting it right now. Sometimes I wake up cowering, turtling into myself to avoid your attack. I've been expecting your axe every second of my life. I remember you trying to teach me to swim. You were so angry at me for not learning fast enough, that part of you was trying to drown me—to teach me a lesson, I guess. And then I was standing in front of a mirror, watching myself cry, feeling as tiny as my little dick from the cold water you couldn't teach me to swim in. Or even to drown in.

"And still, I wish I'd been able to please you, to be a doctor, but I didn't have the aptitude ... or the fucking IQ. We both know that. So I picked the only business that has any real importance in this town.

"I learned about it from a lumpy little tosser in Arizona. Isn't that peculiar? He had no future, not a very impressive past, but he made me feel free. He made me feel ... innocent. He told me I didn't have to be careful. You have no idea. Innocent. Can you even imagine? And for one instant, I actually believed one of those people who is advertised as knowing something.

"What he didn't *tell me was that what he was teaching had sod all to do with show business. He should have said it's an incredible feeling, what he was trying to teach us, but 100 percent silly buggers when it comes to real life. ... And oh, Daddy, if you could only feel what I felt. In the moment ... It's an acid trip. It's hurdling off a cliff. It's hang-gliding—the wind enveloping you, rushing through you, pushing you ... kissing you. And then you're a tiny, breathing post-it to God. It's lovely. It's sailing. It's skittering through a hurricane. It's leaping into death without having to die. ... Except ... later, life—my life anyway—doesn't let you do it anymore. It keeps reminding you that you fucking well* DO *have to die, and after that ... you will*

never fly again. And from then on, everything … EVERYTHING *is … disappointment.*

"I didn't learn the realities of that and of my line of work until long after I'd come home from London—and by that time, it was … well, you know the rest.

"But what do you think? It turns out that just maybe it's not too late after all—that I might still have a chance to be one of the lucky few. I'm getting another shot at it. That's what I was trying to tell you that night. Maybe I'll still be able to find out … who I am. Right now, I open my wallet, look at my driver's license photo, and I don't recognize the face.

"No, that's wrong. I'll be honest; it still looks like you, no matter how many surgeries I get.

"And I don't want to be like you. You're a killer. But I'm not.

"I did not do anything to that boy in camp.

"Look what I found. Is this letter why you stopped even pretending *to care about me? I came across it among your things.*

"Look what I found, you … pathetic piece of papa poop!"

• • •

Dear Dr. and Mrs. Bennett:

My name is Vivian Riley. I am the mother of James Riley, the boy referred to by Ralph McCollough, owner of Camp Cottonwood, in his letter of September 17. The letter was copied to my husband and me. Inasmuch as you have not seen fit to respond, according to Mr. McCollough, I have taken it upon myself to write to you.

What I want from you is some form of satisfaction regarding what happened to our son. I do not wish to sue you or the camp. I hope that will not be necessary. I do not know if anyone else was involved with what happened to Jim. I only know that it happened in the middle of a night when he was supposed to be asleep in his cabin, under your boy's supervision. How deep my son's scars will be, our doctor can only guess. The one thing we know for certain is that scars unquestionably exist.

We need to hear from you in the very near future if litigation is to be avoided.

• • •

"It's signed Vivian Riley, and she gives her address and phone number in Pacific Palisades, California.

"You paid them off, didn't you? I would have known if there'd been a suit. You paid them off and you never forgave me.

"But I never did anything to that kid. I couldn't have. It was Wally. Why didn't you ask me? I would have told you. Why didn't you ever bring it up? Did you just assume I was that kind of a child? Don't you remember me, Daddy? I was your little boy—a long time ago, I know—but how could you forget me? You loved me once! What's inside you that could end up hating your own ... blood? ... Ah, well never mind, I just answered my own question, didn't I?

"But I can forgive you. At least, I can begin to try."

Ben Bennett Jr. got up and lay down, trembling, on his father's bed.

• • •

At 11:38, Tom knocked on Emily's door and found her already in a nightgown, hastily covered with a powder blue cotton robe. On the television, almost silent in the background, a man was selling automatic can openers.

"He's not back," said Tom. "I knocked on the door. He's not there."

She let him in, and he sat down on the chair next to a small maple writing desk. She closed the door and sat opposite him on the edge of the double bed. “I’m sure he’s all right. He just went for a drive.”

“He can be crazy,” said Tom.

“Yeah.”

“If he’s hurt himself, it’s my fault.” He looked away.

“Stop that. If there’s blame, it belongs to both of us.”

“What should we do?”

“Nothing,” she said. “He didn’t have more than a couple of beers at dinner. Go back to your room and get some sleep. We’re shooting tomorrow. Don’t worry about Jimmy. He wasn’t so stoned that he couldn’t drive. He wants this more than any of us. He’s not going to screw it up.”

He tried to look her in the eye, but she didn’t return his gaze. “What happened tonight?”

“Nothing, she said. “We sat around a campfire and got spooked. Like a ghost story. It was catching. We all got to feeling strange.”

“You’re probably right.”

“Nothing out of the ordinary happened. Look.” She pointed at the television set.

On the screen, John Wayne talked to a child in the common room of a large log cabin.

“*The Searchers*,” said Tom. “Did you hear from your brother?”

Emily stared at *The Searchers*. “Yes, he’s here. Thank God. Joanna was ready to kill him, and me. I walked into the office and found her looking through our copy of the *Players Directory* trying to figure out who we might get to replace him. But he’d gotten in while the rest of us were out smoking some serious shit.”

“Did you see him?”

“No. I guess he went to bed right away. Joanna left him a copy of the shooting schedule for tomorrow.”

Tom was staring at her. "Why won't you look at me? What did I do?"

"Nothing." She bit off the word as she turned to him. "You didn't do anything. But you don't really know who I am."

He frowned. "Is it Jimmy?"

"It's *me*. How can you love a woman who can't see you for yourself?"

"You're not talking about your movie star thing, your proso-whatsis, are you? Because that's loony. I looked it up. You don't have such a serious case of it. I know you don't. And anyway, you know *exactly* who I am."

She felt a bewildering pain. It settled, then rose again. She tried to put a name to it, but by then it was only the usual nameless apprehension. "You don't see through my eyes," she said. "My mother told me that's what movies are for. So they're always up there, and you're always safe in your comfortable seat. That way, when anything harsh is being said, it's being said to somebody else—to Katharine Hepburn or Shirley MacLaine. And I know I'm not them." Tears appeared in her eyes. "Nothing that's said to Carole Lombard matters to me. The words were said decades ago, and I'm not Carole Lombard."

"But you take part in life. You're not withdrawn."

"No, you're right. That's what I mean. It works—this thing I've done for as long as I can remember." She drew in a deep breath. "Or it used to." She pressed one hand flat and hard against her forehead, as if trying to prevent something from getting out—or in. "I've been sitting here thinking, not trying to, but thinking anyway."

Tom waited.

"I remembered something about my father and about ... Ben." She shuddered.

"What?"

"I *don't know.*" She shook her head again, as if she were trying to hurl out whatever was stuck inside. "I'm probably still stoned, or ... maybe it's just some kind of panic thing. It's stupid, I understand that, but … I don't know who *anybody* is."

"You're going to be all right. You're going to be fine."

She clenched her eyes shut, opened them, and studied his face as if she were seeing it for the first time. "You really think so?"

He held out a hand to her, palm up. "Whose hand?"

She wiped her eyes, looked down, and slowly reached out to touch it. She could have been demonstrating the difference in size. "Tom's," she said.

He closed his fingers around her hand and held it.

• • •

In his own room, Tom brushed his teeth, but didn't get ready for bed. He tried to keep his mind still, but had no success. He felt exhilaration and rage.

He turned on the television, sat on his bed, and wondered if he should be trying to breathe evenly or something.

On the screen, Jeffrey Hunter and John Wayne stood next to their horses in an overnight camp.

"It's funny," said Hunter, "but last winter when we passed through Fort Wingate, I don't have any recollection of Nawyecky Comanche."

Wayne moved to the other side of the fire. "It's not so funny when you recall what Nawyecka means."

"What's that?"

"Sorta like roundabout. Man says he's goin' one place, means to go t'other."

The next angle on Wayne wasn't right. He was looking directly at the camera.

He said, "What does that suggest to you about wisdom and courage, son?"

"I dunno," said Tom.

Wayne stared at him from inside the television. "Sometimes it takes courage to be smart, but other times, it's the opposite way around and you have no choice but to mislead folks—at least for a while. You can't tell people the straight truth in every case. A constant barrage of that can hurt those you least want to hurt."

"If you say so."

"But it's never smart or courageous to mislead *yourself*. You need to do what you need to do to survive, but somewhere along the line, you've got to face whatever it is. Maybe … when it's all over, I'm your wind of truth."

Tom felt chills between his shoulder blades.

He stood and picked up his keys from the dresser. "I guess I'll head down to the bar and get myself a nightcap."

Without looking back at the television, he walked out into the hall and shut the door behind him.

5

Until the Dodge finished rolling, it was like an out of control Tilt-A-Whirl at the county fair. It slid sideways on its roof across a wide sandy wash, hit a low ridge of sandstone, flipped a final half revolution, and came to rest right side up in a patch of black and silvered scrub grass.

The door was jammed but Jimmy was able to get his seat belt off and open the roll-up window. He thought he remembered sliding through it, hands and head first, and crumpling to the ground where he thought he lay for—he had no idea how long.

• • •

He doesn't feel quite like himself—or maybe it's just that he's not sure whether he's unconscious or dead.

He gets to his feet and makes his way slowly up the wash, casting in the moonlight a ghostly shadow that limps alongside him toward the macadam road.

He doesn't think he has any broken bones but is surprised—and of course, also not—that his body doesn't ache.

He stands at the side of the road, waiting for cars.

The first one doesn't stop. It gives him wide berth, slowing slightly, then speeding up as it passes.

He focuses his attention on the only light he can see, below him, half a mile away.

After five more cars pass him by, he starts toward the light.

• • •

He stands at the front door, afraid to knock. It's an A-frame cabin, little more than a shack, half hidden among pine trees. Lamplight shines from the single window. He doesn't try to work his way over to it. He fears, even if this is some expression of death he's experiencing, that he'd be taken for a prowler.

A streak of indigo cloud passes over the moon, and it seems the only light in the world comes from inside this shack. He thinks of going back to the road, but he's more afraid of being seen running away by whoever is in the cabin than by having to confront them.

He knocks and hears the scraping of a chair being pushed back on a wooden floor, then nothing, no footsteps.

He waits.

He knocks again and hears the scraping again, but more emphatic, as if someone came stocking-footed to the door the first time, saw him standing there through a hidden peephole perhaps, decided he or she didn't want to commune with the bleak, unpromising soul standing alone in the midnight chill, then returned to where he'd been, and sat back down. Now, hearing the second rapping, the person is getting up again, only this time he or she is angry.

With a rattle and wrenching squeak, the door opens.

Jimmy starts to turn away, then, afraid not to look, turns back and sees a man of medium height retreating into the room.

The man says in a soft but firm voice, "I had to make sure you were serious. Come on in."

Jimmy steps inside.

"Close the door."

He does so and turns toward this man, or this specter, sitting now in a pigskin Mexican equipale chair. In front of the chair is a yellow, linoleum-topped table. On the table is a wormwood lamp, a pack of Camels, an old-fashioned cut-glass ashtray, and a Zippo lighter.

Lamplight throws the man's face into shadow. His head and shoulders are outlined in amber-gold. It looks like a shot from a sumptuous Warner Bros. melodrama.

"Sit down," says the man. He points to an old metal folding chair that was once painted red, then leans back in his own chair and lights a cigarette with the Zippo. "What can I do for you?"

Jimmy finds his voice. "I'm dead, right?"

"Would you like a Camel? You're never dead as long as you can walk a mile for a Camel." He extends the pack to Jimmy.

"No, thanks."

"Suit yourself." He takes a deep drag. "Let me guess why you're here."

"All right," says Jimmy. "But just so you know, I didn't roll my car on purpose."

"Bullshit. Yours was even more blatant than mine. At least there was another vehicle involved in mine—some circumstances beyond my control." The man smiles in a way that almost unties the knot in Jimmy's stomach, and says, "So, do you want to make excuses for every unconscious act of your lifetime, or do you want me to tell you why you're here?" Waiting patiently for his guest to answer him, the vision leans forward into the light, still smiling.

Its features are now unmistakable.

Jimmy's stomach clenches again. He sees the man's face clearly now. As if doing an old screwball comedy routine, he shakes his head and blinks his eyes several times. Studying the face by lamplight, he realizes that unless his eyes are lying to him, he *knows* who he's talking to—or who this moment is trying to make him believe he's talking to. "Okay," he says, "Go ahead. Tell me why I'm here."

"You want me to let you know where that picture on Tom's living room wall *really* came from and what it means," says the vision. "You think that's a clue to solving your bigger picture."

"Okay, where did it come from?"

"Sorry. I always wanted to be a guy with the answers, but that never panned out. How about some random information? I've got a little of that."

"Okay, fine. You got any information about why I'm sitting in a cabin, in the middle of nowhere, talking to … *you*?"

"Nope. Got no dope on that either."

Something about James Dean has changed. He still has the charm and the wicked grin. He seems as precocious as ever, but time—or maybe it was death—appears to have made him more accessible, more thoughtful, but also, just as nearsightedly eccentric. "Is the woman a character in the movie?" says Jimmy. "Did you have the mother in the original script? Or was she only an off camera role?"

Dean displays his sweet, girlish smile, shakes his head and shrugs, indicating he doesn't know.

Jimmy concentrates as hard as he can, trying to come up with a question his host might answer. "How does it end? Who is the showdown between?"

Dean looks around at the tiny shack, his brow creasing. "I'd love to help you, but see, they got these rules and if I don't follow them, I don't ever get to get out of here." He tugs at one ear. "I'm only telling you the rules."

"Do you know *anything* about Tom's painting?"

Dean shakes his head. "Just that it's there."

"Then what good are you to me?"

"Not much I guess. And the only mother I spend any time thinking about is the one who had my baby. That, I can talk about. … What's with that look? You mean you never heard?"

Jimmy shakes his head, fleetingly unsettled by an image of a woman in a security guard uniform, and something—he can't remember what—he heard from Emily and Butterworth.

"Shit, I'm a legend. Are you saying you never heard of my child?"

"You never had a child," says Jimmy, "not that I know of. And I'm a student of you."

"Some student, if you don't know about my kid. What year is it?"

"Nineteen seventy-nine … I think."

"Jesus, you look away for five minutes and a generation has passed." He takes a drag on his cigarette and looks toward the darkened window, then at Jimmy again, studying him. "Son of a bitch. She didn't tell anybody. Maybe that's why I'm still in this hovel. Shit!" He looks away, bringing a hand to his forehead as if shading his eyes from sunshine. "I've got to find my son and tell him who he is. I didn't do right by him, and that turns out to be a cardinal mistake on this side."

Jimmy plays along. "How do you know you had a child?"

"Betty was a healthy girl. She was about three months pregnant."

"Betty Merrow?"

"Yes."

"But you didn't meet her until you were shooting the film, did you?"

Dean shakes his head. "I met her around the same time I met Duke, a good while before the shoot began. You can count back as well as me. She was one of his lawyer's secretaries. I went to their offices in downtown LA one day to iron out some details and I met her there. I took her out and then, later, I got her the job on the movie. She wanted to be an actress. I suggested she begin by being script supervisor. She said she'd give it a try." He massages his temple. "It's not easy work, but I was sure she could do it. She was *something*."

Jimmy feels as if he's finally getting somewhere. "So, what happened with her?"

Dean shrugs sadly. "She got pissed off at me." He takes a drag on his Camel. "I got pissed off at her. I moved on. I had a lot of things happening then."

"How did you know she was pregnant?"

"She didn't know I knew." He flashes the mischievous smile. "She wasn't feeling well one day. Script supervising is demanding work, even if a person's done it all her life." He looks at his cigarette. "A guy's smoking a new cigarette in one cut, and in the matching coverage, it's burned down to his fingers. Spoils the illusion. Anyway, one day she didn't catch something. Duke had his sleeves rolled up in one scene and they were not rolled up for the reverse angle. So I yelled at her, and she started sobbing and Duke gave her a few pats on the back—a few too many pats, if you ask me. Then the AD took her to the doctor."

"What happened?"

"The doc sent her home. After we were wrapped for the day, I went to him and asked him what the trouble was. He didn't want to tell me, but I 'prevailed' on him. I told him I needed to know what was going on with my crew—"

"No offense," says Jimmy, interrupting. "But how did you know the baby was yours?"

The martyred actor touches the bridge of his nose. "I was the first man she was ever with. What's that look? She told me so."

Thinking Dean is about as informed on the subject of mothers and babies as he is, Jimmy says, "Of course, you're in my mind anyway."

"Take my word, if you'd known Betty and heard her tell me I was her first, you'd know it was true. The doc confirmed what I'd already guessed. She'd missed two periods. She didn't tell me, but I found out."

He scratches his chin, and Jimmy thinks he looks pathetic. He's unshaven, his hair grown into a longish flattop that splays out like a designer cut from a later time, but without the art. He is dressed in threadbare jeans and a T-shirt.

He stares at Jimmy, then narrows his eyes. "First thing you can do is don't go feeling sorry for me. You're in no position. I may be the one actually gone, but at least I'm awake. It was just dumb luck that I'm the one who died."

"I'm not dead?"

Dean shrugs slightly. "You tried. But I'll allow you're alive, by conventional standards." He looks around the small room and shudders. "I'm only dead by conventional standards." He blows a smoke ring that breaks up as it floats toward the lamp. "I secretly fantasized I was immortal." He shakes his head. "… It turns out I decided to … *test* that."

"But you had a phobia about death."

A bleak smile. "Yeah, well, maybe there was something in me that wanted to get it over with, you know? That urge to hurtle off into eternity and get it out of the way, so you won't have to worry about it anymore. … Anyway, God's truth, I did not want my life to end. I wasn't even going that fast when that Ford Tudor pulled onto the highway. I was just starting to have my success." He groans at the injustice. "I was a mess, sure, but I had everything to live for. I was fascinated with death like most teenagers, but I didn't want to *experience* it yet. When I realized that big old sedan was pulling directly into my path, I was shocked. If you were to ask me if I understood what was going on, deep inside me that day in Cholame, California, I'd have to tell you I did not. There were things I was always pushing down where I wouldn't have to worry about them, but …" He takes a drag on the stub of his Camel and smiles sadly. "But I had more reason to bury things than you."

"What do you mean?"

He looks as pained as Jimmy can ever remember seeing him. "At my house, they used to dress me in long sleeves in July to keep the bruises from showing."

"What happened to you?"

"The details aren't the point," says Dean.

"Well, you don't know what happened to me."

Dean spits a couple of pieces of tobacco out of his mouth and grinds his cigarette out in the ashtray. "No, and neither do you." He gets up, moves to the window, and looks out into the darkness. "I went to camp, too—in a way. I had a hero. I worshipped him."

"The guy who … took you on? Your mentor?"

"Right," says Dean. "He was all things to me. I needed him. I was searching for anyone with the answers. And when I found him, it was like … something in me heard what it needed to, even though most of it wasn't in words, and I jumped at it." He shrugs. "I never knew what I was getting till after I'd bought it." He shakes his head. "And I'm afraid I paid for the wrong set of answers. Which means no answers, no guidelines; zero wisdom—stranded with … nothing." He turns to face Jimmy again. "If you spend your prime learning years just licking your wounds and snarling … you are nowhere. So, now I'm trapped and ignorant like you."

"I'm not trapped."

"Oh, really? You figure you might be dead; you're willing to accept oblivion without even putting up a fight, but you won't come clean to being trapped?"

"They're not the same thing."

"Oh, but they are, good buddy. Play along with me that you're alive. Is this what you want—to live somebody else's life? Unable to let yourself be touched, a sacrifice to your past?"

"I'm not a victim anymore. I have nothing to do with my mother."

"You couldn't have more to do with her if she was your roommate. She lives inside you, lost, unforgiven, and—craziest of all—forgotten." He gazes sadly into eyes nearly the spit of his own. "She inhabits your every decision, every passion, every dream."

Jimmy imagines he hears his own labored breathing. "So what do I do?"

"First off, think about what you *don't* do. Don't—in reexamining it—get too intimate with her. Notions like that should be long past."

"I don't know what you mean."

"You *do* know what I mean. Don't get over-close with mum. Suckling time—which as we both know, you never got much of—is long past. In case anybody should suggest the idea or anything like it, don't *do it*. If *anybody*, and you know who I mean, brings it up again, tell her that everything—as far as our character is concerned—depends on you disengaging from 'mom.' "

"Is that why I'm here? To learn that from you?"

"Yes, that's good! I think maybe you called it. I'm a necessary stop-off for you. Your college. Bill it as graduate work." He laughs. "I like that. The University of James Dean Graduate School of Life—well, and death, of course." He makes a jokey face.

"But what were you looking for—in your life?" says Jimmy, absently wondering why, in the midst of this midnight digression he's trying to understand a ghost that no one dead or alive, including the ghost, will ever understand. "Can you at least tell me what you were looking for? … What you *are* looking for?"

"I don't know," says Dean with his faraway gaze. "Maybe I just wanted to hang on to the dream I'd been lucky enough to …" Faraway morphs into wounded. "Then one day I woke up and realized that it was all temporary—having, as I say, zero wisdom, and not a clue how to write a happy ending for it." He looks like Jim Stark in *Rebel Without a Cause,* vulnerable, imploring. "If I could only finish my movie, it would be the final reel I never got to put in the can. It would mean something deeper than all that overblown teenage angst crap. Do you think you can do it? Do you think *you* can finish it for me?"

"Did you write it?" says Jimmy. "Did you write *Showdown*?"

"It was more or less my idea."

He tells himself the eyes are honest—that if Dean is lying, it would be the eyes that would give him away. "C'mon, answer me. Did you write it?"

"Maybe," says Dean.

"Ye-aah, su-ure. That's what I thought."

"All I want is to finish my picture."

For the first time, Jimmy hears the whining in James Dean's voice.

"That's why all these events and people are converging."

"You have that kind of power?" says Jimmy.

"I have no power at all. But I draw energy like iron filings to a magnet."

6

Jimmy opened his eyes and beheld a state trooper kneeling over him. "Are you all right, sir?" He said it louder. "Are you all *right*? Can you speak to me?"

He went on like that for most of a minute before the message got through to the part of Jimmy's brain responsible for dealing with life's quirkiest moments. Jimmy said, "Yeah. I guess. What happened?"

"You rolled your car. Can you tell me your name?"

"Sure."

"What is it?"

"Pardon?"

"Your name."

"James Dean."

The trooper was silent for a moment. "Is that a joke, sir?"

He reprocessed the question. "Yes ... *yes*. I was kidding. My name's Jimmy Riley. I'm with a film company. We're staying at the Trading Post Motel."

"I see. Well, we're about to load you into an ambulance and take you to Graham Memorial Hospital."

"You don't have to do that," said Jimmy. "I'm fine."

He tried to get up, but the trooper placed a restraining hand on his shoulder. "Sorry. You're gonna get checked out. Also test you for alcohol and drugs."

"You won't find anything."

The trooper contemplated him. "Well, you're a lucky man. You shouldn't have survived this. Can you tell me what happened? How you lost control of your car?"

"I'm not sure. I guess I missed a curve or something."

"There are no curves around here, sir. This road's straight as an arrow."

• • •

Joanna went with Emily to the hospital.

"He's up in X-ray," said the doctor in charge of the emergency room night shift. "We're taking a picture of his left leg. I don't expect to see anything I shouldn't. Just bruises. He's a lucky fellow."

"I hate to ask this," said Joanna with an embarrassed shrug. "He's scheduled to work in a few hours. Will he be able to?"

"We've got to keep him overnight for observation. But sure, I guess. If it's not too strenuous. What kind of work does he do?"

Joanna looked at the floor. "A few easy horseback rides. It shouldn't be much."

The doctor made a wry laughing sound, like simmering lava. "Well, he's going to be pretty stiff for a day or two, but I guess he's okay to do that. I trust you'll let him off the hook if it hurts him too much." As an afterthought, he added, "And that you're not going to ask him to do any galloping."

"Of course," said Emily.

"Yes of course," echoed Joanna, still gazing at the floor.

"You're from LA, huh?"

They both looked at the floor and nodded.

The doctor shook his head and burbled again. "Tell him not to drive so damned fast."

• • •

Tom looked into the blackness outside his window.

"Why aren't you wearing it?"

"I take it off sometimes, at night."

"No, you don't."

Tom scooped up the horseshoe pendant from the dresser and put it on.

"Why'd you tell me you were going down to the bar for a drink?"

"It's an old Nawyecky trick," said Tom. "You know about that."

"Well, that's just swell, but where did you go?"

"To see Philip Hopper is my best guess."

"And what got said?"

Tom frowned. His voice came out in a low moan. "I don't know. All I remember is standing outside his door."

"I told you a long time ago, son, I need you. But you're not giving me any help here. Sometimes you seem to start off in the right direction, but you always lose your grip. Talk about stage fright. And don't tell me I'm the cause of it."

"I'm trying as hard as I can."

"Courage has to be a whole act, pilgrim. It doesn't count unless you complete it. If you don't let me go, I can't let you go, and if I can't do that, what's been the point?"

• • •

The night nurse said in a firm tone of voice, but soft, calculated not to startle him, "I've got to check your temperature, Mr. Riley."

He opened his mouth and she inserted the thermometer.

"Are you happy?" he asked when she'd removed it.

The young nurse smiled in the semidarkness. "Am I happy?" She made a note on his chart. "What do you mean?"

"Well, is everything okay?"

"I'm ready to go home and get some sleep, if that's what you mean."

Jimmy wished he could go to her home and get in her bed with her, but he knew he couldn't do that, so he pictured himself sitting next to her in a lit-up coffee shop, ordering from the same menu and talking about unimportant things.

V
PRODUCTION

1

When Emily woke up, she saw that the day was overcast and was afraid there would be a storm. Then, she remembered she had to perform and was afraid there wouldn't be one. Although Sarah didn't have a lot of dialogue, she would be in most of the scenes in the Eastern sequences, which would begin shooting on the second day.

She tried to comfort herself that she had nothing on the first day's call sheet, but that didn't lessen her nerves, or ease her panic. She was going to be "pretending" to be her brother's wife.

"That is a damned peculiar thing for a human to do. But it shouldn't surprise me. You are peculiar."

"*No,* you're *peculiar.*"

"You *are.*"

"*You are.*"

"I'm rubber and you're glue. Everything bounces off me and sticks to you."

She telephoned Ben's room, got no answer, and had more edgy feelings when she learned he'd been picked up early and driven to location.

She bathed, put on blue jeans and a ribbed, white cotton sweater. Her hair, still wet from washing, was shiny with glints of amber gold in the morning sunlight. Looking at herself in the mirror, she realized she looked quite pretty if she didn't count that she was vibrating.

As she headed down to the lobby, she realized she knew what "butterflies in the stomach" meant, except her butterflies seemed awkward, clunky, lumbering; not yet butterflies, still caterpillars.

• • •

"I always thought improvising for film was bollocks," said Ben Bennett.

Solange was overseeing the setup of four cameras and the placement of more lighting instruments than she'd ever worked with at one time, and hadn't been paying much attention to him.

She blinked her eyes. "Why is that?"

"That's all I need—to see what some thespian git had in his bean the day they were filming. I like to see a little craft and sullen art when I go to the cinema."

"Why are you telling me this? What's the matter with you? I told you we'd be working with improvs. You knew that when you accepted the job."

"Sorry, old girl. It's just that I'm no great shakes at it. When it's used by people who know what they're doing, it can be smashing. I simply meant the self-indulgent kind." He tacked on a tight little laugh. "But, of course, if you know what you're about." He blinked rapidly. "Go ahead and tell one to get stuffed when he talks rubbish." He shrugged. "The truth is I'm a little knackered from lack of sleep just now … and"—he wiggled his eyebrows—"mad as a bag of ferrets."

Solange swallowed hard. "Well, I can see how you might be, not having worked for a while, and when you do, it's with your sister and your old friend."

"Old friend?"

"Jimmy," said Solange. "You were his camp counselor, right?"

"Did you hear that from Emily?" He looked especially bland.

"Both of them."

"Emily *and* Jimmy?" She nodded, and he said, "Why would they tell you that?"

Solange stared at him. "I'm using improvisations. I'm using your inner lives, and your inner lives are made up of every … beg pardon, 'bloody' personal thing about you, 'the bleeding lot.' Do you understand what that means?"

A scowl slipped out from under Ben's smile.

"Why don't you go and relax until you're called for."

"Aah, right. Good-o." He looked off at the crew preparing the east end of the clearing for the shooting. "And when will that be?"

"It'll be *a while*," said Solange. "What are you doing here so early?"

"I got in late last night. And … well, as I say, I couldn't sleep." He smiled ingratiatingly. "So I nicked the first ride out I could. I expect I was just keen to get started."

"Well, get into wardrobe and makeup and we'll come get you when it's time. And don't let me hear any of … whatever that dialect is when you work."

"Could I ask another question?"

"*What*?" said Solange.

"Never mind."

"No, *what*?"

"Do you like me?"

"*Do I LIKE you*?"

"Never mind."

"Do you *care*?" said Solange.

"No," said Ben, a ventriloquist, still-faced. "Just curious."

• • •

Jimmy's call wasn't until two p.m.

Waiting for the doctor to come by on early rounds and release him, he took an envelope out of a pocket of the pants he'd been wearing when he crashed. Mail had been forwarded to him at the Trading Post by the proprietor of his private post office box.

Inside the envelope, along with a letter, was a black-and-white photograph of a trim-looking man, staring pugnaciously at the camera, arms akimbo.

He reread the letter.

Dear Jimmy—

I know you believe I don't think of you much, but I do. I want to communicate with you the same as any mother wants to communicate with her son. I saw a little of that recent mini-series, "Roots," that traces the genealogy of a family of negroes and you popped into my mind.

How do you like this picture of your grandfather? He was twenty-one. Some small-town photographer knew about good camera angles, didn't he? He was very well built—about five foot ten, and so coordinated and could do anything with his hands. He was a wonderful father—wrote long and interesting letters and read constantly. He also liked a good athletic Indian and completely defied my mother on that. He didn't drink at all, but smoked two packs of cigarettes a day, which killed him. Oh sure, he wasn't perfect. He didn't beat me or anything, but sometimes he would dismiss me a little scornfully. I did hate that. It made me want to cry, but I was always too angry.

I have one small picture of Mom in a group but I can't find it right now. She was pretty, wonderful smile, very blonde. She broke her nose when she was twelve and locked herself in her room when the doctor came. I suppose her father was dead then, because he was THE boss and I guess Granny Belle was too busy running her business and supporting the rest of the family to bother too much with any special one. The men all became successful with only grade school educations and married teachers.

I think of Gracie more often than I can tell you and wish I could share this with her too.

Love, Mom

Jimmy looked at the photograph of his grandfather again and closed his eyes. He pictured his mother coming into his room after getting home late on a Saturday night. She was young and beautiful, even with faded lipstick and clumpy mascara, and she gave off the heady smell of cigarettes and perfume. She sat on the edge of his bed, bending over and kissing him, whispering that she loved him as her shiny chestnut hair closed them off together in a silky cocoon.

• • •

Drinking a cup of coffee, Tom sat at the makeup table, looking past the crew setting up, at the vivid colors, even under cloud cover, of a central Arizona morning.

He inhaled deeply. He liked the smell of film locations. He supposed it was from all of the equipment freed from the warehouses and released into the air. In the case of this shoot, whatever it was that created the atmosphere was complemented by creosote, mesquite, pine smoke, and a higher ratio of oxygen to lethal particulates than he was used to.

A young woman named Gretel, with frizzy blonde hair and sparkling green eyes, put his foundation on sparingly. Tom did part of his own makeup because it was a special job that he was accustomed to doing. Gretel didn't mind; she was professionally admiring of his expertise at doing Wayne.

Since Tom, in 1979, was considerably younger than Wayne was in 1955, they needed to replicate the star's middle-aged jowls. Using a damp sponge, then a 3/8-inch flat sable brush, Gretel skillfully applied a pancake base (RO3g), carefully blending above and below the jaw line, shading with RO9g, accenting with P13g, and highlighting with O1.

Tom shadowed the hollows of his cheeks, the area between his jaw and lower lip, and under his chin with Max Factor 27-07c. To suggest a finely drawn hint of something like an Asian influence somewhere far back in Wayne's family tree, he applied a subtle shading of dark brown eyebrow pencil at the outer edges of his eyes.

When they were finished, Gretel stood back to appreciate their joint handiwork and said in a hushed voice, "They won't let me take your picture, but I wish I had one to show people."

In the three-way mirror on the makeup table, a whiptail lizard appeared on a rock eight feet behind them and, swaying hypnotically, stared back at Tom.

He said thank you to Gretel and got up to go to work as the lizard scuttled off the rock and made for a creosote bush.

• • •

Ben lay down in a patch of scrub grass outside his dressing room. It promised to be very warm once the sun got higher. He was wearing his brown twill costume shirt. He didn't mind the heat. Impurity no longer bothered him. He didn't care if the shirt got dirty and sweaty before they began shooting, although he did briefly wonder if it had been washed since being worn by a previous actor, which made him question whether twill was accurate to the historical period of this film.

Bugger me, no need to get me jam-jams in a twist.

He turned his head to the side, looked through a crosshatch of jungly grasses toward the crew at work, and thought about his sister broadcasting things about private family business. It didn't matter that *he* was a something of a showboat … once in a while. He had an excuse; he was an alcoholic. He'd been on the piss so long he couldn't remember how the Serenity Prayer started.

He looked up at a slow-drifting bank of clouds and thought about the boy.

2

They planned to begin with telephoto coverage and long shots for the missing action sequences, then move in, testing Tom's and Jimmy's levels of authenticity as the stars they were impersonating.

It was a complicated shooting schedule. In 1979, the four million dollars Oakland had raised (and partially funded himself) would ordinarily have been enough—given that they were not paying huge star salaries—for the forty-five to fifty minutes of finished film they needed. But much of their work was experimental in nature, so while Emily and Joanna hoped Solange would be able to bring it in on schedule, neither of them really believed that would happen.

Emily was still nervous. Her original feeling of confidence that Solange was sensible and gifted was being eclipsed by her growing fears that she was a little Napoleon—a loose cannon, coming more untethered every day. In nightmares, Emily was banished from Hollywood, made to work dreary jobs: wearing a hairnet, bussing tables in an unfriendly cafeteria; selling newspapers at a teeny Dickensian newsstand in freezing winter; typing a script for a crappy sci-fi movie about space aliens who run out of food and come to our planet to eat all the earthlings, with a predilection for urban dwellers wearing bib overalls. Her father showed up in some of those dreams. "Better wake up. Don't want to lose *this* job. You're not good for much else."

On this first day of shooting, Solange planned to get a series of beauty shots of the landscape and several ride-ins, then use the intervals while the crew was setting up to work with the actors.

Standing outside the door of the mobile production office, Emily looked back at the clearing where they were going to shoot some of the scenes in the final sequence. In the foreground, on the scarred, callused landscape of stone and sand, were the photographic and dolly trucks, a crane truck, a dressing room trailer, a trailer shared by makeup and wardrobe, an all-purpose flatbed truck, and two large vans for electrical. Most of the finale—several nights "on the trail" (two in particular), separated by one day at the end of Barnes's and Gabriel's trek—would be filmed day for night, which calls for a flock of lighting instruments. (The light cast on the actors has to be intense enough to counterbalance the vital day for night filters and create the impression of brilliant nighttime.)

A hawk flew out of some brush and, rising on warm air currents, was swept up into the cloudy sky. A coyote barked in the distance. Emily felt momentarily intoxicated, as if on good champagne, but a delicate vintage, hard to catalog.

The crane operator came down the steps from the honey wagon. Spotting Emily, he pretended he was patting his lower abdomen, instead of zipping up his fly. "What the hell am I working on here?" he said. "You wanna tell me that?"

"I'm afraid that's classified."

"I saw one of the actors just now. In the get-up he's wearing, the dude's a dead ringer for John Wayne. What kind of a picture wants the ghost of John Wayne in it?"

Emily giggled. "Nobody ever asked me that. Where were you when we started putting this thing together?"

The crane operator smiled at her in the way people do at mentally disturbed persons and continued on his way.

Emily watched him go.

We should be able to answer a question like that.

• • •

Solange made some brief comments to the crew and then gave them back to the director of photography, who sent them off to their tasks setting up for the first shot.

The director spoke to the cast: "We've been given a unique opportunity. I'm here to help you, to be your guide." She looked at Jimmy and Tom. "But not your parent. I don't have time to caress you into trusting me. My job is to work you as well as I can and get the best of it on film. Please concentrate on your problems, not mine. Let us worry about camera angles and the lighting. Most of the time, you should hardly be aware a film is being shot."

Emily glanced over her shoulder, back into the trees, but couldn't see any equipment from where she was. She lifted her gaze. Even the cranes were hidden in foliage. Solange was using the technique of her idol, Soviet director and film theorist Sergei Eisenstein, of camouflaging the cameras like a magician.

"I will be making various interior cuts," said Solange, "back to the original film—to reaction shots from scenes we can use better in this context, and of course to the 'attitude shots' of Dean and Wayne. Thank God they were John Ford fans and we have that footage." She nodded to Joanna and Emily. "We'll be using tilts, slow motion, panoramic shots, whatever we have to, to get what we need."

Tom raised his hand like a schoolboy, but she waved him off. "There will be lighting instruments all over the place—don't run into them. And be aware that at any given time, I may be shooting film, I may not. I may have told you we're rolling, I may not—"

Tom raised his hand again.

"—That's a lot of pressure, I know, but don't think of it that way, and for God's sake, don't think of it as coming from me; I don't exist once we roll. You've got enough self-incriminating junk in your own heads to last you till the end of time."

Tom's hand was still in the air.

"*What*? I'm not interested in anyone's random anxieties."

Emily's fists were clenched. *She's goddam Otto Preminger.*

"If you're John Barnes living by yourself in the Old West," Solange went on, "you never know what lies around the corner. You're always expecting to be surprised. And that's good. That's life. Don't waste your energy and our time trying to figure out exactly what the surprise is going to be before you get to it. Does that answer your question?" She didn't wait for a response. "If your subliminal 'self' woke up today, wondering what alchemy has drawn you to this thing we're doing, in the middle of this wilderness people used to call Indian country, the answer is: the power of your unfinished story did. That's what I hope will stay in people's minds."

"But you're talking about different stories," said Tom. "How do you know they're going to ... fit together?"

She looked at him, then the others, without blinking. "The people you're playing—as if your life depends on it, please—have all lived *their* lives hiding from the truth. At this point, they've traveled over two thousand miles to remedy conditions that have become intolerable. You folks need to come a similar distance. Don't worry about your 'characters.' You *were* these characters long before I met you. And you don't need to think about the trek. The only trek I'm concerned with is the one you make back through your own minds by way of your guts. That's what I want to see. Give me everything you can—what you feel in your soul, your heart, your kidneys ... all your ... parts. We'll work from there."

"But *how*?" said Emily. "How do we decide which …?" She stopped herself.

Solange had closed her eyes and gone motionless, her body language was at the still point before an operatic surge, her eyes flashing. "*I don't give a shit how*!"

She held her hands up. "Sorry. I'm sorry. You're my boss; I'm supposed to be civil to you. … I mean, you ask me if an egg is a fruit or a vegetable, and you seem to want me to be patient with a question like that. Look, I'm not just talking to you, Emily, I am talking to this whole cast. Where do you people *come* from that you never *confront* what's going on inside you? What's the *matter* with you? How are we going to get to the meat of this thing if you won't open some wounds? I'm not asking for a full-out hemorrhage …"

She spread her arms, palms up, looking skyward. "Ah well, maybe I am. Maybe blood is what we need. Either way"—she scanned their faces—"how are the people who promote this thing going to sell your movie if you don't give them something to work with, other than a couple of dead movie stars? This story can be, if you will only have the balls to let the bridge clubs in Peoria kiss our unconventional ass, a knock-down, drag-out, ice-pick-to-the-guts spectacle. That's what's going to sell this fucker. Can you *please try* to give me that?"

She took in a deep breath. "So, okay, start modestly. Let whatever's inside you come out. Please! Begin there, all right?"

"But we've got a script," said Emily. "*Most* of one."

"Yesss! And we'll be following the script when we need to."

"You wrote it. I agreed to it."

Solange looked at Emily for several beats, then spoke almost in a whisper. "Do you want ketchup and cardboard cutouts? We can do that. Or do you want a movie with life in it? If it's life you're after, I need you not to worry about any of this while you're acting. That's how you direct amateurs. It doesn't work any other way."

“Wow!” whispered Jimmy.

Emily thought this was some sort of creepy motivational technique, but she was certain that none of these *actors*, with the possible exception of Ben, was old enough or far enough away from actually being amateur that they could easily shrug off her words. “What’s *wrong* with you?” she said to Solange. “Don’t you have the faintest clue how to deal with people? What do you expect this to do to us? Do you want us to lose every bit of confidence we have?” She realized she was yelling.

Solange looked at her with a spreading smile. “There, you see? You’re not as thick as you seem. Yes, my dear. That’s precisely what I want.”

• • •

After the first day, mostly shots of Tom and Jimmy on horseback from several angles and distances, the women in charge knew they had the right cast. It was clear from the videotapes, shot concurrent with the filming, that both Tom and Jimmy (despite his physical stiffness from the car crash) were completely convincing as Wayne and Dean in everything but the close-ups.

On the second day, they moved to a spring-fed patch of wooded land that was to pass for Southeastern Pennsylvania. They went “back East” for the next five days to pick up the first chronological scenes, some of which would be edited in, as flashbacks. Since Scanlan and Sarah had not been in the part of the movie filmed in 1955, they decided to shoot most of their pages up front—to make sure Emily worked out as Sarah, and to establish that their reference points for the final sequences were on the mark. It was a luxury they needed to allow themselves. Solange’s script called for the backstory to be told from different points of view, like Kurosawa’s *Rashomon*, except this was to be only bits and pieces—covered from multiple perspectives—and to be used for heightening the suspense.

They would cover much of the opening with MOS shots, then overdub these scenes—and, where appropriate, the rest of the movie—with nineteenth century American music, as Ken Burns would do ten years later with his *The Civil War* series. Later, they would weave that in with a contemporary score by a composer yet to be chosen.

(MOS is a mysterious old Hollywood term, supposedly deriving—and this is very likely apocryphal—from an unidentified German director of the twenties, meaning with no soundtrack: "mit out sound." Most persuasively, the term developed in the early days of film history from the fact that the noise of the camera was so great and the the power for it was finally placed off-stage in the sound recording room. When a shot was called for that did not want sound, the production sound mixer on stage communicated by intercom to the sound recordist and said, "Roll the motor only,"— which, became "motor only shot," or MOS. Emily preferred Mit Out Sound.)

• • •

In the first sequence, Sarah and Barnes are getting married in a small country church in front of a few extras, picked up from Ocotillo Springs and environs. As they're about to say their vows, the front door of the church is slammed open.

Scanlan.

It was more powerful than they had dreamed. Joanna and Solange both said they thought Ben at this age had a good future as a screen heavy. There was something about his even-featured, but decadent, obsessed bearing that, before he'd acted a lick, was mesmerizing and sinister.

He strode down the aisle, grabbed Sarah's hand, and without even glancing at Barnes, dragged the horrified Emily back up the aisle like chattel, like John Wayne dragging Maureen O'Hara across the countryside in *The Quiet Man.*

Emily, "playing" panic, was beyond persuasive.

The shot then came slowly around from over Tom's shoulder and finally into a close-up of John Barnes and a mock-up background of the church's apse and altar—still to be inserted. This shot would be dissolved, with immaculate timing, into one of their "library" shots: John Wayne, looking crestfallen.

The next day, they began work on a sequence to be used in flashback while Gabriel is telling John Barnes the story of his leaving home to head west. Again, with Gabriel, Solange would insert close-ups of James Dean when they were called for. The sequence was intended to show Gabriel's day-to-day life, and included a scene where he confronts Scanlan and takes off to find Barnes—leaving focus on an enraged Scanlan.

Jimmy had mixed feelings, shooting at this location. It reminded him of his abbreviated summer at camp. Like Camp Cottonwood, this place was surprisingly green in the middle of the otherwise mostly dry Arizona landscape. It also featured one of the same characters from the other time.

But *this* man was the polar opposite of the first. *This* Ben Bennett had an aura of something malevolent, stillborn. Jimmy was almost incapable of looking at him. Being forced to act with, even to just be around Ben Bennett, gave him chills. It was a perfect fit for Gabriel's feelings about Scanlan.

• • •

The rest of the days on the "Eastern" location completed the remaining sequences that were to take place in Pennsylvania: Sarah gathers her belongings and heads west; Scanlan discovers Sarah is gone and, anger becoming obsession, follows her. They also filmed a series of MOS shots of each of the four characters from Tom's painting simply going about the business of living. These were to be used in a pair of montages to show the lives these people led before they started west.

• • •

Back in the desert wilderness, Tom and Jimmy shot a scene between Barnes and Gabriel that Wayne and Dean hadn't gotten to: one of the clearly necessary scenes that didn't exist in the footage that had been shot in 1955.

The tension between the actors continued to be palpable, even more than before. Joanna was happy with it, but all Emily could feel, aside from aggravation with Solange, was the rawness of her own nerves and guilt. Tom and Jimmy gave off the feeling of genuinely hating each other now—Jimmy the most transparently.

Emily knew it was her fault.

"What's wrong, Em?" asked Joanna one evening after they'd watched the dailies.

"Nothing. But how the hell can you and *Mizzzzz Borugian* be so goddam calm?"

"Because it's going well."

"Is it?"

"You know it is."

"I don't know *anything*."

• • •

They worked from sunrise to sunset every day. Twice, they had to stop filming, cover the equipment, and make for the trailers until a desert squall had passed. Several times, they thought a deluge was coming. It usually didn't.

The lines between the days became blurred. They would go back to the motel, quickly eat whatever was served them, fall into their beds, and sooner than they could believe were on their way to the set again.

For Emily, the lightheadedness she'd experienced after the night around the campfire with Hugh Palmer and Gil Kahcheenay seemed to echo in the back of her mind throughout the filming. Day for night shooting amplified it and exaggerated the dislocating effects of their location work.

It does that. It permeates the inner folds of consciousness and gets into the bones, creating a sense of perpetual twilight.

3

OCTOBER, 1979

On the set, living this day—as are the others—in the twilight of day for night, Emily asks Gil Kahcheenay if he knows what's causing her to feel that she's living in a constant state of present time. She had fantasized never having to live in the past again, but hadn't realized that it might cancel all sensations of the future as well—leaving only the instant she was living in.

"There is no beginning, no end," says Gil. "We think we've forgotten our past, but none of it goes away. It's all happening again. Until you see the face of it, it keeps curling back on itself."

"You haven't answered my ... pardon me, my direct question."

"I know that. I'd like to help you, but I can't. You're asking me a question only you can answer, and only when you're ready."

Emily frowns. "And the *tarapo*?"

"Has nothing to do with it. What kind of a shaman would I be if I didn't imply that I have magic?"

"You *told* us you have magic."

He gazes at her with gentle eyes. "The filming will remain in the minds of all of you, forever, as if it's happening now – again and again, front to back, back to front, over and over; now and ..." He smiles and holds a hand out, palm up.

"Will we learn from it?" says Emily.

"Of course."

"And your wind of truth? The lost mirage?" says Emily. "Do we have that to look forward to?"

"Yes, you do. The secret is to recognize it." He looks at some point between Emily and the distant mountains. "You can, right this second, reach out and touch it. You can smell it in the air."

"And we *all* have the ... this ... whatever?"

Gil smiles again.

• • •

Self-consciousness is an inflexible characteristic, obstinate and unbending; it is the number one killer of actors. It comes in ten thousand guises, each marked by a form of posturing that keeps the human being within the actor snugly hidden from view. It conceals the guts of life—mandatory for the audience to see, hear, and mostly feel, if the drama has any chance to rise above the trivial. For as long as it lasts, self-consciousness hides the important stuff as effectively as timidity hides courage.

Improvising only has a chance to work when the actors aren't "thinking." It happens when the material being brought to life takes on a reality more powerful than the performers' consciousness of themselves. It's like tossing a hat on a hat rack. If you just toss it, you have a good chance to hit the target; if you give any thought to it, the hat is probably on its way to the floor.

The clearing: Gabriel, John Barnes, Sarah, and Scanlan.

Scanlan's prop pistol is drawn but not aimed. Each of the principals is trying to look out from Tom's painting through the eyes of his own character.

"What's going on here?" says Solange to Jimmy. "You're an independent author of this moment."

He shakes his head, beyond unhappy with her autocratic style. "I had nothing to do with it," he says. "I see the others, but I don't know anything about them."

"Then why don't you find out? You could start with him." She points at Ben. "The man with the Smith & Wesson. Do you have any questions for him?"

Jimmy looks at Ben. "… No." With a wobbly voice, he says, "It won't solve a thing to talk to him."

"Where's your *outrage*? I've never seen such restraint. Let's not call this *Showdown*. Let's title it *Lay Down and Die*. That way nobody has to hear anything unpleasant, or God forbid, human." She scans all their faces. "Is that what you want?"

Her eyes come to rest on Tom. "He's aiming a gun at you. You're being violated."

Glancing at Ben, Tom says, "I see him. I just don't want to start a bloodbath." He scrapes a hand across his chin and says, "Put it away, please."

Ben holsters the Smith & Wesson.

Solange barks at him: "I didn't tell you to do that."

Emily says, "Don't! You shouldn't talk to him that way!"

"Oh?" Solange turns to her. "Are you afraid he might break? What happens then?"

Emily scowls. "To hell with this. Let's go to Phoenix and cast somebody who's up for this shit. We'll reshoot my scenes. This is just stupid."

"What's stupid about it?" says Solange.

"It makes my skin crawl."

"Which part of it is doing that to you?"

"All of it."

"How do you feel about cockroaches?"

"What?" snaps Emily. "I don't like them."

"They make your skin crawl?"

Emily hisses. "Yesss."

"And you can't see how that might be useful here?"

Emily's eyes dart from Solange to the ground, to several points in the sky, to the mountains in the distance, then back to Solange. She takes in a deep breath and whispers, "All right, lady, let's do this goddam thing."

Jimmy, who has not been looking at Emily, notices Scanlan's hand is still on the pistol and, purposely giving himself no time to think, ad libs: "There was a lie at the core of it, wasn't there? What was wrong with you?"

Ben answers just as impulsively, "I was doing what I had to do."

"Were you just … *afraid*? You were supposed to lead the way, guide me."

Ben, who looks like an aging choirboy caught with his hand in the collection plate, turns to Solange. "What's that mean? I told you I don't do this."

When she doesn't respond, Ben's gaze swings back to Jimmy, who is now immersed, watching him steadily.

Sheet lightning flares in the distance, setting the western sky aglow.

"I don't think you really want solutions," Emily says to Solange. "I think you *want* a bloodbath."

"Yes! I've been telling you that for quite a while now." She looks at Tom. "And I really don't care what shape it takes. Give me *something*!"

"I don't have enough to go on," says Tom. "My character doesn't have enough background. Anyway, why doesn't Barnes get his spirit back? I can't relate to somebody who's just stopped caring."

"He hasn't stopped caring. He has one of the oldest problems in the world. He's gotten lost. He's trying to find his way back.

You have to figure out his path for him. You have to give him his compass. That's your task."

"All right!" says Tom. "John Barnes doesn't know where he came from. So he's never been sure what he's supposed to want."

Solange shakes her head. "He knows. At bottom, everybody knows what they want. John Barnes might be embarrassed he wants it. He might be afraid to let others know he wants it, but he knows. Quick. What does Barnes want?"

"A home."

"And how does he go about getting it?"

"He goes out to find it."

"Where?"

"As far away as he can get."

"So, then does he really want a home?"

Tom moans. "But I have a home."

"Where?"

"Inside of me, but ..."

"But what?"

He looks into the distance, far across the desert. "It's lonely there."

• • •

Edgar Scanlan's first horse, a pewter-gray gelding, has come up lame and lies on his side near a hummock of piñon. Scanlan kneels down next to him.

From another, closer angle the camera sees tears in the man's eyes, hollowed from the hardships of his long journey. He tries to find words to say to his terrified companion. Without looking away or changing the expression on his face, he slips his Smith & Wesson out of the tooled leather holster on his right hip, strokes the horse's head one last time, twists a half revolution away, turns his head, and pulls the trigger.

Still on his knees, crying, he looks across the great expanse of scrubland. The desolation of it grieves him. The smell of sage fills his nostrils. Overcome yet again by the sting of humiliation, he's already forgotten this.

• • •

"What are you up to, Skippy? Where are you going?"

Ben is wearing gray slacks, with a blue blazer over a white oxford cloth shirt and a blue and yellow paisley tie. "That's the thing, you see. I've got to go away."

"Where? What are you dressed up for?"

"I was just trying on some ... 'traveling' clothes. I've got a job."

"What kind of a job?"

"Acting." He can tell his father has been crying. It's because of the dog. The old man has been crying over El Poochino.

Ben Sr. studies his son's face with contempt. "Are you still at that? *Why? You aren't any good at it. It doesn't make you happy."*

Ben inhales deeply, loudly through his nose, as if the sound of it might erase his father's words. "I have mixed feelings right now because I've got to leave you." With methodical care, he takes off his jacket and lays it neatly on the corduroy-covered slipper chair.

• • •

"Ben?" the first AD calls to him. "That's a cut. Please stand in while we re-set. The director will get the walk-out in the next angle."

Ben gets up, holds his hands out in front of him, and sees that there is almost no tremor left.

• • •

Joanna is watching a camera rehearsal—or Solange might be shooting for all she knows—of the scripted sequence that sets up the scene they've spent most of the morning attempting to improvise.

Gil walks over and watches with her.

In one hand, he holds what looks like a photograph album. It's old, made of cowhide, gone dark and brittle with age.

On the set, a woman rides down from the crest of a hill toward the three men.

The shot lasts a long time. It will be mixed with intercuts of each man watching her. Gabriel and Barnes know, even from a distance, that it's Sarah.

Gil watches, fascinated.

Before Sarah arrives in the picture, Barnes looks back at his old antagonist. "What do you want, Scanlan?"

"I've traveled more than two thousand miles to kill you."

"A man would need a lot of hate to come this far to do somethin' so unnecessary."

"It's not personal," says Scanlan, his hand tensing on his Smith & Wesson. "I'm doin' it because—"with the smallest shrug—"It's what I gotta do."

"You can't kill him in front of my mother!" screams Gabriel.

Scanlan looks at the boy, then back at Barnes. "Tomorrow. Right here. Sunrise."

Solange shouts, "That's the cut!"

• • •

Watching the action, Gil says, "I wonder that Emily is not an actress. She has an extraordinary light about her."

"So it seems," says Joanna. "Do you still like to watch movies shoot, after all these years?"

"I like to get away from the goats sometimes."

"What have you got there?" She's looking at the album in his hand. "Photographs?"

Gil smiles. "I thought you'd like to see this." He opens it and flips through several pages of pictures.

"Family?" says Joanna.

Gil beams. "Yes. Four generations."

Tom walks over and joins them.

"Would you like to see my pictures?" Gil asks him.

Tom nods, but he's still preoccupied by the scene he just played.

Gil shows them several pages, pictures of his parents and children, all distinguished looking people, all with Gil's chiseled looks. When he comes to the end: "This is the picture I especially wanted you to see."

He turns to the last page and shows them a color close-up of himself and John Wayne.

Gil looks young and serious, Wayne is laughing.

On a chain around Wayne's neck is a horseshoe with D-U-K-E clearly visible across the center and with what could be emeralds for nails.

Tom's eyes roll back.

He buckles to the ground.

• • •

They work on a sequence in which Gabriel spirits Sarah out of Scanlan's camp, takes her into the clearing, and they talk. It's nearing sunrise, still nighttime to the camera.

Gabriel says, "Ma, why did you do it? Why did you come all this way? You can't *do* nothin'." When Sarah no more than looks at him, resolute in her determination, he says, "You've got to get him to leave or one of them is going to get killed."

Sarah shakes her head. "It's too late."

"What's he want to prove?" says the boy. "It wasn't Barnes's fault anyway. You've got to go back now. If you weren't here, maybe we'd come up with a way they could save face."

"Why do I think you're worried about something else?" says Sarah.

"And cut!" barks Solange.

Emily is startled. "I thought that was a rehearsal."

"Telephoto master," says Solange. "Look back there."

Emily turns to look in the direction she's pointing, but Solange takes her by the arm and forestalls her. "You've got enough to worry about. … Here." She hands Jimmy and Emily loose pages. "I want to try something."

As she skims the scene, Emily goes ashen beneath her makeup.

She turns and heads toward her dressing room. As she strides away, she shouts, "Bullshit! This is *not* what we decided. This is *bullshit*!" She repeats "bullshit" over and over until she's out of earshot.

• • •

Late at night, Joanna stops by the Dude Drop Inn, the Trading Post's bar and restaurant, to get a sandwich, and finds Jimmy alone at a back booth, on the verge of becoming seriously smashed.

"Are you okay?" she asks.

"Yeah, I'm just trying to loosen myself up a little."

"Don't get too loose."

"Do you want to join me?"

She hesitates. "I was going to go up and—" She smiles and raises a hand in surrender. "Sure. Why not?"

After she's had a margarita and finished her sandwich—grilled jack cheese and Ortega chili peppers—and Jimmy has had most of one more large ale, he says, "How's it end? Is Sarah his mother? Did that all get worked out? I know you know."

"You just wanted to get me drunk so I'd 'come across,' right?"

Jimmy smiles. "Maybe. And if she is his mother, they aren't going to be having … *you-know-what* together, are they?"

"Solange would have me pilloried if I said anything."

Jimmy nods. "I know. It's just got me concerned. It's a little hard to work on a character if you don't know what's happening. Maybe it's not that way for everybody, but it is for me."

"Solange thinks that's good," says Joanna. "And we've got to let her do it her way. She's the best." She shrugs, smiling distantly.

"Yes, of course she is. But I don't always see what other people see." He chuckles. "Neither would you if you were me. It's dark and scary in here." He touches his temples with his middle and index fingers.

"A lot of people feel that way."

He nods and takes a gulp of ale. "I think maybe I keep to myself too much."

Joanna smiles uncomfortably. "Yeah, maybe that's it."

"Almost dying in a car accident has made me think. I realize I don't believe in a single conclusion I've ever come to. Whatever my beliefs are, if I were really pressed, I'd give them up in a second. I don't know what I want. I don't want to be alone—I know that. And liars are always alone. I've never been able to be with anybody. I've never been with a woman. … I've never been with a man." He smiles blearily. "I've never been with fucking anybody. I live entirely inside myself."

Joanna doesn't know where to look. "You've *never*, uh …?"

Jimmy squeaks a little laugh and holds his hands up like a burlesque comedian surrendering to the straight man's harmless bullying. "It's okay. I'll be all right." He fixes her with a serious gaze. "Maybe what I'm saying is that I was always too involved with myself, and my mother was right. She said it was all about me. And I guess that's true—here I am babbling at you. I mean, if it weren't true, I'd have found a way to change things, wouldn't I? She always called me selfish and a liar and a lot of other things she was herself. And it didn't take long to figure out—her being the leader and me the follower—that I wasn't going to be able to change the rules of her game. So, I played … you know, *within* them.

"But in order to do that—since it was a rigged game—I learned to cheat and to lie, which made her opinion of me a self-fulfilling prophecy. And pretty soon, I had *become* her—I had let myself be intimidated into seeing out of her … *heartbroken* eyes, and I couldn't bust out of that no matter how hard I tried."

Joanna searches for *anything* to say. "So … so, how does that tie in with being by yourself?"

"If you *are* someone, you want what that person wants. My mother wanted a real man. And so do I—not sexually I don't think. Sexually, I want her, or something like her—in a manner of speaking, you know? But I get confused. I want her, but I don't want to be around her—which kind of limits my options. And so, I stay all by myself, a lonely liar, who wishes with all his heart he was a 'real man.' "

Joanna quietly clears her throat. "Well. It certainly sounds like you have something to deal with there."

He nods, gazing into her eyes. "Uh-huh."

They're both silent for a while. Then, Jimmy says with a tone of final punctuation: "Sometimes, when you don't have anybody of your own to say these things to, you just say them to whoever is kind enough to listen, and try to learn what you can from their body language and the look on their face."

Joanna's look is about the same one a mother gives her child after he's told her about the interesting cult he just joined.

• • •

Tom sits by himself in his darkened motel room.

He's not sure what direction it's coming from, but he hears a strain of Paul McCartney warbling about how to fly, despite having broken wings.

He realizes the old man isn't going to appear this time.

• • •

"What are you doing in Arizona?" he demands of the man in the open doorway of room 153.

Hopper knew he would finally show up.

Until now, beginning with the first time, the time he saw him in the hall, Tom has imagined Hopper as a mischievous rabbit, purposely letting himself be seen by the fox, just as he slips safely into his warren.

"It's late," Hopper says. He yawns and his mouth slips into its habitual contemptuous smirk. "I know you won't mind if I tell you that what I am doing here is your business only insofar as I let it be."

Tom feels as if he is someone else. He reaches out, picks Hopper up, and carries him into the alcove between the outer door and the room. He slams the outer door shut with one foot and pins Hopper against the wall—so that his head is wedged into the corner where the wall meets the ceiling and the header above the entranceway into the bedroom. The only illumination comes from a nightlight through the open bathroom door.

"Were you there?" says Tom.

Even with his head and neck crammed nearly into a right angle with his torso, Hopper's inflections are venomous. "I don't know what you're talking about."

"You had something to do with the first filming, didn't you?"

Like a bratty seven-year-old, Hopper clamps his mouth shut.

"How did you know about this *location …* this *time?" says Tom.*

"You're barking up the wrong tree," says Hopper. "Look to the villain. There's a villain in every story, and it's not me. I may know the villain, but it's not me. Think of the villain in your story."

"Put him down," says a throaty female voice.

Tom looks to the left and sees a form in the darkness, sitting on the furthest bed.

He swings his eyes back to Hopper.

"Do you want me to call the desk?" says the woman.

Hopper looks down at Tom's shrouded eyes. "That won't be necessary. He's doing it again. He's forgetting even as it's happening."

4

The next day, the few cirrus clouds from the night before have merged into cirrostratus and continue to thicken in the western sky. The temperature is dropping and the desert air is still, harbinger of a cloudburst.

Ben has been walking his second horse, Brownie, in the clearing.

He ties the mare to a birch tree with a lead line and halter and walks toward the set.

• • •

On the other side of the clearing, Tom is giving Cimarron a workout.

Riding at a slow trot, he looks out over the patchwork of gulches and canyons to the north and gives in to the exhilaration of being by himself in the midst of God's cathedral.

"Aren't you just some kind of slug, if you do this?" says the old man, riding along next to him on a white stallion instead of his usual chestnut quarter horse. "If you don't ask a few pointy questions at a time like this, how do you learn anything? If you let yourself be satisfied with the simpleminded contentment of some pretty scenery, or spend your life moaning about who you're *not* or how lousy you got treated when you were a kid, then what have you aspired to? What do you have to be proud of ? How are you going to learn to grow up the way a man ought to? History is full of kids who got treated lousy. A lot of them rise above it."

"Leave me alone."

"There are no second chances. You only get one life."

"You keep saying that. What I need to know is how to use the one I've got."

Wayne grins. "Very good, son. Just when I'm losing all hope, you produce an acceptable form of the right question."

"And the answer?"

"Ah, that's the tricky part."

"No disrespect, but how do you know *anything* about *any* of this?"

Wayne looks at him with a rare ironic smile. "I don't. It just feels like I do because I'm John Wayne. John Wayne says things with authority, but John Wayne, you boob, is only an actor. He doesn't know any more than you do. From your POV, he's just a little older—dead, if you want to be technical." He mouths his birth name: 'Marion Morrison.' No wonder I had to be so damned manly."

"But if you don't know—if *you* don't know now—" He studies the old face and thinks for a moment he can see the imprint of all the years of photography it has suffered.

"Disappointing, isn't it?" Wayne shrugs. "Unfortunately, it turns out being dead is no more educational than being a movie star."

"Don't you have some kind of best guess?"

"All right, but listen good because I'm on my way to other regions." He leans in. "My opinion is that you need to stop running away from the *showdowns*. That includes not letting the painful scenes drift away unexamined. Never mind medicine men and mirages on desert winds. If you want to be alive, don't close your eyes to any of it. If you want to arrive at wherever you're riding to, if you want to know whose dream you're dreaming, you'd better do some seeing, *some* listening, and some, absent of all bullshit, remembering."

• • •

"Who are you?" Tom says to the woman in the darkness.

"Well, look at you. You're awake," says Hopper. "You know perfectly well who she is."

"I do not!" What do you want?"

"Did you know she was watching, when you picked up the horseshoe and the painting at my saloon?"

"No! She couldn't *have! She wasn't ..." Tom's eyes are still fixed on the darkened figure of the woman. "You're not who you're trying to make me believe you are!" He looks back and forth between them. "She died! I don't know who she is. You died! Paige Leone died! You* told *me she did!"*

As if he's been studying Jack Nicholson line readings, Hopper says, "I lied. He chuckles. "She was watching. Do you remember that day I pointed to the barstool nearest you?" The chuckle goes falsetto. "And you sat on it. The main room surveillance camera had you framed perfectly. She wanted to see your reaction and she wanted a record of it."

"Reaction to what?"

"To the horseshoe. She wanted to see if you'd remember."

"Remember WHAT?"

"That you'd seen it before. Back when you thought you were pursuing her, but she was stalking you; you spent a night with her. Afterwards, that same night, you asked her about the charm she was wearing on the chain around her neck."

"I don't remember any—" He stops. "—WHY was she 'stalking' me?"

Hopper laughs obscenely. "She wanted to be present when you realized for the second time where the pendant came from."

Tom stares into middle distance, his mouth halfway open. "The second time WHAT?"

"She gave it to your father, but obviously she found a way to take it back. Then, before her 'passing,' she left it to you. ...God, you're dense."

"Why are you saying all this?"

The white stallion rears, pivoting 360 degrees, until "Duke" is facing Tom again.

"Good," says Wayne. " 'Why' is the most productive question human beings ask each other—although not always productive in the way they might expect. So here's one for you. WHY are you not seeing that there's something … OFF about these people? Pay attention. Back it up. One line should do it."

"She gave it to your father," says Hopper, "but obviously she found a way to take it back. Then, before her 'passing,' she left it to you. ...God, you're dense."

"I have no memory of this," says Tom.

"Incorrect, cowboy. You knew the first time you saw it where that pendant came from, but you pushed it down the way you push everything down that scares you. Later, when she left it to you as a bequest, you tried to push it down one more time. But it wouldn't stay there, would it?"

Tom stares at him.

"She knew you'd buried that memory, but she thought it would float back to you when I gave you the picture and the pendant at the Blue Martini."

"WHAT would float back?"

"Have you REALLY never asked yourself why you look so much like the man you make your living impersonating?"

"She thought WHAT would float back?"

"Because you DID remember—for a few seconds. She told me there was a certain look in your eye, that night, *when it registered to you who you had 'gone to bed' with. She wanted you to have the horseshoe, so the memory would come back, and this time stay back, and you'd never again forget what you did."*

"WHAT did I do?" Tom's heart is pounding. "Goddam it, tell me!"

"Oh, you stupid man," says Hopper. "You know by now; you just won't say it." He giggles. "I'll put it another way: when the most famous man who did what you did—guy named Oedipus—realized it, he stabbed his eyes out."

• • •

"Tom's heart is still pounding. He has not fainted."

As he looks again at the woman sitting on the other bed only a few feet away, a familiar voice echoes back from faraway: "So, then do you really WANT a home?"

He looks again at Hopper. "You know what I think?"

Ignoring him, Hopper says, "Do you remember this man?"

"Of course I do," says the woman in the darkness, her voice low and husky.

"I think you're both insane," says Tom.

The white stallion rears up and spins a single revolution. "There is hope for you still," says the movie star.

"By the way," says Hopper, unable to hear any words but his own, "I think this is the moment to say it clearly." Expelling a fine mist of spittle: "Your mother was not killed in a car crash." He looks at the woman. "Tell him your name. He's still not getting it."

"He remembers me," says the woman.

"Who are you?" says Tom.

Hopper hits a light switch and Tom sees her clearly, sitting on the second bed. He recognizes her as the woman Hopper told him had died. She is as lovely as he remembers, but in her mid-forties now, with all the allure of a radiant young girl who has matured into a beautiful woman.

"Tom Manfredo," says Hopper with grinning formality, "meet Betty Merrow."

"No," says Tom. "She's Paige Leone. And she's not dead."

"Doesn't miss a trick," sneers Hopper.

"Either way, she is NOT ... WHO YOU ARE TELLING ME SHE IS."

• • •

"Tom? Better start in. Need you in five for lineup."

Tom looks up, waves to the second AD, and turns back to Wayne. "Why do you believe I'm Tom Manfredo and not ... who they're telling me I am?"

Looking as sheepish as "Duke" can, Wayne says, " 'To D from P.' " He shrugs, "To me from Pappy ... John Ford. I don't know how that woman, Paige Leone—or Betty Merrow as I knew her—got hold of that pendant. I thought I'd lost it. She must have swiped it from me."

"And the picture?" whispers Tom. "What was the picture for?"

"I knew she liked to sketch and to paint. She was pretty good. Why she chose to paint that particular scene I have no idea. ... Well, actually, I guess I do now."

"But I don't understand those people," says Tom, "and I still don't remember what I'm supposed to."

"I know," says Wayne. "That's what you do, just like me, when you get pushed into a corner. You either forget things, or you get pissed off and take 'em way too far. You vent your rage, first on yourself, then on people who don't deserve it, on innocents who aren't guilty of anything apart from being born the way they were—like this poor sap Philip Hopper and his deranged girlfriend—and all on account of you not believing you are who you are, even though you finally know who you are."

"But I only have your word."

"And that misconception, to answer the question that has lately tarried between us," says Wayne, "is why I'm still here. … Okay, first off: when you return to room 153, and they tell you more lies—which they will; they are, after all, two of the three the villains in this piece—just inform them that you are a descendant of a long line of Italian fishermen and a fine human being and that they do not own you."

As older cowboys often do, Wayne readjusts himself in his saddle. "Okay. It looks like I gotta guide you just a little more. Not fifteen minutes ago, on your way to room 153, you picked up a message from the desk. It was from your not so quick on the uptake detective friend … 'Donkey, the Sleuth.' "

"I have no memory of that," says Tom.

"Of course you don't. I told you, that's what you do. … Now lift your right hand, reach into your left shirt pocket, take out what you find there, and read what's written on it."

Tom takes out the telegram he finds in his pocket and opens it.

> "TOM. HAVE LOCATED YOUR OFFICIAL BIRTH RECORD. PARENTS' NAMES: ANTONIO AND PATRICIA MANFREDO. CONGRATULATIONS. YOU ARE YOU. YOUR BUDDY, DONALD KEY."

"So?" says Wayne. "Are you satisfied?"

After a long beat, Tom says … "Maybe." He frowns. "Maybe. … But I'm still a little worried about my state of mind."

"That's okay, you've been through some ... deep manure. But you're gonna be fine now."

"What about those people in room 153?" says Tom.

"The villains?"

"He told me he wasn't a villain."

Wayne grins. "That's why everyone loves you, son. You don't think villains exist."

"Sure, I do. I just don't like to make people feel any worse than they already do. And anyway, this is about something else."

"Right. That's the other thing. Welcome to the world of celebrity, son. You have apparently become one. Don't take it lightly. That woman, who would like you to believe she's your mother and that I am your daddy, is just one example of how insane your fans can be."

"Do I have to go back to … *that room?*"

"You don't have to go anywhere you don't want to go."

" … But why do they do that?"

"I don't know," says Wayne, shaking his head. "I don't think anyone really understands why certain people get carried off into total insanity by even the briefest encounters with luminaries, idols, VIPs … all that crap. If, God forbid, you happen to be someone like me, who has been, for a couple of heartbeats, recognized by most of the humans on the planet, it drives a countless number of those folks altogether doolally.

"You may well become recognized," he continues, "not as me, but as yourself, and you may draw—well, you already have—a few lunatics of your own. First, don't imagine you understand them. There's always a new bunch of crazies around the corner, like the ones in room 153. They want to own you, in some cases, like yours, so they can humiliate you as badly as they feel the world has done it to them."

"But I gotta tell you, they did sort of understand me," says Tom.

"I didn't say they were stupid. And nobody ever said these people can't be gifted at what they do—especially reading weakness. Some of them, like those two in room 153, can create a world that's unnerving in its resemblance to the real one."

"Why do they do it in the first place?"

Wayne emits a shaky old man sigh, is quiet for a beat, then says, "The ones who go to extravagant lengths to do this kind of thing, do it because they feel you already belong to them. The ones with *real* trouble don't just want to see you, they want *you* to see *them*. The couple in room 153 are the reason we hire bodyguards."

"But the story they've concocted, they seem to believe it."

"That's what happens."

"But why? There's no truth in it."

"Doesn't matter. They've convinced themselves. When you're that far gone to begin with, that's all it takes." He looks out across the desert. "I've always hated this kinda thing"—he shakes his head —"but somebody shoulda helped those poor folks when they were still very small."

"You said you knew why she painted that picture. Why?"

"My guess is that somehow she was seeing into the future and realized that in one way or another, you were the closest she would ever get to feeling even a little bit up to scratch in this world." He shrugs. "She had to latch onto that with every ounce of grit she had."

After a silence between them, Tom says, "I gotta go rehearse the next scene." He looks off toward the distant mountains. "But I'm still …"

"A little weak in the knees?" says Wayne.

"That gets to the spirit of it."

Doing his best parody of himself, Wayne says, "Wull, don't be ascared. This is *not* one of those heroic ventures you're going to have to saddle up for. You'll just chew on this one for as long as you need to, then you'll get past it and allow it to slip into routine memory—not the kind that haunts you day and night the rest of your life." He gazes into his protégé's eyes. "I know it's contradictory, it all is, but once you've paid your dues and understand that you've paid them, you do not have to pay them again. You don't have to deny yourself the pleasures of life. That's one of the nice things about having your eyes opened."

Tom sighs and reins Cimarron into a tight turn. "Where are you off to?"

Wayne swivels to face him again and lifts a shoulder. "We don't get shooting schedules over here."

He smiles, raises a hand in salute, turns west, and begins to canter off toward his new dominion.

Tom calls after him, "But I *still* don't understand *why*. *Why* did they do that?"

Almost too far away to be of any further use, Wayne spurs his mount, and as he disappears, booms, "Always a great question, 'Why?' But don't set your heart on too many answers to it. Oh, and one last thing," he adds, "me to you."

"What's that?" whispers Tom.

"I am a myth, Pilgrim. Don't try to make anything real out of me."

• • •

Emily has a recurring nightmare. She's on a stairway, climbing up to the floor above her. It's dark. She can barely see the wrought iron railing or the thick carpeting on the steps. When she reaches the top of the stairs, she sees the arched entrance to a cavernous room. She doesn't think there's any exit from it, or if there is, she can't see it. The back and sides of the room are in forbidding darkness. The only obstacle separating her from this space is a thick velvet rope, the kind that in the old days they used in most movie theater lobbies.

The reason this dream is a nightmare to her is that just as she's about to turn around and retreat back down the stairs, where she's safe, the velvet rope drops, and she knows she has no choice but to go in.

She heads toward the clearing.

5

It's still morning, but it feels like evening. The coming storm, mixed with the sharp smell of sagebrush, charges the air with electricity. The branches of the trees at the edge of the clearing have begun to stir and twist in a rising breeze.

The four actors have assembled fifty feet into the clearing with Solange and some of the crew. With a nod from Solange, everyone but the actors goes off to the edge of the woods to wait.

Solange says to the cast, "This is the payoff scene. Everything's at stake for all of you—right now." Deciding she's begun too bluntly, she adds, "But I don't want you to feel pressured." She laughs. "On the other hand, how can you *not*? There are certain things a director can't put into a rosy light, yes? This is not a rosy scene." She shrugs. "And I'm not reassuring you, am I? Oh, well. Bullshit anyway, let's get on with it.

"So. Scanlan has awakened before sunrise, finds Sarah not in the camp, and comes out to this spot where he's supposed to meet Barnes later. He finds mother and son together."

Jimmy says, "Will we be filming that"—there was an inaudible adjective—"scene … the one Emily and I started to work on?"

"I'd like to say yes, just to watch your face, but my producer"—she nods at Emily—"thinks some parts of our truth may, paradoxically, be better served if they lie beneath the surface. And who knows? Maybe there *are* times when people need to see their truths through at least … *some* kind of filter." She frowns up at the darkening sky. "But only if the spirit of truth is totally intact."

"But is she my mother or isn't she?" says Jimmy. "Don't you think that's an important thing for me to know?"

"That's not the point. The point is there is something tying you to this woman—an umbilical … *cable*—something beyond a normal mother-son relationship. What you need, along with a little luck, is to figure out what that relationship is."

Emily groans. "Stop it. You're embarrassing him."

"I hope so. One of the things you people have going for you is that you're young. You feel these things deeply, and they're still close enough to the surface that you show what you feel—except when you're 'acting.' Then, you're statues."

"Maybe if one time you would just shut up."

She turns to Tom. "Yes?"

"Maybe we could get to something. We've learned lines. Do we get to say the damned lines or not?"

"I don't know. Maybe. Eventually. For now, why don't you tell us what's going on?"

"I don't know what you're talking about."

"Sure you do. Go ahead." She points at Ben. "What's going on with him?"

Tom aims his frown at Ben. "How the hell do I know?"

Ben regards him warily.

Tom sighs, then, gazing at him again, finds himself trying to figure him out. "He's come here this morning, same as me, to see what's going on between these two." He glances at Jimmy and Emily.

"And what does he find?" says Solange.

"He doesn't know." He studies Ben's face carefully. Above them, the sun breaks through the clouds for an instant, blinking like a great eye. "I think Ben's one of those people who's never been able to figure out where he ends and everybody else begins."

The sky grows darker. "A mountain of pain has been triggered by him, and he knows it. That's too much for a man to take."

Ben, silent to this point, takes an impulsive step toward Emily. "Sarah, we're going back."

"I don't want to." She looks at her brother with a mixture of curiosity and dread and notices that he's trembling.

"It's not time to be here yet," says Ben. "I'm not … *We're* not ready for this. It's not dawn. It's not time for the showdown. I can't leave you alone here." He looks vaguely at Jimmy. "With him."

Motionless, Emily stares at him. "I remember a letter." She nods vaguely at Jimmy, but without looking away from Ben. "Why am I remembering this now? There was a letter. Have you remembered it, too? He read it to us. It was his worst rage, ever."

Except for the trembling, Ben is dead still.

"Say something."

Her brother's mouth is locked shut.

Jimmy, watching Ben, hypnotized, says, "But he's okay." He shoots glances at all of them. "Can't you see that? He's been through a lot. He's been in that … prison he's built. He can't help it that people don't like him. It's not his fault. He hasn't done anything to deserve this. When he started off he had such—everyone must have seen it—such … *promise*."

Emily's gaze is still frozen on Ben. "What is it, Skippy? What's wrong with you?"

Ben looks from Jimmy back at his sister. After a bewildered moment, he drinks in a breath and whispers, "You were able to take it. I couldn't."

Sheet lightning flashes in the distance.

Tom says to Solange, "You have to go away. This is not an improv. This has nothing to do with the movie, or you."

Solange starts to speak, but Tom cuts her off, speaking evenly, "Go back to the trucks. We have to finish this."

Solange doesn't move.

Tom whispers with an intensity that silences the desert: "This is for invalids only."

Not looking away from Ben, Emily says, "*Go. Now.*"

Solange would normally be able to think of half a dozen things to say, but staring at Tom, she sees Ethan Edwards's eyes in *The Searchers*, unbendable from his purpose. She turns and walks toward the camera crew and the trucks.

• • •

In the silence, Emily remains concentrated on Ben. She nods at Jimmy. "Why *him*? Why did you do … whatever you … *did* to this … *child*?"

Ben stares at the ground for a long moment, then, with no trace of his RADA accent, says: "It was late … dark. I was stoned. We weren't even thinking about him—or consequences. … What are *consequences*? You don't worry about what's going to happen later, when you know you're going to get "—he looks for the right words—"get *yours*. Nothing makes them happier than … watching you … *bleed*. The only thing in the world that existed that night, that moment, was … *that moment*. Nothing else to worry about." He looks at Emily but doesn't see her. "So. You get to do whatever … it *occurs* to you to do."

• • •

Sheet lightning colors the western sky green and magenta. In his guts, Jimmy recalls the smells, sounds, and excitement of his summer at Camp Cottonwood, and in the same moment, understands how little bearing time has on his life. He wonders why he never grasped that before.

• • •

He walks on a wooded path at night, led by a man he dreads, a man lit by the eerie glow of a camping lantern.

Even though he'd hated him one second earlier, Jimmy now feels that he can trust this man, and he's not afraid, being alone with him. For a moment, he sees him three-dimensionally, as if lit from all sides. In profile, he sees the robot smile. But it's okay. The fullness and depth of the figure, the trustworthy, masculine bearing, persuades Jimmy to feel peaceful, reconciled to whatever is going to happen. Even though the man is only a few years older; against any reason whatever, Jimmy sees him as a ... father. It's more than just crazy, he knows that—like letting himself believe that, up close, Hitler wouldn't have been such a bad guy; that if he really knew you and if you were lucky, he'd like you and then you'd like him, and maybe you'd be pals. Except ...

The light is wrong.

The man is not *only illuminated by light escaping from his own lantern.*

Jimmy turns and follows the diverging beam of light to its source.

He can't see a face, but he recognizes the voice.

"What do you say, mate?"

• • •

"We were in that cabin," Jimmy says to Ben. "Have you thought about it in all these years? Do you remember it? Or did that join all the other forgotten things in your mind? I'd like to know." He studies Ben's face. "Maybe it doesn't matter. Looking into your eyes, I wonder if someone who did what you did could *ever* say to themself, 'Maybe that little boy didn't *like* that.' Or I wonder if the boy has ever thought of hurting me back—even though it wouldn't change anything.'

"And since you can't undo what you did, why am I even talking to you?" He looks away, then back. "I *know* why. So I can tell you just a *little*, just one time, how it was for me.

"We were in that cabin," Jimmy shakes his head, half smiling. "Somewhere inside me, I have *always* remembered it. Your words have been stuck in there … well, ever since. You said to me, 'We've been keeping careful track of you, *mate.* We think you're eligible for the *Cottonwood Rights of Manhood.*' And Wally laughed. He took out his belt and tied my hands to one of the pommels on the side horse. You said to him, 'Jimmy's got a cute little sister, in case he ever decides to say anything.'—I think you were somehow trying to please Wally when you said that. … But then, as he was gagging me and putting on the blindfold, you told me you were 'very, *very* sorry'—and *that* almost made me feel sorry for *YOU, because you really did seem remorseful—*'but that I must never, *ever* tell *anyone,' you said, 'in the camp or away from it, or anywhere, not EVER.'* … And … then, when it was all over, I remember you going to the sink in the corner and washing your hands. … After that, I don't remember anything except … you know, *pain* … and then later … I'm not sure where we were then, you told me to remember what you'd said to me. …But I *didn't*—not for a long time, not until it was either *remember* … or kill … *something.*"

Ben's face flashes lime green. "I've lived with it my whole life. I've already paid."

"What was going through your mind? Did you need that much to hurt … just *anyone*? Why did you pick me?"

"I don't know," says Ben. I've always been sorry … even as it was going on. ... I think I wanted to see … just what it would … *be like.*" His eyes widen. "But *I* didn't *do* anything. It was *him.* It was Wally. He said, 'Let's go fuck with that kid's head.' "

Jimmy moves to within millimeters of his face. "I never thought I'd get a chance like this. People go through their whole lives and never find the means to say what they need to. Or they die young—like my sister. They take drugs and kill themselves because they can't cope with people like you."

Lightning flashes again, closer than before. Ben's blond hair glows for an instant. Thunder rolls across the desert.

"I didn't know," says Tom. "I'm sorry, Jim."

• • •

Emily is still frozen on Ben.

He doesn't move.

"What's wrong with you? It said in your baby book that you had accidents. '*Accidents*?' My God, every trip, every stumble, every fall wasn't a learning experience for us, it wasn't a part of growing up. It was an irreversible error. So, if everything but holding it in is an error, why bother? If all behavior is outlaw behavior, what's the point in *not* being an outlaw? If all behavior is outlaw behavior, then nothing is out of bounds. Is that what you thought?"

Hopelessly typecast in a role he never wanted, Ben can only smirk.

Watching her brother, Emily's eyes fill with horror. "You were *awake*. You were *awake* when he died. The bruises on his throat were *not* from blood thinners."

"Don't make I laugh," says Ben. "It makes I pee I pants." His face flares iridescently as a colossal swath of solid lightning flashes even closer to them, bathing the world in a ghostly, pale green, jukebox glow.

• • •

Ben faces his father and continues massaging the old man's shoulders.

"The real problem," he says, "is that you can't believe anybody, even when they're sincere."

Ben Sr. frowns.

"And I am sincere when I tell you I wouldn't be doing this if I didn't have to leave you." He laughs. "And I guess that's kind of a whopper, too, huh?"

His hands move from the deltoid muscles to the trapezius.

The old man groans and his lips configure themselves into a perfect O.

Afraid his mortal co-creator might say something he doesn't want to hear, Ben brings his thumbs forward to the sternomastoid muscles, then to a point just below the larynx.

As he applies pressure to the trachea, the air that normally passes into the two bronchi that feed oxygen to Dr. Bennett's lungs is stopped.

Ben watches the face and, hands trembling, holds his thumbs in with all of his thirty-four years of rage.

• • •

The face is replaced by Emily's. "It was easy for you," he says. "He didn't even … *like* me. When he started to make us his primary target after mother died, you didn't seem to mind so much. You seemed to have resources, to be able to accept that 'Daddy' was an awful …" He giggles. "well … maybe only a garden variety sadist. But I ... I didn't know what to do with it. Then"—he shoots a look at Jimmy—"when I found the letter your mother sent, I had to do something. So, I killed the cancer at its source."

"You never told me," says Emily, "what was wrong with your original face and the way you used to talk?"

Ben sneers. "Well, I think that's rather obvious." He runs a hand over both sides of his chin line, then rests it briefly on what he's afraid are the beginnings of some puffiness just above where his chin meets his neck. "I had to get away from myself. I'm not a nice man. Never was." He shows her a *GQ* smile. "But I'm neat as a pin."

"Tell me why. *Why* did you do it?"

He considers her solemnly. "It was just something I'd thought about for a long, long time." He shrugs. "I finally got up the courage. And I think he understood. I think, in the end, he understood. As I put my hands around his neck, I saw it in his eyes. They finally … sort of relaxed, and said, 'Okay. Go ahead. I've got it coming. Do it."

• • •

He whirls around and strides off toward his horse.

Emily screams, "Skip-eee!" and charges after him. She falls down, struggles up, takes off after him, and falls again.

Tom has run after her. He swoops her up and, for a millisecond, with the strength that enables people to lift cars in dire circumstances, holds her one-handed over his head. Then, still part of the same motion, he puts both arms around her, swings her back, and gently sets her down.

"It's all right now. It's going to be all right now, love."

• • •

Again, lightning flashes across the sky, followed by a barrage of thunder.

The first AD is signaling them frantically from next to one of the trucks. Tom sees him and says, "We have to take cover!"

When he looks back, Emily and Jimmy are watching Ben get up onto Brownie.

Brownie immediately rears up and unseats him. Ben's foot slips out of the stirrup, and he tumbles to the ground. The mare pulls away and begins to graze nonchalantly at a patch of desert grass.

• • •

Ben's only consolation, in his state of frenzy, is the bliss of contempt he hasn't felt so profoundly since he strangled his father. When he considers what Jimmy and his mother have done to him—the smear of humiliation—when he considers that everything would have been all right if it hadn't been for them, he wonders that he contained himself for as long as he did.

He gets up, slaps the dust off himself, grabs the horse's reins, punches her in the neck as hard as he can, and swings up into the saddle again.

• • •

As he careens toward them, he screams, "*Look at me, Daddy. I'm a player after all.*"

Gathering momentum, they leap over a gully as a new bolt of lightning slashes down from the sky.

Ben and Brownie freeze mid-stride, a paralyzed centaur, steam and smoke rising from them as time stands still.

None of them remembers what they're thinking or even what's around them. But they all carry an image, branded in their minds forever of horse and rider poised in a sickening frieze, then crashing to the ground in a tangled wreckage, the smoldering ruins of two lives struck down from the sky.

• • •

"Jesus God," whispers Rush Mellman, the director of photography. Then to Art Gallagher, his camera operator: "Did you *get* that?"

"I think so. Focus is good. We're still rolling."

"Let it go till we're out of film," says Solange.

Mellman is still staring, open-mouthed. "There's no way he survived that."

"Holy shit." says Gallagher. "Look at *that*."

"What?"

"The horse. It's getting up."

"Not the actor though."

VI
POST-PRODUCTION

Jack Butterworth said that *Showdown* cut together like a dream. Despite Emily's feelings about "smug and ruthless, life-is-a-dance-on-a-tongue-of-fire" Solange Borugian, some would say that it was she who ultimately made the movie work.

When modern viewers see the film, they will probably assume that Edgar Scanlan's death scene was a gripping, macabre trick of computer-generated imagery. They may or may not have learned that the final pick-up shots were completed with a double standing in for Scanlan. They will likely not believe—because aren't all movies make-believe?—that the director filmed, in its entirety, the death of Benjamin Bennett Jr.

Solange had three cameras, two with telephoto lenses, directed at the action. There wasn't as much light as she would have liked, but it was clear in the raw footage that Edgar Scanlan had been struck by lightning.

"I know that's what it looked like," a "knowledgeable" film afficionado will say to his girlfriend, "but take my word for it, that was CGI."

• • •

Jack Butterworth returned to film editing for a few years, but remained outside the Hollywood community. He had a prostate operation in 1993, which, according to Jimmy Riley, he felt as affectionate about as all of his years in "show business."

Jack passed away in 2008.

Joanna Morgan is professor emeritus of film production at USC.

• • •

Emily Bennett and Tom Manfredo are married and live in Tuscany. They own a small winery—although Tom still buys Pepsi by the case—and have a grown daughter named Joanna. (When little Joanna was born, Tom took one look at her and dropped to the floor, unconscious.) Emily and Tom long ago retired from the film trade. They miss Southern California, especially what essayist/memoirist D.J. Waldie calls "the light that breaks hearts in LA." But they don't miss the enduring whirlpool of insanity that is the film business. Orson Welles said of Los Angeles (and the film industry): "The terrible thing about LA is that you sit down, you're twenty-five, and when you get up you're sixty-two."

Emily still sees people as celebrities, but only rarely. When Jimmy asked her "secret," she replied in a letter: "I think when you're surrounded by love, ailments tend to dwindle. It's like light and dark. If you keep introducing more light, after a while, the dark gives up. It has no choice."

As for her other voice, one day she told it to go away, and it did. Mostly.

Occasionally, when she's feeling sad, she talks about regrets that, so far anyway, people haven't gotten the chance to see *Showdown. "All that work," she says, "all the people who came together and made something beautiful—generations of them."*

She also said, "But Showdown is being watched over and someday people will know about it."

• • •

Jimmy Riley's mother, Vivian, died in 2005 of a stroke. Jimmy flew home for the funeral from location in Ireland where he was doing a new film—one of those arty projects he came to be known for. Emily always knew Jimmy would make it. He never married.

When Emily asked him why, he told her he was holding out for a good athletic Indian.

• • •

The reason Solange Borugian was not upset—and didn't want anyone else to be—about the break-in at the Radford offices was that she already had a good idea who was responsible for it.

She had deep connections to her family, but she didn't know everything about them. Like many Armenian-American families, especially first and second generation, hers had remained close. But, as with all families, close or not, there can be a "bad apple," and sometimes the rest of the family is ignorant of the fact.

This particular branch of the Borugian family had a single shady character. He was Solange's father's half-brother. He had never shown himself to be untrustworthy, but in fact he had strong mob connections. Solange learned about this from her mother, who had never trusted Uncle Harry (Harout). Unfortunately, Solange had dropped some prideful hints about what she was working on professionally (*Showdown)*, and in the way those things can happen in close families, this news had drifted into the hollow rift of Uncle Harry's awareness.

As the words about the break-in flowed out of Joanna's mouth, Solange's hackles went up. She wasn't positive, but she was pretty sure by that time that it was distinctly possible good old Uncle Harry was behind it. She figured that the people Uncle Harry was connected with would not want to interrupt the shooting, but she could only pray that they would conclude there was no money to be made by peddling their information to some illicit interest group.

This prayer was not answered. The *interest group* set the wheels in motion to blackmail Keith Oakland and his associates.

They were in for a surprise. The Oakland faction, in the end, voted not to buckle to the pressures of the people Uncle Harry had sold his information to. Instead, they took what, for them at the time, amounted to a very advantageous tax loss.

Emily and Joanna were caught in the middle. The finished film, *Showdown*, has remained unreleased to this day, due to a battery of a legal encumbrances that could sink another *Titanic*.

• • •

No one knows for sure why John Wayne walked away from the original shooting of *Showdown*—if, as many believe, that's what happened. But there are at least a few who think that it was still weighing heavy on James Dean's mind when he said his final words: "That guy's got to stop. He'll see us."

• • •

The revised A-negative of *Showdown* remains in hermetically sealed cans, carefully watched over in a guarded location.

• • •

On a beautiful day in May recently, Emily and Tom were in Siena, doing some shopping. When they were done, they found a place among the mostly kids, students, and tourists on the huge red brick and white travertine stone Piazza del Campo. They lay down in the late afternoon sun, among the hundred or so others, to enjoy the air for a while before starting their drive back home. Tom's hands were braced on the brickwork that slanted down to the Palazzo Pubblico. Emily lay next to him, her head in his lap,

They were approached by a man with a notepad, who sounded American, and who asked, "In the end, who is the showdown really between?" The man added, cryptically, "There are rumors."

In all the years since 1979, neither Tom nor Emily had ever been asked anything about the story of *Showdown.* The very few questions that had gotten through to them had simply been about the rumor of the movie's existence.

Emily looked up at Tom, then still smiling, said to the man, "Niente spoiler."

THE END

A LITTLE HOOPTEDOODLE ABOUT RICHARD BOONE

I worked as an actor with Richard Boone on and off for two-and-a-half years on a Universal television series, *Hec Ramsey*. It was part of the NBC Mystery Movie rotation that included *Columbo, MacMillan and Wife, and McCloud.*

When he wanted to, Boone could be a raconteur. As he got to know me better, he started telling me stories—many of them about other actors he'd worked with. He said that when he was doing *Hombre*, he ran into Paul Newman one day while Newman was in the makeup chair. He said Newman pointed at his own face and with his signature grin, said, "Bluest eyes in the business." When Boone was doing *Night of the Following Day* with Marlon Brando, and the director had been "let go," several of the cast and production team were sitting around, wondering what to do next. In frustration, the producer finally said, "Marlon, who do you want to have direct the rest of this thing." Marlon, sitting on the floor, not looking up, held up one finger, pointed at Boone, and said, "Him." Boone directed the remaining sequences for *Night of the Following Day*.

Boone and I did some drinking together. One Friday afternoon, after we'd finished shooting the close-ups for a scene on Universal sound stage 29, where we shot most of the interiors, he said to me, "You want to go to Hawaii?"

I blinked or something. "When?"

He made a face that suggested I might be a little dense and said, "Now." We hadn't wrapped for the day, which didn't seem to bother him.

If I hadn't had a wife and daughter at home, I would have gone to Hawaii with him that weekend to celebrate … *whatever* he had in mind to celebrate.

I never tried to keep up with him as a drinker. Not many could. I don't know how much he went through on a daily basis, but if whiskey was rain, he'd have needed storm gear. The series took place in 1901 "New Prospect," Oklahoma. Boone, as Hec Ramsey, took orders from Police Chief Oliver Stamp (me). It was still more or less hippy days. The twist for our show was that the older Hec was the hippy. I was his young, hot-tempered, establishment boss. A lot of the humor of the show came from Hec goading Oliver about his by-the-book, meager-of-imagination way of approaching their work.

Our personal relationship began to take on some of the same colors as our characters. As Hec teased Oliver, Boone teased me—adopting a borderline adversarial/friendly, big brotherly attitude. Sometimes it took the form of practical jokes. In one episode, Oliver had a terrible toothache. The script called for him to chug eight ounces of whiskey (tea) to ease the pain before the tooth was pulled. When it was time to shoot my close-up (the wrap shot for the show), Boone had seen to it that the tea actually *was* whiskey. As I downed it, looking, I'm sure, as startled as I felt, I glanced up and saw him off-camera. I later wondered if there was something maybe a little … *off* about me that I was so tickled to see his silent, gleeful laugh.

• • •

I won't waste your time by telling you why I've rewritten what was previously called *Impersonators Anonymous*, except to say: in that version, important pieces of the puzzle were missing. For example, things that are a little ... *off* about some of the characters were not satisfactorily revealed in *Impersonators Anonymous.*

Some sections of *Mit Out Sound* are close to being what they were previously, but the real problem with the first version was that I realized, having started to write this story many years ago—long before I'd made any other stabs at writing novels, that I had not learned the necessary craft. I hadn't completed what some authors refer to as the thousand shitty pages you have to write before you can hope to get good (I did not sell, or try to sell any of my god-awful thousand).

Also, I had not included anything in the first version about Richard Boone being the inspiration for this tale. His wife, Claire—a lovely woman—was still alive (she's passed on since), and I didn't feel good about writing anything about her late husband that might in any way hurt her. Boone's son, Peter, is still, by my standards, a young man (he was a very young man when we shot *Hec Ramsey*), and I'm pretty sure he's not going to feel bad by my mentioning what he already knows, that his father was a brilliant eccentric.

Finally, and most importantly, I wrote the book again because I got elements of the story wrong the first time, and it would have driven me over the edge to leave it that way.

• • •

One day, well into the second year of shooting *Hec Ramsey*, Boone and I were sitting outside his trailer, him on the steps of his Winnebago, me in a canvas chair. We were sipping Bourbon and talking about *Long Day's Journey into Night*, the Eugene O'Neill play he was considering doing. He'd told me I could play the youngest son, Edmund, which would have been fine with me; it's one of those roles almost any young actor longs to play.

He reached behind him and grabbed a picture in a simple silver frame. "Nothin' against you," he said, "but this is the kid who should have played Edmund in the first place. Maybe he would have, if he hadn't gone off on his sorrowful little road trip a year earlier."

He handed the picture to me.

"Well, yeah!" I said. "What are you doing with a picture of James Dean?"

"Somebody else familiar with *Showdown* gave it to me." He revealed an impish grin.

"What's *Showdown*?"

"You never heard that title?" He studied me, then: "Well, I guess I'm not surprised. Most people haven't." He took a drag on his Pall Mall. "But a lot more people than you might imagine know about it. They also know it's more than rumor."

"*But what is it*?" I said.

His grin turned into a distracted half-smile. He took a deep breath and said,

"*Showdown* is the title of the unfinished John Wayne/James Dean film."

I started to laugh. I knew he was sucking me into some kind of urban myth.

"Do not tell *anyone* I mentioned this to you," he said. "I shouldn't have. It's meant to stay a secret." He shrugged. "As much as that's possible with something like this."

He gazed at me for a long moment, then frowned and shook his head, waving me off.

• • •

Sometimes, Boone would get me curious about one of his stories, then like a master fisherman, playing a trout, give me some slack for as long as it pleased him, then lazily pull me in.

One day we had just walked off the set. The crew was making lighting adjustments. I said, "What do you *really* know about that movie you brought up … That was a joke, right? *Showdown*?"

He cleared his throat, studied me with an odd, almost sweet smile, and said, "I know very little about it."

"Yeah, but what? Where did you hear about it?"

He shook his head and looked across the backlot at the "Black Box," the Universal executive office building he from time to time idly discussed the possibility of blowing up. "I saw it," he said. "Well, two or three minutes of it." He frowned and looked back at me, then, at the bottom of his warm, raspy register, intoned, "What the hell."

This is the story he told me:

• • •

"One morning I got up and found a brand-new Cadillac in my driveway. Duke had bought me a car to thank me for doing Sam Houston in *The Alamo*. I'd worked for pocket change since he was producing it and footing the bill. Well, hell, I didn't know what to say. I figured I ought to say thanks for a thing like that, so I jumped into that beautiful black Caddy and drove over to the office he kept in Culver City."

Boone stopped, frowned at me and said. "I don't think I'm going to tell you any more about this—at least right now. I'll just leave it that he showed me a couple minutes of an unedited scene with two actors you'd never in a million years expect to see working together: James Dean and John Wayne."

He smiled at the look on my face. "You want to know any more about it, you're a bright kid, do some research. You gotta pay a price to get into these insider clubs." He gazed at me, musing. "I think you'll do it. I've got a little too much of the male thing, the warrior gene I guess, to really *get* it. But maybe you will." He studied me. "I've got a hunch you will. Then, maybe someday you'll be able to explain it to me." He grinned. "Let's wait and see, shall we?"

Shortly after this conversation, our show was cancelled because TV series work is physically demanding and Boone wasn't as robust as he used to be. He made demands on NBC they couldn't possibly satisfy.

And that was it for *Hec Ramsey.*

I talked to him occasionally until shortly before he died, but we never saw each other again, except once, two years later, on the set of John Wayne's, final film, *The Shootist*.

ACKNOWLEDGEMENTS:

Thank you to my friends, teachers, writers, and colleagues who have with unremitting kindness taught me as much about the craft of writing as I can absorb: Michael Norell, Elizabeth Forsythe Hailey, Kendall Hailey, Harriet Pitts, and Bret Easton Ellis.

For her wise, knowledgeable and warm-hearted counseling and her invaluable help through the whole publication process, Keri Barnum.

I also gratefully acknowledge the contribution of: Pamela Cangioli, Gerry Blanchard, Noralee Carrier Potts, Meghan Pinson, Sunny Chermé Cooper, Claudette Sutherland, Cheryl Laimon, Rosemary Forsyth, and for her sense, sanity, and heart, Michele Winkler. Finally, I've never thanked her before, but I hope somewhere far off or nearby she can hear me— my favorite acting teacher of a bunch of acting teachers, Claribel Baird. She inspired creativity in me on all fronts.

Special thanks to Kevin Cook, the only editor I ever knew who researches as he edits—to the story's benefit. And to Amit Dey, the superb layout artist.

Thank you to Scott, Charlie, and Abigail for being not only my inspiring children, but my true-blue friends.

There aren't enough thank-yous for my wife Linda. She shows me the meaning of the word "care," and has made my life far better than I would have guessed it would be. She is also my first content editor. She reads my most recent pages. It goes like this:

Linda: "I like this and this, but I don't care for this bit."

Me: "What are you talking about? That's the_essence of what I'm trying to say here."

Linda: "Well, it doesn't ring true to me."

Me: "If I cut that I'll be gutting this whole chapter, probably the whole fx#*ing book!"

Linda spreads her hands, palms up.

Me (ten minutes later, grumpy): "Okay, it's gone."

Lastly, I'd like to thank James Dean, John Wayne, and Richard Boone.

ABOUT THE AUTHOR

Rick lenz was an actor for many years, working in regional and New York theatre. He repeated his Broadway role of Igor Sullivan in the movie version of *Cactus Flower*, opposite Goldie Hawn, Ingrid Bergman and Walter Matthau. Other films include *Where Does it Hurt?* (with Peter Sellers), *Melvin and Howard*, *Scandalous John*, and *The Shootist.* For many years he shuttled between playwriting (regional theatre, Off-Broadway, and PBS) and television acting jobs. He was Police Chief Oliver Stamp on *Hec Ramsey* with Richard Boone and played a wide variety of characters in TV movies and series, including multiple appearances on *Murder, She Wrote, Green Acres,* and *Bionic Woman*. He is the author of three previous novels, *The Alexandrite, Hello, Rest of My Life, A Town Called WHY*, and a memoir, *North of Hollywood.* Rick lives in Los Angeles with his wife Linda and an ever-shifting array of animals.

NOTE FROM THE AUTHOR

DEAR READER,

If you enjoyed *Mit Out Sound*, please consider leaving a review on Goodreads, Amazon, BookBub or one of your favorite online book selling sites.

Reviews are so important to an author. It doesn't have to be a long review, a sentence or two is fine, unless of course you'd like to say more.

I'd also love to connect with you online.

Website: www.ricklenz.com
Instagram: @RickLenz
Facebook: @RickLenzAuthor
YouTube: @RickLenz

With great appreciation,

Rick Lenz

www.ingramcontent.com/pod-product-compliance
Lightning Source LLC
Jackson TN
JSHW020105050225
78393JS00004B/10

* 9 7 8 0 9 9 9 6 9 5 3 7 1 *